One Lavender Ribbon

Young Adult Novels
by Heather Burch

Halflings

Guardian

Avenger

One Lavender Ribbon

Heather Burch

Published by

Ⓜ Montlake
Romance

Published by Montlake Romance, Seattle

www.apub.com

ISBN-13: 9781477823149
ISBN-10: 147782314X

Cover design by Laura Klynstra

Library of Congress Control Number: 2014900302

Printed in the United States of America

Dear John,

I'm a writer. Words are my lifeblood and yet I find all of them inadequate to tell you how much I appreciate, need, and love you. If what I'm doing is good, then you made it good. If my words reach beyond the paper veil and into someone's heart, it's because you've reached into mine. And if I live a thousand years, I still won't find words suitable for how I feel.

Your wife,
Heather

Prologue

Present Day

*W*ill sat in the front row, knowing the room was full without turning to see. The unmistakable sense of people squeezing in tighter to pay their final respects and all the sorrowful tension that accompanied them filled the space with an awkward silence.

He glanced down at his fingers. He'd rolled up the little leaflet, something he was sure one shouldn't do at a funeral. Will swallowed the lump in his throat. Grown men weren't supposed to cry. No worries—he was certain he could hold his emotions at a safe and reasonable distance.

Until a tiny little hand slid into his palm.

"Daddy, are you sad?" Giant dark eyes blinked on a small angelic face, now creased with a frown.

It undid him.

Will cleared his throat, a futile attempt to remove the surge wrecking his last shred of composure. "Yes, baby. Daddy's sad."

The frown deepened, causing her eyes to darken and fill with tears. "Then I'm sad too."

He reached down and scooped her into his arms. She strained to look in the casket, but only for a moment, then turned and wrapped her little arms around his neck. Will held her close. If not for the deceased, he wouldn't have his young treasure. Music filled the air. Short breaths warmed a spot on his shirt. "Daddy," she whispered, "when we get home will you tell me the story again about you and Mommy?"

He tilted to look down at her face. "Sure." He'd tell her a thousand times if she wanted. Because there'd been no real life until that day Adrienne Carter knocked on his door with a stack of old letters.

Chapter 1

"Letters," Adrienne Carter whispered, and ran her fingers over the contents of the small open box in her hands. Thunder sounded outside, causing the attic window to rumble. She glanced at it, then above her head to the rafters, where the box had been just moments before. Adrienne adjusted the flashlight under her arm and reached to the floor, where an old broom—her weapon against the onslaught of attic spiders—rested, perched between an empty trunk and a stack of old magazines. With a soft pool of light guiding her, she tilted the broom into the corner, keeping the metal box pressed against her chest. This was something . . . unique. Of that she was certain. The intrigue almost caused her to forget her prior plan of tinkering with the breaker box. If the lights didn't come on soon, she'd return to it; but right now, letters from a distant past waited. And that took precedence over everything else.

The attic door groaned as Adrienne threw her weight into pushing it shut. Old houses didn't always comply with the rules . . . simple things like doors fitting into doorframes, the same frames that had cradled them for nearly a century. This one insisted on puffing up. She'd called her dad and asked about it right after she'd moved in. But he'd just said, "Old houses. They breathe. Humidity and all. It'll fit better in the winter."

Whatever *that* meant. Like southern Florida *had* winters. She'd also consulted the hardware store guy, but he'd just suggested she hire someone to shave off the edges where the frame had scraped until bare wood shone beneath the wood stain. Hire someone. Yes, that's what she needed to do for about a billion jobs in this renovation.

Her feet padded down the attic stairs, through the upstairs hallway, and finally onto the stairs leading to the first level of her new . . . old home.

The flashlight cast shadows as she moved, highlighting and then shrouding various rehab projects in multiple areas, all at different levels of completion. If she ever actually got a few done, she'd throw a party. If, of course, she had any friends. Which she didn't.

Her light skittered across some ominous thing in the corner, causing her to pause halfway down the stairs. Just a sheet thrown over the recliner. Adrienne released the air she'd sucked in hard and scanned the area, orienting herself and looking for other monsters. None.

She hated being without electricity. It always happened at the worst possible time, during window-rattling thunderstorms. Actually, the whole place looked better in the softened radiance— where the scars of life hid behind the muted glow of lantern and flashlight.

The tart bite of fresh paint greeted her at the base of the stairs. Her hand had grown sweaty around the small metal box. Adrienne's heartbeat picked up, and she scurried to the couch to open the first letter.

June 1944

Dear Gracie,

I fear where this war will lead me. I fear the dark unknown that hovers in the distance and takes men captive—if not their flesh, their very hearts. The thought of you keeps me moving forward, forces me to refuse the desperation that threatens. Before we met, I was alive, but empty. From the moment I saw you, there was no doubt you were all my heart had yearned for. My mind slips back to that day. You and Sara were at the park. Your golden hair danced in rhythm to the gentle wind. Your white sundress flowed around you, and as you laughed, all the world sprang to life. I desperately wanted to come and speak to you. But I dared not. Perhaps you were only a figment of my imagination, and if I approached, you would disappear like fog on a cool morning. I watched you walk away and could feel my heart going with you. For many minutes I waited, staring at the horizon, hoping you would reappear over the hillside, but you didn't.

Gracie, of all the things that have brought me suffering, being apart from you is the most excruciating pain I have ever experienced. But please know, I would suffer this a thousand days to spend one day with you. And there will come a time when we will walk together along the ocean, watching sunsets and sunrises. But we will be together in honor. You told me in your last letter that your mother was pleased with my decision to join the Army. I pray it is so. I refuse to be at odds with her. You and Sara are all she has. Of course she wants the best for you. I know you have been melancholy about my decision, but it is the only way.

I will come back to you.

And I make you this promise: upon my return, we will celebrate for an eternity. We will celebrate life and love, and nothing ever, ever will pull us apart again. Pray for me, Gracie. Give Sara my love.

Forever yours,
William

In one long whoosh, all the air left Adrienne's lungs. Her grip softened on the letter as her gaze drifted to a dark spot in the hallway. She stared into the nothingness, unable to focus. Only able to feel. *What's it like to get a letter like this? Have someone hold you in such adoration that he'd die a thousand deaths to spend a day with you?* She couldn't imagine. The love she'd experienced with Eric had proven to be a lonely road on her part and a self-absorbed dictatorship on his part.

Each fingertip throbbed where she touched the letter. The pulses sent unnamable sensations flowing through her, potent and uncommon and able to caress the desperate places of her heart, allowing her to wish. To hope.

Allowing her to dream.

Lightning flashed outside, causing Adrienne to jump. The living room lit up in strobe light flashes, a giant camera snapping photographs of her holding a letter so intimate, she felt like an intruder in her own home. Adrienne pressed the faded page to her heart in an attempt to absorb all that it was. Her free hand reached to touch the rusted metal box that had likely been its home for more years than she'd been alive. Beyond the window, the storm continued its assault.

She drew the envelope closer in the lamplight. For the first time since she'd bought the rundown Victorian house, she was thankful for the quirky wiring. Without it, she'd have never found the letters.

But still, she added calling an electrician to her ever-growing list. She looked at the envelope more closely.

It had grayed over the long years, but the names and addresses were legible, the postmark unmistakable. Nineteen forty-four. That would have been World War II. When she read the address line, her breath caught. Her home, 722 Hidden Beach Road, and the names: To Grace Chandler from William Bryant.

The roar of the ocean momentarily grabbed her attention. She paused and listened to the angry sea as a barrage of palm fronds smacked the side of her house. Adrienne set the box down on the wooden coffee table and leaned back, melting into the couch.

How many times had she entered the attic and flipped the breaker, unaware of the delicate silver package hovering above in the rafters? If not for the spider and Adrienne's ninja skills with the designated spider-broom, the box would still be up there, safely hidden from prying eyes, with an old-fashioned ink pen; a black-and-white photograph; and lastly, the stack of letters tied with a faded lavender ribbon.

Earlier in the night, Adrienne had almost given up on the on-again, off-again wiring and gone to bed, when the lights flickered, went off, and stayed off. But oil lamps made one brave, and the thought of waking at 3:00 a.m. to a house with its own set of imaginary ghosts and strange noises had forced her up the creaky attic stairs. Now she was glad she'd gone. Maybe she was finally getting used to the turn-of-the-century house. And being alone. She hadn't thought about it until her first night in the creaky old Victorian, but she'd never *been* alone. Not ever. She'd gone from her folks' house in Missouri to college with a roommate—four years of fun; and then to being married to Eric—almost six years of torture. But never alone. Until now.

Her neighbor Sammie had warned her about the violent Florida storms and recommended she purchase the lamp along with the candles and flashlights. Oh, she *did* have one friend: Sammie. But the two of them together could hardly be considered a party. There was also Ryan, the college guy who'd helped move in her belongings. They'd shared a few fun dinners and beach strolls, but Ryan wasn't what she needed. Fun college boys might have appealed a few years back, but not now. Even if she did get some major remodeling done on the house, a party with her only two friends would be laced with more obstacles than the clearance section of the lumberyard. No party.

She reached for the oil lamp. The soft flame danced in flickering waves that grew taller as she turned the lever. Shadows snaked to the corners of her living room. *Her* living room. In the house she'd bought after a five-minute inspection. Really, when she thought about it, it was crazy. So she didn't think about it. Messy divorces had a way of tweaking one's common sense. Adrienne had spent the last few months tweaked.

But the house was growing on her. Sort of. It was becoming a home. That's what she told herself. Well, one thing for sure: it looked a whole lot better now than it had when she'd flown down from Chicago and made an immediate offer—which had been accepted almost as fast.

Adrienne touched the edge of the ribbon. "Nice to meet you, Grace Chandler and William Bryant." *Who were they, the faceless names in the letter? Grace had lived in this house. Sara must be her sister. Each had occupied one of these rooms.* She closed her eyes for a moment, listening for the past. *Did they live here long? Did William return from the war?* With the light brighter, she reached into the box and found the photograph. A handsome young man in a crisp Army uniform stood smiling, with a young girl at his side. Adrienne's finger ran along the opposite side, which sported a jagged yellow edge. Someone had ripped that section off. She flipped the photo over. The date, 1942, adorned the back, but no names.

This *could* be William. What about the girl? She couldn't be Grace. The girl in the pretty polka-dotted dress was just a child, years younger than the boy.

He was strikingly good-looking, with an eager grin that made Adrienne want to smile back. Eyes sharp and focused, he looked out at her from inside the picture. Poetry danced in those eyes, not unlike the poetry of the letter. Surely this must be William.

After extinguishing the oil lamp, Adrienne rose and carried the box to the kitchen table. The flashlight tucked beneath her arm fell across a local phone directory—the town was so small it still printed them—splattered with bits of sheetrock dust and spackle. Her fingers gently drummed the tabletop the way they always did when she was considering something ridiculous. William Bryant, WWII veteran, in the directory and still here after so many years? Not likely. Or Grace Chandler? No. It was an eternity ago, yet the words in the letter had come alive in her hands, the love seeming as fresh and new as it must have been when he wrote them.

She chewed her bottom lip. It was nearly raw from her chewing it during the day's work of stripping the fireplace mantle. Since moving to Florida, she'd discovered a few things about herself. One, she was pitifully deficient when it came to renovating houses. And two, when she discovered she was pitifully deficient at something, she gnawed her lips to shreds. One glance at the envelope and her fingers were finding their way through the directory pages. B for Bryant.

Halfway down the page, William Bryant waited.

Chapter 2

*W*illiam Bryant—known to everyone as Pops—rubbed a hand over the fifty-year-old scar on his left leg. Humid mornings brought a stiffness he'd learned to live with but didn't relish. He rose from the bed slowly, letting old bones and joints awaken as he moved to the window and peeled back the curtain. Lonely strands of light sought to illuminate the room, leaving hazy streaks across the space.

A few personal items and pictures sat here and there, but not quite enough to make it feel like home. He tried to keep the room tidy enough to please his grandson Will, yet cozy enough to please himself, but when he'd tripped on a stack of books in the middle of the night, Will's desire for a safe, streamlined area over-ruled Pops's affection for creature comforts.

The notion of a stroll encouraged a second glance out his window. Morning dew cloaked the backyard with a glisten-ing splash of moisture. No walk to the pier this morning, he decided, tossing a look at the gray sky. With the sun's inability to break through the clouds and burn off the dew, everything remained slick. He wasn't afraid of a little moist grass, but Will worried about him, so he would honor his grandson's wishes.

He didn't despair over Will's desire to protect him. Will had sacrificed much of his valued personal space to make room for his only living grandfather. The boy had even forfeited half the library where Pops's treasured books waited for him, meticulously positioned and ready.

He let the curtain fall back in front of the window, bathing the room in quiet darkness. Weather-imprisoned and joints throbbing, he allowed himself the indulgence of self-pity. But sometimes pity, though she had an edge that could cut, was a welcome companion. After all, it was hard for a man like him to admit age was overtaking agility. Time was conquering dexterity.

He had few regrets. At age eighty-one, not too bad. He'd married a good woman. They'd had a beautiful son. And now he had Will. The memories were first rate. So he'd wake up every morning, open his eyes, and see what was in store for him. At this age, what more could he ask for?

One day, he would simply close his eyes and not open them. That's how he envisioned it. Now Will, on the other hand, had a recurring nightmare where Pops took out the boat late at night and drowned. Will was a worrier. Not too much Pops could do or say to change that. "It's just a dream," Pops assured him. He'd even gone into his grandson's room when he heard him thrashing about. Soothed his forehead, like he'd done a thousand times while Will was growing up. Pops understood nightmares. A man didn't survive the second World War and return without knowing the power of bad dreams. But that wouldn't be the end of life for Pops. No. He'd go to sleep and awaken on a fair morning in Glory. Where there wasn't any arthritis, and there wasn't any dew to threaten the path to the pier. Pops smiled.

Weathered fingers reached to the table lamp and fumbled with the switch. He slid his Bible closer, his thumb finding its way down the tattered leather edge.

He read, starting from where he'd stopped the previous morning, pulling the words deep into his soul. He closed the book and felt a quickening, an earnest expectation of something new, something fresh on the horizon.

"I'm not afraid to die." Determination set his jaw as his gaze moved to the window. "But I'm also not afraid to live." William rose, slipped on his shoes, and went downstairs to get the boat key. He was headed for the pier.

By morning, the storm had passed, and the silver box waited. Adrienne slept late, and the aching in her muscles confirmed overwork. Sanding an entire fireplace mantle that had fifty-plus years of layers of paint would do that to a body. She could count off the decades as she sanded. The yellow of the sixties, avocado green of the seventies, and then white. Layers and layers of white. But she'd almost completed the project. Just a few finishing touches remained. The desire for completion had fueled her for the better part of the day. Morning had turned to midday, and midday to dusk as she sanded and scraped like a maniac, shoving loose strands of hair from her eyes, blotting the sweat from her brow, barely stopping to take a break. Now she was wishing she'd used a little wisdom. Every muscle screamed. She needed a massage.

But the new home was finally becoming a warm replacement for the cold marriage she'd endured. Poetic justice. Her divorce settlement had purchased the house and would pay for restoring it while she figured out what she was going to do with the *rest* of her life. For now, the house would be her sole profession and her most appreciated companion. Its beautiful antebellum back porch stretching the length of the house, framed stunning views of the Gulf of Mexico. Gentle waves brushed toward her each morning as she sipped good coffee and contemplated the day's project. But her body bore the abuse the renovation entailed. Adrienne needed to learn to ignore it. Today, she intended to ignore everything about the house. Not that she could pick up a hammer if she wanted to. She couldn't—her muscle groups were all on strike. It wouldn't matter anyway. Her attention had drifted elsewhere. She hurried downstairs, made coffee, and settled into a comfy chair to read. She placed the photograph beside her and dove into the letters.

August 1944

Dear Gracie,

I may be brief with this letter, but I promised to share with you all that I experience. War makes a man different. I've no other way to explain but that. Though this is a gray and dying world around me, there are tiny glimpses of vibrancy on the muted canvas. I live for those splashes of color and light. But I met death today. He stalks us even when we rest, giving no mercy. He knows no bounds. We sat in camp, some talking, others playing cards, awaiting word on our next mission. Runner—we call him that because his father makes moonshine in the South Carolina mountains—was relaxed at a table one moment, then collapsed the next. We've been trained in combat death, but not the kind that sneaks silently into the hallowed place of one's daily order of life. This death touches me deeply because we had stayed up late into the night, talking about the ocean and fishing and life. His plans for return. And mine. I told him of you and Sara and deep-sea fishing on the Gulf. We joked that we would compare fish stories—him on the Atlantic and me on the Gulf. He'd decided to stop running moonshine. I told him that was good. And today he is gone. We've lost many. And more arrive to take their place, but that is the nature of war. And war is the nature of death. But death is not the nature of life. And yet, I am beginning to see that it is. Death is not an anomaly. Life—life is the anomaly. And what a glorious gift it is.

I won't shelter you from what I see. You are strong, Grace. If I don't share with you, I feel there will be a part of me that closes off. I must not let that happen. I won't close any part of myself from you. I love you. Forgive me for loving you so much.

William

By the time she'd finished another letter, Adrienne formed a plan. She grabbed a quick shower and headed out the door, the address scrawled on a scrap of paper and the photograph tucked into her jacket pocket.

She forced her thoughts from the scenarios fluttering through her mind and concentrated on the drive, still loving the fact that she frequently passed things like signs pointing the way to the Gulf beaches and tiny little saltwater tackle shops that looked like a strong wind could drop them. Looking at palm tree–lined roads passed the time.

Less than twenty minutes and she was there. Adrienne chewed the inside of her cheek because her bottom lip couldn't take any more abuse, and regarded the house. Her initial excitement waned. All morning—before the short drive from her home in Bonita Springs to Naples—this had seemed like a good idea. Now, apprehension crawled over her skin like fire ants. This was silly. She pressed her palm to her forehead and scanned the pretty dwelling at 41123 Canal Boulevard. She checked the address against the ornate numbers over the front door. What on Earth would she say? *Hi, I'm a pathetic divorcée who has to live vicariously through letters about people I've never met.* Adrienne put a hand to her stomach. Divorcée. She still hadn't completely reconciled with that. The divorce, yes. Eric—brilliant cardiologist and adulterer—made it easy to walk away, but being a *divorced woman* at age twenty-eight, that was still difficult to swallow. It's not like she was old. She'd married right out of college and now she was *divorced.* Which made her feel like a failure. Her fingers threaded through her hair in an attempt to erase her frustrations, but things like disillusionment and divorce didn't go away easily.

Adrienne threw out a breath and slid from the car, giving the door a good slam to trap the aggravation inside the hot vehicle. Off to the side of the house lay an impressive garden like one might see on the cover of one of those DIY magazines she'd started collecting when she purchased the house. But she didn't have time to examine it now.

Before she could change her mind, she headed to the front porch, her back arrow straight. The crisp white two-story sported pots of flowers arranged on a long front patio. A wooden swing anchored one corner, and the luscious scent of all the brightly colored flowers filled her nose. The wicker patio table and chairs waited for someone to sit, offering colored cushions to sink into. The home was about the size of her towering Victorian monster, but newer and in that beautiful Tuscan style of terra cotta rooftops and stucco walls. Without so much as a pause to catch her breath, she knocked.

When the door swung open, the blood drained from her face. Deep-green eyes greeted her. Beautiful eyes, she noted, for an instant forgetting why she'd come. He was handsome. But sadly, about fifty years too young to be whom she sought.

"Can I help you?" A light smile tilted the corners of his mouth, and his shoulders filled the doorway.

"Yes," she muttered. What had she practiced saying? She couldn't remember. Something about how she'd just moved here and bought a house on Hidden Beach Road in Bonita Springs. For support, she clutched the photo in her jacket pocket. "I'm looking for William Bryant."

He considered her a moment. "I'm William Bryant. But everyone calls me Will."

"Well, the Mr. Bryant I'm looking for is a World War II veteran and—"

"Good ol' war days," she thought he mumbled.

She leaned closer. "Excuse me?"

"Nothing." But it *was* something, and she could see it clearly in the instant of frustration framing his mouth and the slight flare of his nostrils. "I'm certainly no war veteran. Sorry I couldn't help you."

He moved to close the door, and her hand flew up, palm flat against the cool wood. There was something familiar about this man. She rubbed the photo in her pocket. "Look, I'm not trying to cause any problems or anything, but . . . " This wasn't going at all the way she'd imagined. She should just walk away, but the fact was, this man and the William from the letters shared a name. They had to be relatives.

The emerald eyes hardened. "But what?"

"Well, I'd like to talk to Mr. Bryant about his war experience. I have—"

"Let me get this straight. You're looking for a WWII veteran so you can get him to talk to you about the war. And that doesn't seem insensitive to you?"

Adrienne's cheeks heated, and her palms turned clammy. "Insensitive," she echoed. She hadn't even thought of that.

"As I said, I'm no war veteran, and I can't help you with finding this *other* Mr. Bryant. But if I were him, I'd seriously have my doubts about someone who showed up at my doorstep wanting to know about the hardest time of my life."

A strong wind surged around the house and smacked her face with the precise force his words smacked her. She needed to explain, but her voice left her, all that energy going into holding the stranger's door open and fighting to stay erect against the wind's onslaught. Nervous tension flew off her in waves solid enough to drift away upon. She opened her mouth, but nothing came out.

The man stood there like a statue, brows riding high and *daring* her to explain.

Well, when he put it like that, there was no explanation that could suffice.

After a few horrible seconds, his eyes slid from her face to her hand, still flattened against his front door.

Adrienne followed his gaze to her left hand, the tiny band of lighter skin on her ring finger that, after three months of daily sunshine, still didn't match the rest of her flesh. She swallowed the lump rising in her throat.

He noticed. His gaze softened on her, only marginally, but enough for her to feel it.

"Miss, I'm very sorry I can't help you." He offered a weak smile. Maybe it was sincere, maybe not. She'd heard pity before. And she hated it. Worse than anything . . . except maybe Eric's condescension.

He tossed a thumb behind him. "I'm, uh, in the middle of something." But his body language told a different story. The tension around his eyes had lessened, mouth relaxed. A tenderness worked its way toward her.

She plucked her hand from the door, feeling more defiance than despair. She didn't need anyone's pity. "Of course. I'm sorry I bothered you."

"No problem." He almost sounded sincere; the taut muscles of his chest had loosened, releasing some of their strain; his shoulders, broad and tight beneath a T-shirt, dropped a few millimeters.

Expecting him to shut the door and let her leave, Adrienne's gaze fell to the porch floor with its fresh stain. Her fingertips were stained a similar shade. Maybe that's what he'd noticed, not the missing ring on her hand. Walnut stain looked better on porch floors than on skin.

When Will didn't close the door, she glanced up. His head tipped to the side, and his weight fell against the doorjamb. He cocked one foot in front of the other.

Those green eyes probed again, this time filled with sparks of curiosity. It caused a prickly sensation along her neck. *Just close the stupid door! I made a mistake.* She tried to turn and leave. Unfortunately, her feet didn't cooperate. As her upper body pivoted, her lower body stiffened. She felt the frown crease her brow and deepen. Embarrassment flushed her, because Adrienne really, truly wanted to believe in love. It was a shocking realization, one she'd rather not visit while standing on a complete stranger's property. But the words drifted through her mind again. *I know there's real love out there.* The kind she'd read about in William's letters. Now, standing on the front porch of a man she didn't know, her desperation almost overwhelmed her.

Divorcée.

Tiny lines crinkled at the edges of his eyes. "Have we met?"

Absently, she tucked her hair behind her ear. "I don't think so. I've only lived here a few months."

His gaze coasted from her head downward. A smile slashed his face. "You seem familiar."

"I, uh, get that sometimes. People say I favor—" She fumbled with her walnut-stained fingers.

"Angelina Jolie?" he finished for her.

"No, Jennifer Garner."

His eyes narrowed playfully. "I can see that. But your mouth is full, like Angelina's."

Adrienne swallowed hard. Seriously? Mr. Rude and Grumpy wanted to stand around and flirt? No thanks. Mortification caused a person to want to climb into a hole, not play games. She lifted her hand into the air. "Well, as I said, I'm sorry to have bothered you."

He pointed a finger at her. "The bank."

"Excuse me?" *Please, please, feet, step off this porch.*

"You recently opened an account at the bank where I work."

Frowning, she thought back. She had opened a savings account at the Naples branch of her bank. But if this guy had waited on her, surely she would have remembered. "You helped me?"

"No, but I noticed you from my office."

She raised a brow.

He laughed. "Hard not to."

She should say thanks or something. But honestly, this whole interaction had thrown her off her game. Who was she kidding? She didn't have a game. And—she began to realize—she was *really bad* at interacting with men. She stared at a pot of plants to the left and chewed on her stained fingernail. Not with all men. *This* kind of man. The handsome, strong kind that made her stomach tighten a little. Adrienne was going to need practice before entering the dating world.

With Ryan it had been different. He'd shown up in her life right after the divorce and helped her unload her baggage. Well, if a guy sees that much of your baggage and doesn't run off screaming, it sort of endears him to you. But Ryan wasn't the kind of man she could see herself ending up with. A college boy might be a great playmate, but he was a long way from dating material. Too many years of fun still wrestling under his skin.

Adrienne blinked. "Oh, I'm sorry. Got lost in my thoughts there for a second."

A half smile appeared on his face. "Obviously." He stayed positioned in the doorway, his faded jeans stretched over muscular thighs and his T-shirt over a set of pecs that hardly screamed "bank teller". She forced a smile. "It was nice to meet you, William. I really am sorry I interrupted your Saturday morning."

"I go by Will, remember?"

"Will, then." Adrienne drew in a breath and turned to leave. A breeze ruffled her hair as she reached the bottom of his steps.

"Do you live in Naples?" he called out.

She paused, her fingers gripping the railing, and glanced back at him. "Bonita Springs."

"Why'd you go to the Naples branch to open your savings account?"

Her grip tightened on the railing. Well, best to stop this whole flirting thing right here and now. "Why?" she repeated.

"I'm just curious." His brows quirked, and she noticed a tiny dimple on one side of his face.

"You'll think I'm crazy."

His eyes widened. He probably already thought she was crazy.

Adrienne pulled in a breath and let the wind have its way, leaning into the gusts instead of fighting them. "I don't know the area very well. I hardly know anyone who lives here except my next-door neighbor who owns a coffee shop in Bonita, and a guy who helped me move in. Oh, and a myriad of subcontractors that I call when I get myself in over my head. You know what? That's too much info. I went to the bank in Naples to expand my world." She threw her hands up and waited for him to suggest calling the white coats.

Will Bryant ran his tongue over his teeth and gave a quick nod. "Makes sense."

"Okay, so nice to meet you—What did you say?"

He shrugged. "You're new to the area. Makes perfect sense. It's your bank. You need to take ownership. Feel at home at both branches."

She blinked. Wow, *she* didn't fully understand her logic, but he seemed to. Or maybe he was making fun of her. She watched him with suspicious eyes for a long moment.

"I guess I'll see you at the bank sometime?"

She waited a bit before nodding, but he didn't burst out in laughter, so Adrienne let some of the tension in her muscles drain. She took one last look at him, then turned and started toward her car. She didn't look up, but she was pretty certain he still stood there staring at her.

Adrienne gripped the steering wheel and scolded herself. Why hadn't she just called and saved herself from this whole thing? Then again, Will couldn't know how pathetic she was, right? Right. There was no one to judge her. No one knew why she'd really come. That solidified just how alone she was.

Movement in an upstairs window drew her attention.

She saw a hand tilt the curtain. A shadow, a silhouette of someone watched her from the darkened room. Slowly, the fingers released, and the curtain fell into place.

Adrienne turned her attention back to the car and tapped her thumb on the steering wheel. "You'll see me again, Will Bryant."

Will ran up the stairs and got back on his rowing machine, his mind on the woman who'd just left. He remembered seeing her at the bank in all her tanned glory, long dark hair floating down her shoulders and back. Up close, she was even more stunning, with giant coffee-colored eyes. He blew through his workout, thinking about those eyes and wondering what made them so sad. Like she carried the weight of the world on her narrow shoulders, and the load was getting heavy.

He shouldn't have let her leave his house so quickly. She'd pretty much thrown him the proverbial bone. *I'm new in town. Don't really know anyone.* Man, he was dense when it came to women. It hadn't even occurred to him that that might have been an invitation, until she was gone.

Will didn't hear Pops, so he peeked out his upstairs bedroom window, knowing what he'd find. The backyard was too slick for Pops to walk down to the boat, but he had a feeling that's exactly what Pops was doing. Before he could get the window open and call for him, he heard the boat motor come to life. Will shook his head and returned to the rowing machine. An extra-long workout couldn't hurt. After all, it was Saturday.

Thirty minutes later he heard the boat return. He moved to the window and peeled back the shade. The bright Florida sunshine streamed in as his eyes drifted to the canal that began where his backyard ended. A perfect morning. The kind Pops couldn't resist.

Using a hand towel, he dabbed at the sweat he'd accumulated and rubbed menthol cream into his knees. *I shouldn't have to do this yet. I'm only thirty.*

Below, his grandfather tied up the boat at the pier's edge.

Strips of liquefied gold bobbed across the beckoning cobalt water. The thirty-two-foot cuddy cabin bounced in the gentle movement as its own wake caught up to the fiberglass hull and lapped at its sides.

Will shook his head at his grandfather's antics—the way Pops hurried toward the house, all the while glancing around like a teenager creeping in from a forbidden date. Pops fumbled to get the boat key in his pocket, but stopped halfway across the lawn. His gaze traveled the distance from the yard to the second story. The older man forced a smile to hide the guilt.

Will crossed his arms accusingly.

William Senior shrugged and headed to the back door. Although he pushed a hand against his knee, Pops's leg remained stiff with each step. Will knew he'd grown so accustomed to the old injury, the gentle climb through grass and sand was nothing more than a Sunday stroll.

But not for Will. Every time his grandfather negotiated a climb, it reminded him of all the pain the old man had lived through. Pain that the pretty brunette who'd knocked on his door wanted to bring to the forefront of Pops's mind.

If it were up to Will, his grandfather would only trek on safe, level concrete. But Pops was a stubborn man. Kind, but stubborn. He didn't seem to realize that an eighty-year-old body couldn't do everything it once had. And early morning boat trips *alone* topped the list.

Will showered and headed down to the kitchen.

"Morning," Pops said as Will descended the stairs. The morning paper lay at Will's spot.

"Morning, Pops." Will perused the headlines while his grandfather placed a plate of scrambled eggs, bacon, and toast on the table, next to the paper.

Obviously anxious to avoid the conversation sure to ensue, Pops tapped his finger on the newsprint. "There's a lot going on in town this weekend." He rolled up the sleeves of his gray flannel shirt, arthritic fingers fumbling to make the folds smooth. He vanished from the doorway and reappeared with a stepladder.

"Yeah?" Will shook pepper over the eggs and took a bite. "Like what?" But he knew where this conversation was headed. He watched Pops maneuver the ladder under the kitchen light.

"Out at the Animal Sanctuary, they're having a hike."

Will grunted.

"You might like it. You used to hike all the time."

That was before grandma died and I brought you here, Will thought. "Nah, I'm not really in the mood for a hike today."

"It's to raise money for the new shelters." Pops produced a lightbulb from the cupboard.

"It's hot." Will nodded toward the wall thermometer in the kitchen window. "But we can send them a donation to help out, if you'd like." When silence followed, he glanced up at Pops. "Or were you thinking of adopting a pet?"

Pops seemed to consider the suggestion, eyebrows riding high on his forehead. He moved back to the sink. "Would *you* like one?"

Will wasn't interested in dealing with dog or cat hair or the endless responsibility of caring for an animal. But if it would make Pops happy, he'd do it. "If *you* do."

Pops rubbed a hand over his chin.

Will attempted to embrace the idea. "It might be cool to have a dog to take out on the boat with us. And he could keep you company while I'm at work."

Pops nodded. "And dig up my garden and eat our shoes."

Will chuckled. "I think only puppies do that."

They both exhaled and discharged the idea as quickly as they'd welcomed it.

Pops pointed to the advertisement section. "Well, there's also a coupon for a one-man kayak rental at Manatee Park. Five bucks off. And I hear the manatees have moved upriver."

"Pops, I don't want to go see manatees today." This was getting old. Every Saturday brought the same conversation. Today, Will just wanted some downtime. From work, from everything. He dropped his fork on his plate. "Why don't you tell me why you're trying to get rid of me?"

Pops's tender cornflower eyes saddened. "I'm not trying to get rid of you." He slowly settled into the chair, his words so gentle that they shot a bullet of shame through Will's gut.

He leaned over the table and took the older man by the arm. "I'm just teasing. I mean, if you've got some hottie from the senior center coming over or something, I promise to stay out of the way." He slid the lightbulb from Pops's hand and moved to the stepladder, readjusting it under the fixture.

A bright red hue materialized on Pops's cheeks. "I don't have any hottie."

Will smiled. How empty would his world be without his grandfather here? Less frustrating perhaps—especially on Saturday mornings—but completely hollow. He changed the light, giving Pops a nod to flip the switch, and returned to his breakfast, completing yet another task that demonstrated the symbiotic relationship the two men shared.

When Pops had come to live with him after his grandmother died, Will questioned the wisdom in his own offer. Being a busy, dedicated bank executive, did he *really* have time to care for an aging grandfather? Five years later, he couldn't imagine a life that didn't include daily chats, playing checkers on the front porch, and fishing in the Gulf of Mexico.

He patted Pops on the shoulder. "What do *you* want to do today?"

Pops sighed. "I guess we could take the boat out."

"Did you leave any gas in it?" Will asked, voice flat, but the smile that tugged at his lips melted the accusation.

Pops concentrated on a water ring on the table. "Yeah, I think that sounds fun." It was their Saturday ritual. Take the boat down the canal and out into the Gulf of Mexico. Most days they'd fish, catch dinner—anything from red snapper to tuna, and return home at dusk. After dinner, they'd sit on the front porch until the stars came out. It was a good life.

Pops knew this. Yet he constantly insisted on shaking up a perfectly good schedule, a perfectly balanced routine, with ideas like hiking and kayaking. Time to end the inquisition, once and for all. "Seriously, Pops. Why do you keep trying to get me to go do things I'm not in the mood to do? This happens every Saturday."

Pops stopped clearing the dishes and faced him. "Will, you're thirty. And you spend your weekends with an old man."

"I happen to like that old man."

"You're a good young man." Pops wagged a finger and pinned him with a sharp glare. "But you *are* a *young* man. Since I moved here, you've stopped doing so many things you love."

Will shook his head, but Pops continued. "I know you used to go hiking and kayaking, scuba diving."

Will grinned, lifting an index finger. "I went scuba diving last month."

"Yes, and I practically had to force you. You used to go every month." His face clouded. "I've turned you into a geezer."

Will leaned back and laughed. "That's absurd."

"You don't even go to the gym anymore." Pops motioned up the stairs. "You put that metal beast thing in your room, and you work out there."

On the opposite wall, the clock ticked, blinking away moment after moment of time. Precious time. Pops was eighty-one. The death of Will's grandmother, when she was seventy-five, had been sudden. No warning of the illness that took her in a few short weeks. It had rocked Will's world. He wouldn't waste the time he could spend with Pops. He also couldn't tell his grandfather that.

Pops was philosophical and poetic and would somehow twist it into Will just hiding behind the fear of loss. Pops wasn't scared to die.

But Will was terrified of losing him.

Will pressed his palms over his eyes and exhaled. "Look, how can I explain this?" Yes, life had changed five years ago, but Will wasn't a kid anymore. The things that had seemed important to a twenty-five-year-old weren't important to a thirty-year-old. Now, life had meaning. It had purpose. Still, no real way to explain that without it all coming back to Pops and the time they had together. "Five years ago I was working to get the promotion to executive loan manager." Within the same week, he'd received the promotion and welcomed Pops as a roommate. "When I got the job, I knew I had to clean out some clutter in my life."

"The hobbies you had were clutter?" Pops's voice filled with sadness.

"They're a distraction," Will said, hoping Pops believed it. "The job is extremely demanding. Mentally, it's exhausting. Before I got the promotion, I had a lot of pent-up energy to burn. I don't have that now. My life had to become more organized, stream-lined, to be successful in my new position."

"You make a convincing argument." Pops straightened. "But it's an awfully technical and practical way to look at life. And it doesn't sound very lively or exciting."

"Well, everyone can't lead an exciting life. Some of us just have to work hard, be honest and persistent." Will did love his work. And some childish things had to be set aside to do his job to the best of his ability.

It was all good. Orderly. No surprises, no shocks. Everyone wanted that kind of stability, that security, right? And Will wanted time. More time to spend with Pops. But the more of a routine Will and Pops developed, the more troubled his grandfather became. Though Pops didn't say much, Will could sense it. And he wasn't interested in Pops ruining their unspoken yet carved-in-stone Saturday morning plans.

"Sounds like a rut," Pops admitted.

"Maybe I like my rut."

"You know what they say. A rut is just a grave with both ends kicked out."

"Then it's not a rut." Will frowned and tugged at his shirt collar. *Honestly, what thirty-year-old man lived like this?* None he could think of, but it didn't matter. He enjoyed his life. There were worse things than losing a few hobbies. Like regret. Yeah, that was a big one. He'd never have to look back and regret how he'd spent his time. "Look, Pops, things are just the way I want them. If they weren't, I'd make changes."

The older man watched him through narrowed eyes. "So, if I wasn't here, you'd still be doing the same things you are now?"

"No, I'd have to fix my own breakfast."

Pops threw a soft punch into Will's shoulder. "Funny." He grew serious again. "It's not because you're taking care of me?"

Will laughed. "I think you have that backward. You're the one who's taking care of me."

Pops's face lit up. "I guess that's what families do."

Will stiffened and hoped Pops wouldn't notice. He tried to swallow the rock lodged in his throat but couldn't get it down. He rose from the table. *That's what families do.* That's what he did. Certainly what Pops did. Now, Will's mom and dad? Not so. "I'll clean up. Why don't you pack us a couple of sandwiches for the day?"

Pops nodded and pulled the cooler from the pantry. "I heard from your folks. They have to cancel their trip home."

Will nearly dropped the plate he was carrying to the sink. He spun to face Pops. "Are you kidding?"

Pops looked down. Will could tell his grandfather didn't want him to see the disappointment.

"Did they give a reason?" Will asked through gritted teeth and dropped a glass in the sink with a loud clink.

"No." Pops tried to sound cheery, but his voice cracked, betraying him. He forced a smile. "They didn't."

A familiar burn settled in Will's gut.

Pops brushed a hand through the air. "Their work is very important. I don't have to tell you that. It's okay that they can't come. We'll still have us a humdinger of a time."

Will filled the sink with warm bubbly water, keeping his back to Pops because, where his mom and dad were concerned, he had a lousy poker face. They'd let Pops down. Again. How could they do that? How could anyone be so heartless?

In the stark silence that followed, Pops worked to fill the cooler. Will glanced over his shoulder. The slight tremor in Pops's fingers only allowed for slow meticulous movements while working with small things like sandwich bags and Snack Packs.

"It's your birthday, Pops." Will forced out a breath when his anger got the better of him. Peace Corps workers or not, his parents were wrong to devalue Pops's birthday like this. Two years between visits. Two *years*. With each passing day, the gravity of Pops's age weighed. Eighty-one. How many more birthday celebrations did they think he'd be having?

Their trip home from Africa was all Pops had talked about for weeks—making plans, arranging the spare room to their liking. And now, with no explanation, they simply weren't coming. Will's fury burned. But letting Pops know how mad he was would only make matters worse. He forced a smile and glanced over his shoulder. "Humdinger, huh?"

"We'll go to a nice dinner, then maybe hit one of those discothèques," Pops teased.

"A discothèque?" Will laughed, releasing the anger for Pops's sake. He crossed the kitchen and hugged his grandfather's shoulders. "I don't think so. I'm not even sure they have discothèques anymore. But we'll come up with something."

Sun streamed in through the window, bathing them in its light. Pops turned to it, letting it warm him in the cool kitchen. "It's a beautiful morning. I hope the fish are biting."

"They've never let us down."

Pops pivoted enough to look Will in the eye. "You've never let me down."

"I hope I never do."

"Couldn't happen." Pops grinned. "You come from good stock."

The lump, again. The muscles in his jaw tightened. *Even if it did skip a generation.*

"I've got to water the garden before we go. I'll be back in a few minutes."

"After all the rain last night, you need to water?" Will held the cooler lid open and looked inside.

"Can't be too careful," Pops said. "I planted some new seeds. Thought it'd stay cloudy today, but the sun broke through."

"And when you noticed it, you thought it would be a good idea to take the boat out alone?"

Pops brushed at the sides of his pants. "It was just a little trip down the canal."

"Pops, next time I'll go with you." Will studied his grandfather's face. "I'm just trying to protect—"

Pops's sigh cut him off. "I know, protect me. A man who jumped from airplanes during a war, and I need to be protected from slippery grass."

"You'd do the same for me. Now, go water that garden."

Pops nodded. "Right after I change into shorts." With a spring in his step, he headed out of the room, pausing in the doorway.

Will glanced over, wondering what stopped his grandfather's momentum.

Without looking back, Pops said, "Love you, boy."

Will squeezed his eyes shut. All that had gone unsaid over the years about Pops and his war filled the space around Will's heart and filled the room around both men. Will closed the distance. He didn't trust his voice to speak without shattering, so he placed a solid hand on each of Pops's shoulders.

A gentle squeeze created the slightest of tremors through Pops. Pops knew Will was all he had.

Head held high, he stepped away from his grandson and was whistling a tune before he reached the stairs. Through the window, the sun kissed Will's face.

Chapter 3

War was horrific, Adrienne decided, and tried to imagine what it would be like to have someone die right in front of her. Not once, but over and over again. William's letters were changing her. Altering something deep within. And she was starting to wonder if it wasn't a good thing. This—*this* was real life. This was the sacrifice men had made so she could sit around and complain about being lonely or hide in a dilapidated house where the only conversation came from her and the less-than-perfect plumbing. People should live the very best life possible. Too many had died so that others could.

But the letters weren't all about the horrors of war. They were about Gracie and William's undying love. All this she'd learned from reading only a few. He also spoke about Sara, Gracie's younger sister. From all Adrienne gathered, the young girl found trouble around every corner. He talked about Sara getting lost in the dark and stumbling into the neighbor's chicken coop, waking half the town. She'd escaped with her life, but not her dignity. He told the other soldiers about it, and they spent the evening sharing embarrassing stories and laughing harder than they'd thought possible in the middle of a war. *Tell Sara thank you,* he said, *I knew she wouldn't mind me exposing her secret. If there's anything I know about sweet Sara, it's that if she can bring a much-needed smile to another soul, she will. No matter what the cost.*

It was almost noon before Adrienne dressed. She tugged the heavy mahogany front door open and surveyed the world. Yep, another sunny day in paradise. She headed out the door, photo and one of the letters in hand. She could use the advice of a best friend right now. With the windows down, she drove to Sammie's coffee shop, listening to an indie rock station.

The coffee shop was bustling with customers. She couldn't have come at a worse time of day. Sammie was behind the counter, taking an order from a young man. Then she ladled up a bowl of soup. She glanced over her shoulder and threw Adrienne a quick smile.

The scent of espresso and homemade stew floated on the air. Chatter from table after table of people surrounded her. The guy took his food and turned directly to her, giving her a long appreciative stare. Adrienne stepped aside so he could get by. He brushed against her as he passed, going out of his way to make contact. Things like that happened to her sometimes, men trying to catch her attention. Since the divorce, she'd had to remind herself, it was *okay* for someone to find you attractive. She ordered a latte and stood aside while Sammie made it.

Sammie was a tall woman, nearly six feet, and towered over Adrienne's five-foot-four frame. She wore the long, roomy dresses popular in the sixties. Her feet were always clad in flip-flops, her mop of wavy red hair pulled back in a loose ponytail at the nape of her neck. She was thirty-five years old and attractive, but wore little makeup to enhance her natural beauty. Adrienne had never seen her without dangly earrings that made tiny tinkling sounds as she floated around the coffee shop.

She handed the drink to Adrienne. "Here. Go have a seat. I can join you in about ten."

Adrienne positioned herself so the guy who'd bumped her—the one who continued to stare while she waited for her drink—was out of her direct line of vision. "Looks like I caught you at a bad time," Adrienne said when Sammie dropped into the seat across from her.

"I'm making money. As far as I'm concerned, this is a great time. Here, try this and tell me what you think." Sammie held a napkin out, on which sat a small block of bread.

Adrienne crunched into the crouton. "Delicious. Homemade?"

"Of course."

"Garlic, butter, sea salt, something else . . . " She tapped her finger to her chin. She'd grown adept at detecting which spices were in the food she ate. Long, boring dinners with Eric and some hospital department head he was trying to impress had forced Adrienne to look inward for entertainment. With each entrée she ordered, Adrienne would see if she could guess each and every ingredient. If something stumped her, she'd ask the waiter, who then asked the chef. Chefs began to take an interest in the woman who was guessing their secrets. At first, Eric had enjoyed the attention when the chef would leave the kitchen and hover at their table. But he quickly tired of it. To them, Eric was invisible, and she received all the attention. Eric wasn't good at playing wallflower, so Adrienne stopped guessing ingredients and sat quietly like a good little wife should.

"Parmesan," Sammie filled in for her.

"Brilliant."

"Your turn. Let's see it." Sammie rubbed her hands on her apron and reached.

Adrienne handed her the photo but left the letter in her pocket.

"Handsome. Who is he?" Sammie flipped the picture over.

"I'm not sure. It was in the box. I think it's the man who wrote the letters. There's more, but you don't have time right now." Adrienne gestured toward the line of people that was forming at the register.

"1942. Isn't that around the beginning of World War II?" Sammie tapped the photo.

Adrienne nodded. "I think his girlfriend lived in my house at the time. Have any ideas how I can find out more about them?"

Sammie frowned in concentration. "You could go talk to Leo. He owns the diner across town. He's a World War II veteran and has lived here forever. Maybe he knew them." Her eyes fanned to the register, where a young girl was tying an apron around her waist. "My backup person is here. Could you stay for a few more minutes? I want to ask you about something."

"Sure."

Sammie smoothed her skirt. "Listen, Ryan was by earlier."

Adrienne dropped her head to the table, a pool of hair blocking the light.

"Did I say something wrong?" Sammie said.

"No." She peered out from under her hair. "Ryan and I aren't dating anymore."

"Why not? After a while, I never saw you together without a huge smile on your face."

"Right? But let's face it. He was the textbook rebound boyfriend."

Sammie reached up to untangle her hair from her earring. "I don't see how. You didn't even like him at first."

"You mean when his tanned, muscled body showed up at my door to move in my furniture?"

"Yeah, if memory serves, you told me his flirty, polished confidence made you want to throw up." Finally free of the hair strand, Sammie shook her head gently, the tinkling sound of her earrings drifting across the table.

"He did." Adrienne thought back and smiled. But he'd won her over with the genuine charm she'd mistaken for arrogance. That, coupled with a heavy dose of laughter—something her marriage to Eric had denied her—and Ryan became a quick remedy for her pain. But not a long-term remedy. She pulled her bottom lip between her teeth and bit down.

He was a lovely distraction, though, and wasn't looking for a serious relationship; just in it to have a good time—something he'd made clear up front. She'd been relieved.

"And now, suddenly you don't like him. Are you just not into good-looking young men?"

Adrienne sighed. "No, it's not that."

Sammie pushed her hair from her eyes. "Let me try again. Ryan is a terrific guy. But after being in a difficult—and as far as I'm concerned, abusive relationship—you need to get to know yourself before you get to know anyone else."

Adrienne's head snapped up from the table. "Exactly. It's taken me weeks to figure it out, and you nailed it in—what—nine seconds?"

Sammie shrugged. "Easier to see from the outside. So, have you told him?"

Adrienne's shoulder tipped up a little. "Sort of."

"Sorry, Chicago. That's a yes-or-no question."

"I told him I needed time. So we agreed to be friends." She leaned forward. "He seemed okay with that since he wasn't looking for anything serious. Did he tell you differently?"

"No." Sammie's mouth tilted down at the corners. "When your little journey of discovery is over, you two can pick up where you left off. You deserve to have some fun."

Adrienne shook her head. "No, we can't."

"Why not?"

"Being with Ryan is great." She chuckled. "In fact, it's a blast."

"I never really heard the story about how you found him. I've been in Bonita for years and haven't found my Mr. Fun."

"Mary Lathrop, my real estate agent, roped him into being my mover. I kind of suspect she hoped we'd hit it off." Mary had been the dream agent, handling every detail and understanding Adrienne's desire to *for once in her life do something on her own*. "She never told me, but I think she's been through a similar divorce situation."

Sammie nodded. "So Ryan was her way of getting some cosmic justice. A stupid guy dumps you, and you end up with a beefed-up college man to keep you from getting lonely."

Mary had been so attentive, so understanding. The kind of understanding shared only by women whose lives had crumbled because of infidelity. Intentional or not, it *was* payback to all the lousy husbands who had destroyed their marriages over an instant of cowardice. That's what infidelity was, as far as Adrienne was concerned, a coward's way out.

Her mind trailed to the sexy, flirty, smooth young man she'd shared several moonlit walks with. "But being with Ryan . . . it's like I'm back in college." Her words were sad, caught between the fun of youth and the seriousness of adulthood. "I'm twenty-eight years old. I was married for five, almost six years. The college scene just doesn't appeal to me anymore." She blinked several times, studying Sammie's face for insight. "Do I sound like an old crone?"

"No, you sound like a woman. Ryan is—what—twenty-four? Maybe twenty-five? You've led a different life, moved past all that." She closed one eye and pointed a finger at Adrienne. "Just keep in mind, Ryan won't always be a college boy."

A tiny, humorless laugh escaped Adrienne's mouth. "He will to me."

Hands on her hips, Sammie's head tilted to the side. "So what kind of man would be on your list?"

Adrienne's gaze left the coffee shop and watched the traffic out the window. Cars zoomed by, slowing for only a moment as they passed through the flashing yellow light that anchored the edge of the strip mall and the coffee shop.

It couldn't hurt. Sometimes you have to dream. "Someone strong, but not overbearing. Fiercely devoted, but not crazed. Someone who could protect me, but gentle enough to reach into my soul without destroying my spirit."

Sammie rested her chin on her palm. "Sweetheart, if you find Mr. Gentle Hero, let me know. In fact, sign me up for two."

" 'Where have all the poets gone?' " Adrienne wondered aloud.

"What?"

"It's from my favorite poem. 'Where have all the poets gone? Rhyme with passion left unsung, Even now my heart it yearns, Until my poet prince returns.' "

"That's beautiful." Sammie's gaze drifted slowly down to the table. "Your heart wants a soulmate. Hold out for it. Can I ask you a question, Chicago?"

Adrienne ran her fingertip along the rim of her empty latte mug. "Sure."

"Why did you come here?"

"The coffee shop?"

Sammie cast her eyes heavenward. "No. Here."

"Oh, you mean why did I go to a town I've never been and buy a two-story, dilapidated handyman's special? Key word being handy*man's* special?"

Sammie chuckled. "Yeah."

Adrienne pulled a deep breath. If anyone could understand the need for independence, it was Sammie, a woman who seemed to live by her own set of rules. "I needed to know I could do something on my own, something out of the ordinary."

"Why else?"

Adrienne dug a little deeper into her heart. "For once in my life, I didn't want to do what everyone expected of me. Eric expected me to stay in Chicago. Mom expected me to move home to Missouri."

"Bingo." Sammie pointed an index finger at her. "Good girl syndrome. You needed to prove yourself on *your* terms in *your* way. And do you know why?"

Adrienne shook her head.

"Because you're sick of doing what's safe. You wanted to do something dangerous. Unexpected. Something with as much likelihood of failing as succeeding. You're challenging yourself to be a better woman. Way to go, Chicago."

Sammie was right. From the time she was a little girl, Adrienne had been taught to play it safe. First by her mother, who could find the danger in a marshmallow—*Don't ride your bike by the road. Don't cross the street alone. Don't play too close to the picture window.* Then Eric, with a whole new set of rules: *Don't laugh so loud; you sound like a horse. Don't smile so big; it makes you look fake. Don't stand like that; you look like an old woman.*

Oh, she'd been trained to be the perfect daughter, then the perfect wife. It was time to take some risks.

She pushed Eric from her thoughts because he didn't deserve any more of her time. Instead, she stared at the photo, thought about William—risk taker extraordinaire—and tried to imagine him as an eighty-year-old man. Time would have changed his looks, but what about the tender heart and his gift for words? Maybe he'd laugh at the letters, remembering the passion, intensity, and fragility, like spun sugar of young love. Or perhaps his eyes would fill with tears, remembering death and war and pain. She had no way of knowing.

"You thinking about the letters?"

Adrienne crossed her arms in front of her on the table. "Am I that easy to read?"

Sammie tilted her head from side to side. "Pretty much. Which one is your favorite?"

"All the ones I've read." Adrienne rolled her eyes. "But there is one that's particularly haunting." She reached into her jacket pocket.

"You brought it?"

Adrienne's head bobbed up and down. "Thought you might like to hear one. Have you ever heard of Bastogne? William doesn't mention the exact location, but a bit of digging online confirmed that's where his unit would have been."

Sammie's gaze narrowed. "Maybe in high school history class, but that was a long time ago. Battle of the Bulge, right?"

"Listen to this . . . "

December 1944

Dear Gracie,

I am cold. I miss the warmth of your smile and your gentle touch. This is a desolate place. All is silent except for a chilling wind that moans above us. It is a ghost voice taunting us, telling us we will not survive. We are cut off on all sides. The heavily armed German military surrounds us. This is a deep blow, because we had forced the Germans closer and closer to their own border. Their retaliation was swift and unforgiving, an onslaught no one saw coming.

At present, no supplies can reach us. Every attempt has failed. Our rations landed in the German camps. Many nights we go hungry. We must conserve what little food we have. But we are holding the line. If this bulge is broken, the German Army will invade. We have no choice but to do our job, so much rests on the outcome.

I no longer count how many days we've been here. I no longer awaken and think that perhaps today will be our last. Sometimes, it feels like we will never leave. It almost seems like justice that we all die in this hard, unforgiving, frozen ground. So many of us have already fallen. What right do the rest of us have to live?

And yet, I know I will not die here. I will return home. I will return to you. You are the only warmth I have, especially since the winter here is so brutal. Our winter gear did not make it to us, so we are in warm weather uniforms. I don't remember what it's like to awaken without shivering.

I have heard that word reached the States about our previous campaigns. I hear we are called heroes. This seems so strange to me. I am no hero. Yes, we were trained, but when the real drop occurred, we landed splintered and awkward. But somewhere between bullets that sang past us and the ground, our training took over. Once down, we became the unit we were in the States. Rick landed near me, promising to watch my back. We've kept each other alive on more than one occasion. But Rick seems different now. There is a hopelessness that dwells in his eyes. I fear for him. This place will break many of us, if not through open wounds, through those that are hidden.

Gracie, when you write to me next time, tell me about the beach again. In your last letter you told me about you and Sara swimming with the dolphin. It was so wonderful to read,

I almost felt like I was there, the sunshine on my face and you in my arms. You are the one thing that makes this bearable.

All my love,
William

Sammie was quiet for a long time. "You did find a treasure in your attic."

"Yes." Adrienne wondered about William now. Maybe the war had turned him into a bitter, angry old man. Her heart sank a little thinking about that. People changed, but rarely for the better.

Chapter 4

*A*drienne crossed town, headed for Leo's Diner. Her car windows were down, allowing Florida's salty coastal wind to reach in the windows and muss her hair. She relished it. After all, southern Florida was her dream, with its perfect weather and tropical vibe. She'd wanted to move here since they'd vacationed on Sanibel Island a few years back. It's what Eric had promised her, but never delivered. So she was committed to enjoying every sunny day Bonita Springs would produce. It was early June now, and splatters of new flowers were beginning to spring up everywhere. She'd been there since March and didn't think it was possible for everything to get greener, but as summer approached, it had. The rainy season ushered in with it the explosion of new foliage.

She tried to concentrate on what she might plant in her front yard, but thoughts of where she was headed and what she was about to do kept interrupting. Twice she nearly turned the car around and went home. But something compelled her. She knew she was becoming obsessed with this couple, but couldn't help herself. A nagging thought kept haunting her mind. Where was Gracie? These letters were hers. She would never have left them behind.

Leo Sanderson was a wiry, eighty-three-year-old man who still walked to his diner every day. Early each morning, he trekked the block and a half, turned on the open sign, and greeted his regulars while pouring them a cup of his deadly strong coffee. He stayed until two, made the trek home, and did it all again the next day. As he was a well-known Bonita Springs character, Adrienne had heard the stories. She'd only visited the diner a couple times, but he'd made it a point to greet her and offer her coffee on both occasions.

Already having been warned about the brew, now she'd opted for iced tea. She took a seat near the front door and waited to speak with him. It was nearly two o'clock when he finally made his way over. With an upturned palm, she motioned for him to sit. He put the coffee pot down on the Formica table, as was his custom when he'd visit and joke with customers.

They exchanged pleasantries, but she wasn't here for chit-chat. She got right to business and handed him the picture. "Do you know him?"

"Sure do. William Bryant," he said, studying the photo. "I haven't thought about him in years. But we were pretty tight way back when. Several of us local boys enlisted together."

Adrienne leaned closer, heart racing at the confirmation that this was the man she'd hoped was William.

Smoke-stained fingers pointed to the girl. "That would be Sara."

"So, that's what Sara looks like. Can you tell me about Sara and Gracie?"

"William was like me. Poor. His dad owned a local business, but it went under, leaving the family with nothing. William could play ball, though. Probably had a shot at the big time if he hadn't enlisted." He leaned back a little. "'Course, no one knew at the time what the future would hold for baseball. Some said it'd end 'cause of the war."

She thought back to the letters. "He enlisted to please Grace's parents?"

"Gracie's momma. Gracie was her trophy daughter. 'Cause she'd run out of money herself, it was up to Gracie to marry well. William came along and ruined that. Enlisting was his way of being respectable enough to marry. We all had our reasons for signing up."

Leo slid the photo across the table to her. "Why do you want to know all this?"

Adrienne opened her mouth to speak, but no words came out. She couldn't really explain her obsession or why it was so monumentally important to know that this one solitary man got what he so deserved. "I just . . . I found some things in the attic of my house that belong to her. I thought maybe she might like to have them. I don't think they were meant to be left."

For a moment he didn't speak, just studied her with watery gray eyes.

The diner around them grew quiet as the few families that had come in for a late lunch exited the restaurant. She watched a couple of beachgoers slip out the door, the scent of coconut suntan lotion lingering in the air. Her attention went back to Leo. With the deep wrinkles that creased his face and throat, the older man looked every bit of his eighty-three years.

"Gracie's dead. She died in '45."

He continued speaking, but Adrienne heard nothing but the single word that rolled over and over in her mind. Dead. A quick breath escaped her mouth. Regret surged through her, because she'd built the couple a neat little love story in her mind: William returning, the two marrying, having maybe a half-dozen kids, and living out a wonderful life. The tingling sensation started in her nose; tears would follow if she didn't get a grip. She fisted her hands. She should have just read the letters and left it at that. Of course, in the back of her mind she'd known the likelihood of an eighty-something woman still being alive was a fifty-fifty shot at best. But dead since 1945? That meant she'd died just a couple of short years after William left to serve his country.

Sun beaming in the large windows made the restaurant feel stuffy. Suffocating. "How?" she finally managed.

Leo studied her for a long moment. "Look, I don't know why you want to know about Gracie. Honestly, she wasn't worth the time you're spending on her."

Adrienne's eyes widened. How could he say that? Gracie was the woman William Bryant fell in love with, the woman that kept him from giving up during the war.

Leo was perturbed—maybe even angry—and Adrienne felt like she'd somehow opened an old wound.

Scratching his balding head of sparse springy white hairs, he pushed himself away from the table, piercing gray eyes locked on the window pane.

Maybe she didn't have the stomach for this. "I'm sorry."

Leo remained silent.

She shook her head to clear her fear. "I have some letters written by William. He talks about Grace like she was an angel."

Leo flashed a disgusted smile. "Yeah, she was good at making people think of her that way."

Adrienne's eyes fell to the photo. "I thought she loved him."

"Oh, she did." Sarcasm edged his words. "Until he left. Then she quickly fell in love with the new guy in town. William deserved so much more. He's a good man."

Her journey and the hope of William and Gracie ended right here with Leo. For all she knew, they were both dead, and there'd been no one in the upstairs window of Will's house. She'd probably imagined it, just like she imagined a neat tidy life for William and Grace. Then Leo's words sank in. "Did you say he *is* a good man?"

But Leo was taking his own trip into what was proving to be a painful past. "He came home to learn that Gracie had run off with a traveling salesman—a draft dodger no less—and that she died in a car wreck not a hundred miles from town. William lost everything for her."

"The picture. Was it Grace on the other side?"

"I suspect." His hand touched the jagged edge. "Probably tore herself off to give to that poor excuse for a man she ran off with."

Adrienne's head began to pound with slow rhythmic force. She needed to leave. Just go home, stop prying, but even as her mind agreed, her mouth was asking more questions. "What do you mean William lost everything for her?"

"He came home crippled from the war. A hero, though," he added as an afterthought. "Screaming Eagle, one of the best."

The twinkle in Leo's eyes made him seem younger. Or maybe it was a mistiness that accompanied wizened old men as they chatted openly about difficulties most people would never endure. Either way, it was rare. Beautiful, tragic, and very rare.

"I'd like to know more about him, if you don't mind."

Leo shot a glance up to the wall clock. "Sorry. Past my nap time." He rubbed a hand across the back of his neck. "If you want to know more about William, maybe you should go ask him."

"He is still alive, then? Do you think he'd be open to talking with me?" Adrienne blurted.

"Sure. Can that little sports car make it to Naples? Far as I know, he still lives there."

"Naples," she echoed. Her car could make it. She'd just been there last week. "He lives with his grandson, doesn't he?"

Leo nodded. "Need directions?"

"No." She could find William Bryant's house without directions or the help of her GPS. *Will* Bryant. She thought back on the conversation the two had shared. He had never said he didn't know another William Bryant, just that he couldn't help her. "Men," she mumbled. Maybe the younger generation was all the same. In Chicago and here in Bonita Springs, telling half-truths whenever it suited their needs. Like Eric telling her they'd move to Florida. That one wasn't even a half-truth.

Before buying the house, she'd never heard of Bonita Springs, Florida, but had found it while searching property for sale on the Gulf Coast. She'd always wanted to live by the sea. But Eric had refused after promising her in college. Chicago was the only place for a brilliant young cardiologist. Plus, it was on Lake Michigan, so she convinced herself it would *almost* be like living on the coast. But a lake, even a massive one, was vastly different from the ocean. She'd grown to love the city but never sank roots. Her heart yearned for something else. Someplace with sand and salt.

"Thanks for your help, Leo."

"Good luck."

Adrienne bid Leo good-bye with a new zeal squelched only by the pang of sadness about Gracie. But William had returned from the war, and now she couldn't help but wonder what he'd come home to. It had been a bittersweet homecoming, no doubt.

A whole new barrage of questions accompanied her as she drove the palm-lined streets toward home. How could anyone not love a man like William Bryant? Someone with something to hide? The letters were left in the attic. Someone with a secret? It still seemed like they were hidden, not just left behind. Leo assumed Gracie had removed herself from the photo. Sara and William were still in the picture. That was her sister and her boyfriend. But why tear it? Maybe Gracie had given it to someone else, or maybe she'd done it in anger. Adrienne would probably never know.

It was time to put this to rest. Go home and let her imagination finish the story where the letters left off. The reality was no fairy tale. William and Gracie had lived. And as she had so achingly come to understand, especially in the last several months, life was messy. Ugly, even.

But her heart went out to the brave young soldier who'd gone off to fight a war in the hopes of earning the respect of his girl-friend's mother. She wondered if he had recovered from Gracie's betrayal and from the wound that left him crippled.

Adrienne pulled her car into the driveway. She stared at the house. Her house. Perhaps she had learned enough about its history. It was the future she was interested in, not the past. She'd dealt with enough drama in the last months leading up to her divorce. She didn't need to stir up more. She'd keep the letters she'd read, but return the rest to the attic. The words were the treasure. More drama, she couldn't handle.

She turned off her car engine and listened to it tick. Beyond the windows, she could hear birds, but right now their song wasn't soothing. Adrienne understood wounds, scars. She could identify with the kind of pain he must have felt. She and William Bryant had one thing in common. And it was beginning to cut a little too close to her own heart again. Only six years ago, she had thought her world was going to be fairy-tale perfect. But there was no *"happily ever after."*

As she exited the car, the Florida sun shone down on her, showering its approval of her decision. The front door no lon-ger groaned when she opened it. She'd purchased the lubricant and tightened the hinges herself. The house was her project, not a mystery from half a century past.

But when she stepped inside, there on the little table next to the door were the letters. The letters that read like poetry. And she couldn't help herself as her fingers reached out and snatched them up. She went to the kitchen, made some iced tea, and stepped out onto the back deck, to her favorite chair.

The afternoon breeze glided over the water, and rays of light peeked from behind a smattering of clouds. She gazed up at the burning ball, awaiting an accusation, but instead found its warmth kissing her cheeks. The water-cooled air drifted up to her with the aroma of summer riding its wings. She leaned back in the lawn chair, hair dancing across her shoulders and arms. She hoisted the stack of letters to her lap, a contented smile on her face. It was a perfect day to sit and read.

September 1944

Dear Gracie,

Even as I write this, I am reluctant to pen the words. I have walked so many miles since I've been here, and thought of you with each step. You are what keeps me alive and keeps me moving forward when my heart would cry out to stop.

The camp is quiet, most are sleeping or what we've come to know as sleeping. Our numbers have diminished. There is constant shelling from the Germans. But it is not that which scares me. I think what frightens me the most is the dark hopelessness that stalks among the trees, lurking in the shadows. I dare not dwell on it. It is death. No less than a grenade, a strategic bullet, or artillery fire. We have become mechanical in our work. I think this is a blessing. When we watch a friend fall in battle, we grieve, then move on. There is no choice. We must keep moving on.

Gracie, I have a favor to ask of you and Sara. Please don't give up. As long as I know the two of you believe in me, I am able to conquer any foe, be it one German foot soldier or the entire German Army.

Thank you for your last letter. I received it just as we were shipping out. When we invaded Normandy, other letters were lost, as was all of my gear when we made the jump. I am so sorry. Each one is golden to me. But I reread them in my mind over and over. It may be some time before our mail catches up to us again, but please have words for me. Tell me you love me, and remind me of home.

How is sweet Sara? Tell her I often think about the day I found her at the swimming hole. She'd been crying, and my heart went out to her. I've never known a more tender soul than sweet Sara. Please, Gracie, don't forget to let her know that. If you see my parents, tell them I miss them. Like you, they didn't want me to come here, but I will not let them down.

Gracie, you have all the love that's in me.

Forever yours,
William

Adrienne tried to imagine where Grace had sat while she read the letters. Alone in her room? Outside by the shore? And Sara, the tender soul: How did she handle losing William, her friend, the one who found her crying at the swimming hole? Adrienne took a break from the letters to make a sandwich, focusing on William, not on Gracie's betrayal. Soon, she found it easy to approach the letters with the same innocent wonder that first drew her to them and to the heroic stranger she read about.

Enjoying a peanut butter-and-jelly sandwich and cold milk on ice, her gaze fell on the phone directory, where she'd first discovered the address for William Bryant. Leaning against the sink, she balanced her weight on one foot and crossed the other in front of her, then stopped when she realized it was the same posture the man, William—*Everyone calls me Will*—Bryant had assumed when he stood at the doorway of his home in Naples. Slowly, she lifted the sandwich to her lips and took another bite.

Her mind drifted back to William Bryant, the war veteran. Each time a pebble landed in the water, there was a ripple effect. This was a ripple she wasn't sure she could contain. But she knew it was inevitable. Sooner or later, she was going to go back to that house in Naples to knock on the door again. She was too nosy. If she didn't go today, it was only a matter of time. And time, when an eighty-plus-year-old man was involved, was not to be wasted. At the end of the day, the letters belonged to William. He should have them.

Chapter 5

William showered and made his way down the staircase to the library. He held onto the railing as he went, pressing his free hand over his left knee. Years ago he'd learned not to sleep with his good leg propped on his bad, but he must have turned onto his side in the middle of the night—this morning, his knee was screaming. He would attend to his garden later. With Will gone to work, he could spend a few hours reminiscing. Most days he'd study his family albums. Photos of Will as a kid, Charles and Peg, and his darling Betty. Sometimes he'd devote an entire day to one photo album. It was like reliving all the glorious events that made life the indescribable journey it was. But today, he'd revisit the war. He'd remember the friends he'd lost and thank God that his life was spared.

William settled into his grandson's comfy library chair, pulling the desk lamp closer. He removed his reading glasses and rubbed them against the cotton of his shirt. Soft sunlight spilled into the room, warming the book in his hands. Not all memories were good, but they were all important. He pulled a book off the shelf and opened it, remembering how Charles had once asked him whether most of his memories of World War II were good or bad. He hadn't known how to answer. So he hadn't.

He thought back even further. He had lied about his age to enlist. When first approached about becoming a paratrooper, he had asked, "What's that?"

The response came from Rick, a buddy from school who'd just signed up. "You'll make more money."

Well, more money meant more respect from Grace's momma. So William Bryant joined the 101st Airborne. They were an elite group—not by design, but by their extensive training. When others rested, they climbed the hill. When others went on furlough or had weekend passes, they remained to train. What nearly killed them in training saved them in battle.

As with many soldiers in World War II, Normandy was forever carved in his mind. William had watched the plane in front of them get hit by flak, then fall from the sky like a child's dropped rubber ball. His plane took casualties as bullets zinged through the open side door. Explosions lit up the sky, and he wondered morbidly how many paratroopers would hit the ground already dead.

When it was his turn, he jumped into darkness. He couldn't see ocean or beach, but they were falling into hostile territory. No one knew who'd seen them or who would greet them on the ground. But each man knew it would not be the allies.

Normandy was the horrendous battle that it had, in recent years, been portrayed as. But for him, it failed by comparison to Bastogne, a battle that stretched on and on for the 101st. It wasn't just the isolation, but the intense cold, the knowledge that they were surrounded by the German Army, who were far from beaten. By the time the 101st Airborne reached Bastogne, they were no longer the raw recruits they had been in Normandy. After that, they were battle toughened and physically ready to face any enemy. But nothing could have prepared them for Bastogne. The lack of winter gear in the freezing temperatures stole their focus, while starvation stole their morale.

And though he now knew he was safe, knew he was home, sometimes still he'd awaken, thinking he was there again, with the smell of winter pine and death filling his nostrils. Bastogne was as much a psychological battle as a physical one, and some wounds never healed.

Hours passed by. William leaned up from the library chair. Its padded leather seat had conformed to his frame, and as he rose, he realized he'd been there longer than he'd thought.

Sun-weathered hands attempted to rub the wrinkles from his face. He stretched, left the room, and moved slowly to the kitchen. It was important to remember all he'd been through. It made the good times, the good days, that much more precious. He had really spent little time thinking about the war. And he wasn't sure why today it seemed so important, but he had learned not to question motives. If the heart needed to take that journey, it simply did. And today, his heart had needed to.

For years he'd stayed in contact with others from the 101st. But after his wife had passed away, five years earlier, he had just lost touch. Even with Leo. Leo wasn't in the 101st, but he had introduced William to his then-future wife, Betty. They'd shared a long, happy marriage until her passing. He still missed her. Every single day.

Some nights he would even forget she wasn't there. He'd awaken and roll over on his side to draw her near. Instead of her soft form, his hands would grasp only cold blankets. He'd pull them to his face, burying the pain. Yes, he still missed her and probably always would.

Stiffness slowly drained from his joints as he walked to the kitchen counter, where he leaned his weight. The wall clock ticked, its second hand making slow circles around the white face. It was 4:15 and Will would be home soon. William began pulling fresh vegetables from the refrigerator, humming as he did. It was good to be needed.

Will stepped into the kitchen. "How was your day, Pops?"

His grandfather placed a bunch of fresh-picked vegetables on the counter, examining them for signs of injury. "Fine. I'm glad you're home. I was just starting dinner."

Will gestured to the greens. "Are you going to inspect every leaf?"

Pops took as much pride in his garden as many men took in their children. Sometimes he would be out there for hours—meandering through the vegetables, checking for bugs, pulling weeds. Last summer Will had built him custom planters for the smaller veggies, so he didn't have to bend over as far. He'd also built several resting spots, so Pops could relax and enjoy his time in the bountiful jungle of tall plants and tilled earth. Moist and rich, the fresh fragrance of whatever was ripe and blooming floated on the air.

Will wished he could share his grandfather's fascination with the growing process, but he didn't. When sent to the garden, he was usually frustrated that all the inhabitants weren't fully ripened. It was irritating to him to have to search out the best ones. Pops had given strict instructions on how to squeeze, sniff, and feel to see whether a candidate was ready. But they all felt the same to Will. He avoided the garden as much as possible.

Pops, on the other hand, gloried in it. "I'm just glad there wasn't any hail with the storm we got last week. It would have killed these." He lifted a handful of lettuce greens to Will's face and shook them at him. Particles of dirt fluttered to the open newspaper Pops had underneath them.

Will nodded, leaning back slightly. He placed his cell phone, car keys, and loose change on the side table that split the kitchen area and living room. "What can I do to help?" He squirted dish soap into his hands and scrubbed them under the kitchen faucet.

"I've got it all under control," Pops assured him. "I'm going to pick a few red peppers, then slip down to the dock and check on my crab traps."

Will noticed the large pot of water on the stove. "I'll go check the traps."

"No, I have a certain order I do it in." Pops winked. "You'd probably mess up my system."

"Probably." Pops did a lot of the housework. Will was constantly trying to help out, but he'd noticed how much more content the older man was when he was contributing like this. "So what should I do?"

"Why don't you go upstairs and change, and sit and read that novel I bought you." His eyes twinkled. Will used to love to read fiction, but over the years it had slipped away from him.

Why Pops felt it was important to become reacquainted with it, Will couldn't fathom. When he took time to read for pleasure these days, he liked books on self-help. *The Power of Positive Words in Business* and *How to Grow Your Field of Influence*— these were the titles he preferred, not an adventure book about modern-day pirates on the high seas. But if it pleased Pops, he'd read the thing. "Sounds good."

Pops faced him, smiling and nodding. "I'll holler when dinner's ready."

"Okay, if you're sure," he said, as if he needed a little more convincing, "I mean, I feel guilty sitting and reading while you're down here working so hard."

Pops beamed. "You've worked hard all day. I'm just throwing dinner together." He brushed a hand through the air dismissively, but couldn't disguise his pleasure.

Will watched him leave through the back door, humming and swinging the crab bucket. What would he ever do without

Pops? Will grabbed a bottle of ice-cold water and started up the stairs. After all, he had an exciting high-adventure pirate novel waiting for him.

Adrienne hated admitting it, but she'd driven by the house twice since last week, when she was so rudely dismissed by Will Bryant, bank boy. She paused in front of the home, with her heart picking up beats. An admirable garden stretched alongside. Her vantage point gave her a good view, so she admired it, hoping to kick up the courage to go to the door again.

The garden was full and lush and reminded her of the one she had in Chicago, but on a much grander scale. It was anchored by a picket fence that enclosed it in priceless oasis fashion. Tall stalks of a variety of vegetables reached toward the sky. Dots of red, gold, yellow, and purple were visible from under their protective leaves. She tried to count the number of different types of vegetables, but couldn't. There were raised boxes of herbs and ground cover plants, birdbaths, and benches. And the whole thing looked like something you might see in the French countryside. Even from her car she could smell the mint that nestled in one corner.

The scent brought back memories of Chicago—good memories for a change. There were a few things she missed about the Windy City. Her garden topped the list. Then, of course, the museums. She could sit for hours and watch history collide with the present—schoolchildren strolling through the Middle Ages, young couples in love admiring the raw diamonds. Her parents had come to visit her one spring. What had her father said about museums? Oh, yes, *God's family photo album.*

She'd left a few friends in the city as well. But no really close friends. Eric had discouraged her from getting too close to anyone. And the friends she'd left behind would probably have little to nothing in common with her now. The circle of five girls that got together once a week for lunch spent their time discussing what was happening in town, the new theater shows, who had gotten the best deal on a Prada bag or Chanel dress, where the new sushi bar was opening. Adrienne's gaze drifted down over her T-shirt and jeans. *If they could see me now.* It was strange that she didn't miss them more. But she did miss her garden.

She continued to admire the beautifully landscaped, custom wooden boxes of herbs, flowers, and the greenery. She *might* be able to build a smaller version.

That's when she saw him.

Fifty yards beyond the garden on the dock stood a man just about the age she was looking for. She threw the car into park and shaded her eyes with her hand. The evening mist came with the low sun, sneaking up the end of the pier and almost encasing him. It was like a painting, a masterpiece half hidden in the mist's shadow. But the man. He alone was what caused her heart to stop. In what seemed like slow motion, he worked, dragging something up out of the water. Hand over hand, he tugged a drenched rope.

As if he sensed being watched, he turned just enough for her to catch his profile. He was taller than she'd imagined and extremely fit for a man who'd seen so many decades. He worked the rope into a circle on the dock, where little droplets of water pooled on the wooden planks; the motion caused him to face her.

Her fingers shook and something dropped into the pit of her stomach. On shaky legs, Adrienne left the safety of her car. Without thinking about it, or what she might say, or anything, her feet carried her toward him. Past the house, past the vegetable garden with its sharp scent of herbs and earth. She didn't care that she was trespassing. She walked to the edge of the pier, barely noticing the luxurious boat moored there, for her gaze stayed fixed on William.

He pulled in what looked to her like some kind of trap, seemingly unaware that she was standing there as he dropped the trap's contents into a bucket and hoisted the container. He turned fully, as if to head home, but jolted when he saw her. Adrienne's hand flew into her pocket where the photo lay. She stared at it, then back at him. The decay of time had taken its toll, but there was no denying the strong chin, structured features, and high brow.

William.

A friendly smile animated his face. "Evening, young lady. How can I help you?"

This was it. It was him. "I believe I'm looking for you. William Bryant." There was more answer than question as his name rolled off her tongue. More star-struck wonder than she would have thought.

Kind eyes searched her face, a hint of a frown deepening the lines between his brows. "Do we know each other? I'm sorry, I don't recognize you."

"I recognize you." She reached into her pocket and held the photo out to him. "But not from your picture. From the letters."

Ever so slowly he took the photo from her. She watched sixty years of memories flood him, and for an instant, Adrienne was sure her coming was a mistake.

He sat the bucket down gently. Angry crabs bumped and knocked at the sides as he gazed upon his past. Beyond them, the boat rocked, canal water slapping against it. Crickets were beginning their nightly song, their sound intensifying as night fell. Finally, he spoke. "You said you recognized me from my letters?"

She nodded and was struck with the very real possibility that he would have no interest in talking to her. A wave of anxiety washed over. Maybe he would want to retrieve the letters and bid her good-bye.

Of course, that was supposed to be okay. But now that she was here, face to face, the idea of leaving without having even one conversation with this man scared her.

Tender blue eyes, watery from age, studied her as if he read her thoughts. "I think we must have a lot to talk about."

Adrienne sighed relief.

He motioned in front of them toward his back door, just up a slight hill from the pier. As the fog closed in and drained color from the surrounding world, they made their way to the back of the house, with William pressing a hand against his left knee with each step.

They reached the back porch, but Adrienne paused in hesitation, recalling the conversation only a week before with the other William Bryant.

"Something wrong, dear?" He pulled the door open.

"Yes," she said quietly. "Last week I knocked on the front door. The man there was less than forthcoming about your whereabouts."

He frowned for a quick second. "That's Will, my grandson. He's got a heart of gold but tends to be a little overprotective."

Heart of gold, yeah, right. "Well, I don't think he'll be happy I'm here. He was pretty quick to get rid of me."

"Nonsense." He shooed her into the kitchen while crabs smacked the sides of the bucket. "We can talk while I fix dinner. Would that be okay?"

"Um, yes." Adrienne raised and dropped her hands. "That would be fine."

They went inside, and he reached for a stack of newspapers and handed some to Adrienne. She copied him, spreading the papers across the kitchen table, noticing the difference between her hands—smooth and with fingertips tinted by wood stain, and his—wrinkled and age-spotted, with swollen, arthritic knuckles. Somehow, he managed an air of strength despite the obvious frailty.

She couldn't believe she was here. With him. With William. The same man who had invaded Normandy. The same man who had nearly frozen and starved at Bastogne. The man who never gave up. But the most remarkable thing about it—he was everything she'd imagined. Men like him really did exist. Even if they were from generations ago.

Chapter 6

*T*hey were laughing when Will neared the room. He peeked from the living room around the kitchen door to find her and Pops sitting at the table. Her long dark hair shone everywhere the light hit it. Her voice was sultry as it slipped out of that soft, generous mouth. There was a scent of citrus and flowers surrounding her, and if it hadn't been for the pungent aroma of fresh crab, it might have been disarming. Will rubbed a hand over his face, shook his head to clear it, and glanced around the room, trying to erase the vision of the woman he'd met last week. Fat chance. He'd thought about her often in the last seven days. Even caught himself glancing up at work occasionally when he caught a glimpse of dark hair. Ridiculous. Just as ridiculous as her showing up to inquire about his grandfather. Again.

He pulled a breath and stepped fully into the room. The veggies had been chopped and arranged into a salad; the crab had been cleaned and boiled; and now she and Pops sat at the table, breaking open crab legs and removing the meat.

She hadn't knocked on the door this time. Nope, she must have stalked Pops outside. Great. Will was pretty sure his grandfather had already invited her to stay for dinner—fresh crab salad was one of his specialties. Besides, that's just the kind of man Pops was, gracious and ever so trusting.

Will, on the other hand, glared at her accusingly. "I thought I heard voices," he said as he stopped where he could tower over them.

"Will, this is Adrienne Carter." Pops used his elbow to shove a chair out so Will could sit. "She lives in Bonita Springs."

Will nodded but didn't sit down. He'd traded his work attire for old jeans and a white T-shirt. He almost wished he were still in his suit and tie. He felt more authoritative in them, and something about this woman caused him to be slightly off kilter. The suit would help him keep control of the situation. Will pressed his eyes shut. Really? Was he really feeling intimidated by a sprite of a woman who couldn't weigh more than 100 pounds soaking wet? The thought of seeing her soaking wet flashed through his mind. Skin glistening with water, flesh slick, and . . . *whoa there*. Will reined in his thoughts.

"Here," Pops said, trying unsuccessfully to remove the loose bits of crab from his fingers. He reached for the photo. "Isn't that a handsome fellow?"

Will took the picture. He softened, remembering what Pops had looked like years ago when Will was a kid. Not this young, of course, but younger than now. The two of them had always been close. His mind's eye took him back to when he was only five years old, sitting on the floor next to Pops, the two of them coloring for hours until Pops had to have Grandma Betty give him a hand up from the floor. For several moments he stared at the photo, wondering when Pops had gotten old. It seemed like it had happened so fast. Five years ago, in fact.

Laughter once again drew his attention to the present. Will placed the picture on the table with a little more force than necessary and turned his full focus to Adrienne Carter. "So, are you a student doing a paper on World War II?"

"No," Adrienne said, for the first time looking self-conscious about the crab meat she was up to her elbows in. She used her shoulder to brush some of that luscious hair away from her face.

A twinge hit him for being so rude, but hey, this was the last thing Pops needed right now. "Reporter?"

She shook her head, those giant eyes troubled. She glanced to Pops, seemingly searching for help.

"Settle down." Pops said. "She didn't come here for anything like that. Forgive my grandson, but a few years ago, a show about the 101st Airborne was a big hit on TV, and we were inundated with reporters and college students wanting interviews about the war. It was when we found out my wife was sick. Not the best time for interviews."

"I'm so sorry," she said.

Pops turned to Will. "She has some letters that belong to me."

A little of the tension left Will's shoulders.

Pops winked at Adrienne. "Of course, they were in your house. Technically, they belong to you."

She gently touched the older man on the arm. "They're your letters. I wouldn't have it any other way."

Her voice lowered when she said it, rolling over Will like honey on toast. He pulled out the chair and dropped his six-foot frame into it. So he'd misjudged her. "It's nice to meet you, Adrienne," he mumbled.

"You as well, Will." A flash of a smile on that full mouth, and she returned to her job of removing meat from shells.

"Adrienne is staying for dinner," Pops announced.

Will pointed to her hands, covered with bits of crab meat. "I figured so. I really didn't think you were going to have her help make dinner, then ask her to leave before eating it."

Pops winked at her again. "That would be downright rude, wouldn't it?"

Will watched as she pressed her lips together, biting back a smile. She pivoted and swung her feet out from under the table.

Will's eyes trailed down a pair of long, slender legs to the tanned ankles tied with a black sandal strap. Dark pink toes. Sexy feet, especially as she stood, high on the sandals. She leaned over and grabbed the greasy bowl of empty shells.

Will realized he was staring, so he stood up with her, a half-hearted attempt at courtesy. He reached his hand out to take the bowl. "Can I help?" But he only succeeded in making her jump. The two were now face to face at the table edge. The color drained from her cheeks. *Wow*, he thought, *I really must have been a bear the other day to elicit such a response.*

"Uh, yes . . . " She clutched the bowl, but he could see her slippery fingers losing their grip. She pulled it to her, against an apron he'd seen Pops wear many times. Then he saw panic in her eyes as her grip tightened, but the bowl slipped away from her anyway.

It flipped up, over, around, and fell as she clambered, fingers grasping, trying to recover. Empty crab claws showered the floor, then ricocheted, pelting them all with bits of meat and crab water. The bowl didn't break, but turned like a top, its clattering ring echoing through the kitchen until it finally rested.

Adrienne's jaw hung open in shock, her face turning from pink to a deep crimson red. Bits of crab were stuck to her legs and clothes. In her right hand she grasped one mutilated claw.

"Glad I could help," Will said, beginning to chuckle as he heard Pops mumbling that the kitchen floor needed to be mopped anyway.

She blinked big brown eyes. Once, then again, her mind probably trying to catch up with what she'd just done. There was a bit of crab meat caught in her eyelashes. That's when Will laughed, a deep belly laugh, and it rolled right out of him, ridiculous as the mess that was in the kitchen and on the pretty brunette who'd arrived and turned their crab bowl—and their evening—upside down. In five years of making fresh crab, Will had plenty of messes under his belt, but none came close to this, and for some reason, inexplicable and surprising, the look on her face, coupled with the crab stuck in her lashes, unhinged him. She stared at him for a few horrified seconds. Blink, blink went the crab. She must have noticed it there because she blinked harder, her left eye trying to focus on the white sliver, and she actually tried to lean away from it. It dropped onto her cheek, and Adrienne reached up.

"Here, let me." He slid a thumb across her face, trying not to notice how smooth and delicate her skin felt beneath his touch.

"I don't know what to say," she managed.

"How about, where's the mop and broom?" His voice lowered to match hers, creating more intimacy in the moment than he intended.

With the crab meat gone from her cheek, Adrienne took in the carnage. "It's everywhere," she whispered.

"Yeah. You've got a lot of work to do."

Her dark eyes fanned back to his face. He was fighting another full-on laugh when her own glossy lips spread into a smile. Her shoulders rose, and she tried to stifle the laugh but couldn't. Adrienne and Will both dropped to their knees to gather the pieces. Pops grabbed a garbage can as they cleaned up.

Adrienne sprawled on the floor, catlike, with one elbow propped up. Will's gaze danced over those legs again. He noticed her toes were painted meticulously, but her fingernails were worn down and . . . stained. He thought he'd seen that the other day but had dismissed it. Beautiful women—he'd told himself—don't run around with stained fingers.

Adrienne got up, ran her hands under the water at the sink, and reached for the soap a second time.

"That won't work," Will said, sliding beside her. He cut a fresh lemon and gave her half of it. "Try this."

She threw him a half grin. "No thanks, I prefer oranges."

"Ha, ha. It's not to eat." He rubbed a piece over his hands. "It removes the fishy smell."

Her gaze drifted down to his chest. "Does it work on shirts too?" She reached over and plucked a piece of crab meat from his T-shirt.

"Hopefully," he said, and noticed he was smiling again. He liked watching her gaze slide down over him. So she wasn't here to use his grandfather for a story or a thesis. She was simply here to return items that belonged to Pops. That changed the dynamic.

Will tried to keep reminding himself of that, but somewhere in the back of his mind he felt there was more to the pretty brunette's story. Throughout dinner, he couldn't stop his gaze from continually drifting to the klutzy woman with the smoldering eyes. It was almost like she knew his grandfather as well as he did.

"Tell me about yourself, Adrienne," William said, shaking pepper onto his salad. They had settled into a comfortable flow of conversation—until now. She'd never really liked talking about herself. And now that she was a twenty-eight-year-old divorcée, she liked it even less. "I moved here from Chicago," she began slowly. "I've always wanted to live in a beach house in Florida, so in February, I began looking for one." February 14th, to be exact. The day her divorce was final. Happy Valentine's Day.

"Did you have some high-falootin' job in Chicago?"

Will rolled his eyes at her. "He means high-powered job."

She smiled. "I recognized the term. I have a grandfather as well." Taking a bite of salad and crab meat, she looked from the older Mr. Bryant to the younger. Will had seemed so stoic at first, but that had melted somewhere between broken shells flying in the air and squeezing fresh lemons to eradicate the smell.

"No," she said. "No high-falootin' job for me." Side by side, she could see the family resemblance in the two Mr. Bryants, though the contrasts were glaring. William's eyes were a soft blue, the shade of a pale summer sky and soft fuzzy baby blankets. Will's were an intense green that seemed to darken in direct relation to his mood. William's hair was white, but full. Will's hair was dark with loose waves that threatened the business professional cut it was layered into. Hair gel held it in place, and for a brief moment Adrienne wondered what it looked like untamed and windblown.

"So, why now?" William set his fork against his plate.

She lowered hers too, not wanting to discuss what brought her here. Not now and not ever. This night wasn't about her. It was about William. But as her eyes traveled up, it was Will's tender look that held her captive. The green had softened, almost glowing, coaxing her on. Suddenly, she did want to explain. "I was in a divorce months ago. I never wanted to live in Chicago, but he accepted a residency there. We met while he was in med school and married before graduation. He promised that when he finished school we would move to Florida, but he really had no intention of doing so. He'd made up his mind and that was that."

Concern ran across both men's faces. "How long were you married?" Pops asked.

Will shot a look over to him. "She may not be comfortable talking about this, Pops."

Adrienne shook her head. "No, it's okay." She felt like she was in a safe environment, tucked between two men she barely knew. "Five years, almost six."

Pops rubbed a hand over his face, elbows on the table. He threaded his fingers together, chin against them, and leaned slightly toward her. "So sorry, Miss Adrienne. Love is an unpredictable thing. It is beauty and tragedy."

Adrienne took a thoughtful moment. She nodded.

"Pops, you sound like a Hallmark card." The somber mood that had filled the kitchen dissipated. Will glanced at her with an apologetic smile.

She smiled back. And really, didn't she owe William this? She had walked into his life without his consent or approval. "My husband was unfaithful. It was the last straw. So I began looking for a house to remodel here on the Gulf Coast."

"Good for you," William said, rising from the table. "How is the remodel going?"

"Considering I've never done anything like it, I'd have to say it's going well," she said, but noticed Will's eyes had not left her. "Until a week ago."

William pulled a piping-hot pan of cobbler out of the oven and turned. "What happened a week ago?"

"I found your letters." The aroma of homemade crust and fresh fruit made its way to the table. Even though she was full, she salivated.

Pops set the pan down on the stove top. "My letters have distracted you that much?"

She nodded. "I'm afraid so."

"Perhaps I better take them back, or you'll never get your house finished."

Will had grown quiet.

"I don't even remember what I said in them. Sitting down to write a letter was an escape for most of us, like a little mini-vacation from the madness." He sat back down and drifted off to another time and place. "When I had downtime, there were only two options. Write a letter to Gracie or read a letter from Gracie." He reached for the photo on the table. His hand ran along the torn portion. A tiny frown drew his brows together as he examined the jagged edge where Gracie had once completed the photograph.

Adrienne swallowed, her appetite for cobbler gone.

His finger moved from that side of the photo to the other; a gentle smile touched his face, dissolving the struggle she'd just seen. "Sweet Sara," he whispered, lovingly. "She was fourteen when I left. Her mom had just bought her this dress. Gracie and I took her to town and got the picture made. It was the only time I ever saw a dress on Sara."

Adrienne settled into the chair.

Memories danced, catching the light in his soft blue eyes. "She was the original tomboy. Rolled-up pants and hair tied back. You would more likely find her at the fishing hole than at a dress shop. Sara loved to fish." He set the picture on the table.

When Pops's voice cracked, Adrienne's heart crumbled. She looked away, feeling this was too intimate a memory to be privy to. But the silence became stifling, and she looked back to Pops to find his eyes misty.

"I guess she grew up while I was gone." His index finger ran across her picture as if trying to capture her essence. "I just wish I knew what happened to her . . . "

The sadness in his tone pierced Adrienne's heart. "You never saw her after the war?"

"No," he said. "After Gracie died, Sara and her momma packed up and moved back to North Carolina. They were gone just days before I came home."

Adrienne shot a quick look to Will but couldn't read his face. She reached over to Pops and placed her hand on his sun-darkened arm. "I am so sorry about Gracie."

"Love is beauty and tragedy, remember?" He patted her hand. "Gracie's letters got me through the darkest chapters of my life. I would never have survived without her. I still thank God she kept writing. She made a choice to follow a different path, fell in love with someone else, but she kept me alive. And I never knew it from the letters. She still sounded just as in love as the day I left. It wasn't until I got back that I learned . . . " He paused, cleared his throat. "Maybe if I'd made it home quicker, she wouldn't have left town with that other man. She died one month to the day before I got home."

"And Sara was gone too?"

"Sara was gone." He shrugged. "I didn't know how to find her, contact her. We both lost our best friend when we lost Gracie. I wanted to be there for Sara, but she didn't stay in touch with anyone here." He cradled the photo. "Didn't leave an address. It was like she just disappeared."

Years had healed the wound, but not the sorrow. To still hold Gracie in such high regard was remarkable, and Adrienne was once again reminded she was in the company of an extraordinary man.

Will, on the other hand, seemed to have grown increasingly uncomfortable with the conversation. "I didn't know any of that, Pops. Your life is full of mysteries." He stood to clear the dishes.

Pops picked up the cue and stood as well, stretching up slowly, using the table for support. He took the plate from his grandson. "Let me." He motioned toward Adrienne. "Why don't you two go sit on the front porch while I clean up."

But both Will and Adrienne protested and began moving dishes and silverware to the sink. After all the work he'd done already, neither one was willing to let him clean too.

"Fine," William said, sounding tired while the two of them sprang into action. "When you're done, you can go wait for me out front. I'm going to relax for a few minutes in the living room while the cobbler cools. I'll meet you out there when it's ready."

Adrienne slid dishes under running water, rinsing them before placing them in the dishwasher. Without the buffer of Pops in the room, an awkward silence hung in the air. Will hadn't wanted her here in the first place, and blast it all, he was just so irritatingly difficult to get a read on. "I should probably go home. I think I've disrupted enough of your evening," she said.

Will stopped and turned to face her. "I'd like you to stay. Pops is a social creature but doesn't get many visitors. You—you've made it a nice evening for him."

Well, that was unexpected.

Unexpected. A good description for the younger Mr. Bryant. The top of her head barely reached his shoulder, causing her to have to look up to see his eyes. She did and found him to be uncomfortably close. He'd been passing her dishes for the last several minutes, standing close, then moving away. But now there were no more dishes in his hand, and it was just him and his broad shoulders and bright green eyes.

One side of Will's face cracked into a smile. "Besides, Pops would be crushed if you left before having some of his homemade cobbler."

"What about *your* evening? I feel like I'm intruding . . . "

His gaze dropped to her lips for a split second, and Adrienne felt a whoosh of hot blood shoot from her head to her stomach.

"You're not intruding."

Okay, Will seriously needed to turn down the intensity level on those eyes.

As if he'd picked up on her discomfort, he moved away. "In fact, you've been a great help. If you hadn't been here, I would've had to clean all the crab."

"I'm good at cleaning them—just lousy at getting the shells safely to the trash."

"Well, that's a talent that takes years of practice." He recovered the last plate, rinsed it, and handed it to her to slide into the dishwasher.

She tilted her head to the side, eyeing him. "You didn't do so well either." She reached under the sink for the detergent she knew would be there.

"I was distracted," he said, taking it from her and pouring it in.

"Did I distract you?" she teased.

"Yes," he admitted, a mischievous grin animating his face. "I thought you were some nutball."

"Oh, very nice. But now I'm okay?" She slid the lock on the dishwasher, and they nearly bumped heads as both bent to set it to the proper wash cycle.

He shrugged. "We'll see." Will had an amazing smile, and he knew just how to use it, she realized. He motioned for her to follow him outside. The two of them paused in the doorway. "We're headed out, Pops. Let me know when the cobbler's ready to cut."

William mumbled something from farther in the living room. Will shook his head at his grandfather's obvious attempt to leave them alone for a while.

Adrienne and Will stepped outside into the evening air. Two large trees laden with Spanish moss secured the front yard. Tall, spiny trees stood at attention along the edge of the driveway, guardians of the Bryant fortress.

"It's beautiful out here," she said. Tropical bushes and pots of vibrant flowers surrounded them as they moved to sit on the porch swing, where a thousand crickets serenaded.

"I'm sorry about your marriage."

Ugh. They really didn't have to go there again. Tension knotted Adrienne's neck.

Will threaded his hands together. "I see that happen a lot at work, and it's a shame."

The breeze moved the giant palm leaves of the nearby trees as if whispering to the night's sky. "Thank you. You see that at work at the bank?"

"I'm the senior loan officer there."

"Oh," she said, trying to make the connection between divorces and banking.

He seemed to pick up on her confusion. "I handle a lot of business accounts. Couples getting divorced who are joint owners in a business rarely want to stay in business together."

"I guess a lot of businesses sell for that reason, huh?"

"Some, but more often one party will buy out the other. That's where I come in. New business loans, new paperwork." He used his index finger to scrape at the paint on the swing's armrest. It sported a bare section, and she thought he must do that often. "Trust me, I've sat in on my share of 'he said, she said' conversations where both parties are more concerned with hurling accusations at each other than taking care of their incomes and investments."

She frowned. "In the middle of a divorce, income is the least of your worries."

"When it should be at the top of your list."

Adrienne stared at him. *You can't really be this dense. This callous.* "When your world is crumbling around you, you don't stop to think about money."

"I know, and that's a problem. I mean, isn't there enough upheaval with the divorce? I'd think people would want to protect what stability they have."

"Wow. Stability must be really important to you."

He turned to face her. "Isn't it to you?"

Heat rose to her cheeks. "Oh yeah. Absolutely. That's why I bought a house practically sight unseen in a town I've never been, planning to restore what most would condemn. Yeah, I'm all about stability." Her words hung in the air, emotions dredged up and raw.

He sat quietly for a few seconds, his fingers lacing and unlacing in slow, methodical motions. "Sorry, Adrienne. That doesn't sound very stable."

A humorless laugh escaped her lips. "Well, we've discovered I'm all about stability and you're all about compassion."

She watched his brows knot, and then understanding came into his gaze. How could anyone over age *fifteen* not understand what love does to the heart? And the brain.

William Senior stepped out onto the porch just in time. He must have felt the thick tension in the air because he set three bowls of blackberry cobbler on the table and split questioning glances between Will and Adrienne.

The metal chairs scraped against the wooden deck as they pulled them from under the patio table to sit. It was Adrienne who broke the silence. "This looks wonderful, William." She scooped a plump blackberry into her mouth, tangy sweetness zinging her taste buds, helping erase her frustration with Will.

"I've been perfecting this recipe for twelve years." He tilted his head back.

"Come clean, Pops," Will said with a hint of humor and accusation in his tone. "This was Grandma's recipe. You haven't changed it a bit."

"That's not true," Pops corrected. "Sometimes I add the salt first, sometimes the baking powder."

Adrienne laughed. One thing about Will, whether he was frustrating or not, he adored his grandfather.

"And it tastes the same every single time," Will reminded him.

Now that Pops had joined them, the earlier tension dissolved. "William, I have a confession to make."

Both men abandoned their plates and gave her their attention.

She twisted the checkered napkin in her hands. "I wasn't completely sure I'd find you. Or get to talk to you." Her gaze skated to Will. His eyebrows rose.

"What I'm trying to say is, I don't have the letters with me." *And I wasn't about to leave them with Will,* Adrienne added silently. *Even if he admitted to being your grandson.*

William's light-blue eyes smiled at her. "That's okay. You can bring them back another time."

Adrienne shot a quick glance over to Will, but his reaction was unreadable.

William took another bite, "If it isn't too much trouble for you."

"No, I'd love to come back." *Maybe during banking hours, when your aggravating grandson is gone.*

She met Will's gaze and hoped he hadn't read her thoughts. But she didn't find the contempt she'd expected. In fact, he almost seemed glad he hadn't completely run her off.

"You really enjoy those letters don't you?" Pops's light-blue eyes wrinkled at the corners.

"I do," Adrienne whispered.

"Do me a favor then?" Pops rested his elbows on the table, fork hovering over his dessert.

"Anything."

"Make yourself a copy before you bring them back."

Her gaze dropped to the table. "Are you sure? I mean, they're . . . well, intimate."

"I'd be honored to share them with you, Adrienne. Love doesn't always go the way we hope, but that doesn't mean we can stop living. It doesn't mean love isn't a beautiful thing." Aged fingers rubbed swollen knuckles, and his gaze intensified to the point that she thought she might burst. "You understand?"

Don't stop living. Oh, she understood. That was a tall order. One she wasn't completely sure she could manage. Adrienne exhaled and looked away, beyond the yard to a long stretch of road, the road that had brought her here. The road that would later lead her home. It was becoming familiar, each turn, each bump. "I understand."

When there was no more cobbler and no other excuse to stay, Adrienne returned home. It was nearly 10:30, and the cool breeze of a coastal night proved too much for her to resist. She chose a random letter from the stack and went out back, where a moon framed by a million stars shone against the water. Off in the distance, she heard the hum of a motorboat moving slowly along the horizon. Adrienne opened the letter and read.

October 1944

Dear Gracie,

Something I've learned while being here is that a man must have clear vision. Sometimes I wonder what keeps the others going. You keep me going, Grace. The thought of your smile when we'd watch the dolphins play along the sandbar, the wind in your hair, the shimmer of sun on your skin. This would be an impossible task if it weren't for those things. They reach to me, Gracie. Even though you're so far away, I relive your smile, I relive your touch. Over and over I see you there, standing before me, your arms outstretched and waiting. That image keeps me alive.

I look at Rick and Chuck and the others, and I wonder. Do they have a Gracie back home? Someone who powers their ability to get up, keep moving? I won't lie to you. There've been times my heart failed me and I wanted to give up. But you are the strength I lean on, the power that fuels me, from my heart to my mind, to every limb of my body.

Love is a peculiar thing, I think, lending its persuasiveness to every area of a man and giving him the fortitude to live, to thrive, to survive. Thank you for the treasure that is you. Thank you for giving me vision. And most of all, Grace, thank you for loving me.

All my heart,
William

She sighed and smiled. A light breeze lifted Adrienne's hair from her shoulders, dragging the humidity of summer with it, but she didn't mind. This was her home now. She watched as a tiny green frog dove off the end of her back deck. There was much to love about southern Florida. Come to think of it, she really didn't miss Chicago at all.

Chapter 7

Ryan, hi," Adrienne said, eyes wide, pulling the door open. She hadn't expected him to drop by.

Three months before, she had met him on this very porch for the first time, after a long, fitful night's sleep in a huge house that creaked and moaned its own lullaby. Her hair had been a mess, and the sofa she'd slept on had left its imprint on her cheek. She'd pulled the door open to find a muscled, tan grad student stuffed into a Florida State T-shirt, claiming to be one of Mary Lathrop's friends. And so a sort of relationship began. First he'd invited her out with some of his friends. Being lonely, she'd taken the invite after a few panicked hours of consideration. Ryan had been patient with her, treating her more like a friend than a date on numerous occasions. Then the big crowds became smaller, until it was just the two of them. Eeeeeaaaase into dating, her dad had told her. Ryan had seen to that. There'd always be a soft place in her heart for him.

"Hey," he said easily as she motioned for him to come inside. He was still muscular. Still tan. Because they had discussed the boundaries of their relationship, it shouldn't make her uncomfortable that he was here, but it sent little tremors of doubt through her. Adrienne—horrible at confrontation—didn't want to have to figure out their friendship again.

"I was at the coffee shop the other morning, and Sammie told me about all the progress you've made on the house."

What a relief. It's just a friendly visit to check out the ongoing project. Excitement overtook any lingering apprehension. "Do you want to look around?"

He nodded and gave her a dazzling smile. He inspected the living room and glanced into the kitchen. "You've transformed this place. It doesn't seem like the same house."

The living room walls were painted a rich buttery color and the chair rail had received a crisp, new coat of white. She had stripped the ornate fireplace mantel to reveal hand-carved mahogany that, now stained, seemed to glow. In every corner, she'd found the home's expression, the room's personality. It was evolving into a masterpiece far beyond her expectations. Adrienne couldn't hide her delight. "I never really thought I could do it. And there is still a lot of work to be done, but I really think I'm going to be able to pull it off." She didn't mind enlisting the help of professionals whenever a job was too daunting, but she hadn't given up and called in a general contractor like Eric had told her she would. He'd ridiculed her relentlessly when she told him she would spend her divorce settlement money on a dilapidated Victorian monster poised on the Gulf of Mexico.

After a closer examination of the kitchen and discussing what was left to do there, she offered Ryan a glass of iced tea and gestured toward the back deck. Opening the French door caused sea air to slam into Ryan and pushed him closer to Adrienne. She sidestepped and dropped into a lawn chair. They sat and watched waves rush up the shore, chasing tiny birds searching for a meal. She could hear some families farther down the beach. Now and then, she allowed her gaze to drift over to Ryan. Gone was that schoolgirl fluttery feeling, she realized, and was thankful for that. In its place was just the genuine warmth of seeing a friend.

After a few minutes of silence, Ryan turned to her. "So tell me about the letters."

Shocked, Adrienne threw a look his way. Sammie must have told him. Of course, she hadn't asked her not to tell anyone; she'd just expected it. The battle within her began. At first she was reluctant to talk about William Bryant and his story, but as she sat there thinking about war and bravery, it became clear that his was a story that needed to be heard. It was beautiful. It was inspiring.

Over the next hour, she shared William's life with Ryan. Ryan listened, occasionally asking a question, and had actually inserted some interesting facts and tidbits of information. He was a World War II buff. "He's a war hero, Adrienne. The real deal."

She loved the fact that others found William as intriguing as she did. But something had consistently plagued her thoughts after meeting him three nights ago: Grace and the fact she'd continued to write William even though she'd fallen in love with someone else. The last letter was dated 1945. Grace had continued to write for close to two years. Maybe it was as simple as Gracie wanting to have a backup plan if her new love didn't work out. "I got to meet him, you know."

"You mean William?" Ryan took a long drink of tea, cubes of ice clinking as he finished.

"Yes. And I'm going back. I have to pick up some granite samples in Naples tomorrow."

"So you're going to go with granite after all?"

"Yes." Adrienne had agonized over the decision. Beauty versus price and practicality, but in the end, her love of gourmet cooking outweighed any price factor. Even though it stretched her budget to the hilt and left no room for error, granite she would have.

Ryan wiped his hands on his shorts and reached for the letters sitting between them. He rifled through, the old pages delicately and more interested in their contents than her counter choice. "So what's he like?"

"Old. And amazing. As amazing as his letters. Listen to this." She took the stack from him and searched for one. "Their company was being moved from one location to another. They stopped in a village that had been abandoned. They only had a few hours to rest." She unfolded the letter and began to read.

We'd been walking for eleven hours. Though paratroopers are jumpers, we've put more miles on our boots than a lot of foot soldiers. It was a cool night, but not cold. The beauty of the French countryside surrounded us. Had it not been for the remnants of battle, it would have been the most picturesque place I've ever seen. It had been two days since most of us had slept, so being allowed a seven-hour break was a welcome gift.

Then we saw her. She was standing in the doorway of a home that, like the others, had been all but destroyed by the constant shelling that had caused the evacuation of the town. She was a pretty girl, Gracie, reminding me of what Sara may look like in a few years. There were cuts on her arms, but her wounds seemed superficial. We wondered if she'd been left behind accidentally.

We could see she wanted to run, but she stood firm as we moved toward her. She picked up a broom handle as if she would take on the whole lot of us if she needed to. Amos made his way to her first. Being from Louisiana, he spoke some French, so we were able to discover why she was there. Once sure we meant her no harm, she pleaded with us to help her. An elderly woman lay in the small bedroom. The young girl explained that she had been too sick to move, so they stayed there despite the order to evacuate. It got into all our hearts.

Gracie, always remember when one is confronted with a random act of kindness that is neither expected nor ordinary, one is obligated to meet that kindness and exceed it if possible.

So that's what we did. Taking turns, we repaired the roof of her house. The war was nearing its completion, or so we had been told. If we could leave her with enough food for a couple months, she might have a chance. Doc, our medic, examined the girl's grandmother. He left her with some medicine. Most of us only got a couple hours of sleep that night, but what we'd accomplished in that few hours rejuvenated us unlike sleep ever could. It might even be enough to keep us going for the remainder of the war. We've brought so much death, bringing life replaced a bit of what we'd lost.

"Read that part again about a random act of kindness." Ryan leaned his weight on the chair arm.

Adrienne didn't have to read it. She'd probably read it a hundred times and now could quote it without looking. She dropped the paper to her lap. "When one is confronted with a random act of kindness that is neither expected nor ordinary, one is obligated to meet that kindness and exceed it if possible."

"I've never heard anyone talk like that," Ryan admitted, tilting his face to the setting sun.

"People should, though. And live by it as well."

Ryan nodded, leaning back in the flower print cushion on the Adirondack chair. Silence fell over them as they watched a shrimp boat slide across the horizon.

"Can I tell you something?" Adrienne said.

Ryan angled to look at her.

"Meeting him, reading his letters . . . it's changing me." She pressed a hand to her heart. "I don't think I ever thought of love as a force, a thing that gives you power."

Ryan chuckled.

"Sounds stupid, right?" Her eyes rolled.

"Not if it's how you feel." Ryan leaned forward and rested his elbows on his knees. "Tell me about this force, Adrienne."

She shrugged. "I can't. It's elusive."

"Like the green flash?"

Adrienne had heard of the phenomenon that happened on the beach just as the sun set. A green flash, shooting across the horizon and lasting only a couple of seconds. She'd watched the sunset almost every night and had never seen it. "Maybe even more elusive than that. But I'll keep watching for it. I had just about given up on love before the letters. I guess that's how they're changing me."

Ryan leaned back, placed his head against the chair and shut his eyes. "Good. You need it."

"Ryan!"

"What?"

"That's . . . that's not very nice to say." The wind kicked up, annoying little fingerlings of air tossing her hair in too many directions. She gathered it at her nape and trapped the strands against the chair back.

"We're friends, right? So I should be able to talk freely." He paused for half a second. "You're an amazing woman, Adrienne. Some dude is going to be lucky to snag you. But fact is, that jerk in Chicago really did a number on you. So if love is like the green flash, and you've started watching for it again, good for you. You needed it."

Adrienne blinked, unsure what surprised her the most: the fact that she and Ryan were having this conversation or the fact that she kept surrounding herself with blunt people who apparently had no filter on their mouths. She sighed, leaned forward, shook her head violently, and let the wind have its way. "You're right."

"So, let those letters work their magic."

Adrienne settled more deeply into her chair and closed her eyes, copying Ryan's posture. "They are, Ryan. Believe me. They are."

Chapter 8

*A*drienne sat in the dark in the first bedroom at the top of the stairs. This was the smallest of the three bedrooms and, like the others, displayed circa 1930s wallpaper. The crown molding framing the room was painted white but had darkened as years rolled by and time left its mark. This would be the first bedroom she'd remodel, she decided. She had finished much of the downstairs, and it was time to begin the upstairs projects. But that's not why she sat here now.

It had been two weeks since she had first met William Bryant and his irritating grandson. She had returned his letters, but not before making a copy, and then visited while Will was at work. William had invited her back. The two of them struck up a friendship, and she'd returned to visit him four times since. Over the course of time, Adrienne noticed something. He talked more about Sara than he did about Grace.

Adrienne forced Grace from her mind, but couldn't erase Sara so easily. William spoke of her often. She'd heard so much about the sassy tomboy, she felt as though she knew her.

Plunked down on the bed with her arms spread wide, she closed her eyes and imagined her house a half century earlier. This was Sara's room, she was sure. Sara was the sports lover, and Adrienne discovered marks on the wall in the corner of the room where someone had repeatedly bounced a ball enough times to leave rings on the wall and an impression on the hardwood floor.

Sara loved basketball, according to the letters, and at the time of William's departure was hoping to grow tall enough to play with the boys who met every afternoon at the park on the corner.

Suddenly reminded of her own childhood, Adrienne sprang from the bed and flipped on the light.

She examined the doorframes. Her long fingers slid up one doorjamb, scanning as she went, and down the next, looking for the telltale markings she hoped to find.

Children were always intrigued with how much they'd grown. Adrienne's father used to hold a ruler to her head, stand her against the wall, and make a tiny mark, dating it, and she would read each date in awe of how much taller she'd become. At first, Adrienne's mom had been angry that her father was marking up the doorframe. But she'd quickly softened as she watched her child grow up before her eyes. Within a year, it was Adrienne's mom who was calling her over to study the makeshift growth chart.

After working her way around the room and finding nothing, she thought about Sara's mom. She would have been furious if she'd discovered her daughter had written on the wall. Adrienne's eyes fell on the closet.

She pulled the closet door open and tugged the string on the solitary light. The dusty bulb threw a muted glow into the small empty space. Adrienne had to step completely inside to find the notches she was looking for. Standing where Sara's clothes once hung, there they were.

The marks contained no years. Instead, each scribbled line denoted a day and a month. Sara had grown between January and March. But after April, her growth seemed to slow. Then a jump in July. That mark put her close to Adrienne's height. She ran her fingers over the lines, then dropped her weight against the back wall of the closet. The stillness closed around her. She thought about life in the forties. What was it like to be a girl who loved to play ball and fish with live worms? Sure, that was accepted behavior now, but had not been as much back then.

Sara's mom probably hated it. From all Adrienne could gather, Sara's mom wanted girly girls with ribbons and bows and lace. How did she handle having a tomboy for a daughter? Probably not well at all. Adrienne pulled in a breath, tugged her weight off the back wall, and wished she knew more about Sara. As if some great power heard her plea, the rusty nail found its way into her foot.

Adrienne felt the raw sensation of tearing flesh at the same time she tripped. She caught herself by the doorjamb, fingers tight over Sara's growth marks. She glanced down at her bare feet, already knowing by the pain in her left heel what had happened.

The bathroom door was only a few hobbles away. She walked on her toes, bearing as little weight on the injured heel as possible. With her foot propped against the sink and counter, she cleaned the fresh cut. It wasn't deep, so Adrienne poured on rubbing alcohol, sucked in air through her teeth, and wondered how sore it would be the next day. A square bandage covered the wound.

Leaving the bathroom, she discovered a neat red trail of dots from the bath to the bedroom. "Great," she muttered, and snagged an old towel from beneath the sink. She kept a good stash of ratty towels there because she was constantly filthy from the remodel. She'd ruined a set of expensive ones by thinking her hands were clean after refitting a pipe in the kitchen. Blue gunk still decorated that washcloth and hand towel.

Adrienne dropped to her knees at the first bead of blood. She scrubbed each as she moved along, her heel throbbing its own conga beat as she went and her knees screaming for kneepads. At least she didn't have to get a tetanus shot. That little journey had taken place one week after arrival, when a loose nail in the shutters ripped her arm open.

When the last droplet was cleaned—or at least smeared into the pockmarked wood floor enough to be unnoticeable—she stopped at the closet door again to catch her breath. Tiny beads of sweat popped out across her forehead and caused her hair to stick to her temples. Once she was inside the closet, she saw the nail protruding near a final spot of her blood. She moved in carefully, no longer trusting the wood floor, and rubbed the rag against the stain, cautious not to catch her finger on the evil nail.

Loose wood shifted under the pressure of the hand towel. At first, Adrienne thought nothing of the creak, creak, creak sound it made. But something stopped her. She shifted her weight and noticed there were three nails in the floor that looked like they'd been removed and replaced many times. Hair hung in her face, obscuring portions of her view, so she gathered the strands on one side, spun them into a rope, and tucked it beneath the collar of her shirt.

The old plank flooring of the closet was a mix of short scrap pieces. Two pieces were loose enough to wiggle back and forth beneath the wobbly nails. She reached to the protruding spike that had snagged her foot and grabbed it. It slid out easily.

Adrienne adjusted to a more comfortable position and reached between the ill-fitting planks to get a decent grip. The first pulled up easily, groaning as it did. A gaping hole stared back. It was about six inches wide and ten inches long. Though it was covered in dust and cobwebs, she could see the distinct shape of something hidden inside.

She pushed the door open more to illuminate the space and cast a light into the shadowy hole. Brushing aside thoughts of spiders and other creepy crawlies, she reached under the other plank and tugged. It groaned, but wouldn't give. She readjusted herself on her knees and tugged again. It moved only slightly, but it was enough to fuel her intent, so she rocked the plank back and forth until it finally gave up the battle. The scent of dust and decay rose.

Adrienne used her forearm to push back the hair that had escaped. Pieces were matted to her wet brow where even more sweat had accumulated in her struggle. She set this plank on the floor by the first one and reached into the hole.

The book was sheathed in a light cotton material that could once have been a piece of a bedsheet or part of an old dress. The cotton, though threadbare and decomposing, had kept the book safe for a very long time. Dust rose as she unwrapped it and examined the front cover.

It held no lock and looked to be an inexpensive journal. Brittle pages clicked as she pulled the book open to examine its inside cover. It was stiff from years of disuse, but the words were legible and clear. The front cover sported the name she had hoped she would find.

Adrienne hobbled from the room and down the stairs. Maybe she would get all her questions answered now. Maybe this would help her understand about Gracie and her bitter betrayal. And maybe Adrienne could get to know Sara from these pages.

Once at the table, Adrienne flipped the book open and hoped to find page after page of Sara's thoughts.

Writing on page one. Two. Adrienne frowned, her fingers gliding through more pages, empty pages. Her eyes scanned as if her intensity could will words and thoughts into the book. Writing on page three. Her nose tickled with so much dust and she wriggled it, not wanting to sneeze.

Disappointment worked its way through her system. Only a few pages at the front of the book had been written on. *At least those might answer some questions*, she assured herself. But after thirty minutes of reading the same four entries over and over, Adrienne was more confused than ever.

Dear Diary,

I haven't had a diary before, so I'm probably not going to be very good at this. I'm not planning on keeping this going for very long, but I have to have someone to talk to about what I've done.

I didn't mean to hurt anyone, but I know it's going to. Gracie is gone, and Momma is making me move back to North Carolina. I don't want to go. This is where my friends are. I guess I'm probably old enough to tell her no and that I'm staying here, but I won't do that. Besides, when William comes I certainly can't be here. I couldn't bear to look at his face or see his disappointment in me.

I have betrayed everyone I love and don't know how to live with the guilt of that. I can't write any more right now.

Sara

Adrienne pressed her hands against her head. Sara had rambled on for a couple of pages about how she'd betrayed everyone and hated herself for it. The last entry was equally chilling, though it seemed to give the young girl some thin thread of relief.

Dear Diary,

We are leaving today and I am putting these words into my hiding place in the closet. I went and talked to Pastor Luke yesterday. I'm not going to dwell on what I've done anymore.

I'm going to close this diary, put it away, and leave town with Momma. I guess I'm all she has now.

I miss Gracie. No matter how she treated William, I still love her. I wish she could come back. William is coming home from the war in the next few days. He'll be here, but we'll be gone. It's better. It's best that I never see him again.

Sara Chandler

Disappointed, Adrienne walked the inside perimeter of the house, shutting off lights and readying for bed. She changed into a T-shirt and sweats—careful not to pull the bandage from her heel. Her head nuzzled into the pillow, but she knew there would be no restful sleep for her tonight. She tossed and turned, haunted by an inconclusive confession from a girl who couldn't have been more than sixteen or seventeen. Sara was hiding something.

And Adrienne couldn't ignore the strong tug to find out what.

Leo smiled when Adrienne entered the diner, his pot of coffee and a clean cup—albeit stained on the rim—dangling on his crooked finger. He stopped at the table, wiggled those sparse but unruly brows, and poured the cup without asking.

She questioned him with a look.

"Real man's cup of coffee." The cup clinked against the Formica countertop.

"Perhaps you haven't noticed, but I'm not a man at all." Adrienne was growing ever more comfortable with her circle of eighty-year-old friends. And though that fact might alarm most twenty-somethings, she rather liked it.

Leo urged her onward with the dip of his chin and a wink of his eye. "If you've come to pump me for more information, you're gonna have to drink."

"Maybe I just came for the best breakfast in town." She sat back in the booth and crossed her arms over her chest. A couple with three noisy kids, covered with sand from the knees down, passed her table and chose a corner booth.

Leo scrubbed at a weathered cheek. "Nah, I know about you city slickers. Y'all think yogurt and fruit is a proper breakfast. Too busy for a real meal, grabbing a bagel and some awful thing you like to call a *shmear*."

Adrienne laughed.

He threw his hands up. "What self-respecting bread product has a hole through the middle of it?"

"What about donuts?" Leo seemed a bit . . . younger today. Almost as if he wanted to see her again. The thought made her smile inwardly. Maybe he just enjoyed the banter. She could hold her own with most quick-witted people. *She* certainly enjoyed it. Especially now that she didn't have to wonder what Eric thought of her conversations. It felt free. She could joke, tease, chit-chat, even flirt without ever having to wonder if she'd be admonished for it later. Life was good.

"I said *self-respecting* bread product."

Adrienne crossed her legs. "Okay, you got me. I'm here for information. What can you tell me about Sara?"

Leo raised his brows again and stared at the coffee mug but didn't say a word.

Adrienne followed his gaze to the thick liquid in front of her. Was this really the price for a little history? She mustered her strength and lifted the death-brew to her mouth slowly. After one last plea with her eyes—and Leo only rocking back on his heels—she tipped the mug the way one might tip a glass laced with poison.

Leo smirked.

She was quickly invaded by two sensations. First, there was the stinging of heavily acidic fluid sitting on her tongue. Then the pungent aftertaste that remained after swallowing. "Mmm," she forced out, unconvincingly. Her eyes watered.

Leo threw his head back and laughed. "Greenhorn. I guess you've earned a question or two." But he rose from the table and brought back a delicate silver container of milk so cold the shiny creamer had frosted. He poured the milk into the coffee and nudged her to give it another try.

It couldn't possibly help that much, or so her eyes begged, but he was relentless. She drew a long breath and obediently took another sip. It was surprisingly better, or maybe she'd just dulled her taste buds with the first swallow.

"So now you want to know about Sara? Did you find William?"

"Yes, I had dinner with him and his grandson a couple weeks ago."

"Will! I sure owe him a lot."

"You owe a lot to William?" Confusion and bad coffee clouded her mind.

"No, to Will. If it wasn't for him, I wouldn't still have this place. I got pretty sick a few years back, and the bank was breathing down my neck about my business loan. Will worked with me, gave me extra time, kept me from losing it. I'm not sure he didn't even kick in on a few payments; I still don't know how I paid it off so quickly." He gave her a few moments to absorb this before continuing. "But you're not here to talk about that."

Who did I *meet?* she wondered. This didn't sound like the same Will. He was all about business and the bottom line, not pitching in on loans for old, ailing men. At the same time, there were glimpses of sweetness in him. Maybe she'd misjudged him or just judged him too quickly. Then again, there was always a wariness and suspicion behind his deep green eyes that she couldn't discount.

"Sara. She was a sweetheart. You could search the world and not find a sweeter girl. But, oh could she find trouble." He leaned his elbow on the table. "She didn't look for trouble, mind you, just always seemed to end up in the middle of it. Sara had a soft spot for animals. When she'd find a stray, she'd knock on every door in town, trying to find it a good home. Someone dumped a litter of puppies once, and she found them before school, took 'em home and barricaded them in. After all, how much damage could a litter of puppies do to a kitchen in just a few hours?"

"Oh, no." Adrienne smiled.

"Her momma was gone for the day, due back at six that evening. Oh, those pups wreaked havoc on that room. It took six of us to clean up the mess. Needless to say, she refrained from bringing any more strays home."

"Leo," Adrienne said. "Do you think Sara blamed herself for Gracie's death?"

He took a thoughtful moment, then shook his head. "No, why?"

"She left a diary that just had a few pages in it. She talked like she'd done something awful." Adrienne's eyes narrowed to slits. "But I don't think she really did."

He gauged her for a long moment and seemed to disappear in the past, eyes on her, but mind far away. "Did she do something wrong?" Adrienne asked.

He nodded. "Yes."

Adrienne's heart quickened.

"But in doing that she also did something very, very right."

Whoosh, whoosh, whoosh. Blood pounded in Adrienne's ears. "You know her secret."

He nodded, tapping his thumb against the table. "It took me a long time to figure out. And once I did, it was too late. She was gone, and William had moved on."

"It involves William?" she asked. "She mentions that William would never forgive her."

"Before Sara left town to go back to North Carolina, she stopped by to see me. I'd come home about six months before William was scheduled to. She wouldn't give me any details, but she asked me to look out for him." A gentle smile touched his face, and Adrienne could see a tenderness he usually kept hidden.

Adrienne realized she wasn't breathing when black spots materialized before her eyes.

He waited, as if time would fill in the blanks.

Pure intrigue pulled Adrienne forward until she leaned on the table, Leo filling her vision. "What are you trying to say, Leo? Sara asked you to watch out for him?"

"I've never seen a woman more in love."

Adrienne sucked in a breath. "Sara was in love with William. But Sara was just a kid when William left."

He brushed a hand through the air. "We were all kids. Sara was fourteen, only three years younger than William. Five years younger than me. But her skinny, gawky frame that fourteen-year-olds so often have made her seem like more of a kid than a teenager. She had just turned seventeen when William was scheduled to come home." He eyed her closely. "And that's old enough to know if you're truly in love."

"Sara was in love with her sister's boyfriend," Adrienne whispered, her weight dropped against the vinyl booth cushion, her hands clasped in her lap. "What a secret for her to have to carry."

"I suspect it was a heavy load. More so after Gracie died."

It was a moment before Adrienne noticed the change in Leo's demeanor. He wrung his hands, his gaze drifting over different parts of the table. "You see, I didn't know. I didn't know right away. After she left town, I figured it out. But it was too late. I'd gone and introduced William to Betty."

Adrienne's heart sank for Leo, for William, for Sara.

"I felt bad for William. Losing Grace. Sara being gone. His injury . . . "

The wall clock had a flip screen on it that advertised local businesses. From where they sat, they could hear the gentle hum of the neon illuminating it. Adrienne waited for Leo to continue, having to tear her gaze from his watery gray eyes gone dark with shame.

"William got home, and I introduced him to Betty. She was sweet and kind and had lost a brother in the war. After William and Betty became serious, I realized what Sara was hiding." He pursed his lips together. "But it was too late. William had fallen in love with Betty."

Adrienne realized how difficult this admission was for Leo. She could tell he felt somehow responsible.

He rubbed one hand with the other. "I never told him. I never did. I just didn't know how." His eyes found hers and begged for long-sought forgiveness that she couldn't give because he hadn't wronged her. He hadn't wronged anyone, but it seemed he'd carried the weight of this his whole life, and it had taken too much of a toll. His lips pressed into a straight line, and she knew she needed to say something.

Adrienne reached across the table and placed a hand on Leo's arm. "You were a good friend. You did the right thing, Leo." Words. Only words. A sick feeling unfurled in her stomach. She had dredged up enough about the past. It was here that her journey must end. Though she loved hearing about the life William and Leo had led, there was something disturbing about discussing it with them. It was their past. It was the pain and the struggle they had fought through to make it to where they now stood. Each time she spoke with either of them, though their words were in the past tense, their eyes and hearts were reliving each moment.

So her journey was over. She was completely convinced this was the last discussion about it. She was convinced, that is, until Leo spoke again.

His words were like the softest brush of wind and delivered after she had thanked him for his time and stood up from the table to leave. A Prada bag was slung carelessly over her shoulder, and for an instant she wasn't sure that he'd said anything at all. Had it not been for the intensity in his gaze, she might have turned and walked right out of the restaurant.

Then, he repeated the words: "It's not too late. Sara never married."

The pounding began in her heart and worked its way out from her core, causing her entire body to zing with warning and intrigue. "What do you mean?"

"It's not too late for William to know the truth."

The vinyl cushion sighed as she dropped back onto it, her weight slumped against the back of the seat. A silver buckle on her purse clanged against the table. She had been so close to escape. A few more steps and she could have left the mysteries and the madness behind her. She shook her head. "I don't know." Lips pressed tightly together, she contemplated what this could mean to William, who had made peace with the ghosts from his past.

But Leo seemed just as certain as she was uncertain.

"Leo, all these years later. I mean, Sara left. If she was seventeen, she was old enough to stay here at least long enough to see him. She chose to go. I think the news would only hurt William."

He gazed at her through gray and piercing eyes. "Not if Sara got the chance to explain."

Chapter 9

"*W*hat are you doing, Pops?" Will reached into the box his grandfather had filled with vegetables. He plucked a tomato and brought it to his mouth. But Pops moved with lightning speed and snagged it from Will.

"Stay out of this box." Pops turned to face him, to point a finger in Will's face, and that's when he saw the spark. There'd been a spark in Pops's eyes since Adrienne Carter showed up, disrupting their crab shells and their life. "We've got more than we can possibly eat, so I am sending these with Adrienne. She loves to cook, you know?"

"She's coming by this morning?" Uh, had there been a hint of excitement in his tone? Yeah, the way Pops was grinning at him, there must have been. He honestly didn't know why he cared at all. She had returned his grandfather's letters, but Pops kept thinking of excuses for her to drop by. First, it was the book about plumbing, then borrowing some tool he'd dug out of the garage. Now she was stopping by for fresh vegetables. *His* vegetables. Will's mouth watered. That tomato was perfect. This was madness.

She obviously liked Pops, since he'd yet to hear her turn down an invite, but Will couldn't help notice that she always came while he was at work, which meant she wanted nothing to do with him. Will was fine with that. But she was coming today. It was Saturday. She had to know he'd be there. Maybe she'd planned it that way.

He imagined her breezing in, interrupting his morning, smelling like wildflowers and maybe tossing some food on the kitchen floor. The thought brought him back to the night they'd spent sitting at the table and laughing with Pops. He caught himself smiling in his reflection in the window, so he turned it into a scowl. She wouldn't get to him. Not today. He headed out back to the pier. He just wouldn't be here. He'd stay outside. Problem solved. As he left, he could hear Pops mumbling about Adrienne bringing the bait for their fishing trip. Will cast his eyes toward heaven.

As he headed for the boat, he stopped and admired the hard work he'd put in yesterday. The thirty-two-foot cuddy cabin gleamed in the Florida sun. He'd spent the evening before, brush in hand, scrubbing every inch of her, wiping down the teak wood, cleaning the windows, and polishing the chrome. She looked better than a brand new boat. And no one, not even a nosy, too pretty brunette was going to ruin his day out on the water.

"Now these are delicious in a spinach salad. Here's kale, mustard greens, collards." Pops's hands meandered through the box. "'Course, I grew up calling it a wilted lettuce salad, but Will says that sounds terrible. You know how to make one?"

"Yes," Adrienne answered. But her mind was elsewhere. She'd spotted Will in the backyard through the kitchen window and had to fight the urge to go outside and watch him. Bare to the waist, with the Florida sun gleaming off his muscles and looking so *at ease.*

"I always use a little bacon grease for the base of the dressing, but Will tells me that's bad for my cholesterol."

"Mm-hmm," she agreed, leaning to glance out the window again.

"How do you make your dressing?" Pops sniffed a bunch of radishes.

She was aware of words being sent in her direction, but couldn't quite put them together.

"Adrienne, how do you make your dressing?"

She snapped to attention. "Oh, I start with a little olive oil, add some fresh garlic in a skillet, salt, pepper, a dash of sugar."

He nodded, and she could see him ticking off the ingredients in his mind. "A little onion?"

"If I'm in the mood. But usually, just dried minced onion. Fresh is too overpowering."

He shook a finger at her. "Exactly right."

"I add the vinegar just before applying the dressing to the greens." She fingered the different lettuce leaves Pops had given her. "This will be a really nice change. I usually only have fresh spinach for my salad."

"You'll love this mix, then. And do you serve it with mushrooms and croutons?"

"Always. Oh, and a boiled egg. I make homemade croutons, you know."

"Really?"

"I got the recipe from a friend not too long ago. I'll bring you some."

He noticed her stretch to glance out the back window again. "Will's getting the boat ready for the day."

"Uh-huh."

He watched her. She watched Will. "Sure is going to be nice out there. The water's smooth, and the cold front brought in a cool breeze."

"Sounds fabulous." Sort of. Adrienne was terrified of boats. She'd had a bad experience once, and Eric had made fun of her for it. Boats and her—not simpatico. But the naked-to-the-waist man outside? Now *that* she could stare at for hours.

She'd only in the last few months been able to look at men without feeling like she was cheating on her husband. Even though they'd separated practically a year ago and her divorce had been final months ago. One thing she could thank Ryan for, she supposed. Ryan, her furniture-moving grad student with the killer smile and smooth confidence. He'd broken through all those barriers of false propriety, even grabbing and kissing her without warning or invitation on occasion. At first she'd frozen at his touch. But then she'd remembered she wasn't a married woman anymore and she had settled into that first kiss. It was nice. The next one was nice. And the next, and several more after that. Was Will a good kisser? For a horrible second, she thought she might have said that aloud.

She breathed relief when she realized Pops was still up to his elbows in her box of vegetables and still chattering about salad. Her gaze and her mind drifted through the window. Tan skin, rolling muscles, denim shorts cinched around smooth hips. It was hard to breathe.

Pops dislodged himself from the box and leaned forward to pick up the bait bucket Adrienne had brought. "Boy, this thing is heavy."

And before she knew it, she was slipping it from his grasp and trying not to consider how Will's mouth would measure up to Ryan's.

A loose towel in one hand and shirt off, Will wiped the morning dew from the otherwise sparkling boat, the *Miss Betty May*. He scrubbed back and forth, removing the moisture that had settled on her. Aggravation from the week's work dissolved with the brush of his hand. Everything about a boat was therapeutic, even bathing it.

He was almost finished when he noticed he wasn't alone. The wind carried the scent of flowers to him before she spoke a word. He groaned inwardly, reaching for his shirt. He pulled it on and hopped off the boat, his deck shoes grabbing the wooden planks of the pier. "Good morning."

"It is," she returned.

She looked . . . guilty and gorgeous. A purple tank top hugged her upper body, emphasizing her curves. Shorts accentuated those amazing legs. Adrienne's neck glistened with a tiny locket. That neck. The kind he could nuzzle into and not come up for air for hours. It was the curve. Tantalizing, smooth, inviting him to nibble. And there they stood. Wordless, staring at each other. Awkward, but somehow that was okay.

Finally, she blinked. "Um, I brought this down for Pops." She nodded at the bucket of bait she held.

But he didn't take it from her. Instead, he regarded her, wondering just how long she'd been standing there watching him wipe off the boat.

She blinked again, innocently, but below the surface, he could see her squirming. A honey-smooth spot on her throat throbbed. She motioned to the bucket that he had yet to take from her.

But taking it might mean an end to her standing there waiting on him. Watching him. She might disappear back up to the house. No, he didn't really want to rush this. Some of the best things in life were rushed when they shouldn't be. It was a crime, really. He was pretty sure this was one of those moments. "I hope you haven't been standing there long with that heavy bucket." He took his time tucking his shirt into denim shorts. He caught her eyes trail from his chest down to his hand, then quickly snap back up to his face.

"No," she said a little too quickly.

But he *still* didn't take the bucket. "So I didn't keep you waiting?"

"Oh, no." She waved a hand. "I just walked down here."

At that moment, Pops stuck his head out the back door. "Did you fall in, Adrienne? It doesn't take five minutes to drop off a bucket of bait!"

A smile tugged at the corners of his mouth. So she *had* been watching him. Something white hot shot into his gut and curled there.

Cheeks stained crimson, she gestured with her free hand toward the canal. "I was just admiring your . . . your boat. It looks beautiful."

"Thanks."

When she began to move the bucket to her free hand, he reached for it. "Let me take that." This put him in close enough proximity to drag her scent into his lungs. He welcomed it.

"Thank you." She rubbed her palm where red streaks left their mark.

Will dropped the bucket on the deck behind him, bait sloshing. He took her hand in his, drawing her closer. He ran a finger over the lines on her palm. Concern drew his brows together. "I'm sorry. I didn't realize it was so heavy." *Really chivalrous.* But honestly, it wasn't every day he caught a gorgeous woman checking him out. He'd just wanted to enjoy it a little while. But he'd left her there holding a ten-pound bucket. Nice.

Adrienne mumbled an answer he didn't quite catch. For a tiny little thing, she was pretty strong. She hadn't even complained about the bucket. Of course, she *was* remodeling a house.

Couldn't be a wimp and do that. Still, he'd left her under the strain of his bait. Not the most gentlemanly thing he'd ever done. "Really, I'm sorry."

"That's okay," she whispered.

A breeze pushed at her back, pressing her closer to him, lifting her hair and forcing the feminine scent deeper into his lungs. Her smell bounded off his skin in waves. Marking him. He wasn't in any hurry to move away.

Gently, his finger rubbed across the marks on her palm. Odd that he didn't mind this woman's scent invading his nose and clothes. Odd that he hadn't minded her throwing crab claws and meat bits all over his kitchen. "I wouldn't have had my shirt off, but I didn't know you would be coming down here. I thought you were just picking up some vegetables."

"I volunteered to," she said unapologetically, and some brave little flicker caused her dark eyes to dance.

It was unnerving. In a good way. He concentrated his attention on her palm. Soft, smooth flesh, warm beneath his touch.

"Pops was going to bring them, but I thought I should say hello."

"Sounds like a chore." His eyes drifted up to hers. Her irises were espresso colored, but this close and in the bright sunlight, he saw multiple flecks of gold. He'd like to mine that gold, unearth the treasure hidden in her eyes.

"Then let me rephrase it. I *wanted* to say hello."

"Hello, back." Something warm twisted in his stomach. He allowed his fingers to slide up her arm to her shoulder. Once there, he kneaded gently until he felt a tremor run along her flesh. "Did the bucket hurt your arm?"

She shook her head. His finger drifted under the edge of her shoulder strap, scarcely grazing her skin beneath and causing her top to move ever so slightly. It could have been an accident, a mistake. But it wasn't. He wanted to see the response it elicited.

A puff of hot breath was his answer. A face flushed with pink, a further invitation. Her skin was velvet. "Good." He pulled in a breath, reluctant to let go. But what could he do? Continue stroking her? No. Will took a difficult and deliberate step back. The scent of flowers and woman stayed.

Oh, this was a disaster. She had seen him from the house, shirt off, scrubbing the boat. She'd only wanted to talk to him, and now, with his face inches from hers, his body smelling of the sea, his emerald eyes staring into hers, she found that she'd lost all her words.

Standing this close to a sweaty sailor shouldn't make you want to get closer. She had watched his long, lean muscles roll rhythmically as he scrubbed back and forth. So he was tan, lean, and muscled. So what? Lots of guys were. It had actually been his hands that caused the blood to pool in her stomach—even before he'd touched her. Every now and then, he'd take the towel away and with long, slow strokes, slide a hand over the smooth white side of the boat, strong fingers gliding, caressing. Those hands could be lethal to a girl. Those hands could thoroughly wreck her. If, of course, she wanted to be wrecked, which she, Adrienne, didn't. And if, of course, he wanted to wreck her, which *he* didn't.

She'd watched him grab the pail from her sore arm and effortlessly drop it to the deck behind him. Even through his T-shirt, the muscles in his stomach clenched as he lifted, then relaxed. His hand, first on hers, then sliding up her arm, each movement a dizzying dance.

But this wasn't just about looking at Will's body, no matter how good, how perfect it was wiping down the boat. She was also interested in being introduced to the Will Bryant that Leo talked about. She really *did* want to say hello. In fact, if invited, she'd hop right on the boat and spend the day with him. Fear or no fear. She'd go. She'd do it.

As if reading her mind, Will asked, "You want to go along?"

"No, but thank you," she answered without giving herself a moment to consider it. "But Pops is really excited about going out today." Adrienne was a master at redirecting the conversation. She'd spent years redirecting it to Eric. After all, the world hadn't just *revolved* around Eric. He had been its sun, moon, and stars.

"Pops always thinks he's going to land a trophy sailfish."

Will wadded a towel and tossed it onto the deck, then turned back to her. "By the way, I'm really sorry Pops asked you to stop at the bait shop on your way over. I don't know what he was thinking." He rubbed a hand through thick, dark hair that was adorably unkempt. Just as she'd suspected it would be without all that hair gel.

"Oh, I volunteered. It was the least I could do. He's giving me a truck load of vegetables."

Tan fingers spread wide, and his hands fell to rest on his hips. "Sure you won't come along?"

"No, I'm not dressed for it."

His gaze drifted down over her, slowly, lingering on the way. "You're right. Shorts and a tank top are way too formal attire for boat trips."

She opened her mouth to speak, but nothing came out. Tilting her ankle outward drew attention to her four-inch wedge sandals.

His gaze trailed down to them in a long, slow perusal as if he'd been invited to inspect her legs along the way. Goose bumps spread across her thighs and calves everywhere his gaze touched.

"You could slip those off. It's pretty customary to go barefoot on a boat."

"Oh." Well, that was the last of her excuses. One last plea. "It's going to be terribly hot."

"Nonsense." The words came from behind her as Pops stepped past both of them. "If it isn't too hot for an eighty-year-old man, it isn't too hot for you, Miss High-Falootin' City Girl."

Will helped his grandfather onto the boat and returned to her, an inviting grin animating his face. "There's plenty of shade to keep you cool."

Shade? Not likely. There was no shade from his smoldering looks and heat-radiating body. Her gaze moved between Will and the monster of a boat that rested beside them. "I've never been on an ocean boat. I mean, a cruise ship once, but you can't even feel them moving. Smaller boats are . . . kind of scary. I nearly drowned in a canoe."

"The water is supposed to be smooth as glass today. We'll go slow if it makes you feel better." He stretched his hand out to take hers. "You're safe with me."

Safe with him. The words dropped to the ground like lead. She'd never met a man she truly felt safe with, least of all one with eyes able to cut right into her soul, which was kind of how she felt with Will.

When she didn't answer, he whispered, "I promise." His tongue darted out to moisten a mouth gone slack.

And for a quick moment, the world stopped.

Behind them, she could hear Pops uttering something about drowning and canoes.

Without realizing it, her hand slid into Will's. It was the look of utter assurance that brought her enough gumption to actually agree to going. There was certainty in him. And honesty. The warmth of his strong fingers closing around hers urged her into motion, and before she knew what was happening, he was pulling her onto the luxury boat.

Her vegetables and purse sat on the kitchen table. Her car windows were rolled down. Her cell phone left smack in the middle console. But none of that mattered. She was going on an adventure. She and Pops . . . and Will.

Adrienne's mind went to Sara—Sara who loved to fish. She had new information concerning the woman, but for now, she wouldn't breathe a word of it. No good could come of it. If Leo was wrong and Sara had died, it would only bring more sorrow to Pops. The thought of causing him pain was unbearable. So, until she knew for sure, Adrienne would keep the secret buried, just as it had been for over sixty years.

She took a seat at the back of the boat. The leather cushion was soft and padded against her flesh. The gloriously rich wood of the deck shone beneath her bare feet: her dark pink toes tried to grip the wood but failed against the velvet smoothness. Smoothness created by Will's care. She faced the front of the boat, her back straight, her shoulders taut. Pops moved below in the cabin. He'd gone down the stairs and was now humming, but the sound brought her little comfort because the engine rumbled to life, nearly causing her to jump out of her skin. Adrienne reached for something to hold onto.

Will shot her a smile. It faded quickly. "Are you okay?"

She nodded furiously, but could feel the color drain from her face, leaving her bloodless and cold. "No one has ever fallen out, right?"

"No. You really are scared, aren't you?" His gaze dropped to her white-knuckled hands, gripping the cushion so tightly that the leather puckered. "Would you be more comfortable over here by me?"

"No," she admitted, considering her previous reaction to him as he'd rubbed the lines in her palm and teased her shoulder. Oh, he'd made her *feel* things. Comfortable wasn't one of them.

But Will folded the helm seat down so they could sit side by side. "Come on." The sun hit his face, and his eyes sparkled like emeralds.

By the time she was seated, he had slipped past her to untie the mooring lines. As soon as he was back beside her at the helm, he studied her face. "You okay now?"

"Better." Warmth emanated from where his arm touched hers. He took her hands and placed them on a chrome bar in front of her. She felt silly. Like a little girl on her first carousel ride.

He must have sensed her anxiety. "Don't worry. Everybody hangs on at first."

Adrienne was pretty certain everyone didn't. But it was nice of him to say. She liked this Will. Gone was the prickly exterior, and in its place was something endearing. Finally, here was the grandson she would expect William Bryant to have.

Within the first few minutes of rumbling away from the dock, Adrienne wondered what her apprehension had been about. They eased down the cove, homes and foliage disappearing past them as they went, leaves of massive palm trees tilting out over the canal and swaying in the breeze. The boat motor hummed gently, vibrating her feet against the warm wood of the deck. As they approached a curve, Will slowed the engine. He faced her. "We're going out into the Gulf after this last turn. I'll have to speed up."

She nodded, no longer afraid, ready to meet this adventure head on. And stunned at how attentive Will was to her earlier panic. From the moment he'd seen it on her face, it seemed everything had been about making her feel comfortable. Safe. *You're safe with me.*

"The waves will be a little rough until we get through the pass, but that's normal."

She was in good hands.

When he made the corner, her breath left her. As the thick foliage of the canal disappeared, she gazed out at the expanse of blue that stretched on forever before them. Though she often watched boats slide across the water, not one interrupted her view today. The deep blue spanned in a panorama from east to west, sliced only by a golden horizon. Wind saturated with seawater sprinkled her face. The engine moaned louder as Will put his hand to the throttle, moving them beyond the barrier.

Adrienne couldn't speak.

Will smiled over at her. "Cool, huh?"

"It's breathtaking." She squinted into the sun on the water and wished she'd grabbed her sunglasses. "I see this every day from my back deck, but it looks completely different from out here."

They crashed through the waves, and Adrienne worked to find her sea legs. Will and Pops made it look so easy. She gathered enough bravery to move around the deck, but preferred her spot by the captain.

"So we're going fishing." She looked down at the bucket of bait.

He nodded over at her, his tongue moistening his lips. "Uh-huh."

Whew, it was hot. Adrienne was glad for the tank top. She'd almost put on a shirt with short sleeves. Now she was thankful she'd opted for the tank. Will seemed to appreciate it too. "Do we just stop anywhere?"

"No, we have a destination."

"How do you know where to go? I mean, you can't exactly stop for directions."

"Men don't stop for directions anyway." He winked and pointed to a screen in front of them on a dashboard of levers, gauges, and buttons. It looked like a mini computer screen tucked between a compass and the throttle. "This shows us the way."

"That little screen tells us where to go?"

He nodded.

"Wow, too bad you can't fasten those onto people. There would be a lot less heartache and a lot more direction." If she'd had one of those little gadgets she'd have never married Eric.

"I think they only work on water." He pushed a button and the screen made a blip, blip, blip sound. "Besides, we're all already equipped with one."

She frowned. "Mine must be broken." Seeing as how she was a twenty-eight-year-old with not even an inkling of what she was going to do with her life . . . broken compass seemed possible.

"Nah, sometimes it shows us a really clear picture of where we're headed." He pointed to the now garbled screen. "But sometimes it's fuzzy."

"What do you do when it gets fuzzy?" Her screen had been muddled for a long time.

"You stay the course." His eyes left the screen and found her. "In time, everything comes into view, and the course we're meant to steer crystallizes before us."

It wasn't that simple. Maybe one day she would have a picture of the future. But it seemed far away. She'd spent so many years making sure Eric had what he wanted, got what he wanted, went where he wanted . . . well, she didn't even know what things she liked anymore. It had all been about him. She'd grown up thinking that's how marriage was supposed to be. That's what her mother had done. That's what all the women in her family did. Unlike Eric, Adrienne's father never took advantage of the kindness. Adrienne supposed she'd done it all wrong, creating a monster rather than a loving partner. But she wouldn't dwell on that. Each morning she reminded herself that life was a gift, something she'd learned from Pops. Each day was a present to be opened and relished. So today she'd cherish the gift. And do the only other reasonable thing.

Stay the course. Until the screen cleared.

"Can I take you to dinner?" Will's voice cracked. Like the words he'd just spoken surprised him as much as they did her.

Her eyes went to his. "Uh . . . "

"It's just dinner."

Like that made it less intimidating. She needed to answer: No. The answer would be no as soon as she found her voice. "Yes," she said, and that surprised her too. Well, if the screen had cleared at all, this had just succeeded in scrambling the message.

"Where are you taking her?"

Will turned to the doorway where Pops leaned against the wall. The last thing in the world Will needed right now was the third degree from his grandfather. "I made reservations at Palermo's."

"Oh, on the water. She likes the water. And I hear Palermo's is first rate." Pops had caught him in his room, staring into the full-length mirror. "I'm glad you took off the tie. Makes you look snooty."

Will flipped the tie over the hanger and headed for his closet.

"Here, I'll take it," Pops said. When he didn't return, Will dragged a deep breath into his lungs, trying to calm his ragged nerves. He'd been on dates before. Plenty. He was thirty. He'd done his share of dating. But Adrienne was . . .

"What about this shirt?" Pops stood in the closet doorway holding a polo that had seen better days.

"Kind of ratty." Will's heart rate sped up. Was he actually this inept at dressing himself for dinner?

"But Adrienne likes blue."

Heat rose to Will's forehead. "I think a jacket is required."

Pops tilted his head. "It's not a stuffy place is it? Adrienne's a free spirit. She's like the wind, and stuffy places don't appreciate wind."

This really wasn't helping. He'd thought this through, whether Pops knew it or not. Palermo's because they would pamper her and because it had an amazing view of the pier. After dinner they could walk out and see if the night fisherman were catching anything. Perfect remedy for a stuffy dining room. Plus, he wanted Adrienne to be pampered. He wasn't sure why, but he did. Adrienne with her movie-star smile and stained fingers. Adrienne with the giant eyes and all that sadness lurking in the depths of them. "Maybe you need to be going out with her, and I can stay home."

An aged hand curled, one crooked finger pointing at him. "Now that's just silly. Don't get smart with me, young man. You're not too big for me to put you over my knee."

Will chuckled. "I think I am."

Fists to his hips, Pops stared him down, the blue shirt dangling at his side. "Shall I prove it?"

Will's hands flew up in surrender. "No, sir. I know when I'm outmanned." Most things, Will could handle—the three-hundred horsepower luxury boat, the down-and-dirty negotiations of a million-dollar loan app—but when it came to Pops, and a certain hot little brunette, Will felt outmanned. Maybe *outmanned* wasn't the right term where Adrienne was concerned. He certainly felt *matched*. And that was as intriguing as it was sexy.

The smile appeared, then fell from Pops's face. "Did you wash your car? You should never pick up a lady for a date in a dirty car. It's disrespectful."

"Yeah, I drove it through Rub-a-Dub two hours ago."

Pops nodded approvingly. "Got some ideas for conversation? Be sure to ask about her. Ladies make connections face to face."

Will bit back a grin. His grandfather was actually coaching him on dating. "And how do men make connections, Pops?"

He looked up at him as if surprised by the question. "Shoulder to shoulder, Will. Side by side."

Will thought of Pops and the men he was probably shoulder to shoulder with during his time in the war. He quickly brushed that image from his head. "So, do I look all right? I'll try not to ruin the Bryant men's swagger."

A wrinkled face scrunched. "Swagger? You just be a gentleman. Don't forget to open the car door and walk her to her door when you drop her off."

"Got it."

The look on Pops's face turned serious. "Adrienne's special, Will." It wasn't so much a comment as an invitation to agree. He wasn't telling Will anything he didn't already know.

"Yeah. I think she was pretty torn up by that divorce."

"Protect her heart. That's what gentlemen do." Pops's hands brushed Will's shoulders as if dusting him off or maybe smoothing wrinkles from his freshly pressed shirt. Will couldn't help but feel there was more to it than that. Maybe he'd spent too long in the sun today, but Pops's action felt almost like a mantle being placed upon his shoulders.

Slowly, his grandfather turned and headed for the door. "Have a nice time. I won't wait up for you." He darted a glance over his shoulder and winked.

"Are you sure this isn't too much?" Adrienne angled in the antique mirror, looking at her backside and wondering if the dress was just a little too snug.

Sammie turned her by her shoulders. "You look amazing. Really. You'll have him eating out of your hand."

Adrienne pursed her mouth and stuck her stained fingers in Sammie's face. Sammie's eyes widened. "They aren't so bad."

"That was the worst lie I've heard from your mouth."

Sammie turned her to face the mirror. "No one will be looking at your hands."

The white dress was trimmed with tiny silver rope that hung from one shoulder and tucked into the fitted waist. The hem, about two inches above her knee, also sported the silver thread. It was a fairy-tale dress. White and whimsical and almost as tight as a second skin. And scary, she realized. This was a grown-up dress and she was going on a grown-up date. With Ryan, they'd usually just grabbed a burger—both of them in jeans and T-shirts. This was different. Like her first step back into the magical kingdom of dating. Adrienne's hand dropped to her stomach. "I think I'm going to throw up."

"Ooooo, let's see the shoes." Sammie—ignoring her plight—grabbed the shoe box from the bed.

In spite of herself, Adrienne got a little bit excited about the shoes. "I don't know what I was thinking when I bought them the other day. They're totally impractical." Impracticality was a constant in her world in Chicago. Too-tall shoes, too-expensive handbags. It all seemed so ridiculous now. She could buy a brand new toilet for the price of one handbag. Maybe a sink and faucet to go with it. When she realized the comparison she'd just made, the nausea returned in full force, and the excitement waned. Until Sammie plucked the jewels from the velvet-lined box.

"Oh, these are gorgeous." She held the sparkly sandals to the light, where a rainbow of sparks danced in each rhinestone. "Nice call, Chicago. Are you going to talk to Will about Sara and what you've learned?"

"No. I don't know enough yet, and he always seems pretty testy about his grandfather. I think he thinks I'm too nosy already."

"Well, whatever you decide, in these stilettos he'd forgive anything."

Adrienne rolled her eyes. "They're completely impractical, right?"

Sammie nodded, earrings tinkling. "Right. Which is what makes them so awesome. Have fun tonight with Prince Charming."

Adrienne slipped her feet into the tall sandals and paused to look at Sammie. "Oh, he's not all that charming."

"Well, have fun with Prince Mediocre, then."

"He's definitely not mediocre." She moved to the armoire and searched for her white evening bag. "He's . . . well, I don't really know what he is, but he's all it." She checked herself in the mirror once more.

Sammie moved behind her and placed her hands on her upper arms. "It's just a date, Chicago. An important step in your return to singleness, where people go out with one another."

Adrienne looked at her through the mahogany-trimmed antique mirror. "Normal, right?"

"You told me yourself it was different with Ryan. More like going out with a friend. This is a real date. With Prince Normal. Have fun. Have a normal, mediocre, charming night. Whatever. But go. And don't be so worried about it."

Adrienne soothed her hands over her hips, the soft cotton material of her dress cool against her palms. "I would feel better if Pops were going with us."

Sammie's eyes widened and she squeezed Adrienne's shoulders. "Yeah, you know what? *That* sounds crazy. Don't say that again."

The tinkle of their laughter filled the room as Sammie took Adrienne by the hand and dragged her toward her fate.

Will knocked on her front door. He pulled in a breath through his nose and let it escape slowly from his lips, the sound of his own breath calming him. He needed calm right now. His heart rate had slowed to a normal whoosh, whoosh, whoosh—until she opened the door.

The remaining air in his lungs left in one quick burst. His mouth dropped open, and mercy—if someone had held white-hot pokers to his eyes and told him not to look down, he still couldn't have stopped his gaze from traveling over her. White dress. Tiny waist. Legs, legs, legs. And sandals cradling her delicate feet. Had someone just punched him in the chest?

She clutched a small purse in front of her, and her fingers fidgeted with the clasp. Some gentleman he was; he couldn't even form two words.

A second later, Adrienne spun from the doorway, mumbling something about changing.

One brain cell kicked in, and he snagged her by the arm. "Don't you dare."

She pivoted on those high stiletto heels and gave him a sheepish look. "I told Sammie it would be too much. Just a stupid cocktail dress Eric chose for me. I feel totally . . . "

He needed to shut her up. She looked too amazing to be self-conscious. He should kiss her. Without being able to stop himself, his other hand found its way to her opposite arm, and there he stood, staring into those beautiful coffee eyes. Those gorgeous eyes. "Adrienne," he said, little more than a whisper.

This stopped her. Confusion flickered in her gaze. But the self-consciousness was gone. Completely gone, and knowing that he'd chased it away with one word was a heady feeling. He moved closer, making the space between them almost disappear. "You look incredible."

She let out a relieved sigh that rushed into his face and caused him to breathe her in. She smelled like life and anticipation and excitement. All of it spun together and surged into his being, curling in the deepest part of his gut.

A smile appeared on her face. "Thank you."

Sad eyes. His mind and his desire fought. He wanted to kiss her. Right now. Needed to. But all she'd been through . . . Pops's words echoed back to him. *Be a gentleman.* Will made tiny circles on her arms and noted the goose bumps as they appeared across her skin. She wasn't making this any easier—reacting to his every word, his every touch. He released a long surrendering sigh that came from deep in his throat. "We should go."

She blinked, eyes lined with charcoal and magic. "Yes."

Neither moved.

He needed to say more, something else, or he was going to . . . "Are you hungry?"

Her gaze left his and drifted down to the floor, thick lashes creating half moons over her eyes. On the quietest breath, she whispered, "Starved."

Will's throat closed because he knew her words referred to more than just food. It was a heart plea. Anger over her ex-husband's foolishness erupted. How could anyone hurt an amazing woman like this? What had that guy done to her for her to still be this broken? But he knew. In one fateful word—when she'd sat at his house, eating with Pops—she'd uttered all that haunted her. *Unfaithful.* Ultimate betrayal, as far as he was concerned. A woman like this should never suffer that. No one should.

Protect her heart. He could manage that. He hoped.

Every head in the restaurant turned when Adrienne entered the room. She didn't seem to notice. Maybe it made her uncomfortable, so she just ignored the stares. Whatever, it didn't matter to him. It was difficult not to puff up his man chest like a rooster. She was easily the most beautiful thing in town.

He'd asked for the table in the corner overlooking the water and the pier, where the evening's parade of fishermen and their pull-along coolers worked their way to their favorite spots on the wooden structure. The restaurant was lit with soft cascading chandeliers and candles that caused ribbons of flaming light to flicker about the space. The sound and scent of the ocean drifted up to them as they perused the menu.

They did the customary chit-chat before ordering. But Will wasn't one for a lot of surface conversation, so he dove right in. "Tell me about your marriage."

Adrienne nearly choked on her ice water.

"I'm sorry. It's just that . . . " How could he explain? "You still seem so sad about it. But I know you told us he wasn't really a nice guy."

Adrienne dabbed her napkin to her mouth. "I seem sad?"

Yes, and the biggest part of me wants to drag you into my arms and kiss it away. Will reined in his thoughts and cleared his throat. "It's in your eyes."

She looked away and focused on the water beside them. Moonlight flashed and disappeared in a dance with slow-moving, puffy clouds.

"That was an inappropriate question, wasn't it? I'm not great with women." Like she didn't already know that.

"You look like the type that's very smooth with women."

He chuckled. "Looks can be deceiving."

She narrowed her gaze on him. "So can eyes."

"So I misread you?" Will dropped his napkin to his lap. A whisper of a breeze flickered the light on the table as if the wind were changing course.

"Not entirely. I'm *very* sad my marriage didn't work. But I'm very happy to be out of it. It was wrong from the beginning. I kept making excuses for the narcissistic man I chose. Finally, the excuses ran out, and I had to take a hard look at who he really was."

Will leaned forward, resting his arms on the table. "The excuses ran out?" He wanted to keep her talking, there was something intimate about knowing she'd share it with him.

"He was having an affair, and I tried to deny it for a while. Then I confronted him. He told me I was crazy. So I followed him one night."

"Ouch."

One shoulder tipped up. "I knew what I would find. Do you know he actually had the nerve to write his dates on our home calendar in our kitchen? Lunch with Jilly."

Will tried to swallow, but his throat was thick, his heart starting the familiar thrashing of anger toward this destructive man.

"I mean, that's not even a grown-up name. *Jilly.* Dinner with Jilly to discuss new hospital wing. Drinks with Jilly. Like I was too stupid to figure it out."

"Was there anyone you could talk to?"

"My folks in Missouri, but my mom just didn't get it. She thought I should stick it out. 'Be tough, Adrienne, when the smoke clears, you'll be the one he wants to stay with.' Like I'd want him after that." She shook her head, and a cloud of mink hair fluttered around her.

"What about friends in Chicago?"

"All my friends were through Eric. Doctors' wives, society types. They'd have to pick sides and it would put them at odds with their husbands. It wasn't worth it to them or me. I really wasn't close to anyone. Eric was my full-time job." Her gaze drifted out to the water where pillow-soft whitecaps rolled toward the beach. "And even that wasn't enough for him."

"How could anyone cheat on you?" Will hadn't intended to say those words out loud, but there they were, big and bold. He wanted to come around the table and pull Adrienne into his arms. She looked so lonely over there behind the candlelight. There was a seat right beside her. He started to move but stopped. What had Pops told him? Women connect face to face.

Adrienne must have noticed his change in posture. "What?"

"Nothing." He leaned back in his chair and rubbed his hands over the thighs of his pants, a nervous habit.

She pointed at him. "You were going to move, go somewhere." Her fingers ran along the edge of her hair. "Don't worry. I won't think I scared you off. You *asked* about Eric."

Will worked the muscle in his jaw. "I, uh, wanted to come over and sit by you. But I decided not to."

Her dark eyes went inquisitive. "Why?"

"I didn't want you to feel uncomfortable."

"Oh." The candle danced between them, showering spikes of light onto the surroundings and playing in the gold flecks of her eyes. "I think I'd like for you to sit beside me."

Something about her throaty words wrapped around Will's chest and squeezed. For a quick instant he thought about throwing his glass of ice water into his face, just to keep things in perspective. Instead, he stood, moved around the table, and sat by her. Adrienne nuzzled close enough for their arms to touch. And there they sat looking out over the water and neither talking about marriage or divorce.

This was nice. He was nice. The air was nice, the breeze skirting from the water and caressing her skin. All very nice. In fact, Adrienne couldn't remember having a nicer time on a date.

Well, isn't that nice.

Except it wasn't. It was terrifying on a cellular level. If she continued to enjoy herself, some chemical reaction would take place, causing every atom inside her body to split. The fact that she was this freaked out about a date was as alarming as the possible blast. What on earth was *wrong* with her?

"Are you cold?" Will asked, pressing his arm to hers. They'd finished a lovely three-course dinner and now sat quietly as the night water rolled beside them, its soothing sound all but lost in the atmosphere where a string quartet wafted to them from farther in the restaurant.

"I'm comfortable." She smiled. She'd done a lot of that tonight. Smiling at his stories about Pops, his confessions about having an insatiable sweet tooth, everything.

"Would you like to walk out on the pier?"

Rushing for the first time that evening, Adrienne dabbed her mouth a final time, folded her napkin, and was on her feet before she answered.

Will chuckled. "Whoa." But he followed her lead. "Either I'm a really boring date and you can't wait to get out of here, or—"

But her gaze was fastened on the long wooden pier ahead of them that jutted out into the deep abyss. "Do you think they're catching anything? It's hard to tell from so far away. What kind of fish did I catch when we were on the boat?"

"Snook."

"Right. I read somewhere you can catch shark at night. *Shark.* Have you caught a shark before, Will? Has Pops? What's that like?"

"Slow down. I'm only one person. I can answer all your questions, but you've got to take a breath so I can catch up."

Adrienne stopped dead at the edge where salt-worn planks met the concrete of the restaurant's patio.

"What's wrong?"

She stared down at the boards and chewed her bottom lip.

"What is it, Adrienne—?" But then he saw. She tilted her foot, revealing the dangerous spike of her stiletto heel. He took in the multiple cracks along the pier and understood. "Ah. Tripping hazard."

He disappeared in a forward bow. She drew a sharp breath when his hand closed around her ankle and tugged ever so gently.

"Here, let me take them." And out her foot slipped from the first sandal, causing her view of the world to rise four inches above where it had been. The same warm hand closed over her other ankle and slipped her foot from its tall prison. "Better?"

Words formed but didn't escape her mouth.

Instead of letting go of her ankle, his hand closed a bit more. "What's this?" His finger grazed over the band-aid on her heel.

The sensation sent dizzying spikes up her leg. "Just a . . . " Really, she couldn't think with his fingers stroking her like that. "I caught my foot on a nail the other day."

He tilted up and studied her, a little frown creasing his forehead. "A rusty nail?"

"I've had a tetanus shot," she assured him, then rolled her eyes at herself. She really knew how to take an intimate moment and spoil it.

From the indentations that appeared on his cheeks, she had to assume Will was biting back a smile. "That's good. Glad you've had your shots. Does it hurt?"

"No." She reached for the shoes.

"Nah, I got them." And he slipped his hand through the straps, then tucked his fingers in his front pocket, letting the sparkly sandals dangle at his wrist.

Adrienne didn't know whether to be embarrassed or touched. She opted for embarrassingly touched as he held out his other arm for her to take. They strolled toward the end of the pier, where the sea crashed against the pilings and sprayed the deck with fine salty mist.

"Tell me about the canoe." Will didn't offer much transition from one subject to the next. They were either quietly comfortable, or he was diving in face first. The honesty and lack of scheming was something she'd have to get used to. With Eric, everything from his mouth had had an ulterior motive, and she'd had to choose her words carefully, sure she'd have to eat them at some distant date.

"It was a canoe trip set up by a hospital where he'd applied for residency. They were taking all their—as Eric liked to say—all the people that mattered"—Adrienne made air quotes and rolled her eyes—"on this get-in-touch-with-nature excursion."

She paused at the end of the pier and rested her elbows on the worn railing. "Eric, of course, weaseled his way in, even though they hadn't accepted his residency. He'd schmoozed the chief of surgery with expensive dinners we couldn't afford and secured us a spot on the canoe trip."

Will came to rest beside her and used his index finger to trace one of the grooves in the rail—just like she'd seen him do on the porch swing. Adrienne smiled.

"To make a long story short, our canoe tipped in the freezing cold water. We were both hung up on a massive tree branch, most of our bodies submerged in the water, and someone from another canoe tossed a life raft to us and was yelling at Eric to secure it to the branch so they could get to us. They yelled for me to start getting in the raft first while Eric steadied me. But *he* climbed in the raft first, and when it started to tip, he yelled for me to keep hanging on to the branch and the others would come get me. Later he said it was an accident, that I'd slipped from him, but everyone knew the truth."

Her hands flattened on the railing and closed, a firm reminder that she was on level ground. But to her surprise, Will slipped his fingers beneath hers, having to wiggle a bit to get below her grip. His touch was steady. Soothing.

"Water was rushing around my head. I wasn't under it, but the force was intense, and I felt like I was breathing more water with every breath. My feet could barely touch the rocks at the bottom of the river. Each time I thought I might be able to stand and get myself unhooked, the rocks rolled away in the fierce water."

"No wonder you were so scared on the boat." His hand rolled beneath hers, naturally threading their fingers together. Is that why he'd slid his hand under hers rather than on top? Or maybe he wanted her to know that all men weren't like her ex-husband. Some wouldn't let you go. Some you could hold and they wouldn't push you away.

"Well, everyone saw his act of *bravery*. The chief of surgery scolded him in front of the entire staff. Actually used him as an example of who they *don't* want at their facility. Eric blamed me."

"There had to be a bit of satisfaction for you. He got what he deserved. Showing his true colors in front of the very people he tried to impress."

Adrienne shook her head. "I suppose there should have been. Vindication and all. But it just made me sad. Once again I was reminded that the man I chose couldn't protect me. Wouldn't."

Off to the right, commotion drew her attention. The zing of a fishing pole and the murmurs of onlookers around an old fisherman erased Adrienne's train of thought. The man wrestled with whatever bent the pole nearly in two. Excitement crackled down the pier, drawing more attention. Soon, a crowd had gathered as the man tipped the pole up and back as he worked to get the prize out of the water.

A flash of white broke the surface and Adrienne squealed. It was big. The word *shark* was whispered through the crowd of onlookers, and people made way while a few stepped in to help land the beast. Adrienne's hand ached, and she looked down and realized Will's fingers had turned bone white. She released her squeeze on him and tried to keep her grip slack. But when the shark came up over the railing and onto the deck, her fingers clenched in a death grip again.

"How big is he?" she whispered reverently.

"Probably four feet."

"What will the guy do with him? Is it safe for him to be up here with all these people?"

"It's not safe for the shark. He's dinner."

Adrienne stared at the meaty gray beast with the wide mouth. "Are they good eating?"

Good eatin' was a term she'd heard from fishermen since moving to the Gulf. But she still had trouble dropping the "g". Will smiled down at her. "Yep. They're good eatin'. Especially for kids."

Her attention snapped from the gray beast to Will. "Why for kids?"

"No bones. You know, people always worry about giving fish to kids because of the bones. Sharks don't have any. No choking hazard."

For a long time she watched his face. Somehow the excitement of a moment ago melted like the spray of saltwater dissolving into the pier. Adrienne considered Will as a father, taking his son or daughter out on the boat. Teaching him or her about what fish are *good eatin'* and which ones should be thrown back. She could see him in that job. Daddy. It fit.

And that—that right there—was where she backed off. Emotionally, but also physically. Adrienne took a step backward, bare feet shuffling on the smooth, moist wood.

Will quirked a frown. "You okay?"

"Yes," she lied. "Just getting tired. You know, Cinderella and the stroke of midnight."

With her sandals still dangling on his wrist and a hint of understanding in his eyes, he said, "Come on. I'll take you home."

They rode to her house in silence, with just the purr of the car engine to keep them company. It wasn't a strange or forced silence, but an easy one, even though Adrienne had nearly ruined a nice evening by thinking about things she shouldn't. Like how a man she barely knew would fit into the role of daddy to tanned, dark-headed children with sparkling green eyes.

Will walked with her up the steps and onto her porch, where she used an ancient key to unlock her door. "You like going barefoot, don't you?"

She frowned. "Huh?" Then she noticed her sandals dangling from his outstretched finger. "Oh."

When she moved to take them, he drew them out of her reach.

Adrienne's head tilted. "We're a bit too old for games, Mr. Bryant."

His green eyes darkened in the soft pool of light from a porch sconce. "And a bit too young to be too serious." He slid the shoes behind his back, where she'd have to nearly bear-hug him to reach them.

She bit into her lower lip, hiding a smile. Her chin rose, nose tilting into the air. "For your information, I do like to go barefoot."

"What else?"

He moved a millimeter closer, but the nearness seemed much more monumental than a tiny gesture. He literally absorbed the air around her.

She needed to step back but instead stood firm. "I don't know what you mean."

His mouth tipped dangerously close to hers. "What else do you like, Adrienne?" The words were a low rumble against her skin, sending sparks from her chest down into the deepest part of her stomach.

And in that white-hot flash, everything she wanted from a man, from a partner, rushed through her system and scorched her from the inside out. "I . . . I . . . " She'd never been asked that. Never even felt comfortable wondering about that. Pressure from within pushed her backward until she rested firmly against the front door. She felt leveled, naked, but also unashamed to find that she did indeed have an answer to the question.

Adrienne blinked, mind searching for the truth hidden in his words. She had a right to want. She had a right to need. Her eyes found Will's. But something had changed, shifted there in his gaze. Gone was the desire from his eyes, replaced by a solemn look of protection.

He set her shoes on the nearby railing, ran a hand through his dark hair, and pulled in a breath. For a long few seconds, he stared at her, a soft—and if she wasn't mistaking—apologetic smile forming on that delicious mouth of his. But he was also creating distance, much-needed distance if she read him right. Will squared his shoulders and moved toward her. Warm hands closed on her upper arms and his face tilted down until their cheeks met. There, he pressed his face against hers and whispered, "Goodnight, Cinderella." The tiniest peck of a kiss brushed her ear. Will stepped away, leaving her dizzy and glad she was leaning on a solid mahogany door. Whatever that was, whatever had passed between them, was gone. She should be thankful he was such a gentleman. But a tiny part of her wished he hadn't been.

Chapter 10

August 1944

Dear Sara,

I asked Grace to give you this letter. My mind has been on you lately. I imagine you've grown in the time I've been away. Are you still playing ball? Sometimes, some of the guys here get together, and we attempt to play baseball. For a bunch of soldiers, they aren't half bad. And to tell you the truth, they aren't half honest, either. My team hasn't lost a game since we started. And with our victories, the opposing team seems dead-set on rewriting the rules. I've never seen anything like it. You'd laugh if you could see them. But I'm glad you can't. It's a tough place to be, knowing you might play a game with a friend one day and dig his grave the next. But I won't dwell on that. I didn't write to you to tell you about the hardships. Though they are plentiful, I suspect they will forever remind me to be thankful for every day I have.

How's the fishing? Are the snapper biting? I know Joseph Wilmer offered to take you night fishing. Grace told me. But don't you go, Sara. I don't trust that boy. Something in his eyes, like he's always scheming. 'Course, I know it's none of my business, but I'd appreciate it if you wouldn't go. I worry about you enough, sweet Sara. When I get home, we'll borrow Old Man Orlin's boat, and we'll fish all night if you want. But just . . . please don't go till then.

132

*Well, give your sister a hug for me. I hope she's okay.
I know you're taking care of her, keeping her from getting
lonely. You girls stay out of trouble, all right?
And I'll see you soon.*

William

Adrienne folded the letter and placed it in her purse. From the safety of her car, she watched as Sara Chandler sat in the courtyard of the Southern Palms retirement home in Winter Garden, Florida. The older woman reached down and plucked a dead flower from the plant next to her. A small plate of cookies was mostly hidden under the edge of her skirt. Had Sara ever gotten to read that letter? Had Grace shown it to her, or had it become another secret Grace had kept hidden?

Adrienne hoped this wasn't a huge mistake. But the question plagued her, and after her date with Will, she'd searched the Internet for Sara Chandlers with a newfound urgency she couldn't explain. If she admitted the truth—which she wouldn't—concentrating her effort and energy on Sara and Pops kept her from thinking about Will. The near kiss, the brush of lips against her ear. Adrienne had never been around anyone who so *absorbed* the world. Next to Will, other men she'd known just seemed small. Even Ryan, larger-than-life, fun-loving Ryan. She gave her head a good shake, hoping it would settle the fluttery bits of memory of a perfect night, complete with a perfect Prince Charming.

She'd tracked only seventeen Sara Chandlers that had lived in North Carolina and only one that fit the age group. That Sara Chandler had moved to Winter Garden, Florida, just two years back. Going on Leo's assurance that she had never married, it was an easy find.

Sara loved to fish. That's all Adrienne could think about on the boat with Will and Pops and again when the fisherman hauled in the shark. *Sara loved to fish.* And Sara was alive and well and right in front of her eyes. When Adrienne had first called the retirement center, they had been reluctant to give out any information. But when she explained she'd moved into a house that Ms. Chandler once lived in, they were gracious and forthcoming. The receptionist said Sara spoke of Bonita Springs often.

Adrienne had googled directions to the Southern Palms Retirement Village, and now, three hours later—and with a physical description of Sara that proved to be spot-on—here she was. She exited the car but didn't make eye contact. She chose a nearby bench where she could decide which level of stalker she'd become before approaching Sara.

She wasn't sure what could be accomplished by her visit, but Adrienne had come to the conclusion that Pops had a right to know Sara was alive and had once loved him.

And Sara had a right to tell him so.

"Sara!" A screeching voice came from behind the bench where the attractive older woman sat. Adrienne moved so she could hear the conversation passing between Sara and a round woman in a long housecoat, wearing several layers of jewelry.

Sara turned slowly toward the panicked voice, sweeping fine white hair from her eyes. "What is it, Louisa?"

Dressed in a dark pink blouse and white skirt, Sara looked decades younger than the jittery woman wobbling toward her. "Mr. Tibbles has fallen in the tub again."

Adrienne started to stand and rush over to see if she could help, but Sara's look of indifference stopped her. "Louisa, if your cat can get into the bathtub, he can get out."

"No he can't. And I'm just not strong enough to lift him." Louisa's tight mouth pursed, dotted with tangerine lipstick.

Sara sighed and scanned the courtyard. Adrienne dropped her gaze as Sara's eyes landed in her direction. "Fine." She stood from the bench and reached down to scoop up the plate of cookies. Louisa froze.

"You're waiting for those kids!" Louisa hissed, eyes growing wide and wild.

Sara bristled. "So what if I am?"

Louisa pointed a bony finger at her. "You're going to get into trouble."

Sara squared her shoulders. "I'm a grown woman, and I have every right to give away cookies."

Louisa shot a look behind her, then to the left and right. "Well, *I'm* not going to get in trouble for those ragamuffin hooligans."

"I love seeing those kids, and if the management of Southern Palms disagrees, they can try to stop me. I buy the ingredients, I bake the cookies. I can give them to whomever I want."

Well, Sara still had a good measure of that spunk Adrienne had heard Pops talk about.

Louisa crossed her arms. "Are you going to help me or not?"

Sara nodded, left the cookies there, and followed Louisa until she disappeared into one of the apartments. While she was gone, Adrienne moved to stand near Sara's bench, half-hoping she'd come back and half-hoping she wouldn't.

A few minutes later, Sara returned. She was an attractive older woman with straight white hair cut into a blunt style that brushed her shoulders and gave her a distinct air of sophistication.

"May I sit with you?" Adrienne asked.

Sara nodded, smiled, and motioned to the seat beside her.

"Are you Sara Chandler?" Adrienne's nervous fingers were balled in her lap.

"Why, yes."

"I'm Adrienne Carter." She extended her hand.

Sara took her hand and shook it. "Nice to meet you." Then she asked, "Are you here to visit someone?"

"Yes." Adrienne nodded. "I'm here to visit you."

This drew the older woman's awareness, so much so that she pivoted on the bench to give Adrienne her full attention. "Are you the mother of one of the skateboarders? I hope you don't mind the cookies. I was a schoolteacher for years and—"

Adrienne placed a hand over Sara's. "No, I'm not. And I'm sure any good mom would appreciate your having an after-school snack for her child."

The wind caught Sara's hair. She tilted into it, and Adrienne had to wonder if Sara loved Florida sunshine and wind as much as she herself did. Sara's finger traced the platter of cookies. "So many kids are home alone after school."

"Sara, I live in the house on Hidden Beach Road." Before she could stop herself, words spilled from Adrienne's mouth, almost as if in confession. Sara seemed to follow most of the story, but she placed a hand to her heart when Adrienne confessed she'd found a small metal box.

Sara held her hands up and shook her head. "Wait, dear. Wait a second. I searched before we left. I searched everywhere. The box was gone."

"I nearly missed it myself. It was tucked into the rafters above the breaker box. I thought Gracie must have put the box in the attic, but you had it?"

Sara's face paled. "No."

Adrienne waited for the explanation. If Sara knew about the box, she'd read the letters, including the one written to her.

Sara turned away from her, hiding her expression. "It . . . it must have been Momma."

"You meant to take the letters with you after Grace died?"

"William's letters *survived*?" It was a breathy question. One filled with so much desperation, Adrienne didn't feel the need to answer.

Wrinkled hands brushed imaginary lint from her white skirt. "You see, when my mother found me with the letters, she was angry. Furious, in fact. I thought Momma burned them."

Adrienne's voice drew her. "They're safe and sound. Did you hear me, Sara? They're all intact. William has them."

Sara's inhale was a tiny gasp of air. "He's still alive? *William* is still alive?"

Adrienne nodded. "Alive and well. He lives with his grandson in Naples."

A thousand thoughts must have inundated Sara's mind, for her eyes danced around the courtyard as if chasing each one. "He's alive. Oh, that's wonderful. I . . . I returned to Bonita Springs once, three years after leaving with Momma. William was married to Betty Nichols."

Adrienne touched Sara's arm. "That must have been very hard for you."

Clear blue eyes flashed to her. Sara's head shook from side to side. "No. It wasn't hard. William survived the war, made it safely home. He was happy with his wife and a new baby on the way."

Sara's voice dropped as if traveling from far away. "In the last few years, it has simply been easier to assume that William had led a happy life and died a quiet death than to . . . to wonder . . . "

Several moments passed between the two women as Adrienne gave Sara plenty of room to revisit a world she'd likely spent a lifetime forgetting. Slowly, Sara stood up from the bench. Off to their right, young voices drifted closer. "Would you care to come back to my apartment for some tea?" Sara asked. "I'm afraid I'm not in the mood to entertain skateboarders today."

They started across the courtyard, Sara carrying the heavy weight from so long ago. Adrienne could practically see it on her shoulders. Maybe Sara had made peace with what she'd done—fallen in love with her sister's fiancé. But Adrienne had certainly opened a wound, if not that one, some other deep-seated scar from back then.

And now the secret she'd harbored was stabbing her in the heart, all because of Adrienne's intrusion.

They stepped into the apartment, made for a single person but large enough to comfortably entertain a guest. The small living room was decorated with soft sea colors, anchored by a lovely antique bureau that, in spite of its size, fit perfectly on one wall.

After Sara poured the tea, they fell into a conversation about Bonita Springs, how it had grown and changed and how Sara loved it. "I called some of the retirement villages there, but they were pricey. Winter Garden offered everything I needed, though I'd rather be on the Gulf, not inland like here."

"How long has it been since you were there?" Adrienne took the honey offered and put a spoonful into her drink.

"Thirty years, at least."

Adrienne tapped her finger on the porcelain tea cup. "If you would ever like to come to Bonita Springs, I'd be glad to have you visit."

Sara laughed lightly. "It's what, three hours? That's very kind of you, but I don't think these old bones would be up for such a long haul there and back."

"You could spend the night. I have plenty of room." Almost quietly, she added, "We could go visit William."

Sara stared beyond Adrienne to a photo on her wall. It was a snapshot that looked like the Grand Canyon. "I don't think William or Betty would be that excited to see me."

Adrienne swirled the spoon in her tea. "Betty passed away five years ago. You would be going to see William. And I think he would be very happy about that."

It was a long, long way down to the bottom of that canyon. And if Adrienne was right, Sara was wishing she could enter the picture and jump off the edge.

Sara shook her head. "No."

"Sara, I know about the diary."

Suddenly, Sara stood up from the table. She walked into the kitchen and stood at the sink, fingers splayed on the cool countertop, her back to Adrienne.

"You shouldn't be ashamed of falling in love with William. He's quite an incredible man."

Sara spun, a hardness in her eyes so solid, it surprised Adrienne. "I. Left. Him."

Adrienne set her tea on the table, wondering if the older woman might shatter into a million pieces.

Sara shook her head slowly. "Do you understand me? I left. He was wounded, had lost Grace, and I *left* him."

Adrienne shook her head. "You had no choice, Sara. Your mother made you go."

"No. We weren't supposed to leave for another week. But I found out William was coming home, and I told her that if she wanted me to go, we had to leave before he got there."

The words swirled around Adrienne as she tried to catch up to what Sara was admitting. "You were ashamed . . . "

"I was a coward. I fell for him. I fell so hard. If I hadn't loved him, maybe Grace would have . . . maybe things could have been different for all of us."

Adrienne stood and walked to her. "Sara, you can't help how you feel. Don't you think it's time William knew?"

Sara was shaking, and the tremors became more violent with each breath.

Adrienne touched her shoulders. "Would you just consider it? Please, I know this is a lot to ask, but William, he's such a wonderful man . . . "

Sara pulled away from her and stared out the kitchen window, the muscles of her throat stretched tight.

Giving her a moment, Adrienne dug in her purse. "I'm writing down my phone number." Her hand fell across the copy of the letter from William, but she pushed it aside. There was no way Sara was ready to see it. That was obvious. Adrienne would keep the letter to herself. She held out the scrap of paper with her number. Sara stared at it as if it might strike. Adrienne held her ground. Finally, Sara took the paper.

"Can I return and visit you, again? I promise not to drop any more news like this if I do. But I feel like I know you. I live in your house. May I come back?"

Sara turned away once more. She placed Adrienne's phone number on the kitchen counter. When Adrienne thought she'd surely tell her no, Sara faced her and forced a smile. "I suppose."

"I'd like to. I've heard so much about you from the letters and from William. It would be an honor to get to know the girl he cared so much for. But today, I've taken enough of your time." Adrienne placed her purse on her arm. She paused at the front door. "Please consider coming to visit. Good-bye, Sara."

The door clicked shut. The air conditioner kicked on, the only sound other than the whispers and accusations from the past. Still in a haze of memories, Sara watched from her window as Adrienne walked to her car. A group of boys devoured the cookies on the bench smack-dab in the middle of the retirement center's courtyard. Seeing them always made her smile. But not today.

Sara shuffled to the bureau across the room and withdrew a key from the high cabinet. Hands trembling, she placed the key in the bottom lock and listened for the click. Her eyes closed and her heart bled. For the first time in years, she opened the desk drawer and lifted out the letters from her long-ago home. Without untying the lavender ribbon, she slid one from the stack. They had no envelopes and were adorned with no postmarks. Simple pages, tri-folded and aged by the years. Fear and sorrow fought for dominance in a heart she'd thought had healed. Sara clenched her teeth and opened the letter.

Dear William, it began. Sara continued to read.

One thing Adrienne was good at was damage control. She'd unfairly dropped a horrible bombshell on Sara—and she wouldn't blame the woman for not forgiving her—but now, only two weeks later, the two women were conspiring against the nursing home. Sara made no mention of William. Adrienne didn't push the subject.

Instead, they invaded the grocery store and bought enough products to fund a bakery. "Bootlegging" them, Sara liked to refer to it as. The management of Southern Palms didn't want kids skateboarding on the property, so feeding them was frowned upon, much as one might be warned against feeding bears or seagulls or stray cats. Sara was fearless in her efforts to keep the youngsters coming by. The management had scared the other residents into submission, but not her. Why couldn't she be that fearless in going to visit William?

"I finished the upstairs bedroom. *Your* old room." Adrienne had painted it Sara's favorite color. "It's lavender."

"Lovely, Adrienne. I bet the house looks marvelous." Sara tucked her hair behind an ear. The apartment was warm from the oven's heat and filled with the delicious scent of fresh-baked goods.

Though her second visit had been more out of guilt than for fun, Adrienne was really enjoying Sara's company. Since Adrienne's own mother was usually too busy keeping up appearances or trying to fix her daughter, Adrienne hadn't grown up with someone who wanted to let her be herself. Sara was like that: no nonsense, speaking her mind, and allowing others to simply be. "I was hoping you might come and see the house." This was it. Her last-ditch effort to get Sara to Bonita Springs. And more importantly, closer to William.

Sara plunked the bottle of vanilla extract down on the kitchen counter. When she answered, her words were clipped. "Adrienne, I've given this a lot of thought. I don't want to see William. My life is what I chose. I cared for him at one time, but those feelings are dead and I don't want to revisit them. From what you've said, William has made peace—even with Gracie's betrayal. I've caused him enough pain. I won't be the source of more."

Adrienne brushed flour from her cheek. "Okay. I understand." She returned to her job of placing warm, gooey chocolate-chip cookies on a wide platter while Sara finished putting away ingredients. "I'll drop it . . . for now."

"My mind is made up."

"*Okay.* Now, let's go find some skateboarders." They headed out, platter of cookies in hand. "You can't blame me for trying."

Just before they stepped into the bright sunlight, Adrienne watched Sara's gaze shift to the antique bureau in her living room.

"Sara, is everything okay?"

For an instant, something white-hot flashed in the older woman's eyes, but she quickly blinked it away. "Yes. Yes, of course."

Adrienne frowned, noticed how Sara's face had paled, as if her question had scared the color out of her skin. "You sure?"

"Everything's perfect, dear." But Sara refused to make eye contact.

Though Sara was good at harboring secrets, Adrienne was equally skilled at drawing them out.

Chapter 11

"orning, Pops." Adrienne reached through the doorway and dropped a kiss on the older man's cheek.

He rubbed the spot with his fingertips and motioned her inside. "Hooey, I could get used to that. Made breakfast for you."

From the top of the stairs, a voice drifted down. Will's voice. And hearing it sent little sparks zinging through Adrienne's body. "It's unfair that you two are sending me off to work."

Hand resting on the railing, he came down the steps with his suit jacket slung over his free arm, looking dangerously sexy. Whew! Someone needed to turn on the ceiling fan. "Good morning, Will." She hoped her voice was smooth but figured it wasn't.

"It would be if I could ditch work and go to the garden show with you two."

Pops waved a hand through the air. "Oh, poo. You hate the garden show. All those snooty women in floppy hats."

Will's eyes skated to Adrienne. He winked.

Pops yammered on. "Last time I made you go, you told me if you ever had to go again, to just shoot you instead, that it'd be less painful."

"Well, maybe I like the company better this time."

"And maybe that's why I don't need you this time." Pops threaded his arm through Adrienne's and led her to the kitchen.

She gave Will a "take-that glance," complete with brows high and mouth tilted down.

He rolled his eyes. "You two have fun while I'm slaving away at work."

"Yeah, we will," Pops said, holding tight to Adrienne. "Don't catch cold from all that air conditioning. Be careful not to get a nasty paper cut."

Will left, mumbling about life being unfair. Adrienne dove into a nice plate of eggs and toast, and when she was just about finished, Pops scooted his chair a little closer. "Before we leave, could I . . . talk to you about something?"

Adrienne wiped her mouth with a checkered napkin. "Sure, Pops."

"Something I want to show you." His uncertainty was clear in the tone of his voice, the way he tilted his head from side to side.

"What's the matter?"

"Nothing." Weathered hands rubbed together, and his brow furrowed. Pops left the room, leaving Adrienne wondering what had gotten him so upset.

He returned with his stack of letters and drew the bottom one out. Right away, Adrienne noticed it was written on a completely different kind of paper. This page was thicker, unlike the thin aerogrammes William used to write to Grace. She'd never seen this letter before.

With gentle hands, Pops took the handwritten note, unfolded it, and gave it to Adrienne.

Her eyes asked the question.

Pops nodded. "You can read it aloud."

When her gaze fell to the opening, Adrienne pulled a deep breath. *"Dear William,"* She'd only seen letters *from* William, never one *to* him.

His hand fell over hers, stopping her. "It's the only letter from Grace that survived. I lost a whole stack of them at Normandy when I lost my gear in the jump. When I got injured and they moved me from place to place, the rest of the letters disappeared. I made it home with this one but never really understood it. Thought maybe you could help me."

Adrienne pulled a deep breath and began again.

Dear William,

Is it wrong of me to hope? To dream? Is it wrong of me to want you all for myself? I've become a selfish, evil girl. To share you is unthinkable. With each passing day, I visualize your return. I see you there on the steps of the train station in your uniform, with the smile that keeps my heart beating. Will you know me? Will you recognize me? The woman you love? The woman who loves you more than life?

There is no second of any passing day that I don't consider the change we've both undergone. You left a boy but will come home a man. And when you left, I was a girl. But I'm a woman now. Things were simpler in days gone by, when our world was new and fresh with each adventure. Swimming in the bay, fishing from the shore. You and I were different then. Closer than any two people could ever be.

And yet, in your absence, we've grown together and not apart. I know you don't understand this fully, but one day you will. One day you'll know my secret. You'll know I've loved you forever and forever. I will until the breath of life leaves me. I'm forever yours."

Across the room, the clock ticked, and a strong breeze pushed against the house. Adrienne's heart raced. This sounded like . . . like a letter, but not from Grace. But that was impossible. Surely, William would have recognized a different handwriting.

He interrupted her thoughts. "What do you think, Adrienne?"

She couldn't look at the page anymore, so she folded it and placed it on the table. "I wish I knew, Pops."

He pushed back in his chair. "I'd practically forgotten about it until I read some of the letters you gave me. It's been stuck in a photo album for years. Betty made me keep it."

"She did?"

"Yep. Said it was important to remember the past. She couldn't make heads or tails of it either, just said she was thankful we met and I was heartbroken enough to fall in love with her." He chuckled.

"I'm sure that's not why you fell in love with Betty."

"No, it wasn't. She was a precious soul, my Betty. A good, good woman." He nodded, emphasizing the fact. "This was the last letter I got from Grace. She sure doesn't sound in love with another man."

"No, she doesn't," Adrienne echoed.

Weathered hands folded together on the table. He rubbed the pad of his thumb over the knuckles of his other hand as if the answer were right there in the folds of his skin. "Well, time's a wastin'. Let's get to that garden show."

They stood up from the table, and Pops slipped the letter back into the stack.

They left the house with the heavy intrigue of a puzzle unsolved plaguing Adrienne's mind. Somewhere in her heart, she knew Sara had the answer.

"Congratulations, Will." Victoria Philips sidled into his bank office and took a seat across from him. She spread her arms like wings across the back of the chair and pushed out her chest, stretching the material of her sweater.

"Thank you." He glanced down at the crystal award he'd received earlier in the day.

Victoria wore a business skirt that she let slide far above her knees as she sat down. Usually, he enjoyed the sensual purr of her voice. Today it didn't have the desired effect. "Youngest executive in Naples Bank and Trust history to receive the esteemed award. How are you planning to celebrate?"

Celebrate? He wasn't planning to. Receiving the award was celebration enough.

When he floundered, she spoke up. "Since you're too dumbstruck to make a plan, let me help. Some of us are getting together later to have a going-away party for Jonathan. Why don't you come along? I'll buy you a drink." With exaggeration, she tossed her blonde hair, and one brow rose, seductively. "Maybe even two."

Intriguing, but he couldn't help wondering why the sudden interest in him. He'd thought of asking her out in the past, but Victoria had made it clear that he was far too wholesome for her taste. The woman needed excitement. And sadly, he wasn't the life of the party. In fact, he was rarely found at a party. Because alcohol seemed to be the hub of most office get-togethers, he rarely enjoyed the gushing camaraderie that accompanied those gatherings. Somewhere along the way, the invitations had ceased. It was his own doing, of course, but there was a little sting that accompanied it as well. He had no clue why Victoria was suddenly taking an interest. Or why his interest in her had just as suddenly taken a nosedive.

He decided he'd attend this party with Victoria. She—and her sweater—*really* seemed like they wanted him to go. Just as he opened his mouth to make the arrangements, Adrienne Carter flashed into his mind. He pushed her aside. There was no commitment between them. Just a nice dinner date that had rocked his world and kept him up late at night trying to remember the scent of her hair.

Victoria was a hot ticket with a great body accentuated by designer clothes and abundant confidence. He liked the idea of walking into a room with her on his arm. But again, picturing this, it was Adrienne's face he saw.

He thought back to their day of fishing. At first she'd been scared. Scared of everything. He'd soothed her nerves. And their time together had been something tight sweaters and silk skirts couldn't match.

In a most direct manner, he said to Victoria, "Why now?"

She flashed a quick smile and blinked. "What do you mean?"

"You've never seemed interested in me."

Her hands came down from the chair, heavily mascaraed eyes narrowing on him. "There's something different about you lately."

"What is it?"

She pursed her mouth. "I'm not sure, but it's hot."

He stifled a chuckle. *Hot.* There was nothing different about him. Maybe she'd just worked her way through all the other guys at the bank, and he was the only one left.

"You seem . . . I don't know. Confident. Sexually, I mean. I've just noticed it in the last month or so."

Confident *sexually*? Really? After seven years of working at the bank, suddenly he'd gotten in touch with his inner lion, king of the beasts, his alpha male prowess? He almost laughed out loud. Nothing had changed in the last month. Except, of course, the presence of Adrienne Carter in his life. But that couldn't possibly have anything to do with this. Victoria had a screw loose.

She licked her lips. "So, we have a date?"

"No," he said, sure he'd completely lost his mind, but suddenly uninterested in the flirty blonde that right now just seemed too desperate. "I have plans tonight. I'm really sorry."

Victoria's red-stained mouth hung open in an O shape. She quirked a frown, obviously not accustomed to being turned down and having to assimilate it into her being. She rose from the chair, body as stiff as if he'd jerked every ounce of confidence from her, and rushed out.

Jonathan stepped in as she left. He eyed her as she stormed past. "She doesn't look happy."

Jon was a good friend and a good guy who loved sports and his wife. When the higher-ups had overlooked him, it was Will who had convinced them to give Jon the much-deserved position of branch manager at a bank across town.

"I take it you're not coming to my going-away party?" Jon dropped into the chair Victoria had vacated.

"You're only moving across town. Is a party really necessary?" Will straightened the calendar on his desk. The promotion was hard earned and deserved. A celebration was in good order.

Jon moved his chair so that both men could gaze out the glass wall that separated the office. Other than the brightly colored tie Jon wore, the two men were identically dressed in dark suits, polished black shoes, and crisp white shirts. From their vantage point they could see the entire bank. They both studied Victoria. "So why did you turn her down? I thought you sort of liked her."

Will rested his hands on the cherry desk. "Me too. But when it came down to it, not as much as I thought." Again, Adrienne sashayed into his mind.

"Well, I never thought you two were a good match anyway."

"Why is that?" Will asked.

"Come on." Jon leaned an elbow on the desk. "You spend almost as much time on that boat of yours as she does putting on her makeup. You two are from different worlds."

"I thought we were from the same world." Will made a sweeping arc around him.

"You mean *banking*?" Jon laughed and shook his head. "Let me guess: You thought that just because you work together, you would share the same interests?"

Will shrugged. "I thought there would be a lot in common to build on."

Jon raised his brows. "To build a *relationship* on? That's the stupidest thing I've ever heard. Man, you don't pick who you fall in love with." He started to say more but stopped abruptly as an attractive brunette entered the bank, after pausing to hold the door for an elderly woman using a walker.

"Wow, look at her," Jon mumbled.

Both men watched Adrienne swoop down to rescue a paper the old woman had dropped. Will didn't fight the grin that worked its way across his face. He was beginning to enjoy the surge that circled his midsection and squeezed whenever he saw her.

Adrienne wore a snug-fitting dress that was the color of a vibrant sunset. The brilliance of the garment accentuated her tanned arms and legs. The contrast played on the sun streaks of her dark hair. When she saw Will, a wide smile spread across the mouth that had recently interrupted his dreams.

Will smiled back. As Adrienne passed Victoria making her way toward his office, the blonde paled by comparison, disappearing like background music when the real concert began. Adrienne was the symphony and Victoria, a practice instrument.

"She's here for you?" Jon pointed at her.

"I certainly hope so." Will reached over and lowered Jon's hand. "Don't get any ideas. She's just a friend of the family."

"I'm a married man. I don't get the luxury of ideas."

Adrienne spoke to one of the tellers and pointed at Will. The lowest part of Will's belly twisted. She sat down in the waiting area, skirt hiking just enough to reveal her knee.

Jon rubbed a hand over his face. "My family never had friends like that. No wonder you turned Victoria down."

Will nodded for Jon to get out, then tugged at the collar of his shirt. His tie was too tight. It rubbed against his throat, irritating his skin. For a few moments he fumbled with papers on his desk, trying to look like the busy bank executive he was. He jotted a note, straightened the stack. He stood, sucked in his gut, and motioned for Adrienne to come into his office.

"I hope it's okay that I stopped by." Man, she smelled good. And all that deliciousness invaded every corner of his universe.

"Of course." Someone must have turned off the air conditioning. A trickle of sweat ran down his shoulder blades.

"I wanted to thank you for the boat trip and the fishing with Pops and for dinner. It was the most amazing day . . . and night." When she said *amazing*, her eyes rounded and rolled, encompassing everything around her, drawing it into her orbit and forever altering it. *Oh boy, this could get bad.* Frankly, he loved that he'd given her the *most amazing day . . . and night.* It made him swell with pride.

Beyond the window, the entire bank seemed interested in this exchange. Busybodies. Or maybe they were all just interested in her. Like he'd been the first time she'd entered the bank, and like every guy at the restaurant. "I had a great time too. You going on the boat is all Pops has talked about. I should be jealous, you know."

She frowned, little lines creasing an otherwise smooth forehead.

"I've been taking Pops fishing for years, but you've claimed all the fanfare."

"Oh." A blush flushed her cheeks, making her face even more alive. Her dark eyes flitted around the room. "Your office is beautiful."

"Thank you."

"Um, Pops is the other reason I stopped by."

What next? he wondered, not minding sharing his grandfather with this woman. Maybe she wanted to plan a picnic or a trip to the beach. Adrienne in a bikini. Yeah, he could like that.

"After I found the letters, I also discovered a diary."

"Oh?" Will stiffened, recalling a few nights before, when he had found Pops distraught, alone in the library, reading the letters and poking through the photo albums that—as far as Will was concerned—needed to stay shut.

"It belongs to Sara. That was Gracie's younger sister. The thing is, Sara lives in Winter Garden, but she's afraid to talk to Pops because—"

He held his hands up, feeling blood rush to his face as his heart rate escalated. "You've talked to this woman?"

"Yes. But she's afraid to come visit."

Anger shot down his spine. "You actually asked her to come visit Pops?"

Adrienne nodded slowly, face darkening with questions.

"Look"—Will pushed himself back from the desk—"I don't know why you think you have the right, but you can't keep butting into his life like this."

"You don't understand." Her voice was faint, and had he not been so angry, it might have cut its way into him. But this was a dangerous path Adrienne kept trying to travel, and it was Pops who suffered all the turmoil of her impulsiveness.

"No, *you* don't understand. You returned the letters—fine. But you need to back off! Sure, when you come over, Pops is all smiles and ready to talk about the summer he spent with Gracie. He's ready to talk about the war. But when you leave, he crashes. That past almost killed him."

Adrienne's eyes registered shock. And pain.

He forged on before he lost the battle with those doe eyes and backed down. "And you keep showing up, reopening that wound, time after time. It's heartless, Adrienne. You may be enjoying it, but it's killing him."

She stared at the floor, shoulders curled forward. When she looked up, her eyes were full of tears, unshed and causing her irises to swim.

He'd probably gone too far. But she had also gone too far. Will had made a promise to himself five years ago when Grandma Betty died. A promise to protect his grandfather. And that's what he was doing now.

He even remembered exactly when and why he'd made that vow. It was the day after the funeral, and he'd stopped at Pop's house to check on him. The front door was open, so he'd walked on in. It wasn't until he'd reached the master bedroom that he had found Pops.

The sound of sobbing had drifted from the walk-in closet and out the bedroom door. The gut-wrenching wail of a broken man echoed in the room. But there was no way to ease his grandfather's pain. Nothing could replace what Pops had lost. As he listened, Will had realized his own cheeks were wet with tears, half from the sound he heard, half from the inability to help. Moving to the closet door, he saw his grandfather's face buried in his grandmother's clothes, clenched tightly between his fists. Will had watched as the man who had always been a pillar of strength crumbled, just a shell clinging to a shadow. At that moment, Will had vowed to protect Pops for the rest of his life. Never again would his hero be alone. Never again would he be broken. Will couldn't control everything, but this was well within his power. It had been an easy commitment to keep. Until now.

Until Adrienne Carter.

"I thought I was doing the right thing," Adrienne said softly. A little unsteady, she stood from the chair. "I'm sorry for causing problems. It wasn't my intention."

Will opened his mouth to speak, to tell her something, anything to erase a little bit of the hurt he could see reflected in her eyes. No. It had to be this way.

She walked out of his office, head down, eyes scanning the floor. She paused at the front door and threw one last apologetic glance back toward Will.

And it broke his heart. But, he reminded himself, he was doing the right thing. He ignored the fact that as she left, a little part of his heart went with her.

Chapter 12

$\mathcal{A}$ bag of groceries still in her arms, Adrienne pressed a hand to her face, barely believing what she heard. She had just stepped in the house, coming from the store, when her cell phone began to ring. Now, she stood frozen, unable to move, unable to escape. And listening to Sara chatter on about wanting to see William. About how one of the skateboarders had told her life was about do-overs. How she knew, knew in her heart, she *had* to see him.

If only Sara had called yesterday, before the disastrous meeting with Will at the bank. Heat rose to Adrienne's face as a wave of nausea crept through her stomach.

Could there be any worse timing? Twenty-four hours ago she'd sat in Will's office and was told she was heartlessly hurting an old man. Twenty-four hours ago, she'd made the decision to distance herself from all of them. For good.

Sara rattled on and on about William having a right to know the truth.

Lies aren't so bad. Adrienne shifted the groceries. *They're nice and safe. Buried things don't stink until you dig them up.* But it was too late for that. Adrienne had prodded and pressed, and now she was reaping the fruit of the seed sown. The biggest problem of all: Adrienne was the only link to William.

After talking to Will at the bank, she wanted nothing more to do with them. Any of them. Will, William, or even Sara, for that matter. She wasn't sure how she'd let this get so out of hand.

All she'd wanted to do was meet the man who wrote the beautiful letters.

This was exactly why she'd always played it safe instead of acting out of selfish motives. She'd wanted to *believe* in something again. To believe in love again. Well, love had gotten her six years of pain and sorrow and now she was imposing that hurt on innocent people. Ruining them. Destroying them. All so she could *pretend* there were happy endings.

Adrienne rubbed her hand across the back of her neck. "Sara, I'm in the middle of something. Can I call you back?" The lie was the truth by a thin margin. She was in the middle of realizing what a complete and utter fool she was.

The other end of the line was quiet for a moment. "Of course, dear." Sara was obviously trying to mask the concern in her voice. After all, this great reunion is what she'd been begging Sara to do.

Adrienne rolled her eyes and forced an attempt at cheer. "This is great news," she lied. "Um, let me call you back when I'm done."

Sara said good-bye, and Adrienne hung up the phone.

Still clutching the grocery bag, she meandered—zombie-like—to the living room and dropped onto the couch. The house was quiet. The tart scent of oranges rose from the bag. They'd probably smashed the bagels. Bagels made her think of shmear. Shmear made her think of Leo. Leo made her think of William. She groaned and loosened her grip.

Over and over she considered stopping this escapade. But it was too late for that now. No matter what she did, people were going to get hurt. Adrienne closed her eyes and shoved the bag away. She thought of Will. Fiercely devoted, pleading with her to butt out. She thought of Pops. *"But when you leave, he crashes,"* Will had said. She thought of Sara, majestic and elegant, but draped in the shame that had cloaked her for so many years. This was finally a chance for her to be free.

She bent at the waist and buried her face in a pillow. *No matter what I do, someone is going to get hurt.* Will, William, and Sara were at risk. And Adrienne herself was on the line too. She knew she could lose the best, most precious friendships she'd ever had.

Will headed outside, where the warm sun shone against the rich green of the garden. Though the sky was perfect, offering the kind of day that could lend itself to a long boat trip, his heart was heavy. Had been for days. Nothing seemed to help, not even putting the throttle on wide open and attacking the waves with the determination of a bull.

"Have you heard from Adrienne this week?" Will asked as Pops knelt to pick a ripe tomato. The garden was lush, thanks largely to an unusually wet summer. Various leaves were so thick and dense, they had to dig through the greenery to find the ripe vegetables hiding within.

"No, I haven't." Pops pushed his hand against his thigh to rise, then placed the tomato in the basket Will held. "Must be real busy working on her house these days."

Will couldn't help but notice the sadness that slipped into his grandfather's words. Guilt stabbed him. "It's my fault she hasn't been around."

Pops used his forearm to hold foliage out of his way. "That so?" He plucked another tomato.

"Last week she came to my office. We, uh, got into a little argument. I didn't mean to run her off completely."

"You ever notice the honeybees out here?"

Will frowned. Had Pops not even heard him? He'd just confessed to running Adrienne off. "Uh, no."

"But they're around." Pops took him by the arm and dropped his voice. "Look right over there."

Will followed his gaze to a nearby tree trunk where a bevy of bees crawled along the bark.

"You see, bees love nectar. And the garden is the best place to get a variety. When we come out here, they move away, but they don't leave. They're right there just waiting for our invitation to come back." Pops light-blue eyes landed on Will. "You understand?"

"Yeah, Pops. You don't think I ran her off completely. She'll come back."

Pops ran his arm over his brow and looked up at the sun, a bright burning ball hanging in the afternoon sky. "Well, I suspect you could take it that way. But I was just talking about honeybees." His eyes twinkled, and a half-smile deepened the curves around his mouth.

Pops held a tomato up in Will's face. "Nothing sweeter than this," he said. "Except maybe for honey."

Will nodded. Could Pops be right? Maybe Adrienne would be back. He just wanted her to stop dredging up the past. But Will never had been good with subtlety. Wrecking ball, his dad used to call him.

Pops loved Adrienne's visits, that was for sure. And since she'd been coming over, Pops seemed so alive, younger even. But when Adrienne and Pops would venture into some deep discussion about the war or Gracie, it took too much of a toll on him. When those topics came up, he seemed to melt into a somber mood that sometimes lasted for hours. It wasn't healthy.

But Will knew his words to her had been unusually harsh. And he hated himself for handling it so badly. Fact was, he missed her. He missed pulling into the driveway and seeing her red sports car there on any given afternoon. Even if, in the beginning, she rushed off as soon as Will hit the door. He missed walking past her in the kitchen and brushing against her soft skin. And her scent. He'd catch himself pulling in that citrusy floral aroma whenever she came near. A toss of her head or a swift movement would send an intense wave of it to him. And when he woke in the night, it was there. Probably residue from his dreams, but it made it difficult to keep her out of his thoughts. And then there were her lips. Man, he couldn't seem to keep his eyes off them, just waiting for her to bite the lower one or slowly run her tongue along the inner edge.

It had only been a week since he'd gotten rid of her, but it had already been too long. And somewhere deep inside, he feared he'd chased her off for good, no matter what Pops thought. He had drawn a line that—beneath her idealistic surface—she was just too sweet to cross. Adrienne was gone. He'd made sure of it.

He put an arm around Pops's shoulder, and they walked back to the house, the smell of fresh tomatoes a poor replacement for Adrienne's scent.

But Will had a plan. Having watched his grandfather's mood deteriorate over the last several days, he'd decided to do something special for him. He'd leave work on Friday at noon, pick up Pops, and the two of them would cruise down to the Keys. It was a three-hour trip by boat. They'd talked about doing it for years. It was sure to lift Pops's spirits. And if he was lucky, really lucky, it would leave the garden empty enough for the honeybees to return.

Adrienne put Sara off for a week, hoping that if she kept coming up with excuses, Sara would give up. Her plan failed miserably. It was now Friday morning and she was headed to Winter Garden. They would be at Will's house by noon, giving William and Sara until five o'clock to sort things out. Adrienne chose Friday on purpose. If the meeting went badly, William wouldn't be alone the following day. She knew Will would be furious with her, but she also knew it was a risk she had to take. The more she talked to Sara, the more she realized that a terrible wrong had been committed, but it might only take an afternoon to correct. If not, two very dear elderly people were going to have their hearts ripped from their chests yet again, all because of her nosiness. The notion sickened her.

Adrienne picked Sara up at nine o'clock. The older woman was dressed in a floral print blouse and khaki skirt. Sara was pretty and didn't look her seventy-eight years. Her straight hair was cut in a flattering style that fell just below her collar. One swoop in the front gave it a youthful yet sophisticated edge. As Adrienne opened the passenger door and saw the beaming face, all hesitation about this meeting dissolved.

"Are you nervous?" She adjusted the air so it wouldn't blast her in the face.

Sara wore soft pink lipstick and had enhanced her eyes with a charcoal liner. She smoothed her skirt. "Not yet." She sounded more like a teenager going on her first date than an old woman. "But I'm sure I will be by the time we get there."

Adrienne patted Sara's lap and put the car into drive. "You look beautiful. I thought you didn't like to wear dresses. It's all I've seen you in."

"Goodness, when I was a kid, my mom couldn't get me in a dress. But I grew to love them as I got older."

Three hours and a side trip to Starbucks later, they were sitting in front of William's house. Sara flopped the mirror down again, studying her reflection. "We should have let him know we were coming."

Adrienne gave her a long look. "I couldn't tell him, Sara. What if you backed out? He'd have been crushed."

Tension filled the car, pressing so hard Adrienne thought the windows might burst. She attempted to calm Sara's sudden onset of fear but couldn't. Honestly, she was as nervous as Sara. Neither of them knew what kind of reception they would receive. "He knows I might be stopping by today."

Sara studied her with pale gray eyes. "No, we should have told him *I* was coming. This is a mistake."

A movement in front of the car caught both their attention. They realized with horror that William was opening the front door.

"Oh!" Sara scrambled, curling her fingers together over her chest. "I'm not ready."

Adrienne put a calming hand on her arm.

Sara turned to her, eyes wild with panic. "I can't do this."

Adrienne took her hand and squeezed. "It's okay." She shot a quick glance back to the house where William stood, one hand to his forehead and squinting in the sun at Adrienne's car.

Sara's breath came in short spurts.

"Calm down. I can go talk to him first." Adrienne tried to judge whether this was what a heart attack looked like. "Let him know you're out here."

Sara started nodding and didn't seem able to stop until Adrienne left the car.

William hugged Adrienne as she reached the top of the steps. She felt her muscles stiffen with anxiety, and he pulled his head back and frowned. "What's wrong, honey?"

"I need to talk to you about something, William." She shook her head. "And I'm not sure how you're going to take it."

He dropped his arms from her. "Okay, come inside."

"Actually, there's someone with me."

Pops's gaze went back to her car, but the glare made Sara impossible to see. He squeezed Adrienne's hand. "Whoever it is, you two wait here on the porch, and I'll go shut off the teapot."

After he disappeared into the house, Adrienne motioned for Sara, who left the car and walked toward the steps like a death row inmate, arms tight to her sides, hands fisted in the material of her garment.

"It's going to be okay," Adrienne whispered.

Sara moved as far from the front door as possible, choosing a seat in the corner, where the porch banister gave her something to grip. It looked like a good knock against her would shatter her entire body like cracked glass.

William stepped outside. Adrienne rushed to stand beside him as his eyes roamed to the far end of the porch. A frown deepened as he looked from Adrienne to the older woman on the porch swing.

"Grace," he whispered.

Fire shot through Adrienne. Oh, no. She took his arm forcefully. "William, it's Sara."

A hand came up, half-covering his mouth. Confused eyes found Adrienne, then returned to the woman waiting in the corner. Slowly, she stood. When she did, he stumbled one step back. Adrienne could feel the years and memories flood him.

"It's Sara. She's come to see you. William, she has something she needs to tell you."

Adrienne sent a coaxing look to Sara, but she shrank away. A stray cat skittered behind the older woman, who looked more like a marble statue than a human being. The color had left her cheeks, and her skirt was wrinkled at the hips from her fingers clinging desperately to the cotton. But something, some unnamable strength gathered in Sara's soft eyes. Her chin tipped back, and her hands flattened.

"I . . . I wanted to say," Sara's voice cracked on each word. "William, I never told you, but I was in love with you. I think Gracie knew it and stepped aside. I think she went to that other boy because—because of me."

What? That's not what Sara was supposed to be saying. "William, what Sara is trying to say, is—"

Sara took a step toward him. "It's my fault. It's all my fault. The fact she left, the fact she died. And not only that."

Adrienne's hopes of a tender, beautiful reunion of two people who once cared for one another crumbled around her feet.

Sara—who had certainly found the words she had misplaced in the car—forged on, as if the confession were cleansing her soul with each new admission. Her head shook. "Not only that. I *knew* you were coming home, and I made Momma agree to leave before you got there. I was ashamed. So ashamed, and I couldn't face you."

Pops's look was unreadable. One hand moved to brush across his forehead. Watery eyes blinked as if trying to sort the pieces of her confession. A confusion-filled silence stretched to the point of torture. "You were in love with me? But you *left* when you knew I was coming home?"

White hair framed a face so covered with shame and regret, Adrienne wanted to go to her, but she dared not. Pops didn't seem stable. He'd swayed more than once since she'd grabbed his arm.

He clambered to hold the doorframe. "It was all a lie, your momma making you leave town?"

Sara nodded.

Slowly, William's shoulder shifted and he pulled from Adrienne's grip. His gaze skated across the yard for a long few moments, then came to rest on Sara, then Adrienne, before he focused on the porch floor. Time ticked by, with no words or actions to fill the void, until it seemed the very air would explode under the pressure. Sara and Adrienne remained frozen. William pressed his lips together, blinked, and started to turn. His hand pivoted on the doorway as he silently moved into the house, leaving a deathly hollow emptiness where he'd been.

Chapter 13

*T*he day turned breezeless. No sounds except for that of a lone seagull in the distance. Sara dropped into the seat at the end of the porch, haloed by flowers and greenery, her eyes wide and filling with unshed tears.

Adrienne's heart shattered, and she moved to the spot where a bloodless oval face stared through the planks of the floor.

"I've hurt him again," Sara whispered through trembling lips.

Adrienne gripped Sara's hands as much to console the woman as herself. "I thought it would go better." Her apology was such a pitiful token, a worthless token. She'd watched the two of them crack and break, the past too painful a place to trudge through.

Sara, eyes swimming, said, "I want to go home now."

Adrienne's heart cracked a little more. For a split second she envisioned Sara sitting in her living room, staring into nothingness. The woman had been happy, content before Adrienne showed up. She took Sara by the arm and lifted her, trying to give strength.

But a shuffle at the front door drew her attention.

There Pops stood, staring at the two women on his porch. First his eyes rested on Adrienne, then shifted to Sara, the woman who had loved him.

Sara's face crumpled under the pressure of decades of unspoken words. All the years of shame washed over her in wave upon wave of buried secrets and forbidden love. She took a step toward William but stopped.

"Sara?" he whispered.

She swallowed and shot a quick glance to Adrienne.

Unable to give her any indication of William's reaction, Adrienne shrugged apologetically.

William ran a hand over his face, brow furrowed. "Why didn't you tell me?" he demanded.

Sara's eyes were rimmed with red, her head hung low. "I . . . "

He took a shaky step toward her. "It changes everything." He began to move to the far end of the porch where she stood, but stopped and sucked in a deep breath. "I could have been there for you. When Gracie died, I could have helped you through it."

Shock registered on Sara's face. Bit by painstaking bit, her body released its tension. "You . . . you're not mad?"

Pops ran his hand over his thighs. "Furious. Mad to the core of my being, but what of it? I'm old, Sara. I don't have time to waste. You're here. On my porch. And you're trying to right the wrong."

A tiny smile appeared on Sara's mouth.

William put a trembling hand to his lips. "Sweet Sara." He reached his arms out wide and shuffled toward her.

Adrienne pressed her mouth together in an attempt to fight back the tears as the two met in the center of the porch. William lifted his hands to Sara's upper arms as if he were soaking her in, remembering her as the younger woman he'd known so many years ago. He pulled her close into the circle of his arms, and she rested her head against his chest and cried.

He hugged her, touching her shoulders, then cupping her face in his hands as if he couldn't believe she was there. With weathered thumbs, he wiped the tears that ran down her cheeks.

"I'm so sorry," Sara whispered, white hair dusting her shoulders. Some loose strands lay across her face, but she didn't bother to sweep them back. "I'm so sorry, William."

He shook his head and had to tilt her chin up so that she would look him eye to eye. "No, Sara, *I'm* sorry for not trying to find you after I came home."

They held each other, crying, laughing, and crying again. And Adrienne cried too. Standing there on the porch, she stopped fighting the tears. For several moments they stayed there, the two old bodies pressed together, swaying gently from side to side as a lifetime of deceit dissolved like salt in hot water.

Wiping her eyes, she noticed the black Mercedes in the driveway. Adrienne's heart stopped beating, blood turned to ice in her veins. She recognized the car. But her mind was reeling. He shouldn't be home this early. And it looked like he'd been sitting there a while.

William took Sara by the hand. "Come on inside. We have a lot to talk about." Completely unaware of his grandson's early return, and equally oblivious to Adrienne, William led Sara into the house, lightly cradling her arm with the caution one might use to hold a butterfly.

Eyes focused on the black Mercedes looming in the driveway, terror spiked through Adrienne. But equally startling and quick on its heels, something protective erupted within her. If Will wanted to be furious at her for interfering, that was fine. But there was no way in the world she was going to let him spoil this reunion. She squared her shoulders and descended the steps, ready for the fight. Fight was something that didn't come naturally to her, so the sudden rush of adrenalin caused her hands to fist. She wasn't a fighter. She was a conformer. In each and every situation she *conformed* to what everyone else needed or wanted.

Well, not this time. Her teeth were pressed so tightly together, her jaw ached.

The sun beat down on her as she walked across the lawn to his window. When she reached him, he was sitting in the car, staring straight ahead, hands gripping the steering wheel so hard that his knuckles were white. Finally, he shot her a look.

"Get in," he said.

For a moment she could only stare at him.

"Get in," he said again.

Confusion flickered through her, and she threw a look at the house, the sight of Pops and Sara and their tender embrace still fresh in her mind.

His words drew her back. "Don't you think they need some time alone?"

She didn't really know what to do. People had been murdered and ditched for less. And this whole new *fight* thing left her uncertain.

His eyes softened. "Adrienne, come on. You're safe with me."

Her thoughts drifted back to the fishing trip, his strong hands helping her onto the boat. How tenderly he slid the pole into her grasp and gave gentle tugs on the line to teach her what a bite felt like. She'd been scared when the engine rumbled to life, and he had eased her fears by moving her to the seat beside him. She was too much of a chicken to remove the fish from her hook, so he'd held the slimy thing with his own hands and wrapped her hand in a towel so she could remove the hook without having to feel the fish wiggling against her. She'd been safe then.

And she was safe now. Before making a conscious decision, she moved to the passenger side of the car and slipped in beside him. Cool air hit her as she pulled her seatbelt on. When he put the car in reverse, she said, "Should I let them know we're leaving?"

He shook his head, resting an arm on the back of her seat as he backed out of the driveway. "Honestly, it'll probably be hours before they realize you're gone." An edge of accusation in his words bit into her.

She fell silent, the hum of the engine accompanying them as Will drove toward the edge of town. The midday sun was an orange bulb above, cut only occasionally by thin ribbons of cotton clouds against the blue sky. Will's vehicle smelled like him. It was a calming scent of leather and man. Right now, she was too nervous to enjoy it.

When they turned onto a gravel road, Adrienne chanced a curious glance at him. She swallowed as they passed the small sign that sent a chill down her back. Loose pebbles and shells crunched beneath the tires as they moved slowly through the woods.

The cemetery opened up before them, covering acres of gently rolling green meadow. He stopped the car and lowered the windows. The smell of fresh earth, heating in the summer sun, drifted inside—a stark reminder they were at a cemetery. Adrienne noticed the section to the left, obviously the oldest part of the graveyard. Though kept in good repair, the century-old headstones leaned with the weight of years, some sinking into the soft ground.

"So you want to fill me in on what happened back there?"

She swallowed. "Will I find myself in a shallow grave if I do?"

A buzzing sound drew her attention, and a bug shot into the window. Adrienne jumped, arms flailing. Will grabbed her hands, trapping them on her lap. "No, no, no. It's just a honeybee."

She stopped, but failed to see how that information should make her feel better. Bees had stingers.

The oval-shaped bug fluttered to a stop on the passenger visor.

Will chuckled. "A honeybee." He shook his head and drew a deep breath.

Uncertain about . . . well, everything right now, Adrienne told him about Sara and William and the whole sordid story. "By the end, Pops was really happy she came." Adrienne added that for good measure.

Silence followed. Flowers dotted the landscape and were bunched at the heads of several graves. Over the hillside, Adrienne could see for what seemed like miles.

She searched Will's profile for an explanation as to why the cemetery.

"I haven't been back here since my grandma died. I should be ashamed of that, but I never really understood why people visit graves." His hands rested on the steering wheel until he reached to shut the engine off. "A grave represents death. Wouldn't you want to remember somebody's life?"

Adrienne opted to remain quiet, unsure whether he sought an answer or not. And unsure about how he felt about this whole thing. He was so unreadable sometimes.

He studied her for a moment, then fixed his gaze on a point in front of them. The engine clicked as the dust the car stirred up settled around them.

Will pointed to a hill beyond the cemetery. "See that?"

It was a gray house encircled by a white picket fence. From where they sat, they could see a family sitting in the yard. A small child played in a sandbox.

"That's Pops's house." He stared for a few moments, as memories from his childhood seemed to flood him. "It took me three months to talk him into moving in with me. But I couldn't bear to think of him spending every evening sitting on his back porch alone, staring at Grandma's grave."

If Adrienne could possibly feel any worse about what she'd inadvertently put this man through, she did.

He angled to look at her. "I didn't bring you here to show you a cemetery, Adrienne. In fact, when I turned onto the road leading here, I wasn't sure why. But . . . you gave my grandfather a gift today. In one afternoon, you gave Pops something I've been trying to give him for five years."

When she searched his eyes, Will said simply, "Hope." He reached over and lightly touched her cheek.

The warmth of his hand eased her anxiety.

"Thank you." She'd taken a horrible risk. It could have gone either way. Adrienne exhaled the breath she'd been holding. "I know this can't be easy for you. I can't even imagine how hard it's been to watch Pops grieve for his wife."

Will nodded. "I just don't want to see him hurt anymore. Come with me."

They stepped out of the vehicle. It was a quiet afternoon at Wainwright Cemetery. He paused at the front of the car and leaned against the warm hood, so Adrienne did too. She looked out over the hundred or so tombstones that stood like miniature pillars of the lives each represented. It was eerily peaceful.

Will broke the silence. "Pops is so strong. He's the strongest man I've ever known."

She looked over at him, his crisp white dress shirt now unbuttoned at the neck, where a tie had undoubtedly been. He looked so good, and he was opening up to her, and that felt *so* right. And here they were, sharing intimate things and feelings, and that felt new and perfect. She wanted to bury her head in the hollow of his throat, as much for herself as for him. Before she realized it, she was leaning toward him. She quickly caught herself.

Oh. Oh dear. She chanced a look up to his face. He remained unfazed, staring out over the horizon. She took his preoccupation as an invitation to study the contour of his jaw, the way his throat curved, the capable shoulders. He began rolling up his sleeves, and she watched his arms where lean muscles flexed under tan skin. She was instantly reminded of how he'd looked wiping down the boat when drops of sweat gathered on his shoulders and chest. He had athletic muscles, now hidden under a dress shirt, but she'd seen them up close, so she let her mind play with the memory.

But the moment stretched and Adrienne had to wonder how she could be so caught up in him when he was all caught up in staring out over the cemetery. *He* didn't even know she was still there. Didn't know what he was doing to her. *I'm invisible.* The thought irritated her. "Thank you for not being angry with me."

He leaned back, resting his palms on the hood of the car. Upper body outstretched, he moved his arm so it crisscrossed her back so closely they were nearly touching. It brought his face near hers. "You're welcome," he whispered, eyes locking on her mouth. And suddenly, he *was* all there, in her space and completely focused on her as if there were nothing in the world but the two of them.

Invisible was better.

His hot breath feathered against her throat. She needed to say something. Maybe something sexy. "I don't think it's bad that you haven't been back here." *Oh, that was brilliant. The kind of words men can't resist.*

He slowly turned his eyes away from her to focus on the cemetery again.

"No?" he said. "My dad thinks it is. Of course, it's just like him to be more concerned with the dead than the living."

Adrienne frowned. She'd never heard Will speak of his father. For that matter, she had never heard Pops speak of his son. "Where is your dad?"

"My parents work for the Peace Corps. They're in a place called Senegal in West Africa. They live there." The last words were clipped, and though Adrienne was curious, now was not the time to press. The muscle in Will's jaw flexed. He might be trying to sound flippant, but there was a distinct sadness in his tone.

A breeze moved from the hills, causing her hair to float into her eyes. Adrienne brushed at it. "Like I said, I don't think it's bad that you haven't come here. The grieving process is different for everyone. The very thing that might bring peace to one person might bring despair to another. Besides, you're here now."

He nodded and looked at her. Will took his time searching her features, his gaze drifting down to her lips again.

The intensity of the moment was almost more than she could bear. She pressed her lips together, suddenly feeling self-conscious. It was like he was inspecting her. He seemed to have a preoccupation with her lips. That in itself made this whole exchange much more unnerving. He wasn't stealing glances or being coy. He was unabashedly scrutinizing every inch of her face. There was a raw honesty to it that made her want to run. But even more, it made her want to stay right there.

And in that second, she made a choice. He was leaving the ball in her court.

Adrienne leaned closer.

Will's eyes darkened. The muscles of his face tightened, but not in a bad way—in a sort of excited anticipation. He reached a hand to her cheek and brushed his thumb over her mouth, watching it slide against the skin. He swallowed, moistened his lips, and leaned in, stopping just an inch or so short of kissing her. This wasn't him *stopping* her. No, this wasn't stopping, this was him *taunting* her. But she held firm even though the intensity of his eyes beckoned. She didn't move except to lick lips that had grown dry from the short little breaths she'd taken. That did it.

He closed the distance, mouth meeting and quickly taking hers. She melted into him. There was no gentle exploration. No soft kisses. He simply surged forward, his body moving, shifting so that he held her fully against him. He did this like he did everything. With purpose. With fervency. With passion.

Her eyes closed, her body consumed by such a simple thing as a first kiss. His chest rose against hers, and as she tilted her head, his arms closed around her more fully than before. Adrienne felt dizzy. She needed to breathe, but it was impossible. His hands found their way to her face and he cupped her cheeks, then pushed his face away to gaze at her. Suddenly his lips were gone from hers.

Adrienne sucked a deep breath, devouring the air around her. When her eyes fluttered open, there he was. Emerald eyes certain, unapologetic, and . . . happy. His hands were cool on her face, thumbs making tiny little circles as she tried to catch up to what had just happened. She was no fifteen-year-old. This was not her *first* first kiss. After all, she was a *divorcée*. What had he just done to her, and did he *know* what he'd done?

His eyes twinkled, and his mouth twitched on one side. Oh, yeah. He knew.

He came at her again, this time slowly, and dropped a peck on her mouth. He knew *exactly*. Then his face was gone from her direct vision. His hands were gone from her cheeks. He remained seated beside her, but the moment was all but a memory. And she was left alone with her racing heart.

"Where's her grave?" Adrienne asked when she finally felt words were possible.

He leaned forward, dragging his arm from behind her and pointed off to the right. "Over there, under that tree." It was a beautiful section of the cemetery, dappled with shade trees and calmingly inviting.

She turned to look at him. "Would you like to go visit it? I'll go with you." She took his hand in hers and added sweetly, "You're safe with me."

Will nodded a knowing smile at the words he'd spoken to her on more than one occasion. Though she might have been scared, she'd trusted him. Now he would do the same for her. And he'd deal with the kiss later. What it meant. Why he'd been unable to stop himself. This was definitely a gray area, and he wasn't accustomed to gray. That was more his dad's territory; his dad saw shades of gray where Will saw black and white. For instance, his dad thought it was okay for them to cancel out on Pops's birthday—to him that landed somewhere in the gray area. For Will, you were either committed to the man who raised you or you were not. Missing the birthday of someone Pops's age was unforgivable. Black and white. Period.

But with Adrienne, everything was different. He was having to find the gray space around the absolutes. She was delicate, still hurting from a bad divorce, and he couldn't just grab and take what he wanted. No matter how *badly* he wanted it.

They walked away from the car, hand in hand, heading toward the big oak tree. The sun was hot on his back, but he barely noticed. It paled by comparison to the warmth that was seeping into his soul.

Chapter 14

*P*ops and Sara were both beaming when Will and Adrienne stepped past them into the kitchen. The older couple chatted at the table, talking faster than used car salesmen, their faces alight with the excitement of remembrance.

"We picked up dinner," Will announced. Cold salad from Leo's Diner. He needed cold after the heat from the sunny walk with Adrienne at the graveyard.

Kissed at the cemetery. A really romantic way to treat the lady in your life. The lady in his life. He toyed with that for a few moments. He'd used other words to describe her. First it was *meddling do-gooder*, then *intriguing woman with the sad eyes and banging body*, then *interrupter of his dreams*. Yes, he could see her as the lady in his life and like *everything* that mattered in his life, he needed more.

"Tuna salad for you, Pops?"

But Pops didn't answer. He was engaged in a conversation with Sara, still holding her hand.

Will winked at Adrienne. "That's great, Will," he said, mimicking his grandfather's voice. "I'd help with dinner, but my hands are full."

Adrienne hit him with an empty paper bag. "Stop that," she hissed.

Will pointed to the couple behind him, eyes wide. "What? They didn't hear a word."

She pointed an accusing finger at him but failed to hide her smile. "Still, it's not very nice."

He liked being scolded by her. With a free hand, she reached into the bag. He caught her fingers for a brief moment and squeezed. A sexy gaze drifted slowly to his eyes. Expecting to throw her off, he'd failed. She'd thrown him with that flirty dark look, though. This woman could level him with her eyes. Slam him flat on his back. On his back with Adrienne and her sultry smile lingering above him? Yeah, he could get into that.

"Be nice," she mouthed, and he wondered if she'd read his thoughts, until she tipped her head toward Pops and Sara. Oh, them.

"They didn't hear me." He raised his voice. "They don't even know we're here. Do you, Pops?"

Finally, two gray heads turned, faces questioning. "I'm sorry, Will. Were you saying something?"

Will and Adrienne laughed.

The older couple shrugged and continued their conversation about the good ol' days and how they missed things like pouring peanuts in Pepsi.

The moon sifted through the kitchen window, complementing the soft glow from the living room and washing the space in gentle luminous shades. Pops and Sara both looked so happy. Will understood. He was pretty happy himself. His plan to surprise Pops with a trip to the Keys was gloriously wrecked. Wrecked by the sultry brunette who had invaded his life.

He thought back to earlier in the day when they'd leaned on the hood of his car, her body so close to his. He'd stretched out to rest his hands on the hood, but it was only a ploy to get closer to her. He'd wanted to kiss her. Had to kiss her. But she was the one who had finalized it, meeting his mouth with an equal amount of anticipation. The thought stirred him.

No, he wouldn't visit the Keys this weekend. That much was sure. Adrienne and Sara were returning in the morning. The four of them would spend the day together.

Will's dad filtered into his thoughts. At the cemetery, he'd almost told Adrienne just what he thought of his parents and their ridiculous decision to live so far away. He just couldn't understand how his parents could value people a continent away more than they valued Pops. More than they valued him. The rawness of the abandonment stung. After all, it had been years since they'd left this country. But he rarely thought of it—chose not to dwell on it—except when they did things like cancel a trip home when they knew, *had* to know, how important it was to Pops. It was selfish beyond belief. Pretty much the polar opposite of what they said they stood for. Sure, they were leading a life of sacrifice. And Pops was the one who suffered for it.

The smell of coffee and toasted bagels warmed the kitchen as morning sunshine poked through the windows. The foursome had gathered to make plans for the day. Pops wore a bright blue T-shirt that made his eyes even more alive, and Will was dressed in a beige polo that stretched across his fine chest.

"What about the zoo?" Pops asked.

Sara's face lit up. "Oh, I haven't been to the zoo in years."

Pops's eyes sparkled. "Remember the circus when it came to town?"

"Oh, dear." Sara pressed her hands over her face. She peered through her fingertips. "Go on; tell them."

Pops leaned back in the kitchen chair. "Sara snuck over to the circus grounds late at night and befriended a caged monkey."

"Poor thing." She faced Adrienne. "He looked skinny. I started slipping bananas and mangos into the cage."

Pops laughed. "And two days later, when the circus started and the monkey was supposed to be performing, he spotted Sara in the crowd, broke free, and went straight to her. It took three men to pull that monkey off Sara's lap."

Sara shrugged. "The audience loved it."

"Her momma received a letter stating Sara wasn't welcome to return to the Caldwell and Cannon Circus *ever* again."

They all laughed.

"It's supposed to be cooler today," Will said.

His glittery eyes were becoming easier and easier for Adrienne to read. Will was judging the older couple's ability to walk the many acres encompassing the Naples Zoo. He questioned Adrienne with a look.

Picking up on his concern, she turned to Sara. "It wouldn't be too much for you?"

Sara shook her head, looking decades younger than her almost eighty years. She clapped her hands together. "It would be wonderful."

"What about you, Pops?" Will sat hot coffee in front of him.

"Sounds good to me."

Adrienne nodded in agreement. A dot of cream cheese decorated her fingertip, so she popped the finger into her mouth. "Sounds fun, I haven't been there yet." The zoo was on the top of her list of places to visit. Known around the country as a top destination for seeing a variety of zoo animals and plant life, the draw had been great. But sadly, not as forceful as leaky pipes, rotting banisters, and peeling paint.

She smiled over at Will who had stopped all motion. His eyes were locked on her finger, still hovering near her mouth, the swirl of cream cheese gone. *Oops.* She bit back a smile, but this only made him look . . . hungrier.

They drove to the zoo, with happy chatter filling the car. Even the parking lot was partially shaded by the giant tropical plants that fenced the perimeter. A souvenir store housed the ticket counter where Will paid the admission. Pops and Sara hovered over a bin filled with soft stuffed animals. Adrienne watched as Pops held a fluffy bear to Sara's cheek. She hugged it, then held it out for him. Glancing left, then right, Pops gave the thing a quick hug and dropped it back into the bin. Sara giggled with delight.

They stepped through the entrance, and Sara stopped, with a hand over her heart. The traffic backed up behind her. "Gracious. I feel like I'm in a *Jurassic Park* movie."

Adrienne touched the older woman's shoulder and tilted back. "Well, hopefully, there aren't any dinosaurs to chase us."

Pops stepped closer to them. "No worries, ladies. We will protect you."

The pathway twisted and twined while the towering plants curved over their heads in long, graceful, jungle-green arcs. "It looks like a rain forest," Adrienne said, remembering the one she'd visited in Belize. She shielded her eyes to gaze up, up, up to the tops of the massive trees.

Pops unfolded a map and studied it. "Which way first? There's a lot to see."

"Lead the way, Pops," Will said when the others shrugged. "You've got the map."

Sara pointed to a sign. "I don't want to miss the monkeys. They're my favorite."

Pops took her by the arm. "If sweet Sara wants monkeys, then she shall have monkeys. But no feeding them, okay?"

Copying his grandfather, Will offered his arm to Adrienne, so she slid her arm through his and enjoyed the warmth and scent of the man beside her. There was something special about the Bryant men, she realized. Though there were many differences, there were striking similarities. Intensity, for one. Pops was all about Sara. Yesterday in the cemetery, Will had been all about Adrienne, kissing her, soaking her in. That's what it had felt like to her, like she was a warm bath that he'd just lowered himself into, invading, but also savoring. To her delight, Adrienne discovered she *liked* to be savored.

For most of the day, Will and Adrienne walked together, a few yards behind Pops and Sara, giving the older couple plenty of room to get reacquainted.

Forever the gentleman, Pops gave detailed attention to Sara, holding her hand or cradling her arm as they strolled along. Even stepping ahead to kick a discarded cup out her path. It was sweet, intimate, the stuff of movies. And the apple didn't fall far from the tree. The way Will showered attention on Adrienne was something he'd obviously learned to do from William, the patriarch of the Bryant clan.

Will leaned on a fence, half-watching the lions, half watching Adrienne. One of the lions stretched, his powerful legs and shoulders growing tight beneath the yellow fur.

In two months it would be Pops's birthday. He wanted to involve Adrienne in the plans he was making, but reluctance stopped him because she was as skittish as a wildcat, and he couldn't bear for Pops to have any more rejection. Would Adrienne still be hanging around in two months? He hoped. But who knew?

"I think they're amazing." Adrienne's fingers twined in the chain-link fence. "Did you know the females do the hunting?" She tipped her head to look at him, dark hair spilling over her shoulders and onto the spaghetti-strap tank top she wore.

"The females usually tend to have sharper claws." He glanced down at her hands. "That's true of most species."

She gave him an evil look.

Why did he love to torment her so? He hadn't done silly things like this since he was a kid. In fact, he couldn't remember being this silly when he *was* a kid. *Poor Will, always so serious. Lighten up, kiddo*, his dad would say.

"There's a lion pride in Africa that can take down an elephant," Will said after they listened to a zookeeper rattle off lion facts. When the keeper produced several pieces of meat on the end of a long stick, Adrienne leaned away from the fence.

"They kill it?"

"Mm-hmm. It's the only pride known to man that can kill a full-grown elephant." He turned slightly to lean on the fence. "I heard about it when I was in Africa."

"Did you go there to see your parents in Senegal?" She pivoted too, half-facing him, half-facing the enclosure. When one of the lions stood, she leaned back again, even though there was a double fence separating her from the cats.

He closed a protective arm around her waist. "They were in Tanzania back then. I visited one summer during college. We went on a safari."

He watched as the idea played across her face. "*This* close to *those* animals with *no* fence. Sounds exciting, but yikes."

"I loved it."

"I bet it was hard to come home."

He shook his head. "I was ready by the end of summer." He didn't want to venture into this conversation but needed to if he was going to ask for her help—which is what he'd decided to do somewhere around the time he'd slid his arm around her trim waist. "I figured they would move back home after Grandma died, but nope." He couldn't help the contempt in his voice.

"You don't approve of them being there?" Adrienne's fingertip ran along a jagged edge of the chain-link fence.

"I know it's important work, don't get me wrong."

She moved that fingertip to his jaw and ran it from his earlobe to his chin. "Sounds like you've practiced saying that."

He shrugged, or it might have been a shudder from the whisper-soft pad of her finger on his jaw. He wondered if her fingertip tasted like ice cream. "Well, just because I know it, doesn't mean I believe it in my heart. Even though I know I should."

"How long have they been there?"

"In Africa? Since my first year at college. They've served in several countries there. About eleven, twelve years now."

"That's a long time." She took a thoughtful moment. "It's got to be very rewarding."

"I guess," he mumbled. "They were supposed to be home in a couple months. Now they say they can't. It's Pops's birthday . . . "

"Oh," Adrienne said, looking across the walkway where Pops and Sara sat on a park bench. "He must be crushed."

Will's eyes followed hers to the man who was, in all ways, his hero. Pops had one arm draped around Sara's delicate shoulders. With the other hand he pointed to Sara's beloved monkeys on the island adjacent to the lions. Will watched the couple laugh in delight as one of the gray and brown monkeys did a backward somersault from a tree branch. "Well, he's too good of a man to let them know how upset he is."

Adrienne's mouth tipped into a bow-shaped frown. He wanted to kiss the frown away, taste those pouty lips. Instead, he concentrated on the anger he felt toward his father for not making more of an effort to get home. "Anyway, I want to have a party for Pops, and I was wondering if you would help me plan it."

She gazed up at him, eyes sparkling. The bow became a smile, a heart-melting, mind-blowing, world-rocking smile. "I would love to. Can we tell Sara?"

"Sure, but I want it to be a surprise. Pops has never had a surprise party before."

She tilted her head. "He must be so proud of you." Adrienne placed her hand on his shoulder, letting her fingertips rest against his collarbone. She stretched up on her tiptoes and planted a kiss on his cheek. "I would love to help."

Adrienne worked like a maniac to finish the baseboards in the upstairs hall. She still needed to sand and paint the ones downstairs, but the long corridor, with no furniture to buffer its emptiness, made these much more noticeable. She'd worked up a good sweat when the doorbell rang.

"I'm coming," she hollered from the top of the steps. She'd invited Sammie over to see the lavender room and, well, to apologize for being a friend MIA.

Adrienne flung the door open and hugged her friend. "I'm so glad you came over. I thought you might be angry with me."

Sammie frowned. "Why?"

"Well, I haven't called you very often lately."

Sammie waved a hand in front of her face and passed Adrienne on the way to the kitchen table. "Oh, please. I'm not one of those needy friends who get their feelings bruised if you don't call and let me know you need to go to the bathroom."

"Thanks." Adrienne giggled and followed with, "I think."

"I stopped by Saturday."

"I was gone."

"With Will, no doubt?"

Adrienne nodded.

"He's becoming quite a habit."

"I know," Adrienne said. "I'm sorry . . . "

"Stop that. Stop apologizing for having a life." Sammie tilted her chin up. "That's all you're doing. So please don't apologize for being human."

Adrienne pressed her lips together.

Sammie's hands went to her hips, cinching the waist of the brown and green dress she wore. "I'm surprised you think me so shallow."

"I don't." Adrienne's face dropped. "It's just that I haven't really had a close friend since college. When I tried to make connections in Chicago, it made Eric crazy. Sammie, I know we've only known each other for the few months I've been here, but . . . I think you're the best friend I've ever had. Am I pathetic?"

Sammie grinned. "No, Chicago. You were in an abusive relationship where your world had to orbit around Eric. *He's* pathetic. You? You're magnificent."

Adrienne hugged her again, catching Sammie off guard.

An uncomfortable moment stretched out between them. "But I have to admit, it doesn't say much for your taste in friends."

Adrienne laughed.

Sammie, usually tough edged, slid an arm around Adrienne's shoulder. "You've been a great friend too," she admitted, jostling her a little. "Now, tell me all about Mr. Wonderful. We can look at the lavender room when we're done."

The two women sat at the kitchen table, which was cluttered with paint samples. Adrienne's next project was the master bedroom. "I don't know what to say about him." Her finger traced an edge of a robin's egg blue paint chip. "It's all been something of a whirlwind."

"But you care for him?"

Adrienne looked at Sammie. "I do."

"But . . ."

"At first, he was really suspicious of me. Somewhere along the way, I think that dissolved." She held the paint chip out for Sammie to inspect; Sammie made a horrified face and tossed it into the trash can nearby.

"You think the suspicion dissolved?"

"He never wants to talk about the past." She held up another, a soft butter cream. Sammie made a *meh* face.

"So he doesn't like to talk about the past. Prison record?" Sammie teased.

Adrienne rolled her eyes. "No, nothing like that."

Sammie shrugged. "For some people, it's just easier to concentrate on the future. If they have issues, dwelling on the past retards their growth." Sammie plucked a forest-green paint chip from the group and held it up. "This one."

Adrienne took it, considering her bedroom in deep green. She preferred the shade of Will's eyes. "He has *major* issues with his parents."

"Honestly, Chicago, don't you think most people do?" Sammie shrugged. "So, basically, you have a grown man who has issues with his parents and won't deal with the past? This doesn't really seem like cause for alarm."

But Adrienne was somewhere else. Her mind was on her five-year marriage to a self-absorbed womanizer. She couldn't fathom how it had taken her so long to see it. "Eric never spoke of the past. If it was painful, he just stuffed it away deep in his heart. The problem with that is, the heart still hurts. And that pain would come out. *Lash out* at whoever was in the way."

Sammie studied her. "Do you think Will is like Eric?"

"I don't know, but one thing I do know is that I will never be in a volatile relationship like that again. Never." She laughed without humor. "You know, whenever I didn't do exactly what he wanted, he would say, 'Can't you see how much trouble you're causing?'"

Sammie sat quietly, letting Adrienne vent her frustration.

Adrienne placed a hand to her heart. "How much trouble *I'm* causing." She shook her head, eyes sad. "That's what he said to me when I told him I wanted a divorce. Not 'I love you. I made a mistake. I'm sorry, you're the one I want . . .' No 'Can't you see how much trouble you're causing?'"

"I'm sorry, honey," Sammie said. "From what you've told me, that doesn't really sound like Will."

Adrienne met her gaze. "I think it's a little too early to tell."

"So how are you going to find out?"

"Time, I guess."

Sammie smiled. "He's worth the investment?"

"I'm counting on it."

Sammie reached over and squeezed her hand. "I think maybe he is. And by the way, when do I get to meet Mr. Hopefully Wonderful?"

Adrienne grinned. "I'm working on that."

Was he Mr. Hopefully Wonderful? Adrienne wasn't sure yet. But she had hopes.

Hope. One more thing William's letters had taught her was about never ever giving up hope. So when Sammie left, Adrienne scrounged through the copied letters and found her new favorite.

January 1945

Dear Gracie,

Sometimes I fear I will forget your beautiful face or the sound of your voice. It seems so long since I've held you in my arms, so long since I've heard the sound of your words. At night, I close my eyes tight. I remember and relive every moment we've shared. Though my mind fails me, I have hope. It is the one force that I can depend on, the thing that doesn't let me down.

How many ways can we count hope? It is every breath we breathe and every beat of our hearts. Hope is the flower that refuses to die off though winter's chill lays claim. Hope is the rushing river, moving the earth and watering the banks. It is more than strength; it fills any vessel and it strengthens any fight. I won't fall to despair, Grace. Hope keeps my feet moving. And though doubt tries to fill my mind, hope has taken me captive. I am its slave. And because I am, my soul is under obligation—hope blooms in me. I hope it is still blooming in you.

I love you,
William

Will drove to Sammie's coffee shop, with the Florida wind surging through his car windows and rustling his hair. Until Adrienne, he'd always used the air conditioning in the car to stay cool, but after watching her soaking up the coast's salty breeze, he had a new appreciation for it. The scent of orange groves drifted from the distance, and he knew the wind must be blowing in just the right direction to carry the citrus smell. It made his mouth water. Watching Adrienne sashay into the coffee shop while he parked his car made his mouth water more.

She introduced him to Sammie, and after a few minutes of friendly conversation, Sammie shooed them to a table nestled in the corner, where he could get her alone.

"What about a luau?" Adrienne suggested, flipping through a party magazine.

Will took a bite of turkey on wheat and considered the idea. "Yeah, Pops would love that. How do we do it?"

"Uh," Adrienne's eyes darted around the room. "We'll need decorations, music, food. Oh, I went to a luau once and they used an old canoe as a buffet."

He stared at her. "Wait, did you say a canoe as a buffet?"

A yellow pencil twirled around her finger. "You know. Fill the bottom with ice and set the trays of food on top. It looked really good." Her eyes rolled. "If we can get a canoe."

"I've got a kayak that's no longer water worthy, would that work?"

Her palm rested against her cheek. "Maybe, I'd have to look at it."

"It's in my garage. Can you drop by later?" He liked this. The easy flow of conversation and planning and the fact that he could ask her to drop by later.

"Sure, but won't Pops think it's a little weird that we're hanging out in the garage?"

He shrugged. "Nah, I'll think of something to tell him. Besides, he's been a little preoccupied." This was all good. He decided to not worry about her skittishness. It seemed to be fading anyway. None of that at the zoo. Not even an inkling.

They both grinned. Will realized how nice it was having someone in his world, someone like her.

"He and Sara are on and off the phone all evening. After I got home last night, he called her twice."

"It's really so sweet, watching them." Adrienne toyed with her lunch. She'd ordered a chicken salad sandwich but barely ate it. No wonder she stayed so tiny. The woman didn't eat. Except cookie-dough ice cream. She'd devoured that like a gladiator.

Adrienne nibbled the croissant.

"And then she called him once." His face scanned Adrienne's. "It's so good to see him happy. I was starting to worry about him."

"What do you mean?" She took a sip of the vanilla Coke Sammie made for her.

"I don't know, but it seemed like he was spending more and more time looking at those stupid photo albums and books from the war. I'm just glad he can finally close that chapter of his life."

Adrienne tapped the edge of the table, eyes covered by caterpillar lashes. "It's not a crime to want to remember your past."

"Who *would* want to remember? It's depressing and it's gone. What good can come of bringing it up?" Of all the people in the world, she should understand. Hadn't she just experienced years of pain in a bad marriage? *Does she sit around and dwell on it all the time? Maybe that's why she still seems sad.* "People need to learn to let go," he said aloud.

The nostrils on her dainty nose flared. Anger. This was anger. He'd never seen it on her before. "Those things shape who we are now. Good things and bad."

She was even more gorgeous mad, with the gold flecks in her eyes turning to molten lava and stirring.

She leaned forward. "Are you even listening to me?"

Not really. He wasn't interested in traveling down this path, so instead of answering, he ate a potato chip.

"You're *not* listening to me." She tilted her head and ran her slender hand through all that mink-dark hair. "What we learn from our mistakes makes us better people."

"That's probably easy to say for someone who lives in the past more than the present." *Uh-oh.* He hadn't meant to say that out loud.

The flick of her brows confirmed that his words stung. She pushed her food away. "What do you mean?"

He shrugged. "You spent a week reading my grandfather's letters instead of working on your house. You apparently let everything around you go so you could stroll through someone else's history." He could see the fire, knew he'd said the wrong thing, but man, could this woman get his engine cranking.

"First of all, I didn't just quit *living* so I could sit and *read* for a week straight." She threw her hands up. "You really run hot and cold, you know that? And even if I had, so what? I can appreciate what Pops and those other men went through. That war shaped our world."

Will swallowed.

She shook her head and leaned forward, capturing him. "Do you even know anything about your grandfather's war experience?"

He opened his mouth to answer, but she forged on, anger fueling each word. "Do you know he was part of one of the most highly decorated units in the *entire* war? Did you know he spent weeks freezing in the woods at Bastogne? Did you know his company was involved in *every major battle* in Europe?" With the last sentence, she used her index finger to tap the table for emphasis. For a moment, she looked at him like she'd never really seen him before. "Do you even know your grandfather?" Or maybe like she'd seen him all along.

That was a stupid question and one she had no business asking. His anger flared to match hers. "Do *you* think *you* know him just because you read some letters?" He'd lived with Pops for nearly five years. Of course he knew him. He knew what kind of cereal he ate. What sports shows he liked to watch. He'd practically grown up at Pops's house, spending every summer there. Pops had attended every one of Will's baseball games. Junior high, high school, he was always there, on the top row, on his feet cheering Will on. When Will was small, every night at bedtime Pops had told him amazing stories about . . .

Blood drained from Will's face. He had to look away as a sickening feeling roiled through his gut. *Pops had told him amazing stories about soldiers in a land far away.* Will searched his memory, mouth going dry. And Will loved them, loved every word, *hung on* every word. When had those stories ended? Did Will get too old to appreciate them? He tried desperately to remember even one detail but failed. Only faint shadows remained where there was once vivid life. It was like trying to capture sand in a screen that was being pounded by a steady rain.

For an instant, Will was reminded of the stack of books Pops had tripped on in his room. Will had moved them downstairs to the library. He remembered the deep sadness that had appeared across Pops's face. But Pops had quickly blinked it away and joked about how much easier it would be to read them in the comfortable library. Will hadn't paid attention to the titles. Frankly, he hadn't cared about the old stack of books. History books. *World War II* books. Now he realized what they were. It was a history Pops himself helped write.

He shoved the sandwich away while Adrienne sat quietly as if her little outburst had shocked her as much as it shook him. Some kids stepped into the coffee shop, laughing and joking about seeing a shark at the beach, but he didn't care. For five years he'd done everything in his power to make a good home for his grandfather.

Will drew a ragged breath and slumped against the chair. Though caring for Pops physically, he'd left Pops's emotional well-being to starve. His eyes met hers slowly. She was right. He didn't even know his grandfather.

Sure, he knew his favorite cereal, how he liked his eggs, what tennis shoes he preferred to buy, what kinds of birds he watched out his window. He knew that Pops wasn't an easy man to stop, and if he wanted to take the boat out alone—even on dewy, hazy mornings—he did it. But he knew little to nothing about the man Pops had once been.

Will rubbed a hand over his face. "It caused him so much pain, I just thought he wanted to forget it." His words slipped out quietly. Almost as an afterthought he added, "That's what I would want."

Adrienne exhaled. "Even though the past may be painful, it's okay to remember it. That's how we heal."

Will wiped his mouth, tossed the napkin on his plate, and slid back his chair. "Adrienne, would you mind if we pick this up another day. I'm . . . I gotta go. I'm sorry."

He started to step past her, but she caught his hand, her grasp firm. "Will," she whispered, "It's never too late to learn about someone we love."

She'd read him like a book.

He swallowed. "I owe him that much, don't I?"

She shook her head, sending shimmery lips into a fit of sparkles. "Don't do it for him. Do it for yourself. You're missing out."

For an instant he wanted to pull her up into his arms. But one hug, one kiss, one press of his body to hers would only light a fire he couldn't tend to right now. Instead, he rubbed his thumb over her clasped hand and lifted it to his lips. In the short time they'd known each other, she'd given him so much. Yes, sometimes her antics were risky. Some of the things she'd done could have backfired and had devastating consequences. But right now all he could feel was appreciation for her taking risks most people never would.

But a small, quiet voice in the back of his head warned that her lucky streak could eventually end.

Chapter 15

*I*t was after dinner when Will asked Pops if he had any war medals.

Pops nearly dropped the dish he was carrying to the sink. He turned to give Will his complete attention, watching the younger man a full minute before he spoke. "Yes." It was a lonely word, filled with caution.

"Do you have many?" Will urged.

Pops's shoulder tipped up in a tentative shrug. "My fair share, I suspect."

Will nodded thoughtfully. From the kitchen table, where he sat, he could see the picture window in the living room. He watched as a pair of headlights moved past the house. "Could I see them sometime?"

A smile formed on Pops's face. His eyes became alive. "Yes," he said, voice quivering slightly. "I would love for you to see them."

"I didn't think you liked to talk about the war," Will confessed. He ran a hand through his hair. "I've always tried to keep you from having to."

Pops moved to the table and sat down. "The only reason I've kept so quiet about it is because it seems to bother you so. I just always thought maybe you didn't approve of war, any kind of war, for any reason." He shook his head. "So many young people don't anymore."

A flush of guilt fanned over Will.

Pops squared his shoulders. "But I don't want to shove my past in a drawer and pretend it never happened. I'm proud of what I did. I'm proud of the country I served. I saw firsthand how far Hitler's cruelty reached." He got lost in the pain of that memory for a moment, then forged on. "Look around you. If we hadn't entered the war when we did, who knows what our world might be like now. *This* world. Every day you enjoy the freedom I fought to protect. What greater honor than for a soldier to fight for his own family?" Tender blue eyes, now misty, studied his grandson. "I made a better world for you, Will. Why should I want to forget that?"

Will nodded. "It just seems so painful to you."

"Closing up a wound that's not ready will only poison the whole body. Wounds have to heal in their own time. They have to breathe." His tone changed slightly. "Will, sometimes I think maybe you have a hard time dealing with painful things in your own life. Though hitting it head-on is never easy, you can't shove everything in a briefcase and go on like it didn't happen."

Both men knew he was talking about Will's parents. "I know." Will tried to force a smile. "Wounds have to breathe."

Pops patted his hand.

But even as Will agreed with him, he wasn't sure he could ever let this one go. His parents had ditched him. Not once, but twice. They had chosen people they didn't even know over their own family. That was unforgivable. Besides, if it was poisoning him, surely he'd know it.

Two hours later, after Pops had gone to bed, Will sat in his leather library chair, surrounded not only by the books *he* loved but by an entire world he'd never encountered. He reached across the desk and pulled the stack of letters toward him.

July 1944

Dear Gracie,

I met a hero yesterday. I didn't know he was a hero at the time, but I sit here now because of the choice he made last night. His name was Samuel. I think he was from Michigan. His company dropped near us into a hot DZ.

Most of his boys made it out, but a couple didn't. From our vantage point, we covered them. Running low to the ground, Samuel dropped into the foxhole with me and Rusty. We were celebrating because Rusty had gotten word that his baby boy had been born. We talked while we fought. Samuel was a marksman. He could pick off a German soldier with a head shot from a hundred yards, barely taking a second to aim. The enemy was dropping back, and we thought the fight was over, until we realized they had flanked us. With bullets and grenades everywhere, it took a minute to regroup and know where to shoot. That's when we saw it. The grenade dropped into the foxhole with us. My eyes met Samuel's just before he jumped. I can't explain the horror of what happened next, but I can say, I am alive. As is Rusty. And Samuel's CO is writing a letter to Samuel's wife and parents.

What kind of mighty spirit dwells within a man that he would lay down his life for those he's just met? I don't feel worthy to stand with the men I stand with. All I can do is pray I don't let them down.

I make a promise to the men who are serving beside me. I will never forget you. I will never forget what you gave. I have no way to honor these men, save this. I will tell their story to my children and my grandchildren. I will tell of their heroic deeds and because I will, a part of them will live forever. What other gift can I give?

William

Will dropped the letter slowly, conflict seeping into every fiber of his being. Hearing about this man's sacrifice, this man he owes his very life to, tore at him. But more hurtful still was the fact that his grandfather had been unable to keep a promise he'd made to himself and the men he fought with because of Will's stubborn, narrow-minded view. "I'm sorry, Pops," he mumbled for no one to hear. "It won't happen anymore."

Will stayed in the cool library, a single light illuminating the desk, and he read until he could read no more. By 3:00 a.m., his eyes were burning and puffy, no longer able to focus on the page. He'd read every letter. Some he'd read twice. He shut the light off, flooding the space with darkness, and ascended the stairs.

All this time he'd been dwelling in a house with a man he only half-knew. Negotiating the hallway slowly, he paused at the closed door of Pops's room. Beyond it, he could hear his breathing. Will placed a hand flat against the door.

Sure, Pops had always been a hero to Will, as grandfathers are to their grandchildren. But Pops was a hero to his country too. It was time for Will to show his appreciation.

Will made plans but kept it a secret. Even from Adrienne. He simply told her, Sara, and Pops it was a surprise and to dress like you would if you were going to a carnival. The trio had speculated, but they weren't even close. Will drove toward Adrienne's house, fighting a grin. If he was going to learn who Pops was, he wanted to learn up close, not just from descriptions and photographs. In the days since he'd first shown interest in Pops's military history, they had sat up many a late night, with Pops giving an account of what it was like, really like, during the war. But Will wanted more. He wanted to see the gun Pops carried, touch the clothes he'd worn. He wanted to put a parachute on his own shoulders and imagine what it might feel like to jump from an airplane into hostile territory. Of course, much of this would have to be left to his imagination—fantasy not being one of his stronger attributes. But the Air Force event would be the perfect catalyst to jump-start the process.

It was fun to have a secret. The others seemed pleased too, with the idea of a surprise and with Will's newly discovered child-like wonder. He'd never been given to whimsy. Even as a kid.

From the time Will was three, he'd started carrying a wallet. By the age of twelve, he kept a meticulous daily planner. Each Christmas he would ask for money. When neighborhood kids wanted to do something spontaneous, it was Will who would point out the negatives, the problems, the possible trouble that could accompany. Before long, he wasn't at the top of the list of kids to play with.

Maybe that's why he and Pops had always been so close. The problem was, their relationship had always been about Will. *What do you want to do, Will? What would you like for lunch? Where do you want to go?* But now, now it was time to even things up a bit.

They picked up the ladies, and Will punched the address into his GPS as everyone settled into the car, both women climbed into the backseat. Pops held the door open for Sara. Will gave Adrienne a wink. "Bring a jacket?"

Adrienne lifted her arm to show him the white cotton hoodie. "Can't imagine I'll need it unless you're driving us about seven hundred miles north."

"It could get cool this evening."

"We really are making a day of it," Sara said.

"Will it be a late night?" Adrienne adjusted her sunglasses over her eyes.

"Shouldn't be too late. Why? You have a hot date tomorrow or something?" Will teased.

"A very hot date."

Even though he knew she was joking behind those giant, round Hollywood sunglasses, hearing her even tease about having a date disturbed him—on a level deeper than he cared to admit.

"With a paint brush," she added, ink-dark hair falling from her tipped shoulder.

"I'm sure it will keep a few days."

She shook her head. "Nope. Gotta be tomorrow. I've rented extension ladders, and they're being delivered in the morning."

Concern caused him to look into the rearview mirror at her. "Do you have any idea what the heat index will be tomorrow?"

"I'll be fine," she quipped.

"Oh, Adrienne," Sara piped up from beside her, "William and I will cancel our picnic and help."

Will's fingers tightened on the steering wheel. "Um, excuse me. Is anyone listening to me? Heat. Index."

"Sure," Pops said. "We can take the boat out anytime for a picnic. Instead of heading over at dawn to pick you up, Sara, we'll just stay and help Adrienne."

"No one is helping Adrienne!" Will forced all the frustration in one quick breath. "Can't you tell the rental place no? To bring the ladders another day? And why are you painting your house? It looks like it was just painted."

"The walls are freshly painted, but I opted to do the trim, windows, and doors myself."

"Well, that was a stupid idea." The words slipped right out before he could stop them. "If you were going to save money and do something yourself, why not the walls? They're the easy part."

Sara threaded her fingers together. "I think we might be seeing the difference between men and women here. To me, the trim work would seem much less daunting."

Pops grunted. "Not really. It's a two-story. All those eaves and having to move a ladder every ten feet or so. I'm afraid I have to agree with Will on this one."

Sara lifted her hands in surrender. "Difference between men and women."

Will flipped the air on arctic. The interior of the car had grown stifling. "No one paints on a day like tomorrow. Too dangerous. With the heat index, I'm sure the rental place can make arrangements. Can't you just call them?"

Adrienne's cheek twitched, and she said in a whisper, "It's not really up for debate."

He couldn't read her behind those infuriating glasses, but the straight line of her mouth suggested her disapproval of his nosiness. "And no, I'm not going to cancel. Without twenty-four-hour notice, they keep your deposit."

"So, you're determined to do this, no matter the danger?" Will spat.

In the backseat, she readied for a fight, he could tell. It was in the tilt of her chin, the square of her shoulders. "Absolutely."

"Fine. I'll be over at five o'clock."

She frowned, brows dropping beneath the top of her shades. "Why?"

"To help."

Her head tilted like she'd never ever in a million years expected him to actually offer to help. "Pops, you and Sara go out on the boat, have your wonderful picnic, and we can all meet up at Adrienne's for dinner. Something easy. Maybe pizza. You two could pick it up on your way over. We can make sun tea while we work on the house. No doubt it will be hot enough. You can have my car tomorrow, and I'll take your truck, Pops—in case we need anything from the lumberyard."

Adrienne opened her mouth. Closed it. Opened it again. And there it stayed in a confused O.

As an afterthought, he added, "Would that be *okay* with you, Adrienne?"

She placed her lips together.

Will held up a finger. "But, we can't work through the hottest part of the day. We can work until noon, and then we take a long break. Evening we can work as long as the sun gives light. Agreed?" He didn't expect her to answer.

She didn't disappoint. Just sat there staring with giant mirrored bug eyes at some unknown spot, thinking her unknown thoughts and looking like a model waiting for the photographer to snap pictures.

"Great, then. It's settled." He loosened his grip on the steering wheel and turned on the radio to keep them company as he drove toward Tampa and Pops's past.

Will's face split into a smile as Pops stepped out of the car and headed toward the Air Force base and the daylong military celebration. Even from the parking lot, they could see the planes that lined the runway. As they entered, they were asked whether any were veterans of foreign wars. Pops was given a purple badge to wear on his lapel.

"How'd you know about this, Will?" Pops asked, using his hand to shield his face from the sun.

"Internet. They do this every year." Will grinned. Adrienne and Sara had to be prodded along; they both stopped frequently to gaze at the planes, helicopters, and midway that resembled a carnival.

Once inside, they meandered through the tables of military memorabilia. Every war that had been fought by American troops was represented, but the group spent most of their time in the World War II section.

Military personnel were stationed at each area to answer questions and give general information about the displays. Before long, they had worked their way to the landing strip that held five planes and one helicopter. Each was anchored with an information table and personnel. The planes were opened up to facilitate tours of the interiors.

While Pops and Sara examined a Hummer, Will snagged Adrienne by the hand and dragged her beside the airstrip, where a hangar blocked them from the crowd.

"What are you doing?" she giggled, turning into him.

He gripped the belt loops of her jeans and pulled her close. "Have I told you how great you look today?"

"Hmm, not that I remember."

"Well, you do. Those jeans are deadly."

She blinked innocently. "That doesn't sound good. Maybe I shouldn't have worn them."

"You should wear them all the time." His eyes sparkled with mischief. "But, uh, if you're suggesting ditching them, go ahead. I won't stop you."

The moment turned serious. Adrienne placed a hand to his cheek.

"What? What's wrong?" He searched her eyes, wanting to place a label on the sweet, sad look that entered them.

"Nothing." Her fingertips slipped smoothly back and forth on his skin. "Nothing at all. I just want to remember this moment. It's . . . nice."

"It is nice." His hands slid with agonizing slowness from her hips to the small of her back, where they trapped her body against his.

Will licked his lips.

Adrienne's eyes fluttered. "Kiss me."

"What?" Had he heard her right? Or was that just what he'd wanted her to say, so he'd imagined it?

"Kiss me, Will Bryant. We're never going to keep our attention on the festival if you don't go ahead and get it over with."

Something about *that* command from *this* woman tightened Will's chest. For the briefest of instants, he imagined waking beside her, not once, not twice, but every day. This woman who could surprise him with such a simple command as *kiss me*.

Will closed his mouth over hers and sank his hands deeply into the hair at her nape. Mink-soft strands curled around his fingers while Adrienne curled around his heart.

Will stood under the propellers of an Apache helicopter that loomed over him like a giant locust waiting for the appropriate moment to whip out a lightning-fast tongue and swallow him whole. He had always thought the Apaches were cool, but now, being dwarfed by its size and ominous presence, he couldn't imagine the sound those blades must generate.

"Invades every cell of your body," came a reply from behind him.

Will turned and squinted to see a young military man, standing at ease—which didn't look at ease to him—gazing up at the sinister aircraft. He smiled.

"I bet it would. How'd you know what I was thinking?" Will split his glances between the soldier and the Apache.

"It's what I thought when I first laid eyes on her." And both men admired the power before them. Will threw a thumb toward it. "You fly one?"

The young man nodded. "Yes, sir. Warrant Officer Roger Patterson." He spoke in an abrupt, no-nonsense military tone, but pride threaded his words.

"Air Force?"

"Army," Patterson corrected.

"What's it like?"

The young officer met his gaze fully. "It's like heaven. Except in combat, then it's . . . well, like hell."

"This one still used?"

The young man nodded. "Just got back from the Middle East."

Will's brows rose. "Really?" There was still war, of course. But as life went on, it was sometimes easy to forget that.

"Yes, sir." He motioned for Will to follow him. "She took some fire here. Scattered fire, nothing too bad. But when they got her back to base, they discovered some frayed wires, a few too many to patch."

Will copied him, running a hand along the holes. *Bullet holes.*

Patterson patted the side of the aircraft like one might pat a favorite pet. "Until they track down why and how the wires frayed, she's on vacation." He pointed to the front of the craft. "See that turret gun?"

He couldn't miss it. "You mean the cannon?"

The young man laughed. "Yes, it's linked to the pilot's helmet. As the pilot's head turns, so does the gun."

"That would come in handy during rush-hour traffic," Will joked.

"That's why they don't allow us to take them home, sir."

Will shook the young man's hand as Pops, Sara, and Adrienne—who just *had* to stop and buy an Air Force ball cap and T-shirt—caught up to him. He thanked the young man for the information and followed Pops to the next aircraft. A large cargo plane waited at the end of the runway. It dwarfed the rest.

They toured the other planes before coming to the C-47. Will stepped up first, then took Adrienne's hand, tugging her inside. Looking around and above them in the cylindrical cave, he wondered how many men had jumped from this craft. How many men had died after leaving this tunnel encased in Army drab? Pops helped Sara onto the platform. Footsteps echoed on metal floorboards as they moved toward the front, silently absorbing the plane's secrets.

Will looked at Pops. "Been in one like this before?"

Pops ran an open hand along the green wall. "Many times."

Weathered fingers examined the seats, the netting, touching each article like he knew it. "This is a C-47. Not the biggest toy on the playground, but it gets the job done. Ninety-five-foot wingspan, sixty-four feet long, sixteen feet high." Pops rubbed his chin, gaze floating somewhere above. "Funny that I still recall those dimensions. Anyway, it carried about thirty seated passengers, or two or three jeeps. Let me tell you, you never forget your first combat jump. Ours was Normandy." He walked to the open side door of the plane. "We'd done practice jumps on many occasions, but the first real jump . . . "

Sara moved to stand next to him.

Pops's words trailed off for a moment. "There's the noise of the plane, everything flapping and banging against the walls. The wind, it takes your breath away. Anything that's not fastened down becomes a missile. Door open, your commander screaming, 'Go, go, go!' You jump. And you hear this whoosh of air." He shook his head. "It's so loud you can't believe it's only air. And you're moving, gaining speed with each second until you pull the cord. Everything starts to get quiet. And you're no longer careening down, you're floating. You look at the ground and your heart rate picks up again. You don't know who saw you, and you know before the jump that it's a hot DZ."

Adrienne shot a questioning look over to Will. "DZ?" Like him, she had to have seen it in the letters, but didn't know what it meant.

"Means drop zone," he whispered, leaning toward her.

She nodded.

Pops shrugged. "Once on the ground you find out real quick who knows you're there."

Will leaned out the side door. "I can't believe you jumped out of these." He turned to face his grandfather. "You jumped out of *airplanes*, Pops! I wouldn't do that even if I wasn't landing in a war zone, but you did it with people shooting at you."

Pops nodded. "I never claimed to be the sharpest knife in the drawer."

"Did you ever want to back out?" Adrienne asked, fisting her hands in Will's shirt and tugging him back inside the aircraft.

Pops studied the roof of the plane. "Every jump. Especially Normandy." He moved across the aircraft. "Here's where I sat on the way." He pointed to the seat beside his. "And Rick sat there, Rusty, Eli, Baxter." He tossed the names out as his finger darted around the interior. I never saw Eli or Baxter alive again."

A mournful silence surrounded them.

"We were being dropped behind enemy lines. I can't explain what that feels like. You land already cut off by the enemy. Your only prayer is to advance, complete the objective. Our job was to take out key targets to soften the firepower on the beach. If the sea invasion failed, we didn't have a chance. We knew what was awaiting us when we landed." He leaned against the wall by the open door. "Normandy was by far the hardest jump I ever made."

Sara moved closer to him. "You wrote about Normandy in some of your letters. Back at home, we were watching the newsreels about it." She shook her head as if to shake off the memory of sixty-odd years earlier. "I was so scared for you."

Pops released her hand and put an arm around her shoulder tenderly. "Sweet Sara."

When another group of spectators entered the back of the plane, Will stepped out, with the others following. But he watched Pops stop in the doorway and glance at the hull. One long, meaningful look. Will felt the emotion. Pops was saying one last good-bye.

Chapter 16

It was strange, really. The sounds, the smells. Half a century had passed, but the scent of fresh gear, hearing the crunch of military boots on the ground, the faint taste of aircraft smoke that floated on the air and stung the back of your throat. If he closed his eyes and imagined hard enough, he was a raw recruit again, waiting to go to war. Eager, able, hopeful.

They'd spent another twenty minutes outside the plane, with Pops giving a play-by-play of battle after battle. Will was enthralled. Sara and Adrienne had finally grown weary of the graphic account and had gone back to the main boardwalk to get drinks, leaving Pops and Will alone at the end of the runway.

"I remember you telling me war stories when I was little."

"I did," Pop's said proudly. "When your parents brought you home from the hospital, you were so small." Pops lifted his hands palm side up. "Your whole body fit in my two hands."

Will smiled.

Pops stared at his palms. If he concentrated hard enough, he could still see, still feel the tiny form of his newborn grandchild. "Your mom and dad said I shouldn't tell a tiny baby war stories. But I did it anyway."

"They didn't like you to talk about it?"

Pops grinned. "Nah. Just wasn't proper dialogue for a newborn."

Will looked out over the planes. "Why did you stop? The last story I remember, I was probably ten or eleven."

Pops's eyes followed the trail to the six military aircraft in front of him. "You were getting older. G.I. Joe was out. You wanted to hear about mutated Ninja reptiles and Spiderman."

"I'm sorry, Pops. I didn't know the stories were real. I didn't know they were about you." Will reached down and plucked a small shell from the ground, rolling it over and over in his hand. "I wish I had grown up with them."

Regret wasn't a welcome visitor in Pops's world. He hated Will feeling this way.

Will's gaze narrowed. "But Mom and Dad didn't make you stop telling the stories?"

Careful, here. Will rarely brought up his parents. Now, an inquisition about them. "No, why would you think that?"

Will shrugged. "I don't know. Their whole mission is about bringing *peace* to the world."

Pops took a stern stance, planting his feet firmly and his hands on his hips. "Your mom and dad are soldiers, just like me."

Will smirked. "I guess. I don't want to talk about them right now; today is about you. I feel like I've missed out on such an important part of your life. Now I just want to know everything about it, Pops."

Appreciation surged as William stood looking over airplanes with his grandson at his side, reflecting on all that was. He was a man who'd lived out his years. He had a wonderful son and a caring grandson. The woman he had once loved like a sister had come back into his life. If he were to die right now, he would be content. No, not just content, he would be fulfilled. If only he could help reconcile son and grandson, it would be perfect.

In all honesty, he didn't know what the problem was. But over the past several years, Will's attitude toward his parents had disintegrated. Sure, fathers and sons often had their difficulties. But Will's words and actions suggested a deep-rooted hurt that pushed far beyond normal father–son struggles. On many occasions he'd tried to discuss it with him, but Will always shut the conversation down. He considered approaching the subject now. One glance at his grandson's face stopped him. Will was dealing with enough for today. But William offered up a silent prayer. *I'd like to see my family intact again. If not today, then before I die.*

"Are we staying for the fireworks?" Adrienne asked excitedly. She and Sara had returned with lemonade slushies, and now the four of them were making their way to the bandstand where the Air Force band was warming up.

Will claimed a drink. "If Pops and Sara feel like it."

They sat down. Adrienne grinned and chewed the end of her straw.

"What's on your mind?" Will asked, noticing how the cold of the slushie had made her lips red and a little swollen. Slushies *rocked*.

"Nothing." She blinked innocently. "Just a little surprise for Pops later."

Will eyed her suspiciously. The man on the bandstand began to speak, and Will's attention left Adrienne and her icy-hot mouth. He drank the tart lemonade as the man talked about patriotism and America.

Minutes into his monologue, the announcer took out a list. "We have several guests here today who we would like to recognize now." He talked about a young man who had just returned from Afghanistan, a high-ranking Air Force colonel, but it was the next name that drew Will's attention.

"Today, we have a member of the acclaimed 101st Airborne that was active in World War II. William Bryant was a para-trooper involved in each major battle during the campaign in Europe, including Normandy and Bastogne. William Bryant, please stand."

For a moment, Pops just sat still, like he was unsure whether it was his name he'd heard. But Sara on one side and Adrienne on the other were tugging at his arm for him to rise. Pops stood, and as he did, a roar in the crowd echoed around them.

Mouth agape, he glanced around as, all over the stadium, people were clapping and cheering. They began to stand with him. Pops slowly raised a hand to them in stunned appreciation. It was a full two minutes before the crowd began to sit back down, their roar fading slowly. Unable to speak, Pops sat as well.

And Will watched him. He'd seen the color drain from Pops's cheeks as he was commanded to stand. He'd watched as Pops placed a hand over his heart, trying to swallow back the emotion at being singled out. This wasn't Pops's style. And he was an old man.

Will's anger began a slow burn deep in his gut. He kept a close eye on him later as they walked to the car.

The night air swirled, carrying the scent of hot dogs and funnel cakes. Will pressed the button on his car keys, and the headlights flashed on, one row out. The gentlemen helped the ladies into the vehicle, and Will stored Adrienne's purchases in the trunk. He moved to the driver's-side door. Once out of the artificial light, and with Adrienne and Sara tucked safely inside the car, Pops slumped against the trunk.

Will rushed back to him. "What's wrong?"

Pops sucked in a ragged breath. "I was doing fine until the bandstand." Tender blue eyes studied the younger man. "I'm sorry, Will. I try to be so strong."

Will forced down a lump in his throat.

Pops's head dropped, fingers lacing together in embarrassment. "I don't want you to see me like this."

It was useless. It was too late. Will could see how delicate his grandfather really was. "When he called my name, it was just too much for me to handle." A choked sob followed, and Will took a firmer grip on his grandfather, shoring him up.

What was appropriate contact between two men quickly fell by the wayside as Will unlaced Pops fingers and held the older man in his arms. Another choked sob was accompanied by two more, as strong, able shoulders rose and fell under the weight of grief. Then, as quickly as the tears had come, they were gone.

Pops took a handkerchief from his back pocket and wiped his face. "Grown-up bawl baby," he mumbled, pressing the cloth to his cheeks.

"No," Will assured. "Bravest man I know."

Though both women had witnessed the embrace, neither was quick to talk about it. When Pops began to cry, Sara reached over to Adrienne in the backseat and took her hand. The four of them drove back to Naples in silence.

Will helped Sara from the car while Adrienne searched for her house keys. Sara had given Pops a peck on the cheek and was already at the front door.

Sure both of the older people were out of earshot, Will turned on Adrienne. "Why did you do that?" he hissed.

Shocked, she abandoned her search, frowning until she realized he was talking about the bandstand. "I passed a table where they were asking about veterans. I told them about Pops. It was to honor him."

Will threw an angry glance toward the car. "He nearly broke down. You need to start using some better judgment in your decisions. The day was hard enough on Pops. You seem to forget he's over eighty years old."

Adrienne glanced toward the car. "I'm sorry. I didn't think—"

"Well, please try to next time." He walked back to the car while she slowly walked up to the house.

Back in the vehicle, Pops stared at him. "You and Adrienne have a tiff?"

"Nothing I can't handle," he said, backing out and wishing the leather smell of his car could erase the floral scent of her that still hung in the air. Once on the main road, he turned the radio on.

Soft music filled the car, relieving the silence. With a finger, Pops traced the stitching of the leather seat. "Listen, Will, I want to apologize."

Will's eyes left the road. "For what?" Bonita Springs disappeared around them, bathed only in the artificial light of the streetlamps and brightened storefronts.

Pops kept his gaze strictly focused on the seat. "For earlier. I should explain."

"No, Pops," Will said tenderly. "You don't have to explain."

"I want to." The resolve in Pops's tone stopped any argument. One quick glance, and Will knew he needed to say this.

"Coming home from the war is like your birthday and Christmas all rolled up in one." Lips framed with wrinkles pressed together. "At least that's what I thought. I'd heard stories about entire towns shutting down and having a parade to welcome a soldier home."

Will smiled at him.

Pops brushed his hands on his pants. "Call it romanticizing, but I just expected . . . " They turned onto a side road. With no moonlight outside, their conversation was illuminated only by the unnatural glow of the dashboard. "Look, when I got home, there was no one there to greet me. No one."

Will's heart sank into his stomach, and he was glad the dash light was faint. He'd hate for Pops to see the horror on his face.

Pops swallowed. "Tonight I feel like I got the homecoming I missed back then." He looked over at his grandson. "That may sound silly to you, but it's how I feel."

Will couldn't breathe. His lungs were denying his body oxygen. He wondered if he would ever learn to keep his mouth shut. "That's why you reacted to it?"

Pops smiled. "You mean my crying fit at the back of the car?"

"I would hardly call it a crying fit."

Pops patted the seat. "Whatever you would call it. It was the perfect ending to a perfect day. Thank you, Will. For making all this happen."

Will couldn't take the credit for the bandstand. He could, however, take the blame for once again accusing Adrienne when he should be thanking her. He ran a hand through his hair, stiffening at the thought of having to apologize. Again.

Pops noticed his demeanor. "Don't worry. If you messed things up with Adrienne, I'm sure she'll give you a chance to fix it."

Will smiled over at him and said wryly, "How do you know I'm the one that messed up?"

"You're the man. We're always the ones that mess up."

"Honeybees have stingers, you know?" Will said.

"That's why honey is so sweet."

"It's worth the sting. Is that what you're trying to tell me?"

"I guess you'll find out."

Will sighed. Yes, he was hopelessly caught in her orbit. "Guess I will, Pops."

The two women had stayed quiet for the first few minutes inside the house. Adrienne flitted from room to room, turning on lights. Sara seemed unusually distracted. "Everything all right?" she asked the older woman.

"What? Oh, yes." Sara followed her into the lavender room.

"Do you think Pops is okay?" Adrienne asked, shaking a thick down pillow into a plum pillow case.

Sara nodded from across the bed. "I'm sure." After fluffing the pillow on her side, she nestled it at the head of the antique sleigh bed purchased for the room.

Adrienne stifled a yawn. It had been a long day. "You've fallen in love with him all over again, haven't you?"

Sara took the pillow back up and hugged it to herself. "No," she said.

"I don't believe you, Sara." Adrienne tucked stray wisps of hair behind her ear and regarded the older woman.

Sara used her palm to smooth the cotton bedspread. "The truth is, I never fell out of love with him."

Adrienne sat at the edge of the bed and drew one foot up under her knee. "What do you see for the two of you?"

Sara blinked, a crimson stain darkening her face. "Whatever do you mean?"

"Well, I don't know." Adrienne threw her hands into the air. "He feels the same."

Sara dropped slowly onto the bed. "I don't know that you're right."

"Of course I'm right." She tipped her shoulder. "The way he looks at you, how he holds your hand."

Sara scooted so she could look at Adrienne fully. "When I hear his voice, my heart beats faster. This warm, thick liquid moves through my veins when he touches me. But—"

"But what?"

Sara pushed hair from her face. "He doesn't look at me like he used to look at Gracie."

"I'm sure that's not true."

Sara's gaze drifted around the room. "It is. Gracie was perfect. She had the poise of a swan while I was more of an . . . "—she scrunched her nose—"an ugly duckling and a klutz."

"Sara, I can't imagine you as an ugly duckling and certainly not a klutz. You're so elegant."

Sara gave her an appreciative smile.

"I mean it. Everything about you is beautiful."

Sara's voice dropped. "Not everything."

Chills spread over Adrienne's arms, though she had no clue why. Then she thought about the letter. The note from Grace that Pops had salvaged. She'd intended to ask Sara about it but had lost her nerve. Now it seemed that fateful note could be somehow connected to Sara's admission. Now was the time.

"Sara, Pops had one letter from Grace. It was the last letter sent to him."

Sara's gaze dropped to the floor.

"I read it. It sounded . . . it really sounded like a woman in love. But it was right before Grace died."

Sara remained silent.

"I wondered if you might know anything about that letter?"

Sara stood slowly and moved to the far wall where her suitcase sat open; clothes ruffled as she dug through the blouses and skirts. One deep breath, and she turned to face Adrienne, a stack of letters in her hand.

Adrienne blinked, trying to assimilate the idea of this new stack with the ones she'd found from William. "Sara, what are those?"

"Grace never wrote to William. I begged her to. I pleaded, but she wouldn't."

A muddled picture of the past began to clear before Adrienne. She wasn't sure she liked what she saw. But what could she do now? Forge on. Clarify her suspicions. "Sara, *you* wrote the letters? The letters from Grace?"

"Every single word." A lone tear trickled down her cheek. "It was such a deceitful, evil thing to do. But he'd gone there for her. If he knew the truth, I was afraid he'd never survive."

"But you told William Grace lost interest in him because of you. Because you loved him."

"Over the years, it was just easier to believe she'd landed in another man's arms because of me. Truthfully, she had no intention of waiting for William."

Adrienne couldn't speak. Couldn't even move.

"Oh, I loved him from the first day he found me crying at the riverside." Her thumbs caressed the letters in her hand. "But I fell deeper and deeper in love reading his letters. I grew up on those letters. Became a woman."

"And you wrote him back."

"Yes. We grew closer and closer, sharing the war, sharing home. I poured my heart into those words. But . . . but never my secret."

"And with each letter, you had to sign Grace's name at the bottom. Oh, Sara." Adrienne moved closer. "I'm so sorry."

When the older woman moved to hide the letters behind her, Adrienne stepped toward her and gently took hold of her wrist. "If you wrote the letters from Grace, what are these?"

Sara forced out a long breath. "These are the letters from me. The ones I never sent. They've been in a locked drawer in my bureau for years."

"The antique bureau in your living room, right? I've noticed you looking at it now and then. I thought it held a secret, but not this."

Sara held out the stack of letters, and Adrienne took it, feeling as if she held another treasure in her hands. Yet the burden weighed heavily. And Adrienne didn't know what to do with them. If she could burn them and never have to tell Pops the truth, that seemed the best—albeit most deceitful—course of action. She understood how easy it must have been for Sara to fall into this deception. The truth was a beast with sharpened claws.

A tiny smile appeared on Sara's face. "Go ahead. Read one."

Adrienne froze. By reading them, even one, she became part of the fraud. Her fingertips grew sweaty with her indecision. Somewhere inside, her heart made the choice her mind couldn't. She slid one letter from beneath the ribbon. The remaining pages she set on the nearby bookshelf. Adrienne unfolded the page and read.

Dear William,

Sometimes I marvel at the selfishness that burdens my soul. I am drowning, slipping silently into quicksand made by my own hands. Lies are hideous things. I feel as though I'm living a dual life. One of a careful daughter, another of a secret lover.

If it weren't for my intense love for you, I'd stop. I'd give up this charade. I'd tell Momma and Gracie the truth. But I won't. So much rests on my ability to keep the two very separate parts of my life far from each other. Maybe you understand. You of all people always understand my thoughts and feelings. And you—the young man who left town as the son of a merchant but will return to me as a battle-toughened hero. Your country honors your sacrifice. Even in the streets, the children tell tales of the brave 101st. And what is that like for you? Knowing your most inner being—the poet I know and love—must take second place to the hero you are called? You, William, are leading a dual life as well.

In it all, we have each other. That makes it worth every scorn I may one day face. Worth every ounce of shame I feel when my mother or my sister look upon me with suspicious eyes. You're worth it all, William. You hold my heart in your gentle hands. You have since the day we met. And if it is up to me, you always will.

Your true love,
Sara

There were no words. What feeble encouragement could Adrienne give after reading a letter that honest, that intimate, that private? With a tear tickling the corner of her eye, she said, "Sara, you have to show him."

Old fingers darted out and snatched the letter. "And what, Adrienne? He has forgiven me for so much. Where does his charity run out?"

"Why didn't you let him know when you first saw him again?" Adrienne wasn't trying to accuse—just understand.

"It's unforgivable. What I did. He wrote such intimate things, private things in those letters." Sara shook her head. "When I got the opportunity to see him again, I couldn't . . . just couldn't. Do you have any idea what it was like writing him with my mother and my sister in the next room? Always wondering when they'd find out. What my mother would do to me?"

"But Sara—"

"No. I won't hear it." She turned away, closing off the conversation. When she looked over her shoulder at Adrienne, tears glistened in her eyes. "I finally have him in my life. Do you know what that means to me? How many years I hoped for this, knowing there was no way, no *possible way* I could spend my life with the man I love?"

Adrienne ran her hands through her hair. She wouldn't convince Sara tonight. "Someday, Sara. He'll need to know."

She nodded. "Please, can we talk about something else?"

Adrienne tipped her head, letting the intensity go. "As I was saying earlier, everything about you is beautiful."

With an appreciative smile, Sara's nearly untraceable Southern accent thickened. "Well, Momma did have her rules." She walked to the bed and grabbed the pillow, then placed it on top of her head and began to stroll across the room, elbows at her sides, fingertips out.

Adrienne clapped. "Bravo."

"Gracefully, my darling," she instructed as Adrienne put a pillow on her head. It fell off.

"This is too easy." Sara tossed the pillow onto the bed and reached for a book from the narrow bookshelf by the window. She balanced it and walked, making smooth twists and turns. Again, Adrienne followed her lead, laughing as she had to reach up time and time again to steady the book that slid from her like an ill-fitting crown.

Book still perfectly balanced, Sara bent her knees and swept down in one graceful motion to pick up a shoe from the floor. "Momma taught us how to walk like a lady, sit like a lady, descend the stairs like a lady."

"There's a proper way to descend the stairs?" Adrienne laughed and rolled her eyes, glad for the change of topic. "Boy, I've got a lot to learn."

"Of course," Sara said, nose high. "Knees together as if connected. Hand lightly on the banister, stand tall, and float down the stairs. I was a bitter disappointment to Momma." She tipped her head forward, letting the book slide into her hands.

Adrienne's book slid off on its own. "All that training must have taken root somewhere. You're more graceful than any woman I know."

"I suppose. Somewhere between knobby, skinned-up knees and the womanly body I prayed for and didn't think I'd ever get." Her eyes left Adrienne. "Gracie didn't have to work at it. Beauty, elegance just came naturally to her. But for once, I wanted to be Cinderella at the ball. I just always ended up playing in the mud puddle when the coach arrived."

Adrienne closed the gap between them. She rested her hands on Sara's shoulders.

"William always thought of me like a kid sister." She practically whispered the words, biting back the pain that edged her eyes. "What if he still does?"

Adrienne shook her head. "He doesn't. I can see it even if you can't. Besides," she grinned, "Cinderella always gets the handsome prince."

"Always?"

Adrienne nodded.

"What about your handsome prince?"

Pulling her bottom lip between her teeth, Adrienne stiffened. "My handsome prince is acting like a toad right now." He was the last thing she wanted to think about. It had been a magical day until . . .

"Acting like a toad?" Sara tapped her index finger on her chin. "I think a kiss rectifies that."

"I'd rather kiss a toad."

Sara yawned and Adrienne took it as a cue to work her way to the bedroom door. "Well, you'll get your chance bright and early tomorrow morning."

She stopped dead in her tracks. Slowly, she turned to face the older woman. "You don't actually believe he's still coming, do you?"

Sara's eyes were troubled. "Of course he is. He was very worried about you overdoing it in the heat. People don't just toss you aside because they get mad at you. Goodness, Adrienne. That's not really what you expected, is it?"

It wasn't just what she expected, it was what she knew would happen.

Chapter 17

A shimmering black horse galloped beneath Adrienne. Even from her place astride him, she was aware of the shine of dark velvet hide and rolling muscles. No saddle to separate her from the animal that was as tuned to her thoughts as any she could ever hope would be.

And together they ran. They ran so hard and fast that all the world, green and beautiful, disappeared behind them. Her hair—splayed in brilliant fashion—moved in tandem with the horse's mane. All this she saw as if watching from above, but also felt and experienced as the two of them fled from the draining world around.

Far ahead a fence appeared. With it, cold. She willed the horse forward, but he slowed. Adrienne raked her bare feet against his midsection, along the ribs swelling and shrinking with each heavy breath. Still the horse slowed as snow dusted the dreamy world with fine white powder. She remembered Chicago, remembered being so cold she'd thought she'd never thaw. When the stallion came to an abrupt stop at the fence line, Adrienne threw herself off and ran to the gate, already freezing over in the chill. Her hands fumbled with the lock, but it wouldn't budge. Nor would her feet. She looked down to see snow and ice working their way up, encasing her ankles, sliding up her legs. She screamed and tossed, trying to break their torturous hold.

Bang, bang, bang.

Her gaze shot left, but all she saw was the winded stallion and the ghost-white puffs of air that left his nostrils and vanished into the snow-whitened air.

Bang, bang, bang.

She stirred. Someone was far down the fencerow hammering it, trying to break it down. In one strong jerk of her body, she threw herself in hopes of breaking free of her icy prison.

Wham! Disoriented, she tried to look around, but all she saw was dark. Her side ached. Something was over her head. Adrienne kicked off the covers and realized she'd landed on her floor by her bed. The dream was still fresh, and she pushed all the blankets away because the sense of entrapment still clung to her like cobwebs.

A hazy digital clock read 4:50. A hand on her side, she sat down at the edge of the bed trying to make sense of the dream. The horse, the running—it felt so free, *she* felt so free, so alive.

Bang, bang, bang.

She nearly dropped again. Her gaze shot to the window, then back to the clock. In a rush, she ran out of the room, flipping lights as she went. Before she could pull the door open, she looked down to make sure she was dressed. T-shirt and sweats.

She flipped on the porch light and swung the door open to a grinning Will. Really. He had the nerve to smile.

She face palmed her forehead. "What are you doing here?"

He held out a bouquet of flowers. Wildflowers, her favorite, and an array of shapes and colors. "I'm here to apologize."

When she stood there stoically, crossing her arms over her chest, he added, "And paint."

"It's four fifty in the morning." A spray of three Gerbera daisies fought for her attention in the center of the bouquet, but she resisted and held eye contact—bleary as he might seem—with Will.

He shrugged. "I told you I'd be here at five o'clock."

She shook her head, noticed the tangles at the ends of her hair, and refused to smooth it. "I thought you were joking."

His eyes darkened. "I never joke about work."

In a taunt, he held the flowers out to her and shook them back and forth, his brows tilting upward at the inner edges. "I think they're thirsty."

She reached out. "Give me those. You'll shake every petal off them if you're not careful." Of course, she'd grabbed them with an equal amount of force.

Will bit back a smile. She spun from the door and headed to the kitchen. "Not a morning person?" He called to her.

She stopped and angled her gaze to him, eyes narrow. "I thought you were here to apologize."

"I thought I did."

She cradled the bundle to her. Gerbera daisies really were the most beautiful flowers on the planet. "No. You said you were here to apologize. You never said you were sorry, what you were sorry for, or how you came to realize you *should* apologize."

"Not gonna let me off the hook, are you?"

"Not on your life. If you wanted mercy, you should have brought dark chocolate with these." She disappeared into the kitchen.

"Duly noted. I'll keep that in mind for our next spat." Will sank onto a wooden rocking chair in her living room.

She tilted her head around the corner and stared at him. "Our next spat?"

"Well, Pops called it a tiff. But my mom always referred to their fights as spats. I don't actually know what either word means." The chair squeaked as he rocked back and forth. "This is a great chair."

But Adrienne was lost in the fact that Will Bryant was comparing their heated conversation—if she could even call it that—to one of his *parents'* spats. That fell well inside *couples territory*, and she hadn't asked for a deed. Which made him a squatter. Oh dear, she really needed coffee.

She put the flowers in a fine crystal vase and ground fresh coffee beans, aware of him rocking away in the other room. Aware that he felt so *comfortable* in her house that he'd slid right in and claimed a spot. Speaking of spots, her side hurt.

"Are you all right?"

She jumped when she heard his voice from the door. He stepped into her kitchen as she turned to face him.

He pointed to her hand, still rubbing her hip.

"I had a bad dream."

"Must have been something to cause pain you *still feel*."

"I fell out of bed when I heard . . . I guess I heard you banging on the door. But . . . " Adrienne kneaded her bottom lip. "I think you were in my dream, tearing down the fence." She stared over at him, and he remained quiet, letting her sort the scattered pieces. "You were the one. The horse couldn't do it. Couldn't jump it. And with the snow and ice we were going to be trapped there."

His brows rose.

"Frozen," she whispered. "Like Sleeping Beauty."

Will nodded, but she could see the doubt.

"Do you think dreams have meaning?"

"No." The one word from his lips was so final, so solid, Adrienne blinked.

"Never?"

Will ran a hand through his hair. "I sure hope not."

"Why?"

He waited several seconds before answering. "I have a recurring dream about Pops."

Adrienne dropped her weight against the counter. "What happens?"

"He dies." His voice broke a little as he said it. As did Adrienne's heart.

"He, uh, takes the boat out late at night. I try to stop him, but he won't listen. The boat runs aground. I'm not there, but I can see it in the dream like I'm watching through a window. He drowns."

All the air left Adrienne's lungs. "I'm sorry, Will. I'm sure it doesn't mean anything."

He tried to smile. "What about your dream with the horse and fence and me?"

"No. It doesn't mean anything either. There's no fence for you to tear down." Now she wished she hadn't even brought it up.

"Hey, I'm only getting paid for painting, not fence removal."

She smiled and pulled two mugs from the cupboard. "You're not getting paid at all."

Suddenly he was right behind her. "Oh, yes I am." It was a growl wrapped in a promise.

And it curled her flesh from her ears to her toes. She grabbed a kitchen knife from the counter and turned to face him. "About that apology . . . "

He raised his hands in surrender and took a step back. But before he could say more, Adrienne spoke, "You're forgiven."

He used the back of his hand to push the knife aside and came so close only a whisper separated them. "Thank you." He dropped a kiss on the top of her head.

Adrienne caught her appearance in the small round mirror on the far wall. "I . . . I need to go change." He was all fresh and showered and smelling like soap and leather, and she smelled like sweaty nightmare girl.

She hurried out of the kitchen. "Help yourself to coffee. Be back in a few."

They spent the day painting, chatting, and making two trips to the lumberyard in Pops's truck. Adrienne worked on windows and doors while Will mastered the soffits around the roofline. In true Florida weather fashion, cloud cover rolled in at noon, shaming the weathermen and giving Will and Adrienne ample time to complete the task.

He'd brought clothes to change into, so she offered him the master bath to shower and get ready for a fun evening of pizza and visiting with Pops and Sara. The house looked great. Adrienne noticed the light, almost airiness of the space around her heart. She placed a hand there, first concerned because it felt so foreign, so alien. But this wasn't a bad thing. This was . . . joy. Even the renovation hadn't brought her that, but somewhere around the time she started setting the table and thinking about hearing the details of Pops's and Sara's day, this odd sensation arrived. And she didn't want it to leave. Ever. Adrienne rubbed her hand back and forth over her heart, hoping this wasn't some kind of sick joke, hoping there wasn't an insurmountable fence just ahead.

Sara and Pops stayed inseparable for the next few weekends. The older couple's activities usually included Will and Adrienne, though occasionally Adrienne would decline, saying she couldn't leave the house project at hand. The problem was, when she did that, Will missed her. Badly. Even though they were meeting regularly throughout the week to plan the birthday party for Pops, he missed seeing her on the weekends.

The party was only five weeks away now. But it was growing more and more difficult to keep everything hidden from Pops. "Maybe we should have the party at my house." Standing up from her back deck, Adrienne swept her arm across her forehead. The hot Florida sun was unmerciful as they worked together to build a stand for the kayak.

"It would keep us from having to move this thing." She kicked the leg of the stand that would hold the Polynesian food.

Will stood, using Adrienne as an anchor to pull his weight up from the seated position he'd been in. He turned her to him while she attempted to keep the hair off her face. Tiny droplets of sweat glistened across her brow. She was beautiful in her cutoff jeans, paint-splattered T-shirt, and work boots. A utility belt hung low on her hips, drawing attention to the hourglass curves below her waist. "It would be easier—everything is already here."

She nodded. "I think it would be perfect. We can set things up on the back deck but maybe trail lights out onto the beach. We can put some extra beach chairs around." She threw out an exasperated breath when the wind tossed her hair back into her face.

Will reached up and smoothed the strays. He licked his lips and leaned in for a kiss.

"Will, come on." She deflected him. "I'm gross."

One brow arched as he looked her up and down. "Though many words might describe you, gross is not one of them. Let's go for a swim." He motioned to the beach and clamped a hand in her nail gun pouch.

She shook her head. "We have too much work to do."

He slipped the buckle open and dropped her utility belt on the deck behind him. "I know. But you need to try out the mask and snorkel I bought you." He'd purchased it last week at the dive shop.

Her face lit up. "You did?"

Ahhh. There it was—all those specks in her eyes sparkling with fresh excitement. This time he captured her mouth in a kiss. "That's not all. I got you a brochure about learning how to scuba dive." His hands landed on those fine hips where the tool belt had been.

"What?" She blinked up at him, the mix of excitement and surprise an intoxicating brew.

"At the dive shop, Ky, the owner, asked if I'd be interested in volunteering to help instruct at Kalanu Camp." He couldn't resist the urge to pull her body a little closer as he spoke. She came willingly.

"I've heard of that. It's a camp for troubled kids, right?"

"Yep. The course is run through the college, and lots of students who are certified divers volunteer, but when he asked, I just jumped right in."

One eye closed partially. "How spontaneous of you."

The growl again, and he tipped closer to her. "Yes, it was. And now you owe me."

She flattened her hands against his chest. "What?"

He leaned until his forehead rested against hers. "All this spontaneity . . . I blame you."

Her tongue slipped out of her mouth and ran over her lips. "It looks good on you. You should do it more often." Her voice had dipped dangerously low.

"Okay." With a smooth motion, he swept her into his arms and headed toward the ocean while she laughed, kicked, and pleaded.

"Will! Put me down! We don't have time for this." With half-hearted effort, she beat her fists against his chest, but gave up when he took the first steps into the water. "At least let me go get a swimsuit on."

"Okay," he agreed. "I'll get mine from the car."

She stared up at the hot sun. "Just a quick swim, all right?"

She was back on the beach before he was, and glanced down at her suit, making sure everything was covered. Adrienne waded out into the water and dove under, hair trailing behind her. Saltwater felt different from freshwater. It felt different from a swimming pool. It had more substance, and the buoyancy it gave her created the sensation of flying. Before moving here, it had been years since she'd been in the ocean, and she wasn't really sure how well she'd like it. But after diving in the very first time, she was reacquainted with an old friend. She swam around, letting tiny tropical fish gather around her legs. She watched them dart about in the clear blue-green water, silvery casings catching the sun. With childlike whimsy, she tried to catch one, and another. It was a futile attempt. They would zip away from her, then return after only moments as if mocking her inability to snag even the tiniest of fish.

She stood in water up to her chest, when a wave washed over her. The water rose to her throat. Her shoulders stayed exposed, the sun warming them and drying the little droplets across her shoulders.

"You know how to work one of these?"

The voice came from behind her. She spun and Will moved out to her in the surf. Two scuba masks with snorkels attached were slung over his right forearm.

"How hard can it be?" she asked, trying not to notice how the water rippled up on his exposed body. She watched the lean muscles and enjoyed the sensation it caused within her. A wave rushed up on him, leaving tiny rivulets to trail down over a tanned chest and lines of clear-cut stomach muscles.

He handed her a mask, and she tried to put it on without jabbing herself in the eyes with the dangling snorkel.

"Ouch." She winced as the rubber mask strap tangled into her hair.

He reached up and released her from the trap.

She relented. "Okay, so maybe it's a little harder than it looks."

"Here," he said softly, moving just close enough to help balance her in the surf. His face was near hers, his breath fanning against her throat and chest. She was thankful for the waves that washed away the sensation, but right on its heels was another puff of air. "Let's make sure this fits you." He folded the strap backward and placed the mask to her face. "Can you hold it on with no strap?"

She shrugged.

"Breathe in through your nose just a little. If the mask fits right, it will make just enough suction to hold it in place."

She followed his instructions, and surprisingly the mask stayed put when he removed his hand.

"Now, do what I do." He demonstrated the proper way to put the mask on without ripping out half a head of hair. He positioned the snorkel in his mouth. "Got it?"

She nodded, snorkel end bobbing above her.

"When a wave comes over us," he said, removing his mouthpiece, "the water from it is going to rush into the end of the snorkel." He laughed when her eyes widened in fear. "Don't worry."

But the panic caused her to spit out the mouthpiece and even stand a little higher.

"Seriously. It's nothing to worry about."

She cocked a brow in answer.

"I get it. This is a beginner class. Okay, close your eyes." He moved closer to her, his arms gently circling her midsection.

She instinctively tensed.

"Relax," he whispered against her. "I'm trying to show you something."

I just bet. Against her better judgment, she allowed the tension to drain from her muscles as they swayed, the water moving their bodies together. The ocean had its own rhythm, and as her breathing slowed, she became a part of that rhythm. She was aware when a wave was coming, and she realized her body reacted as if she and the water were one. Wow. She finally had her sea legs. They'd evaded her on the boat.

His words were a whisper, barely audible over the rush of air and water moving around them. "See, you'll know when a wave is coming." His hands and arms were warm where they touched her skin. "Breathe in before the wave reaches you. If water gets into your snorkel, you just breathe out quickly and it will shoot the water back out."

With her eyes still closed, she nodded. She could feel his hands tightening, drawing her straight down, deeper into the water. Once her mask was under, she opened her eyes, scarcely believing this was the same world she'd watched from the surface. A rush of cool water enveloped her head, introducing her to the silence and beauty of the world beneath.

They swam around for a time, Will pointing out one type of fish, then another. A few times, the water washed up over the snorkel, but like a pro she followed his instructions and shot it right back out.

She studied a small fish circling around her knees. Will gestured to her and opened his fingers to reveal a clam shell. He motioned for her to come up out of the water. With the snorkel finally out of her mouth, Adrienne popped up above the surface, a string of exclamations tumbling from her salty lips.

"Did you see that fish? It was as big as my hand." She continued on, describing the surroundings beneath them as if he hadn't been there.

He laughed. "I know." He held the clam shell out to her.

She took it, examined it, tried to separate the two pieces. "It's connected."

"Yeah." He slid it from her hand. "Come on, I want to show you something cool."

Still a little breathless, she slipped the mask back on and followed him under the water.

With one hand, he pried open the shell. As if on cue, a cloud of fish instantly swarmed around the small shell, extracting its contents. Her gaze shot to Will in amazement. After the feeding frenzy, many of the fish remained and seemed as curious about her as she was about them. They swam toward the mask, looked into her eyes, then swam away. She'd never seen such a concentration of brightly colored slippery bodies. Slowly, Will held out another shell.

With his free hand he reached for hers, then dropped the shell into her palm. He kept a firm grasp on her wrist so she wouldn't drop the meal as feathery fish tickled across her skin. They bumped or nudged her hand. She tried to withdraw, but he held her steadfast. Soon, she had grown accustomed to the feel of live fish bumping and jostling about as they aggressively devoured the contents of the mollusk.

An hour later, she and Will sat on her back steps, wrapped in big beach towels. The sun was getting ready to set on the horizon, and its movement sparked a shower of vibrant colors. The powdery blue sky turned to deep purple, dark pink, and finally orangey-yellow, a heavenly fireworks display for their benefit.

Will stood and lit the torches on her deck. He sat back down beside her. "Are you cold?" he whispered against her ear.

She snuggled toward him. "No, I'm very warm."

"Listen, I want to thank you for everything you've done for us."

She looked over, giving him her full attention. "What do you mean?" The setting sun was beautiful, but so was Will.

He shrugged. "I can't explain it, but you've made my relationship with Pops even better." His face left hers, and he focused on the water. "Also, you forced me to take a hard look at myself, and I didn't really like what I saw."

She watched him. Will Bryant was growing and changing right before her eyes. "Will, can we talk about your parents?"

Slam, slam, slam, slam. Four walls came up. But she'd spent enough time resisting the urge to dive into this conversation. Those walls wouldn't deter her.

"Look, I know you struggle with their decision to stay in Africa. I just want to understand."

He stared at the darkening water. "Do you remember your senior year of high school?"

"Sure," she said. "Everybody does. It's your last year of being a kid. Everything that happens, good or bad, is golden because you know it's the last time you'll experience it."

"You know what I remember about my senior year?" He didn't give her time to answer. "I remember my mom and dad selling eighty percent of our furniture. I remember them celebrating when they got their passports. I remember them spending countless hours a day learning some obscure language for people they didn't even know."

"You feel like your parents' going to work overseas was more important to them than your senior year?" A cold breeze snuck up the side of her legs, and she pulled the towel closer.

He faced her. "I think that for an entire year I was brutally reminded that if it wasn't for me, they would have left long ago.

It was like a yearlong celebration that I would finally be out of their way."

"Are you sure that's how they felt? Have they said that?"

"Some things are louder when they're not said."

"And some things are bitterly misunderstood when they're not said." So many things she should have said to Eric early on in their marriage. Maybe it would have kept him from becoming such a tyrant.

"I know that," he conceded. "But you can't really have a heart-to-heart on a crackling satellite phone from five thousand miles away."

Will pivoted so he could lean forward, elbows resting on his thighs. "I have wanted to ask my dad why. My parents aren't cruel people by nature. I know they love me. But their actions . . . "

Adrienne nodded and reached around him. Her gaze followed his to the dark water, the glow of the moon melding with the torches and creating fire sparks of illumination. Surprising herself, she put her hands on Will's face and turned him to look at her. So much pain in those green eyes. She started to lean forward to kiss him but stopped. Again, the eyes. She wanted to ease that pain. Be the answer. Be his answer. Letting the beach towel fall away, she pushed her lips against his. Their faces came together in a sweet, tender movement. Warm, strong hands slid over her back to cradle her against him.

She was crushed inside his capable hold, feeling safer than she'd ever felt before, unconcerned about her salt-sticky body or the mess that was her hair. Because Will . . . well, Will made everything better. She didn't have to care about her appearance, and that was liberating.

Her hands slid upward slowly, tangling into his hair. She was slipping, spiraling down an oiled slide into a vat of rich sweetness. And she was almost there, almost lost when he broke the kiss.

Hungry green eyes captured her as she dragged her lids open. He brushed his thumb across her mouth, but the spell was broken. Such a gentleman. Just like his grandfather.

Will pulled a deep breath and exhaled a shaky one. "You are the most captivatingly beautiful woman I've ever dated."

Trying to calm the tribal drum that had replaced her heartbeat, she opted for humor. If she gave herself to anything else, they'd end up . . . well, they'd end up doing something she wasn't sure she was ready for. "Who says I'm dating you?"

"You better be or this is completely scandalous." His fingertips played with the end of her wind-dried hair.

"I haven't had enough scandal in my life."

"Nor have I," he said in a playful tone. "Let's see how much trouble we can cause together."

His hands fell to her hips where one tug pulled her closer. Her bottom scooted across the deck, and a throaty giggle escaped her mouth. She pressed her hands against his chest, eyes widening. "Okay, maybe I'm *not* cut out for scandal."

He nuzzled against her neck, lips finding the hollow below her jaw. "I could help ruin you," he growled, hot breath scorching her skin. And oh, she *so* believed it. "Or, of course, there is the alternative."

"Okay, okay. I'm dating you." She pointed an index finger at him. "But only to avoid scandal."

He sank his hands into her hair.

There was an intensity about this man that drove her nuts. She was about to move out of its trajectory, put some space between them, but instead she found herself moving toward his mouth again. He seemed lost somewhere in his scrutiny of her hair and how it slid from her shoulders. But he caught her moving in. All his attention focused on her mouth until it pressed firmly to his. The kiss deepened, her fingers grazing the planes of his cheeks.

She broke the kiss quickly. It wasn't like her to be the aggressor. It wasn't like her at all. But something about him made her feel safe, like she *could* take the risk. Like she *had* to take the risk. He made her feel strong. Powerful. And power was a beautiful thing . . . when it wasn't misused.

"Don't do that," he whispered.

"What?" she managed, her own voice sounding foreign.

"Don't feel embarrassed about kissing me."

Was she really that easy to read? After all, this wasn't their first kiss. But this time, she'd surprised herself. "I'm not, I just . . . "

"Adrienne." He stood and pulled her up to meet him. "Can I admit something to you?"

"Anything." Blood surged into her stiff limbs, and she realized how long they'd been sitting on the deck.

"I'm scared."

She frowned—it seemed so out of place, this admission from this man. Out of place and raw.

"I'm scared of how I'm beginning to feel about you." His hands slid up and down her arms.

"I won't hurt you, Will." That much was true. She'd never hurt anyone intentionally, do to him what Eric had done to her.

"No, I'm not scared for me. I'm scared for you." He shook his head. "I know it doesn't make sense but I . . . I want you. Maybe more than I've ever wanted anything. The trouble is, I'm a really driven man. And I'm worried I'll get too selfish and not put your best interest before my own. You've gotten under my skin and in my blood."

Was he actually saying he was afraid he cared about her *too much*? This wasn't really a bad problem to have, unless . . . No. She stopped that train of thought.

Will read her silence and stepped away. Hands on the deck rail, he stared out at the water.

The light of a torch danced across his features. Adrienne tried to continue to gauge the words. He was actually saying he cared so much for her that his own selfishness could get in the way. If that confession was meant to make her turn and run, it did the opposite. His admission meant a desire to control it. So he had a natural bend toward selfishness. Big deal. He knew it, and better yet, he wanted to change it.

Adrienne stepped to him, fingertips grazing first over his back, then his arms. On her tiptoes, she glanced over his shoulder toward the dark water. Seeing nothing out there, she laid her head against his back and listened to him breathe.

Chapter 18

"I'm not too sure about the sushi," Pops said, looking down at the accumulation of odd and unusual ingredients for the sushi rolls Adrienne was preparing. "But that chicken smells divine."

"The sushi is just to nibble on. Will said you'd never tried it."

It was a Tuesday night, and she'd invited Will and Pops over for an Asian-infused gourmet dinner. Sara was back in Winter Garden, though her weekends in Bonita Springs were getting longer and longer.

Pops used a chopstick to lift the edge of a piece of sushi. Adrienne had taken a class at a chef school when she lived in Chicago. Weeknights without Sara seemed dull and boring, so she'd planned the sushi gathering, wanting to try out her culinary skills on someone who would appreciate her effort. The two Bryant men were the perfect victims.

At one time during her marriage, Adrienne had wanted to attend culinary school. Eric had laughed at her. His words still stung. *Culinary school? Why? So you can make gourmet meals for the cat? Please, Adrienne, be serious. The last thing in the world I want is a fry cook as a wife.* If Adrienne were a fry cook, she'd be proud of it. She thought of Leo and what a service he'd offered by feeding families all these years. It was a noble profession. As were so many Eric had always made fun of. How had she ever fallen in love with him?

Pops, still skeptical, used his finger to poke the seaweed. "There's a reason I've never tried it. Doesn't raw fish carry salmonella?"

"These are California rolls." She grinned over at him, placing a delicate mound of wasabi by the now completed roll. "No fish," she added when his quizzical look didn't change.

"That's good. Where I come from, raw fish has a different name."

Wiping her hands on her apron. "What name?"

"We call it bait."

"Funny, Pops."

He pointed to the green pyramid. "That's guacamole?"

"No, wasabi. It's very hot Japanese horseradish."

"I thought you'd jumped to a different continent." Pops really did seem younger than when she'd first met him. Ah, what love could do. Her back patio was lit with torches, and their light flashed now and then into the kitchen window, catching her attention. Soft music floated from the living room, completing the atmosphere. The scent of roasting chicken and fresh rosemary filled the house.

Adrienne checked the contents of the oven, lifting the tinfoil and peeking beneath; then she attacked the refrigerator.

Will stepped behind her. "What are you looking for?"

"Soy sauce." She rummaged through the doors like a raccoon. "I must be out."

"I'll go get some," Will said, reaching for his car keys. "Want to ride along, Pops?"

The older man shot a glance over to Adrienne, still tucked in the fridge. She was mumbling about mustard, mayo, minced garlic.

"No," Pops said, "I'll just stay here."

Once Will was gone, Pops and Adrienne moved out to the back deck to wait for the chicken to finish cooking.

"Adrienne, I was hoping I'd get a chance to talk to you." A sailboat moved silently along the horizon and looked like it could drop off the edge of the world if it veered in the wrong direction.

She turned toward him. "What is it, Pops?"

"I've never really gotten the chance to thank you for all you've done for me." He added, "For us."

"I feel like I'm the one who has benefited from all that's happened." She leaned toward him. "I gained a wonderful set of friends."

"Well, we're all pretty fond of you." His gaze narrowed. "Especially Will."

"Pops, can I ask you something?"

He nodded.

"What happened between Will and his parents?"

The older man shrugged and shook his head, sadness entering his blue eyes. "Nothing happened. That's what's so frustrating about it. Will is an incredible young man. Will's parents are wonderful. Somewhere along the way, things just got strained."

"Would you tell me about them?"

He smiled. "Charles and Peg are ordinary people making an extraordinary difference. You know they're in Senegal?"

She nodded.

"Well, the area where they work used to have a child mortality rate of seventy percent."

She straightened. "That's awful."

"Yeah," he agreed. "No fresh water. Between that and disease, the children didn't stand a chance." He let this sink in before he continued. "They began setting up medical teams first, sending over doctors, nurses, and medical personnel."

"They sound like amazing people. I hope I get to meet them someday."

"I'm sure you will." He thought for a moment. "They were supposed to be coming home in about a month, but won't be able to. There's a lot of unrest in the country right now, but . . . " He rubbed his chin. "I don't think that's why they cancelled."

"Why, then?"

"I don't know. I just know I'm distressed by it because I thought it would be a great opportunity for Will and Charles to sit down and talk."

Adrienne reached over and squeezed his hand. "Well, miracles can happen," she said, trying to lift the older man's spirits. "How can I learn more about them?"

"Lots of information is online. Also, I have some photos at the house."

"Thanks, Pops."

"No, it's you who deserves the thanks. You're like our personal guardian angel."

"You're the angel, Pops." She thought about the soldier Pops had been. "I'm honored to know you, Mr. Bryant."

This seemed to catch him off guard, and he straightened. "I'm honored as well." Age-weathered fingers rubbed against his thighs in the same manner she'd watched Will's do many times.

He winked over at her. "Life is about relationships. The rest is all gravy. Hey, maybe gravy would make that sushi taste good."

Adrienne laughed. "Oh, Pops."

They stayed on the back deck until the very last bits of sunlight drained from the horizon, and only the stars and torchlight lit the world around.

Will and Pops went home, and Adrienne left the dishes in the sink while she dug through William's letters in search of one. When she found it, she sat down at the table where Pops and Will had been just minutes before.

October 1944

Dear Gracie,

This may seem a strange topic, but it's been going over and over in my head. When I come home and we become man and wife, how many children will we have? We've never discussed it. I don't even know if you want a whole house full of kids or just one or two. Would you like a girl or a boy? I'd be happy with either. A little princess who looks like you. A boy I can toss a ball with and take fishing.

For a bunch of men in a foreign land with a job to do, we sure do talk about home. No, not talk, we dream. We dream with our eyes wide open and our hearts bare. We dream out loud, Gracie, and though a lot of teasing and ribbing goes on here, we don't tease each other about that. There's nothing funny about a soldier trying to remember home.

Come to think of it, we do harass Rick. He swears he's going to marry Marlene Dietrich. Says he met her once in California. She was hiding under an awning in a downpour.

He says the two of them had quite a nice time waiting out the storm.

I guess that's what we're all doing, isn't it? Waiting out the storm.

I'm ready to build a life with you, Grace. Ready to hear the sound of babies crying, children laughing. Ready to smell fresh bread baking in the kitchen and fresh fish frying in the skillet. Think about it, Grace. When this is over, we'll build a life around our dreams.

A boy, I think. Yes. I can see us having a boy.

Your future husband,
William

Adrienne pressed a hand to her heart. All those years ago, Pops had wanted a son. She retrieved her laptop from the front closet. She'd started storing it there after having to have sheetrock dust removed from her PC by a computer repair shop in town.

While it booted up, she thought of Pops and the son he spoke of in the letter, the son he knew he'd have, only it would be with a different woman than Grace. She narrowed her search to Africa and typed in "Charles and Peg Bryant." Her computer screen illuminated the kitchen with a warm but mechanical glow as she studied photos of the couple.

Will favored his father but had his mother's wavy, dark hair. They were an attractive couple and seemed most alive in the pictures that sported a dozen dark-headed, dark-skinned children. Adrienne studied the schoolhouse. It looked like concrete, with holes for windows and doors. Special attention was given to photo after photo of the water reservoir and villagers filling everything from bowls to gourds with the clear liquid. Once she reached the bottom of the page, the good feeling dissolved. Concern drew her brows together as she read the words *Charles and Peggy Bryant's funding has been cut in half. This was effective in January; however, they have continued their work with little interruption. If you'd like to donate to this important cause, contact us.*

Could that be why they weren't able to come back for Pops's birthday? Adrienne tapped her index finger on her bottom lip. Of course, she should leave this alone. It wasn't her place—as Will was always so quick to remind her—to get involved.

Adrienne stared at her kitchen counters, wondering what two airline tickets from Africa might cost. Her gaze fell to the granite samples stashed in the corner. She let out a long, agonizing sigh. Granite probably wasn't that great after all. She chewed on the inside corner of her mouth. Did she really want granite or was she just getting it because it was the counter choice du jour? But she knew the answer. She had wanted granite countertops since she'd taken the gourmet cooking class.

While struggling with the choice that lay in front of her, Adrienne was reminded of something she'd once read. "When one is confronted with a random act of kindness that is neither expected nor ordinary, one is obligated to meet that kindness and exceed it if possible."

She squared her shoulders, smiled to herself, and typed in "International Airlines."

After getting the ticket prices, she looked up the number and was now speaking to a Peace Corps representative.

"I'm interested in information about a couple in Africa. Their names are Charles and Peggy Bryant." After being connected to the right person, Adrienne asked when the Bryants were planning to come back to the States.

"The Bryants will not be stateside for nearly a year."

Adrienne could hear the woman typing something on the other end of the line.

"Actually, they put in a request for a trip next month; however, due to funding, they withdrew the request."

Adrienne's heart began to beat harder. "Would it be too late if they still wanted to make the trip?"

There was silence on the other end of the line for a moment. "You mean, if enough money were to come in to cover the tickets? No, it wouldn't be too late. We encourage our people to get back to the States when they can."

"Is there a way you can find out if they still want to come?"

"Yes. Are you interested in giving a monetary gift toward their trip?"

"No, ma'am." Adrienne threw one last look over at the granite samples in the corner. Strangely, the desire to have a granite countertop had lost much of its previous luster. "I'd like to pay for their entire trip home."

Silence again, but only for a moment. "That's very generous of you!" the woman stammered. "I can contact them by e-mail today."

Adrienne could hear the smile the woman was undoubtedly wearing. She smiled too, feeling more fulfillment than granite countertops could ever give her.

The two women made arrangements to speak the following day. By then she would know whether the Bryants would still make the trip.

The first call from Peg Bryant came late at night. "Is this Adrienne Carter?"

"Yes, it is." The gentle hum in the receiver confirmed the far-away call. Adrienne had just finished replacing a section of rotten wood she'd discovered in the back of a kitchen cupboard, and her hands and hair were dotted with sawdust from the project.

"This is Peg. Peg Bryant."

"Hello." Quickly forgetting the dust trail she left as she went, Adrienne settled into her rocking chair in the living room. The one Will had so comfortably rested in. It really was a great chair. Great house. Filled now with people and life. Parties and plans. "I feel like I know you, Peg. I've studied the pictures of you and Charles online."

"It's wonderful to get the chance to talk to you, Adrienne. We are so looking forward to coming home, and you alone made it possible."

Adrienne smiled.

"We receive letters from Pops regularly. He can't say enough about you." The phone line crackled, and for a horrible instant, Adrienne thought the conversation would be cut short.

"He's very special. But honestly, since Sara has come back into his life, I'm surprised he says anything about me."

There was a pause. Did Peg and Charles not know about Sara?

"I'm sorry, Adrienne. Got distracted there for a second. Yes, Sara. He is quite fond of her."

The phone line buzzed and crackled. Adrienne gripped the receiver tightly as if she were able to stabilize the voice coming through the miles. Peg continued on. "I mainly wanted to tell you thank you. We're looking forward to meeting you."

"If it's okay, I'll plan to pick you up at the airport. Don't want to spoil the surprise for Pops . . . or for Will," she added as an afterthought.

"I can't wait to get there."

"It won't be long now. Thanks so much for calling, Peg."

Adrienne hung up and hoped the next five weeks would pass quickly. She wasn't planning to tell Will his parents were coming.

When the doorbell rang, Adrienne jumped. She wasn't expecting anyone, so she rose, hand to her heart, and paused at the window to glance outside. What she saw made her mouth drop open. She slung the door open. Gerbera daisies filled her vision. Somewhere behind them was a delivery person, but all she could see were two arms cradling the vase and legs as if the bouquet had grown limbs.

"Adrienne Carter?" The voice was strained.

"Yes!" Before he could say more, she took the bouquet from him.

The flowers brought the room to life with the vibrant orange, deep red, and sunny yellow of the Gerbera daisies. Adrienne placed them on the dark wood end table adjacent to her rocking chair, her new favorite place to sit. In the bunch, she found a small card. It read, "For you, honeybee."

They were from Will. Whatever was his preoccupation with bees, she didn't know. She only hoped that after five weeks' time, he wouldn't be nursing a nasty sting.

"I think you need more flowers," Will said, stepping inside her house. His gaze scanned from one side of the room to the other. "Yes. Definitely more flowers."

"You're spoiling me. A girl could get used to this." She closed the door behind him and turned in case he wanted to kiss her. Which had become his habit. A lingering kiss, hands warm and firm against her hips.

"I'm hoping a girl does." He moved in and with one deep sweep of his head stole her breath and weakened her knees. It was almost enough to frighten away the anxiety growing with each passing day.

"Help yourself to coffee. I've got to rinse out a paintbrush. Be right back." She floated upstairs on the wings of his hello kiss, pushing away the thoughts that nibbled at her. Truth was, Adrienne was torn. On one hand, excitement fueled her work. She'd remodeled the upstairs guest bathroom with touches of the vibrant colors inspired by designs from Africa. Charles and Peg were coming. She had been e-mailing them on a regular basis but only heard from them once a week, Internet access not being as easy for them as for her. Arrangements were made. She'd pick them up at the airport late Friday night. They'd stay with her until Saturday, the day of the party. Neither Will nor Pops knew they were coming. In this, there was method to her madness. Perhaps Will would be tenderhearted, getting to see them unexpectedly. Maybe he wouldn't have time to sort through all the different ways to avoid talking to his father. Maybe he wouldn't kill Adrienne for interfering again.

Water swirled in her bathroom sink as she rinsed the brush. She knew there was a strong possibility this would blow up in her face. It was a huge gamble. So far, things had worked out in her schemes, but each time she felt more and more like she was on the chopping block. Though this scared her, there was something that scared her even worse. The last time Will got mad at her for interfering, something in Adrienne's heart had snapped. Something deep within her had changed. There was a disconnected resolve she didn't particularly like but couldn't eradicate.

Will is not like Eric, she whispered to her mirror reflection. But in the deepest part of her heart, she knew she was almost done giving him chances to prove that.

Other than that nasty little revelation, things between her and Will were great. They had met regularly to finish the party plans over the past five weeks. The party planning was just an excuse to get together. They both knew it. They had agreed on every detail—even Sammie catering the bash—and had grown more and more excited as the day approached.

Adrienne bounced down the stairs to find him examining her clipboard list of things to do before the party. For a hot second, she panicked, but she breathed a sigh of relief when she remembered she kept the other list in the drawer, *the list of things to do before picking up Charles and Peg.*

"Can you stay for lunch?" she asked, slipping the clipboard from him.

"Wish I could." He took it back, tossed it onto the couch, and pulled Adrienne into his arms. "I'm just dropping off some things at the Bonita Springs bank branch. Thought I'd drop by."

She liked this: his wanting to see her so badly, he dropped by when he was supposed to be working.

"The party is almost here, and Pops doesn't have a clue," he said.

The party is almost here. Those words dropped into her stomach and burned like acid.

His hands laced together at the small of her back. "Well, I better get going." With a long exhale, he started to release her.

Adrienne grabbed him by the shoulders, tipped her head back, and pressed her mouth to his.

For a moment, he must have been surprised, but settled deeper and deeper into the kiss until his hands were roaming her back and tangling in the loose strands of her hair. Finally, he broke the kiss. "If you're trying to get rid of me, you're failing."

She shook her head. "No, Will. I'm not trying to get rid of you." Adrienne's heart pounded from more than just the kiss. She needed to tell him about his parents. Now was the time. This might be her last chance. "I just ... "

He tilted her chin with his thumb and finger. "I know. You love the flowers, but you're not used to someone spoiling you, right?"

She swallowed the words she needed to speak. "Right."

Will kissed the tip of her nose. "I'll see you Saturday."

She nodded and followed him to the door, knowing that if things played out the way she expected, she might never get to kiss him again.

By Friday evening, everything was set. She'd picked up Sara early that morning and zipped to the airport that evening. Adrienne's special touches in the upstairs bath were not lost on Charles and Peg. Charles had gone on and on about how the space looked, and even grabbed and hugged her. The two were loving, touchy people, reminding Adrienne of her own father. Now the three ladies sat on the back deck, listening to soft island music and the sound of crashing waves.

Sara stood up from her beach chair. "I'd love to stay up late with you two, but tomorrow is a big day. I need my beauty sleep."

"I won't be far behind you, Sara." Adrienne squeezed her hand as she walked past.

"Sleep well, Sara," Peg added. They watched as she disappeared into the house.

"What's it like?" Adrienne asked, handing Peg a cup of tea. "To live so far from home?"

Peg sipped the drink as the bright moon danced on the water. "At first, I cried all the time."

Adrienne stopped what she was doing and looked directly at her. "Really?"

Peg nodded and ran her fingertips through her wavy, dark hair. It was cut into a short bob that reached her shoulders when she shrugged. Her legs, tan and lean, stretched in front of her on the footstool. Crossed at the ankle, she seemed very much at home in the hard-backed wooden chair. "Being so far away from Will was gut wrenching in the beginning. I worried about him constantly."

Adrienne smiled, wondering what that would be like—creating a being that is an expression of both you and the person you love and watching him grow. For a moment, she remembered a trip to the park when she'd seen a little girl fall off the monkey bars. Adrienne had watched the girl's mother clean the wound, wiping her own tears as much as her child's. What was it like to love someone more than life itself?

"But now," Peg continued, "now, when I'm there, it feels like I'm home. And when I'm here, it feels like I'm home."

Adrienne liked this woman with her sweet, tender spirit and her spine of steel. Every now and then, with a certain glint in her eye, she looked like Will. "Will favors you," Adrienne said when she realized she'd been staring. "I didn't see it at first, but he does."

"I don't see it myself, but people have always said that." Peg thought a moment. "He acts like me too."

"Really?"

She nodded, eyes twinkling. "We're organized. Particular. We're planners." She leaned over the table and lowered her voice. "Everything Charles is not."

Adrienne remembered the airport as Charles had lumbered along, haphazardly fumbling with the same number of suitcases Peg was effortlessly rolling behind her. He had lost his wallet and then found it, only to discover his passport was missing. He found the passport and noticed his driver's license was gone. Once everything was back in order and in its proper place, they were able to leave. By the time they got to the car, his wallet had gone missing again. Of course, this, coupled with his cheery disposition about it, made him that much more endearing.

"So opposites do attract?" Adrienne said.

"For us, yes. I adore him. And I can beat him at basketball," she threw in as an afterthought. "That's always good for the female ego."

"You two are very fortunate to have each other."

"We are." Peg studied her. "It's also quite a blessing that you have come into our lives, Adrienne."

"Well . . . "—she squirmed—"I don't know that it's *that* much of a blessing."

"I do," Peg said regally. "There are no coincidences. Everything happens for a reason. It was no sheer accident you came into Will's life."

Uncomfortable now, Adrienne toyed with the edge of her cup, wondering how everyone would feel tomorrow. "Pops and Sara were reunited. There's no doubt that was meant to be."

They both pivoted as the back door opened. Charles's gentle face popped out. "Honey, have you seen my reading glasses?"

Peg reached for his hand. "Bottom left corner of your suitcase." One quick squeeze, and she unwound her fingers from his.

"How about my planner?"

"Jacket pocket," she returned.

"And my toothbru—"

"In the brown carry-on."

He gave her a smile that conveyed every emotion from "I love you" to "I could never survive a day without your help." It was a look Adrienne knew was reserved only for his wife.

When he disappeared into the house, Adrienne grinned. "Wow, you really are organized."

Peg nodded. "Where were we? Oh yes, I was getting ready to tell you not to forget there's a destiny in all of this for you." Seeming to sense the gravity of her words, she laughed.

Peg spoke of destiny as if she had a window into it. Adrienne wished she could spend more time with her. *Make tonight count,* her mind teased. *By tomorrow, you'll be saying good-bye to all of them.*

Chapter 19

Sammie dropped off the birthday cake. She'd be back within an hour with the food. Guests were going to arrive at noon, and Will was planning on getting there by ten o'clock. Adrienne gripped the kitchen counter until her fingers ached. For the thousandth time, her gaze skittered to the wall clock. Knots tightened in her stomach each time the minute hand circled. She wasn't in a party mood.

She should have told him.

This was a rotten deception that could be looked at as nothing but a rotten deception. For five weeks, she'd met him for coffee or lunch, all the while knowing his parents were coming, but not breathing a word of it. She tried to scrub the frown from between her brows and hoped for the best. After all, it was Will who wanted his parents to come in the first place. He had been upset that they weren't coming. So maybe . . .

No. She was grasping at straws. Whether he'd be happy or angry, their being here was beside the point. She'd known and she hadn't told him. There was going to be a reckoning for that. Her eyes flashed to the clock again.

And the time for reckoning was upon her.

She'd just finished cleaning up from breakfast when the doorbell rang. It was 10:05. She took a moment to brace herself. It was just enough time for Peg to get to the door.

"Will!" Peg screeched and threw her arms around her son.

Adrienne peeked around the kitchen wall, as Will stood frozen, arms flat against his sides.

"What are you doing here?" he finally managed, a smile beginning to form.

Peg motioned behind her. "This is all Adrienne's doing," she said excitedly.

Adrienne swallowed and slunk back farther behind the wall.

"Really?" His eyes followed his mother's gesture.

Adrienne watched the smile disappear completely as his gaze bore through her.

Peg was dragging him into the house, pulling him to the couch, and chatting about everything from how hot it had been in Africa to how Will looked thin—had he been eating right? "You aren't living on coffee, are you? You know you can't skip meals and stay healthy."

Adrienne leaned her head against the wall, wondering where the regal, majestic woman she'd had tea with had gone. The doting, exuberant Peg rambled on and on, and honestly, Adrienne just wanted her to shut up and for this whole mess that she, Adrienne, had created to go away.

She listened from the safety of the kitchen as mother and son talked. Will was genuinely happy to see his mom; that much was obvious. She could hear it in his voice. But the ten minutes she worked in her kitchen only increased her dread about the inevitable confrontation.

Adrienne snapped to full attention when she heard Peg say, "I'm going to go let your father know you're here. He can't wait to see you!"

"Great," Will said, disguising most of the tension in his voice. "I'll go to the car to get the chairs I brought over." Then, loud enough for her to hear and cringe, he added, "Maybe *Adrienne* could help me."

She shuffled out of the kitchen and followed him, a prisoner led down death row. The late morning sun heated her flesh. Rather than walk beside him, she fell in line behind Will—away from all that anger on his face. At the trunk of the car, he turned on her. "What's the matter with you?"

She thought she'd be hurt by his words but found she wasn't. A seabird flew above them, its call echoing off her ears. She wanted to tune into that—the bird, the sky, anything but Will. He'd reacted exactly the way she thought he would. Exactly the way *Eric* would.

When she didn't answer, his anger flared.

"How long have you known they were coming?" He waited only a moment. Through gritted teeth, he asked again, "How long?"

She wouldn't lie. For stability, she rested her hip against his car. "Five weeks."

He threw his hands up. "And what—you forgot to mention it?"

"I was afraid you would be upset."

"Oh, I am upset!" His eyes narrowed on her. "Do you really think that every time there is a problem, you can just play God and make it all work out? You need a reality check." He stared down her road as if he couldn't stomach looking at her.

But rather than feel hurt by it, she got mad. *Mad* was a fairly new sensation for Adrienne, filled with power and control. Her hand rested against her stomach where the seed had first taken root and now had grown to full-fledged fury. "They're here for Pops. And if you don't like it, too bad. You're the one that wanted them here, remember? You were mad they weren't coming; now you're mad they did come. Maybe it's *you* that needs a reality check." She poked his chest with her index finger.

Several shades of surprise appeared across his face. She'd met his anger with an equal amount of her own. It took him a minute to grasp. A moment later, his shock dissolved.

The muscle in his jaw flexed as Adrienne stared him down.

"I'm going to get through this day because it's for Pops, but I swear, you have no idea how much trouble you're causing." He turned from her and started pulling lawn chairs from the back of his car.

Adrienne was only barely aware of his motions. His words echoed back to her over and over. *You have no idea how much trouble you're causing.* Is that really what he'd just said to her? Those were the exact words she'd heard from Eric so many times.

Will was on the front porch now. He carried two chairs and dragged another behind him. That far away, he was out of earshot, but it didn't stop her words. "You don't have to worry, Will. I'll never cause you trouble again."

Even though there was an agonizing amount of tension between Will and Adrienne, the party came off without a hitch. Pops had been overwhelmed by the group that included his only son and daughter-in-law. Father and son came together in a warm embrace as Pops took Charles's face in his hands as if his son were an apparition. Once convinced, Pops hugged him again, reaching also for Peg, the daughter-in-law he loved so dearly. There was such excitement in the room, no one noticed the hurtful looks that passed between the two who had made it all possible. She steered clear of him, and he returned the favor.

The house and backyard were decorated in Polynesian style to perfection, complete with music and torches that lined a golden path to the ocean. By all standards, it was over the top. No detail had been overlooked. Will, staring at the tiny umbrella topping his fruity frozen drink, wished he could have enjoyed it. His gaze was fixed on the ocean, calm with small, rolling waves that tossed water and sand onto the shoreline. Yes, he'd like to be enjoying the party. Instead, he slipped outside to take a walk. Stepping off the back deck, he threw a glance at the house where Adrienne and family, *his family*, were sitting together laughing and talking. He was furious at her, of course. But, sadly he had to admit, he was pretty furious at himself as well. He thought back to the look in her eye as he'd told her she shouldn't interfere. First, her anger had met his. But after that, there came a point when she seemed completely dead to his words. A veil fell over her face that took all emotion with it. He couldn't even remember what he'd said that had spawned her reaction. But that look was unmistakable. It was complete resolve. Utter detachment.

And it terrified him. In the time since he'd known her, Adrienne had become a driving force in his life, a force he enjoyed and wanted to maintain. But the woman had to learn to mind her own business. It was a trust issue. He didn't easily give his trust. And he certainly didn't extend it to those who trampled it.

Pops's voice drifted from the back patio. "Will?"

He turned, took one look at the smile on Pops's face, and fought the urge to forgive Adrienne. With a hand pressed to his knee, Pops descended the stairs and stepped out to his grandson. "Beautiful day."

Will nodded. "You look good, Pops."

"Having Charles and Peg here was a wonderful surprise." Pops bent at the waist and found a shell of respectable size. He lobbed it into the water.

"All Adrienne's doing. She didn't let me know." He grabbed a similar-sized shell and sent it flying into the waves, both men raising a hand to their foreheads to shield their eyes as they tried to gauge the distance.

"Well, you can't blame her for that. You're a bit grouchy about your folks." Pops glanced at him from the corner of his eye. "You seemed happy to see them."

Will forced a breath. "Yeah. I am. You seem happy too, Pops. Does Sara have anything to do with that?"

His face turned crimson. "Yes, sir."

"What are you going to do about it?"

Pops gave his grandson his full attention.

"You love her, don't you?"

Pops's hands dipped deep into his pockets. Will heard change jingling. "Yes, I do."

"She loves you too."

A deep frown set into Pops's brow. "Sweet Sara fell in love with a teenager. I'm not him anymore. She fell in love with the past. Can't build a future on a resurrected dream."

Will scratched his head. "So, you're gonna let her get away?"

"No. I just want to know she can love this old man."

Will draped an arm around his shoulder. "Who wouldn't love this old man?"

"Come on inside. I'm getting ready to cut the cake. Thank goodness they didn't have candles, or it'd outshine the sun."

Side by side, they returned to the house, the sun's glow heating their backs. One thing Will couldn't escape was the joy his grandfather felt having Sara in his life. Adrienne had certainly gotten that one right. Will never expected Pops would find love again. No matter how angry Will got at Adrienne, she'd made that relationship possible. Nothing could take that away.

The timer on the oven ticked away minutes to another batch of mini-tarts. Adrienne stared out the window absently. The noise from the party seemed far off now. Someone was saying something behind her.

"Are you all right?" Sammie asked.

"Yeah," she managed.

Her friend placed her hands on Adrienne's shoulders and gently turned her. She smiled softly. "You're a terrible liar."

Adrienne nodded. "Will you help me get through the rest of the day? It's agonizing. Worse than I imagined."

Sammie nodded knowingly. "Of course. Come on." She motioned toward the living room. "Pops wants to make an announcement."

Adrienne breathed deep in an effort to lift some of the heaviness. She painted on her happy face and stood just inside the room, letting the doorjamb shore her up.

Most everyone was sitting or standing in the living room, where the smell of fresh paint was all but drowned out by the scent of party food. Plates and cups rested on knees. Will and his parents sat on the couch, three sets of wavy hair for her to stare at. That was a relief—at least she wouldn't have to look at his face. Sammie squeezed her shoulder, coaxing her forward, but Adrienne planted her feet and wouldn't budge. She remained at the doorway of the kitchen. In the room, but not part of it.

Her gaze floated across the scene. People chatting, laughing, joking, the beautiful muted roar that only comes from family gatherings. And it was all here, in her house, a place that was crumbling just a few months before. The room itself swelled with pride. This house was meant to be filled with people. Pops's voice drew her attention.

"First," he said, gesturing toward Adrienne, "I want to thank Adrienne for hosting this wonderful birthday party for me." He began to clap, and the room joined him. Will didn't move.

"And Sammie for the best food I've eaten in a while." Pops thought a moment. "It is my party, so would you mind indulging me?"

Everyone smiled. Charles spoke, "Go ahead, Dad."

Peg set her cup on the coffee table and took Charles's hand.

Pops rubbed the bridge of his nose. "I'm an old man. I've lived through a war, buried a spouse, and seen my share of heartache." He blinked several times, the room silent enough that one could almost hear the whisper of lashes meeting weathered skin. "But when I look around this room, I feel I must be the most blessed man on Earth." His gaze fell on Sara. "And I've always thought that life should be lived. It's not a spectator sport. Even at my age, life has so much to offer."

Sara nodded in agreement.

"A few minutes ago, my grandson reminded me of that."

He pulled a handkerchief from his back pocket. "Sixty-some years ago, I met two lovely young women, Grace and Sara."

Adrienne's eyes shot to Sara. She could actually see the older woman tense. Splitting her glances between the two people, she wondered why Pops would bring up Gracie, especially here, knowing how responsible Sara felt for Grace's death. Sara tried to smile but was shrinking, old fingers lacing together in the chair where she sat board straight. Her silver-white hair was swept to the side, and her legs elegantly crossed at the ankle. She could be posing for a portrait, if not for the air of apprehension hovering around her.

"That Sara." Pops shook his head. "Oh, she was a spitfire. No fear in sweet Sara. No fear at all. And I'm hoping that's how she still is. Because . . . "

No one breathed as he crossed the room and took her by the hand. "Because I'm getting ready to ask her to marry me."

Sara tilted forward, and Adrienne wondered if she would topple out of the chair. The room's atmosphere grew heavy with anticipation. Sara withdrew her hand from William's and stood.

Horrified eyes found Adrienne's. As much as the older woman silently pleaded for Adrienne to rescue her, Adrienne silently pleaded for Sara not to make a monumental mistake. *Say yes, Sara. Say yes. You two can sort out the details later.*

Sara smoothed her skirt, gaze landing firmly on William. "I . . ."

Sara, this is what you want. A chance to spend the rest of your life with the man you love. Don't throw it away over shame about the letters.

Pops's head tilted forward, awaiting her response.

Everyone else in the room seemed frozen, waiting for Sara to speak; Adrienne clenched her teeth hard. *Please, Sara. Please.*

"I . . . I can't." A head of straight white hair swung back and forth as if the word weren't enough. "I'm sorry, William." Her voice cracked on the last word.

Pops staggered a step backward as Sara rushed past him to the stairs. She gripped the banister and hurried up, the clomping of her feet on each step the only sound other than a mournful sigh from Pops.

Moments ticked past. When Adrienne turned her gaze to Pops, Will was standing at his side, a firm grip on the man. But Will's eyes were burning holes through Adrienne. She pressed into the wall at her back, wishing she could melt into it.

Pops rubbed a hand over his face. "That, uh, didn't go quite the way I anticipated."

When his lips pressed together hard, and he fought the tears that threatened, Adrienne rushed forward. "Pops, Sara is just—"

Will reached out and took a firm hold on her arm. His tone, a quiet roar. "That's enough, Adrienne."

She pulled away from him, ignoring his command. "Just give her some time. She needs—she just needs a little time."

Will stepped in to block her. "I said, that's enough."

There was a deadly threat in his voice. Pops glanced between the two, both trying to protect him, both failing and ready to come to blows. "Will, I believe I might like to head on home now." He drew away from Will and shuffled toward the front door.

"Sure, Pops."

Will threw an accusatory look in his parents' direction. "Come on."

Charles and Peg had stood. Peg brushed a tear from her cheek. "You want us to go—"

He pointed a finger at Pops's back, a threat still evident. "He needs you."

Charles nodded. "I'll go gather our things."

"No. We're leaving now. We'll get your stuff tomorrow. If you can sleep in a tent in the middle of the jungle, I think you can manage one night without your suitcase."

Moments later, Adrienne's house was empty of the Bryant family. No one bothered to close the front door. What did it matter? Doors were meant to be open. Except the doors to the heart. Those should remain shut at all costs.

Chapter 20

*W*ill worked his dive gear into his bag, wishing the deep burn in his stomach would go away. He'd sat up late with Pops, his mom and dad alongside as the four of them wasted the hours until bedtime. He had to admit, his parents knew how to care for someone hurting. His mom made tea and served it while the men assembled on the front porch. Pops had removed his watch and tapped it against his leg, held it to his ear, then tapped it again. Charles took the timepiece and used a pocket knife to open the back. He worked methodically, cleaning out dust and then rewinding the watch. When he finished, he handed it back to Pops. Pops remained quiet, but that was okay. There was more power, more strength, Will realized, in quiet comfort than in words, when the company was comprised of those most loved.

Yes, his mom and dad had their strengths. Will glanced at the house from his driveway once his dive gear was packed and loaded into his trunk. He considered going back in and making sure Pops would be okay. But a niggling little voice inside told him to let his mom and dad have some time alone with Pops. It'd be good for all of them.

Heartache was heartache, no matter the age of the recipient. Sara remained on the back deck for most of the morning. Her eyes were swollen and red. Adrienne figured a sleepless night was the culprit. She hadn't slept much herself and had repeatedly gone to Sara's door. She never knocked, just listened for the sound of the older woman breathing. Once, in the wee hours of the morning, she had stood there several minutes, listening to the old woman cry.

"Would you like more coffee, Sara?" she asked, sticking her head out the back door.

Haunted eyes trailed down to the full cup in her hands. "Oh, no dear."

Adrienne stepped out. "I'm sure that's cold. Let me take it for you."

Frail fingers lifted the cup to Adrienne. "You were right. I should have told him."

Adrienne swallowed hard and dropped quietly into the chair adjacent to Sara.

"But I never expected . . . a marriage proposal. That changed everything."

The full cup was abandoned on the side table as Adrienne reached to take Sara's hand. "How did things change?"

She brushed the soft white hair from her face. "We were building a friendship, maybe even falling in love, but . . . you can't go into a marriage with a lie like that between you. And now it's too late." Sara focused her attention down the beach.

Adrienne followed her gaze and noticed the man tossing a bait net into the water. It was mesmerizing, really. The way he folded and draped the net over his shoulder, how it spun outward and into a perfect circle as he cast. "I'm sure the two of you will work things out and get beyond this."

Sara pivoted to look at her. "There's no getting beyond this. I ruined it again. Second chances are wonderful if you know what to do with them."

Adrienne had no more words of encouragement, so she stayed quiet.

"Don't let love slip through your fingers, Adrienne. When the net is cast upon you, don't get spooked and scurry away." Sara turned back to the beach. "It's a lonely ocean when you're all alone."

Adrienne's heart shattered into a few more jagged pieces. So much so, she barely heard the doorbell. Heavily laden with Sara's grief, she ambled to the door. Shock registered first in her fingers and toes, then shot a path directly to her heart. "Will," she whispered.

He was a statue, eyes cool, body board straight. "Wasn't my idea to come. Pops wants to see Sara." Adrienne moved out of the way as Pops, then Charles, and then Peg moved past her. Will was last.

Adrienne forced her attention to Pops, not Will. "She'll be so happy to see you. She's out on the back deck."

"Thank you." With his shoulders hunched forward, he shuffled to the back of the house.

Adrienne searched Peg's face for an answer.

"He feels he owes her an apology. Leaving the way he did."

Beside his mother, Will made a disgusted sound. "She's the one who stormed off."

Peg whipped around to face her son. "William Jefferson Bryant!"

Adrienne's eyes rounded.

"Yes, she stormed off. After a *proposal*. A *marriage* proposal, Will. You may not understand, but for women, that's a very big deal. Monumental, in fact. No matter how old you are."

A dimple in Will's cheek quirked, his jaw muscle furiously working.

Oh dear. And Adrienne thought *she'd* had a rough morning.

When Pops and Sara stood to walk down the beach, Adrienne offered coffee to the others left behind. She could only imagine the conversation going on outside, but she knew she had to tell them about the letters. Sara was breaking the news to Pops—of this she was certain. But she wouldn't force the old woman to repeat it again. So she explained. The fact that Grace wouldn't write. And how Sara had feared William wouldn't have the will to survive without the hope letters from home could bring. All of it. Charles and Peg took it in with little response, but Will's frown became a scowl. "Did you know this the whole time?"

"No, Will," Adrienne huffed. "I found out the night of the military celebration. Sara knew she'd have to tell him one day, but she thought they were still building a friendship."

His chin jutted forward. "A friendship based on lies."

Adrienne's anger flared. "Look, life isn't as easy as you seem to think. And love complicates everything. Sara made a mistake." She stepped toward him, squaring off and daring him to stop her. "She has been in love with him since she was fourteen years old. Do you know why Sara never married?"

Will swallowed and leaned back, out of the trajectory of her words that seemed to be pelting him like little poison darts.

Adrienne took his movement as an invitation to take one more step toward him. "She never got over Pops. Her whole life. Sixty years of loving a man she thought she'd never have." When she realized she'd moved so close that their bodies were nearly touching, she pulled a breath and took a step back.

Will remained silent.

"She was terrified of losing him again, and if you can't understand that, you're far more heartless than I ever imagined."

Will opened his mouth, but no words came. He rubbed a hand across his chin and muttered, "Okay."

Peg reached up from the couch and took her son by the hand. "You can't protect Pops from everything."

Adrienne watched him flash a tiny smile at his mother.

After what felt like an eternity—but couldn't have been more than twenty minutes—Pops and Sara returned. Unable to read their body language from a distance, Adrienne sighed with relief when they topped the beach steps and Pops's hand slid into Sara's.

He paused in the living room, resting a palm on the fireplace mantle. "I've never been a brilliant man. Average, I'd call myself. But I'm not ashamed of that. Right proud, I am. I've made it my life goal to be a good man. That's about all. The good Lord has always smiled down on me. And once again, I find myself obtaining what I don't deserve. Years back, two girls moved here from North Carolina with their momma.

"Many a lazy afternoon was spent on the water. Swimming or fishing," he said.

He glanced back at the others. "I know I'm rambling, but it's important to me that you all understand." No one moved or made a sound.

"I joined the Army in '42. And someone from home began to write to me." As if suddenly reliving the war, Pops gripped the mantle more tightly to stabilize himself. "Unless you've experienced war, you can't imagine it—the uncertainty, the stark reality of death that accompanies every breathing moment. We men had only each other. We fought for each other, we even cried for each other"—his gaze fell to the floor—"and sometimes we died for each other. Maybe that's why the letters were so important to me. It reminded me that there was another world. I loved the men I served with, loved them like brothers. We were connected on a level only men in battle can understand. But I'd joined that war for another purpose. And as I would read the letters from home, I was reminded of that. I was reminded about the scent of magnolia in the summertime, blackberries in the spring, the ocean water crashing against the sand. And as I read those letters, I fell in love. Love for real." His gaze went to Sara again. "Do you hear me, Sara? I fell in love with you sixty years ago through the letters."

She no longer hid the tears. With one blink, they silently slipped down her cheeks.

"And that's why I want my family to hear me when I ask this." He moved to her and took her hand, pulling her up into his arms. Once face to face, he said, "Sara, will you marry me?"

Her voice was shaky, but no one could mistake the words. "Yes—yes, I will."

Bittersweet happiness mingled with the pain of Adrienne's own personal loss. The two warring factions fought their way through her body. She chose to dwell on the happiness. It had all begun with a letter, a simple handwritten letter, faded from long ago, and a determination to right the wrongs of the past. Though there'd been devastating bumps in this rocky road, things were turning out beautifully for Sara and Pops. And horribly for her. Refusing to let herself wallow in it, she moved toward them, arms outstretched, and hugged the family she had to say good-bye to.

He'd wanted to leave Adrienne's house but was unable to get anyone on board with that plan. Everyone was all "Oooh-aaah, let's make wedding plans." Had they failed to remember this woman had lied to Pops? For years?

Will ran an angry hand through his hair and left the happy family inside. Storm clouds gathered on the horizon, a warning to remain on land. Wind kicked sand onto his legs as he cast a glance through the window, where he spotted Pops waltzing in the kitchen with a delighted Sara.

Okay, fine. Maybe Adrienne *did* have a better handle on what his family needed. Maybe he *didn't* always know what was best. Will picked up a shell. He examined it for a moment, then tossed it into the sea, just as Pops had done the day before.

Whether he wanted to admit it or not, Will knew that Adrienne was the best thing to ever walk into his life. If the two of them could just be airlifted to a secluded island, they'd have a shot. Will slipped his hands into his pockets and was strolling down the beach when his father's voice drifted out to him. Will closed his eyes.

"Wait up, Will," Charles said, trying to bridge the gap between them. He was smiling when he made it to his son. "Can I walk along with you?"

Will gestured around him. "It's a public beach."

Charles swallowed and let his gaze fall to the sand. His words were low, lacking the initial cheer. "I mean, would you mind company?"

Guilt shot through Will. This was his father. And he loved him. He just was so *angry* with him. "Sure, Dad. I'd like company," he managed, and almost meant it.

Charles knelt to examine a coconut washed up on shore. "I need to talk to you, Will." He rose and buried his hands in his own pockets, mimicking Will. Charles stared out to the horizon. "I've needed to for a long time."

Will bristled.

Charles' gaze moved to his son, tentatively. "Why are you so angry with me?"

Will could avert this discussion. He'd done it many times. But in the last couple of months he'd learned some things. And one of the biggest lessons was about things not always being as they appeared.

"Dad, it's not that I'm angry."

"No," Charles interrupted, uncharacteristically, "It is, but I don't know why."

Will stared at him. "Are you kidding?"

The look in Charles's eyes conveyed only confusion.

Will shook his head. "You ditched us, Dad. Not once, but twice."

Charles frowned, still not getting it.

"You left your family for people you don't even know. You did it once, and then when Pops needed you most, you did it again. For *strangers*, Dad."

The older man slowly turned from Will. Tears stung his eyes as he stared at the storm clouds.

Studying his face, Will could see the lines, now deeper than he remembered. How long had his dad had the streaks of white-gray hair that peppered his temples? Suddenly, his dad looked old. Frail. As if Will's confession had aged him twenty years right before his eyes.

Charles spoke, but it was barely more than a whisper. "I've never been good at sports," he said in a mumbling tone, and Will wondered if his dad had lost it. "I can't play basketball or baseball. Your mom beats me on the court."

Alarmed by his father's babbling, Will said, "What?"

But his dad was somewhere else, conversing with no one. "I'm a lousy fisherman. I get seasick when I even think about the water."

Will's tone drew his attention. "Dad," he said sharply, "what are you talking about?"

Charles turned to face him. "I've always been so proud of your relationship with my dad." He corrected himself. "I mean, it made me a bit uncomfortable, but not in a bad way. I just . . . " He lifted his shoulders and dropped them. "I just always felt like an outsider looking in. I envied your closeness. You're like a carbon copy of him. Baseball and all. I would probably be jealous if it weren't for the joy I get watching you two together."

Will tried to follow the conversation.

Charles straightened, chin tilting up. "My father and my son, closer than brothers."

In Will's entire life, he had never wondered how his relationship to Pops might make his dad feel. Charles Bryant was an intelligent man, but more bookish than physical. He couldn't hit a ball or catch a Frisbee. Those things just weren't natural for him. Fixing watches, though—well, that was in his power. And not just watches, but fixing computer programs and explaining the laws of physics so that a layperson could understand—that's what Charles was great at. Will and Pops, on the other hand, were good at any sport thrown their way. Guilt, once again, tickled its way through Will's system.

"When your grandma died, we were making arrangements to come home for good. I found out that you were planning on having Pops move in with you and—"

Will's anger was tempered only marginally. This wasn't a viable excuse. "And what, Dad? You just changed your plans? Yes, I wanted Pops to live with me, but you should have tried to stop me. You should have fought for him." That's what this was really about. His parents should have fought to keep Pops.

"Do you actually think you would have let me? Your mind was made up." He placed a hand on Will's shoulder. "Will, everyone has a mission in life. You and Pops being together is right. But"— he shook his head—"If I had known you resented it—"

Will cut him off. "I don't resent it. I love that Pops is with me. I just don't understand how you could leave him."

"When Pops found out we were making plans to return for good, he was angry. Our work in the field is very important to him. He said the people there needed us much more than he did. He said he'd never forgive us for coming back and leaving them. Reality set in, and I knew I really couldn't offer him very much. We don't share any of the same interests. I can't take him fishing or boating. I agonized over what to do. One night, I had a dream. I saw you and Pops walking to your boat. It might sound silly, but I knew what to do. I just knew."

Charles pulled in a ragged breath and picked up a clam shell. He dusted sand particles from it and flung it out into the water. It went a third of the distance Will's shell had. "I should have talked to you about it, though. I guess this is the hardest part of being stationed overseas." He turned to face his son. "A lot of people raise their families in the field. Many kids grow up that way and love it. They have two homelands. But we didn't want that for you. We wanted you to grow up near your grandparents, playing ball and going to movies with your friends. We weren't planning on going into the field until you were out of college, but you were so independent. You didn't seem like you needed us. Didn't seem like you had needed us since you were fourteen and got your first job. Your senior year, the opening came up. It was a year out, so you would be off at college. It just seemed like the right opportunity."

Why had Will never heard these things? He wasn't the ball and chain that kept his parents from leaving sooner. It was their love for him and Grandma and Pops that had kept him stateside. They wanted him to grow up here.

Charles placed both hands on Will's upper arms and stared at him with intense blue eyes. "If I had known how you felt . . . "

"I never knew some of your decisions were based on what was best for me. Dad, I'm so sorry."

His dad hugged him. "Well, Mom and I figured we'd only get five or six years in the field until we'd need to come home for good. But maybe we should have waited to leave in the first place."

"Why only five or six years?"

"Again, you're the timeline. We were going to wait until you were out of college. We figured the natural order of things would come into play. After college comes marriage and . . . " He watched his son. "You don't really think your mother is going to live thirty hours away from her grandbabies, do you?"

"Well, I've probably bought you some time." He pushed his fingers through his hair.

"Adrienne is quite an amazing woman, isn't she? I wouldn't give up on her," Will's father cast a glance at his son.

"She may have given up on me."

"Time will tell," Charles said. "Will, I'm really glad we talked."

"Me too, Dad. It changes everything." Will placed his arm around his father's shoulder, and they slowly walked back to the house, enjoying the warmth of the sun that illuminated the world around them.

As he stepped onto the back patio, finding the perfect vision of Adrienne, who looked up from the kitchen sink, another storm gathered, this one in the depths of her coffee-colored eyes.

Her mind was made up. As slow as molasses, resolve worked its way through her system and pushed out every thought of second chances. She'd watched Will and his father walk back into the house and could see the weight had lifted off both men's shoulders. Reunited. Which probably only meant one thing.

As he stepped into the kitchen, where she had been neatly tucked away, Adrienne turned to face him.

"Can I talk to you?" he asked.

Her head tilted back slightly—like she was readying for a punch. "Sure." She let him take her by the hand into the formal dining room that offered slightly more privacy than the busy kitchen.

He drew a breath. "You were right in getting Mom and Dad here."

The room was freshly painted, all but the floorboards where she'd run out of paint. It was hardly noticeable. You had to search to find the dark grimy area. But Adrienne knew it was there. And though the rest of the room looked gorgeous, filthy floorboards were all she could see.

His eyes began to plead when he saw her detached expression remain unchanged.

She had sensed the joy welling up in him when he first drew her into the room. The joy a man has when his whole world is in perfect order. But now she saw concern beginning to seep through the cracks. "When will I ever learn to listen to your gut instincts? Pops is happy. He and Sara are together. I understand where my dad is coming from. You were right."

Dark eyes narrowed. "Oh, I was right?"

"Yes." He reached for her, but she stepped back.

Her face remained stoic.

"I'm trying to apologize here."

She cut him off. "So, do it."

A frown drew his brows together. "I'm sorry, Adrienne. Truly."

"No problem," she said, words clipped. She wiped her hands on a kitchen towel as they spoke. But she fiercely held his gaze.

His eyes flashed concern, trying and failing to gauge this reaction. "Okay," he began slowly, "you're still mad. I understand."

She tossed the towel onto the table. "I'm not mad. I expected it, I was right, and now it's over." Her voice was solid and even.

"Well," he stammered, "you've got a knack for repairing people. I just want you to know that, from now on, I won't question your judgment about things." Laughter from the next room drifted into the dining area to them. It deadened as it collided with the tension-filled space.

She blinked. "Not necessary."

"It *is* necessary if we're going to be together. I really care about you, Adrienne. You've brought me so much joy. I want you to know that I'll trust you."

Trust. What an easy five-letter word to say. "Thanks, but it really isn't necessary."

"I feel like what we have is special. I want to protect it." He moved a little closer to her. "If we're going to have a relationship—"

She cut him off. "We're not, okay? We aren't going to have a relationship. We aren't in a relationship and we never will be, all right?" She watched as her words registered in his eyes, on his face, in his heart.

"But—"

"Look, Will, why would I choose to be in a relationship with someone who always initially thinks the worst of me? Sure, you always come back and apologize, but it's just too painful, and I'm not willing to go through it anymore. Do you know what it feels like to have to walk on eggshells every moment of your life? I do, and I can't go there again. I won't." She swallowed hard and looked away from the agony in his eyes. "I'm sorry, Will. I really am, but I just can't."

He pressed his lips together. His eyes pleaded with her, but she wouldn't relent. She couldn't. She'd spent five, nearly six years with Eric, hoping things would get better. Those personality traits didn't improve. They only got worse.

It was almost over. He'd walk out of her life and she could move on, live a nice, quiet, peace-filled life. Paint those floorboards.

Then he said the unthinkable. His words, soft as a whisper but cutting as a knife. "But I love you."

She pulled in a sharp breath. She hadn't prepared for that. She hadn't geared her heart or her mind to challenge that. A sickening cold rolled through her, leaving a wake of raw nerve endings. She tried to hold onto her convictions but could feel them slipping. "It doesn't matter," she whispered back, and it nearly killed her. "Sometimes love isn't enough."

It looked like he'd just taken a bullet to the gut. A fist closed over his heart, his gaze bewildered, searching her as if she hadn't heard his admission of love.

Her eyes dropped from him, unable to look at the pain. Slowly, she turned and went back into the kitchen, leaving him standing by the table, shoulders slumped, eyes hollow.

Safely in the kitchen, her body began to tremble. Though heated by the sun-warmed window, she'd grown cold. Not the outward coldness of a brisk winter wind or an ice skating rink or the ocean on a cool night. She felt the internal chill that spread from the inside out. She felt the chill of utter loneliness.

Putting her hands on her upper arms, she hugged herself, willing warmth into her shaking body. But no matter how cold and lonely, she knew she'd done the right thing. She'd heard of people putting themselves right back into the very situations they hated, but she'd never understood it before, not until now. She loved him too. Loved him with all her heart, but how could she be independent and strong when he questioned her on everything?

Love and trust, she decided, were definitely two different things. And now, neither was in her foreseeable future.

From the mailbox, Adrienne took in the picturesque home before her. A Victorian beach house. Nearly remodeled and shining like a beacon. No granite, though. But it had been worth it. Her fingers ran over the check in her hand. She'd had to fight with the granite salesman to get her deposit back and had almost written it off as a loss, when finally he conceded. It had been two months since the birthday party, and Adrienne stood at the edge of her perfectly manicured lawn, check in her hand. She'd take it to the bank later and send it to help Charles and Peg's mission.

Pops and Sara were going to marry in three months. Will's parents would be back for the ceremony. While stateside, their full funding had been reinstated. It would be nice seeing them.

She closed the mailbox door and tipped her head back, letting the breeze lift her hair from her face. She wished it could blow away her gloom. Adrienne missed the busy lifestyle she'd had when she was a constant in the Bryant family. But she'd thrown herself into her work, and the house gleamed with the fruit of her labor. Though it sparkled, it was as lonely as she was. She could sense it. It needed the warmth of a family, the touch of voices, and the caress of people. She could give it none of these things. This failure added to the despair.

She'd seen Will a few times. He always tried to make conversation, but she always shut him down. It was just better to stay away as much as possible. It was painful to him and poison to her.

Things would have been okay if Sara hadn't asked her to be the maid of honor. Adrienne knew this would inevitably throw her and Will together at some point.

She missed him. Adrienne sluggishly pulled herself up the front steps of her house. She missed him every day. Glancing at the now glowing front porch, she wondered if she should sell.

Chewing the inside corner of her mouth, she played with that idea. *Yes, sell it. The work is almost done. Why not? You could move on.* The wind picked up around her, the breeze carrying a scent of honeysuckle and mint, but underlying it was something she cherished even more. It was the tantalizing promise of a fresh start.

Wind still in her hair as she entered the house, she called Mary Lathrop. They discussed the details and decided that the house would go on the market in two months. That gave Adrienne time to finish the last of the remodel and would keep her here for the wedding a month later.

"I expect it to sell quickly," Mary assured her.

Adrienne figured it would. It had been a prime, though dilapidated, property when she bought it. Now, the perfect location sported a perfect Victorian home.

Then what? A stack of magazines waited for her perusal, strewn across the living room floor. She carried them to their stand by the kitchen island. One ad slid from a booklet and fluttered to the tile. She watched it turn, then twist, and finally come to rest near the trash can. She scooped it up and held it over the can. Fingertips covering half of the words on the advertisement, she momentarily froze. "No," she mumbled, and tossed the ad as she spun on her heels. But the ad hit the floor yet again. The movement grabbed her attention, and she pivoted.

Culinary School—why not you? stared up at her from the Italian tile floor. She stared back at it, arms folded over her chest and hip cocked.

Why not me? She tapped her index finger on her chin. This time, she moved the ad to the kitchen table. She loved to cook and had an aptitude for blending ingredients into tantalizing concoctions that made others gush. *Why not me?* she asked herself and tucked hair behind her ear. A hint of a smile formed.

Adrienne began to plan her future.

Fifteen minutes after beginning her journey, the phone rang. It was Sammie. "Hey, Chicago. Busy?"

Yes, Adrienne thought. *I'm quite busy planning my future, which excludes you and all the other people I've grown to love here.* But instead she said, "No, just ran to the mailbox."

"Can you come to the coffee shop?"

"I guess," Adrienne replied, but knew she wasn't the best of company.

"Good, there's something going on here that you should see."

Adrienne headed up the stairs, wondering what could be so fascinating to cause straightforward Sammie to sound mysterious and . . . excited. There was a time when words like "something going on that you should see" would have sparked Adrienne's imagination. A sucker for an enigma, her mind would have contemplated every possible scenario from a natural disaster to a traveling circus taking up residence in Sammie's parking lot.

But not any more. Those things seemed childish and silly now that she was busy nursing a broken heart. It was safer to just grab her keys and make the five-minute drive without trying to guess. Guessing only led to disappointment.

Sammie had kept a close eye on her for the first month after the break-up—if you could call it that—with Will, but in the last several weeks, Sammie put away the mother-hen attitude and was back to being a somewhat more normal best friend.

Adrienne drove to the coffee shop, but when she saw the multitude of cars that filled the parking lot, she quickly scanned for lion cages and freak-show trailers. There were none to be found. Just normal vehicles and people. People everywhere. She had to park nearly a block away. Stepping inside the crowded coffee shop, she quickly spotted Sammie's flash of red hair. She sidestepped a large group and said, "What's going on?"

Sammie pointed, face beaming. "Here comes Ryan. He can explain."

Adrienne frowned.

Ryan met the two women and reached out to hug Adrienne. "Remember the letter about the random act of kindness?"

She nodded. "William's letter, yes."

"Well, we published that part of it in the university's newspaper with a challenge to be inspired." Ryan gestured with arms outstretched. "All these people heeded the call. They're going today to Northside Elementary School to paint and clean it for the upcoming school year."

Looking around, Adrienne noticed most of the people were young and college age, and all of them were dressed to work.

"This is amazing. Why Northside?"

"They have the least amount of funding and the greatest need." Sammie grabbed her arms, eyes going wide. "Adrienne, don't you see what a difference you've made?"

Adrienne stepped back a little, tried to pull from her grasp. "Me?"

"Yes, if you hadn't found those letters, if you hadn't taken it upon yourself to find William, none of this would have happened."

Adrienne stared at the floor. A lot of things wouldn't have happened, like her broken heart.

Sammie's attention was drawn to the door. She started waving vigorously behind her.

But Adrienne continued to examine the grout in the coffee shop's tile floor as she considered age-old letters inspiring young people. Finally, the vision of scores of people painting and cleaning took root. Excitement quickly followed. "Ryan, congratulations. This is an amazing thing you've done."

"I didn't do this. I just told the reporter. This was all put together by him." He pointed behind her.

Adrienne spun around. And met Will face to face. All the breath left her lungs.

Will reached past her to shake Ryan's hand. "Thanks for coming. I've got those paint tarps in the back of my car. I left the trunk open."

Ryan disappeared and Adrienne blinked, trying to understand.

"Can you believe this?" Will said with a wide sweeping gesture. He smiled, and the entire room melted away from them. "I thought maybe fifteen or twenty people might show up, if we were lucky."

"How?" This whole *Will and Ryan on the same project with Sammie in the middle of it* thing was like a weird dream.

"When I saw the article at the college, I contacted the reporter. The scuba team was already looking for more ways to reach out to the community. You remember sitting in on one of our meetings, right?"

"Right," she barely mumbled.

"When I told the reporter who I was, he wanted to do another article, one about Pops. We agreed. With the stipulation that we put forth a precedent. Be Inspired. Do something out of the ordinary, a random act of kindness. We offered people to join us here to work on Northside School."

A coy grin slashed Adrienne's face. "An article about Pops, huh?"

Will's green eyes sparkled. "Yes. It's important to remember the past, Adrienne. The past shapes who we are."

Those were *her* words. Words from, oh, what felt like an eternity ago. Words Adrienne had said to Will. Words that had changed him. And now, the challenge to allow the same phrase to change *her* was evident. He wasn't talking about kids or schools or acts of kindness. Will held her gaze as if those green globes could strip away every ounce of her reserve. Maybe they could, there was so much power in this man. Beside him she felt small. A thought struck her. "Who's paying for all this?"

Will blinked, looked away. Tried to catch someone's attention across the room. He was . . . uncomfortable, and the reality of that intrigued Adrienne.

"Well, we better get started," he said.

When he walked past, Adrienne caught his arm. "*You're* paying for it?"

Will didn't answer. White-hot sparks burst from where her skin contacted his. She could practically see them. Adrienne wanted to pull her hand away, but the electricity between them caused her fingers to tremble, not release. His response was a quiver that rumbled from him . . . right into her. Skin to skin, the heat burned, but still she couldn't draw away. Will looked down into her face. His lips were parted; he smelled like the leather from his car and that essence she had never quite been able to name. Or resist.

"Come with me," he whispered, and though Adrienne knew he was offering her to join the group, there was another offer beneath. Something that made her feel stripped of all inhibitions—something that made her feel powerful, womanly. Though she knew she shouldn't, she dragged those words deep into herself, let them scratch and scrape in her innermost being, let her mind trail down a dangerous path. How could she have felt so small next to this man only moments ago, yet now—well, now she felt able to conquer the world. Sara's words drifted into her head: "The ocean's a lonely place when you're all alone."

Adrienne squared her shoulders. Mustered her courage. She might have to sort out all the underlying questions and innuendos that had filled Will's words later, but she could answer the surface question. "I'm in." She released Will's arm.

Until she spoke, Adrienne had forgotten Sammie was there. "You can practically remodel the whole thing with a group like this. There's got to be a hundred people here."

As Adrienne took her hand from his arm, Will seemed as though he left—unwillingly—that dark, intimate place they'd just been. He smiled. "It will sparkle when we're done. We've even gotten an okay to paint some murals on the walls. Those kids won't recognize their school building."

Adrienne imagined small children stepping into the freshly painted school. What would it be like to watch little faces and happy eyes study the murals painted especially for them?

"Will, this really is wonderful," she said. "Congratulations."

His eyes locked on hers again. And once more, her heart stopped beating.

She swallowed hard, suddenly aware of her disheveled appearance and annoyed with herself for being aware. She'd already been dressed to paint, having planned to work on her house. She hadn't changed when she got the call from Sammie.

Will pulled half of his lower lip into his mouth. A soft curve lit the opposite side of his face, and for one more flash, she was the only person in the universe. "I'm glad you're coming along."

"Well . . . " She rolled her eyes. "I did have some extremely urgent things I was going to do for *myself.* But suddenly, I feel inspired."

Chapter 21

A bad day painting was better than a good day wallowing in self-pity. But it wasn't a bad day painting. It had, in fact, been a great morale booster. She'd worked, scrubbed, and cleaned along with all the people who had joined in Will's quest. She'd steered clear of him for most of the day, making the entire thing tolerable on the heart level. Adrienne returned home feeling good, really good about how she'd spent her day.

By nightfall, she and Sammie were swapping stories about the school project. "It's going to be on the local news."

"That's great. Maybe even more people will be inspired." Adrienne said.

Sammie nodded, rubbing her elbow. "Boy, I hate getting old. My elbow's on fire."

"Well, I never saw you take a break all day. I'll get us some iced tea." Adrienne disappeared into the kitchen.

Sammie eyed her. "Are you saying this wound is self-inflicted?"

"I'm just saying I have aspirin if you want it."

"Nah." Sammie waved a hand dismissively. "I'll rub some castor oil on it when I get home."

Sammie and her home remedies. "Castor oil. Yuck," Adrienne said as she handed Sammie a tea. Sweat had already accumulated along the side of the glass. When she flipped her mop of red hair out of the way and took a drink, some of the condensation gathered and ran along her hand.

"This is really good."

"Sun tea." Adrienne had finally gotten used to the humidity and the fact that even inside, water rapidly condensed on a glass.

"I noticed Ryan painting near you a lot. I think Will noticed it too. Wonder what he thought of that?" Her friend took another long drink.

"I can't care what Will thought."

"So, you and Ryan?"

But Adrienne was already shaking her head. "No."

Sammie gauged her with narrowed eyes.

The scrutiny was unbearable. "There's just nothing there."

"Hmm." She poked her elbow and winced.

Adrienne shrugged. "I almost wish there were. But I just don't feel for him like—"

"Like you do for Will?"

"I was going to say like I should." Adrienne reached for a cork coaster and placed her tea on the coffee table.

"So, it's not Will that you're in love with?"

Adrienne made a pouty face. "Actually, I do love Will. Okay, I said it. I love him, I love him, I love him." She paused, letting the words fall to the ground and die. "But it doesn't change anything."

"Honey." Sammie tilted toward her, long red hair tumbling forward. "It changes everything."

"I don't see how."

Sammie leaned back, stretching her arms out at her sides and resting them on the couch pillows. "Tell me something: Why did you break it off with Will?"

No psychoanalysis, please. It wasn't something she could explain in an instant.

"So you wouldn't get hurt, right?" Sammie filled in for her, tipping the palm of one hand up toward the ceiling.

"To super simplify it, yes, I guess." Adrienne didn't want to talk about this. She'd redirected the subject a dozen times with Sammie, and she could do it again.

"But you failed. You're already hurt. You're in love with him, Adrienne. Don't you think that deserves a chance? Isn't it worth fighting for?"

But Adrienne didn't want to fight. She simply wanted to exist and enjoy life and not have to watch her back. She couldn't blame Sammie for what she was trying to do, In fact, she loved her for it. But it was a dead issue. She wouldn't risk the betrayal. And that's exactly what it was. A betrayal.

Slowly, she shook her head. "Is it worth it? Probably to most people." She stood up from her chair and moved toward the edge of the room.

Sammie turned on the couch to keep her in view.

"But not to me." Adrienne went into the kitchen for a few minutes, then returned with a glass of water and two aspirin.

Sammie sighed and took them from her.

It was a setup. Adrienne knew it. She'd sensed it coming and knew exactly how she would respond. Sara was on the other end of the telephone line, bubbling about the wedding plans and the honeymoon and all the fun that accompanied the special day. Sara had lost seven pounds, which she was now spouting off about. She talked about cutting down on red meat and blah, blah,

blah. Adrienne brushed a hand through her hair, the recipient of her own disgust. Why couldn't she just put her feelings aside and be happy for the two without feeling sorry for herself?

"Anyway," Sara crooned, "I need you to come with me and Pops and Will. We're going to have brunch at the Naples Elite Beach Resort. We need to finalize everything for the rehearsal, ceremony, and reception." Sara continued her spiel about healthy eating.

Adrienne leaned her head against the living room wall. She'd go, of course. She had to. She wouldn't disappoint Pops and Sara for anything. It was just so hard to be around Will. Of course, it was hard not to be around him, as well. Though over two months had passed since the birthday party, Adrienne still found herself thinking about him on a daily basis. She heaved an angry breath forcing him from her thoughts. Again.

"Are you all right, dear?" Sara asked, evidently concerned.

"Oh." She snapped to attention, not wanting the older woman to know how uncomfortable these situations made her. "Yes, great. I would love to go along. I've heard so much about the brunch at the Naples Elite."

"We'll pick you up Saturday morning around ten."

"Oh, *this* Saturday," she scrambled. "I have some errands to do, so I'll just meet you there."

"All right," Sara replied. "Thank you again, Adrienne."

But she didn't feel deserving of thanks or appreciation of any kind.

She just felt trapped.

By the time Saturday morning arrived, Will had changed his mind three times about what he would wear to brunch. After trying a dress shirt and linen pants once more, he opted for a polo shirt and jeans. Adrienne seemed to always comment on how good he looked in jeans. *This is stupid,* he told himself. *As if a magic pair of pants is going to make her fall in love with you.*

The host escorted them to their table, but Will wasn't hungry. His stomach was a tight wad of nerves that made food seem repulsive. He sat so that he could watch the door. When she entered, his heart started pounding.

A filmy white sundress floated around her hips. Tall wedge sandals elongated her legs, highlighting the muscle tone in her slender calves. Her skin was a little darker, and the dark hair that feathered across her shoulders moved as she stepped. She was stunning.

Adrienne reached the table and hugged Pops first, then Sara. Turning to Will, she stepped around the table and gave him a courtesy hug as well. He breathed deeply, her scent, her life force—everything about her surged into his system.

"Good to see you, Will."

"You as well." He tried to sound casual, but, in a word, he was bankrupt. Completely and utterly bankrupt. Would he ever get over this woman? No. And honestly, he didn't want to. He had told his father that he would never give up on Adrienne. And he meant it. He still meant it. Seeing her again—after their little sticky-hot moment at Sammie's—just solidified his commitment. There was no other woman in the world for him. She was it. She was everything.

They ate overlooking the bay. Outside, the water glistened in anticipation of the cruisers, fishing boats, and clippers beginning to set sail. Sea spray reached upward to cool the sun-heated deck. Its overspray salted the restaurant window.

Pops and Sara were going to be wed at this very hotel. Will's folks were coming home for it, and all should be right in the world. If only he had the woman he loved where she should be. In his arms, at his side.

He stole glances at Adrienne. She was unreadable, untraceable as she chatted about the remodel and the upcoming wedding. She had successfully buried whatever was going on in her mind beneath a friendly—albeit steel-hard—smile. From all outward appearances, she was having a great time visiting with Pops and Sara and even him, for that matter. Which ticked him off. She shouldn't be all casual and elegant and happy when he was being leveled inside. Each laugh, each flicker of her lashes, pounded away at him like a wrecking ball against a condemned building.

Disappointment stabbed his chest. They'd had something special, something unique, but she must be over him. Whatever they had shared—powerful as it may have been at the time—seemed gone. Then again, Adrienne Carter was a complex woman, one that could not easily be read by outward signs. A woman with layers. When Pops and Sara left the table to walk out to the balcony, a thick silence stretched between them.

"Thanks for coming," he blurted.

She smiled. "I wouldn't have missed it."

"It means a lot to Pops and Sara." His hands were sweating. "And I'm glad I got to see you."

Her eyes came to meet his across the table. "Will, for Pops and Sara's sake, I hope things can be . . . " She fumbled for the right words, then continued, "congenial between us."

Congenial. The word dropped into the pit of his stomach and gnawed. So that was it. Where he stood with the woman he loved. The world around darkened, leaving only a tiny pinprick of light. "Okay, if you think that's best for now." Was he agreeing with her? No. It wasn't best. Now or ever. What was best was for him to spend the rest of his life with this woman. But Adrienne couldn't be pushed. She'd spent too many years being pushed by people, and he never, ever wanted to be lumped into that group. She had to reach the right conclusion on her own. Simply, it was out of his hands. But he also wouldn't let her lie to herself. That's what she was doing. His eyes drilled into her.

Her gaze on him was strong, sure, but when she blinked, the first crack emerged, then another. Her shoulders dropped a tiny degree, and there it was, the old fire pushing, tearing its way to the surface—just like it had at the coffee shop.

This was his chance. Will leaned in and trapped her, meeting her forced certainty with a dose of his own. "Is that what you really want?"

She swallowed but held his gaze. "It is." Then she blinked several times and looked away.

There was a flash, something in her eyes. He saw the lie. Her heart betrayed her, brilliant as a neon sign. For now, that would have to do. All he knew was that he'd never give up on her. That tiny spark let him know there was a chance. Slim, but a chance nonetheless. Even if it was only a seed.

"I guess your remodel is almost done?"

"Almost finished." She seemed grateful for the change of topic. Adrienne sipped her coffee.

"It's been a long project, hasn't it?"

She nodded, looking over to the large bay window where Pops and Sara stood holding hands, watching seagulls dance and tip their wings into the wind searching for breakfast.

"What next?"

"I'm going to sell it." She attempted to sound casual, but there was a finality in her tone. "I may be moving. I've applied to a cooking school in Tallahassee."

For a moment, he couldn't speak. The thought of her leaving the area had never occurred to him. How could he convince her they should be together if she wasn't even here? Cold lightning blasted into his chest. "I didn't know. Does Pops know this?"

"No one knows yet," she admitted. "Well, my real estate agent and now you."

His mind swam in a murky pool. "They're going to be disappointed. They care so much for you."

"I care for them too."

Again, her eyes were telling a different story than her words. She didn't just care for them, she loved them like family. Her heart wasn't pleased with this decision, and he fought to offer reasons why she shouldn't go. "You have friends here. Sammie." It was a pathetic attempt. But he had to try something.

She nodded. "Well, if the house sells quickly, I'll have enough money to get into the school and rent an apartment. I've put all of my divorce settlement into the house, so I need to sell it to move on."

He stared at her, and heat crawled up his neck.

Adrienne rolled her eyes. "*If* I get accepted."

Her amused detachment caused more than a little concern. He told her she had friends and all she could say was "If the house sells quickly, I'll have enough money to get into the school"? This was all wrong, and he wasn't hiding his panic well.

She noticed, chewed her lip, and tapped her coffee cup absently with her fingernail. "It's not that I'm *trying* to leave here, but that's where the school is located. Since I already have a business degree, I could open a catering business." Her eyes dropped again. "I've always been interested in that."

"I, uh, hope it works out for you, Adrienne," he managed, but his voice cracked. There was little sincerity in his words. Things were quickly spiraling out of control, and there wasn't a thing he could do about it, wasn't a thing he could do about her because of everything Adrienne needed, independence topped the list.

When Pops and Sara returned, they discussed final arrangements concerning the wedding. Adrienne pulled a small notebook from her bag. "Since the wedding is at three o'clock on Saturday, the hotel wondered if we could do the rehearsal on Friday morning. It works better with their schedule, and I thought it would be good to get it done and have the afternoon to rest before the big day."

Pops and Sara agreed, but Will's mind was far away. He'd been little help in this meeting, and though feeling useless, he couldn't seem to shake it.

After another thirty minutes of chatter, Adrienne slammed her notebook shut. "I think that's it!"

The four of them left the restaurant, Will, Pops, and Sara heading to Will's car and Adrienne getting into her car. After shutting Sara's door, Will rested his hand on the hood and watched as the woman he loved pulled out of the parking lot, the *flash, flash, flash* of her turn signal reminding him that she was headed in the opposite direction. Away from the people she loved. Away from him.

"Moving?" Sammie asked, hands on hips. "Were you planning to tell me?"

Adrienne waved her in the front door. "Nothing is set in stone yet. I may not even get accepted into the school."

Sammie sailed into the kitchen and dropped the two bags of coffee beans she'd brought on the counter. "But you *are* selling the house?"

Adrienne answered her with a gentle nod and quiet words. "Yes, I am."

Sammie rushed back out and slumped into a chair at the table.

Adrienne sat across from her. "I just decided this. I haven't had a chance to talk to you about it yet."

"You know what I think?" Sammie countered, hurt lacing her words. "I think this is a cop-out. I think you're scared to stay here because of Will, and you're running away."

Adrienne toyed with the edge of the salmon-colored place mat. "Maybe."

Sammie leaned forward. "You love him, and you're scared you'll give in if you're here. So you're just going to remove yourself from the threat."

She was right. And Adrienne couldn't deny it. She also wouldn't change it. "My mind is made up, Sammie."

Sammie heaved a sigh. "Can I tell you how I feel about this?"

Adrienne smirked. "I thought you just did."

"When you came here, you said you wanted to work on who you are as a person. You wanted to be a stronger woman. And over and over I've watched you make tough decisions and burst through layer upon layer of weaknesses. But this isn't one of those times. Now, when there is something on the line, something really worth fighting for, you're just shrinking back into that old cocoon. It won't fit anymore, Chicago. It's a coffin. And now that you've grown, it's too small. It will suffocate you. And it won't take very long."

Coldness snaked through Adrienne's veins.

Sammie brushed at her skirt with frustration. "You have no idea how often I've envied you. You're young, you're beautiful, you've got so much going for you. But, I gotta tell ya, Chicago. I'd rather be a used-up, broken-down coffee-shop owner that lived life to its fullest than a young woman who refuses to live at all."

Adrienne threw up her hands. "That's what I'm trying to do. Live my life."

Sammie pressed her palms against the table. "Look, I'm not trying to scold you. I just think that he continued to grow and you stopped."

"What do you mean?" She'd grown. *Was* growing, changing, becoming the kind of woman she wanted to be.

Except, maybe she wasn't.

Maybe all these decisions about taking her life in her own hands, steering her own ship really was a cop-out. It nearly killed her to sit at the table with Will and watch Pops and Sara on the balcony of the restaurant. All of them happy, moving forward while she . . . well, was her decision to sell and move an attempt to outrun the pain? The memories that were so fresh here? When she looked at the ocean from her back deck, all she saw was Will and Pops. She envisioned catching fish and throwing crab claws on their kitchen floor. When she walked upstairs, all she saw was Sara walking around with a book on her head, instructing Adrienne how to be a lady. All these things were just ghosts— ghosts from a past that had nothing to do with her future.

It didn't matter that it hurt so bad. She wasn't quitting. A quitter would curl up inside herself, inside her shell, and never come back out. Adrienne was trying to move on. Wasn't that brave? At least a little? Sammie's insulting words stung. "What do you mean he kept growing and I stopped?" There was a bite to her tone that she wouldn't apologize for or feel bad about. Sammie was out of line.

"You told me that you were going to give Will time to change. You said that his big hang-up was that he didn't deal with things, and he just let them fester. His parents being the biggest wound.

But he's made peace with that. He's even made the choice to embrace Pops's past, though it's painful to both of them. Kiddo, the young man has jumped through hoops."

Adrienne stared blankly at her.

"For you. He wasn't asking to grow, but he made the choice to when you confronted him with it. *You* came here to grow, but now you're running away."

Adrienne wanted out. Sammie couldn't understand. No one could.

She shrugged. "So he got mad when you did something that could have ultimately caused a lot of pain. Big deal. You took a risk with people you barely knew, but these are also people he's fiercely devoted to. How else should he react? You sort of set the precedent, don't you think? Then he reconciled with his parents. And instead of appreciating all he went through, you slammed the door in his face."

Shock kept Adrienne from breathing. Everything around her was going dark, the haze closing in on her field of vision until all she could see was the woman she called *friend*.

Sammie suddenly stood from the table. "You know what? I've said all I'm going to say. You're still letting Eric run your life. I feel sorry for you, Adrienne." And Sammie left.

Adrienne stared at the bowl of fruit that sat in the center of the table. The apples were going bad. Tracing the ugly, brown spots, she reached over and plucked them one by one from the basket. The oranges still looked good. She loved the oranges here. She loved the selection of fresh tropical fruit that was available at the grocery store on the corner and the farmers market in the parking lot every Saturday morning downtown.

Her eyes scanned the house. This house. Her house. The one she'd found while searching "property for sale, Florida Gulf Coast."

Adrienne had made the offer with her entire being screaming to back out. There was strength within her that—though buried under the dirty blanket of Eric's abuse—had been unearthed. She'd given the house time, love, and a fair portion of her blood. It had all been worth it. She could let it go. After all, it had given to her as well. She had learned she could make it on her own. She was strong. And even though she loved this house, loved this town, and, heaven knew, she'd fallen in love with several people here, she'd be okay. Without a second thought, she tossed the apples into the trash. Besides, Tallahassee had grocery stores too.

The morning of the rehearsal, the day before the wedding, Adrienne's nerves were pounding out their own rhythm. She wanted everything to go perfectly. *It will*, she kept telling herself as she willed the butterflies from her stomach. Mary Lathrop had called her to say they had an offer on the house, but Adrienne couldn't be bothered with that right now. Two weeks ago, she'd received the acceptance letter from the culinary school but was shocked at her own lack of enthusiasm over it. It was what she had wanted. She should be excited.

It's the wedding, she decided. She and Sara had spent countless hours on every detail, and in all honesty, Adrienne was tired. That was the reason for the lack of enthusiasm. Once she got some rest, she'd be excited about her new adventure. Of course she would.

Adrienne stepped into the ballroom and gasped. Though she'd been there late the night before, putting on the finishing touches, she'd been too tired to appreciate the space as a whole. Her energy had gone into things like adjusting a spray of white lilies until they were just right and spreading a shimmering white rope along the edge of the seats to let guests know where to sit.

Was this really the same room she'd barely noticed last night? Shades of white from warm winter to soft, billowy cotton were repeated in every portion of the decorated space. The elegance of her surroundings made her smile. It was perfect, and Pops and Sara were going to love it.

The rehearsal went smoothly, with gushing remarks from each new person who entered the room. Sara hugged her, thanking her and telling her that if she'd had a daughter, she would have wanted her to be just like Adrienne.

But Sara seemed reluctant to let go and hung there for a moment, arms draped over Adrienne's shoulders. When the older woman released her, Adrienne scanned her eyes. Though Sara was trying to hide it, Adrienne could see the exhaustion on Sara's face. It was masked by the quick smile that sparkled, but beyond the façade, there was desperation.

As Sara glided across the room, dread crept into Adrienne's being. Had the bride-to-be just stumbled a bit? Sara reached a table and leaned there for a few moments before continuing on. Something was wrong. This woman had outwalked all of them at both the zoo and the Air Force celebration.

On top of that, Sara looked pale. Understandably—Adrienne herself was exhausted, and Sara had kept up a steady pace with her through the work and decorating. But Sara was in her late seventies.

Again, Adrienne watched her lean against a table. By the time the rehearsal was over, Adrienne decided to insist Sara go straight home with her to rest.

But it was too late. As Adrienne began to move to the entrance door where the happy couple were standing and talking, Sara's eyes fell on her across the room. A moment later they were rolling back as she collapsed to the ground.

First, Sara's weight slumped against Pops, who took a steady hold on her despite the confusion registering on his face.

Adrienne broke into a run and dropped beside her. Sara lay unconscious in a pool of soft white silk. Her skin had paled to a disturbing deathly white. Pops had lowered her to the ground and knelt beside her. "Sara? Sara!" He choked on the name. Will dropped too, and there they all were, surrounding the bride. Pops ran his hand over Sara's still arm, mumbling incoherent words. The man who'd cheated death for over eighty years was crumbling.

Somewhere behind her, Adrienne heard someone say an ambulance was on the way. Various hotel personnel bustled in and out, but none were able to help. Sara lay quietly.

Peg screamed as she entered the room. She and Charles had gone to check the hotel room arrangements for Pops and to make sure he and Sara were booked into the honeymoon suite.

Charles dropped beside them all on the floor. "Is she breathing?"

Will removed his suit jacket and placed it under her head as Adrienne held Sara's hand. It felt cold. Thin and cold like tree branches in winter. Vaguely aware of what was happening around her, Adrienne caught tiny snatches of conversation. People talking, gasping, wishing they could hurry an ambulance that would move on its own schedule, and no amount of looking at one's watch would change it. But the only thing Adrienne heard clearly—and each word sliced into her heart—was Pops's choked sobs as he cried, "No, please God, no. Not again."

Chapter 22

What must it be like to lose a spouse? Pops had already suffered that tragedy once; it seemed unthinkable that he might have to again. Adrienne sat in the small, brown chapel of the Naples Hospital, finally understanding Will's fierce desire to protect his grandfather. For it was in the moment of Sara's collapse that she'd looked into Pops's eyes and seen the horror of death. Living beyond your friends, your parents, outliving so many who'd died too young. As Pops slumped to the floor holding Sara, Adrienne understood loss on a profound level, a level that transcended her years. And the pain of it was unbearable as she watched the gentle man with the soft, blue eyes falter as his world tumbled down around him like leaves on an autumn day.

And it was all her fault. It truly was. Unforgivable.

At the hospital, they were notified it would be at least an hour before they knew anything. From across the room, she had watched as Charles and Will stood on each side of Pops, shoring him up. When Will's accusing eyes met hers, she left the room. By the time she found the chapel at the far end of the building, she was nearly running. Trying to outrun the pain she'd caused. He'd been right all along. What a bitter, bitter way to find out.

The chapel was a narrow room with cushioned pews. She couldn't remember ever being in a church inside a hospital. She sat and tried to draw peace, but her heart only filled with accusation. Softly glowing bulbs above lit the space, showering the walls and floor with gentle soothing light. It helped, if only slightly. Yet this felt like a safe place.

Adrienne turned as a mother and small child entered and moved to the front. They sat across from her, and she could see the weight of uncertainty upon them. The child, who'd been clutching a teddy bear, dropped to her knees, set the bear aside, and with eyes squeezed shut began to pray. Adrienne watched. Did children's prayers work better? All that hope, all that faith in those little innocent bodies. Could their heartfelt prayer reach deeper into heaven? Probably. When they were finished, the mother and child silently slipped out of the room. Adrienne was alone once again, as questions assailed her.

Why hadn't she insisted Sara go to the doctor this morning? She'd seen how pale Sara was, saw her struggling to maintain her strength. If Adrienne had spoken up, maybe things would be different. She looked at her watch, a gift from Pops and Sara for all the help on the wedding. Her fingers toyed with the gold band as tears blurred the numbers.

If it weren't for the deep love she felt for this family, especially Sara, she'd leave. Leave right now before Will got a chance to shred her with his words. They were right—they were all right, including Eric: All she did was cause trouble. Sure, she had good intentions. The very kind that paved the road to hell. Now she understood why.

But she didn't leave. Wouldn't run. Maybe she was a coward, but she wasn't heartless. Alone in the chapel as the *family* huddled in the waiting room. She was an outsider who had forced her way into lives already recovering from one tragedy. Now she'd brought another.

Adrienne closed her eyes when she heard the chapel door close behind her. It was him. She steeled herself. She could hear his footsteps on the soft carpet as he made his way to her.

She was in the first pew, and instead of towering over her, he knelt.

When he gently cradled her hands in his, she slowly looked up to meet his gaze.

She's gone, she knew he was going to say. *Sara's dead*. The words rolled through her before he could speak. Scenes flashed through her mind of a funeral, Pops sitting by a grave, alone once again. Grief and regret flooded every inch of her body.

He gently squeezed her hands. "Adrienne?" he questioned, soft as a whisper.

She must be gone, why else would he not be screaming at her? Adrienne began to tremble. It started in her chest, her heart, the center of her being, and rippled outward. "Tell me," she finally managed through gritted teeth.

He flashed a moment of puzzlement, then answered. "We . . . we don't know anything yet."

Relief engulfed her as the tension in her muscles released.

His eyes were green velvet, tender as a petal on a flower. "But you need to know something."

She blinked, causing her vision to clear. Such softness from Will she couldn't fathom. Maybe she was losing her mind.

He made tiny circles on her hands with his thumbs. "I wanted to find you to make sure you're not somehow blaming yourself for this."

Confusion spread through her system. "What do you mean?"

One hand slipped up to cup her face. "Listen to me. No matter what happens to Sara, you gave her and Pops a beautiful gift by bringing them together."

When she tried to look away, his hand held her face steadfast.

"No matter how long or short that time might be."

She stared at him, uncertain if he was really the Will Bryant she knew. He couldn't be.

"Adrienne, no one is guaranteed a tomorrow. Life is a precious and delicate thing. At the very best, it's a vapor. Pops spent a lifetime with the woman he loved. Now he's had a chance to love a woman from a lifetime ago." He moved from in front of her to the seat beside her and turned her to look at him. "Adrienne, you did the right thing."

She shook her head, closed her eyes. Tried to get the disjointed pieces to fall together, but they didn't. He was wrong. She hadn't done the right thing at all. Pops and Will had had a good life before she came along with the letters. She should have left those letters in the box in her attic.

His voice rose. "Do you hear me? You did the right thing."

She nodded absently in an attempt to make him stop talking. This wasn't right. Wasn't *normal*. He *should* be yelling at her. And *she* should learn her lesson.

"I want to hear you say it."

Say it? No. She tried to slide away, but he wouldn't let her. "I can't. I can't because I can't believe that this much pain could be right."

He took her hand and placed it over his heart. "Love is always the right thing. I've learned that now. I trust you, Adrienne. And I think you were right. Sometimes love isn't enough alone. But love and trust together? You can't walk away from that."

He had to stop talking. Had to stop saying these words because though everything else was chaos, the words made sense.

"Sometimes love comes with pain. But you can't just stop loving. You might as well be dead if you do."

Her eyes were dry now, burning. "So love *isn't* enough."

He smiled and despite her fear, his warmth found a crack into her and forced its way through.

Will squeezed her closer. "No, love isn't just enough. *Real* love is everything."

His lips made their way to hers, and he kissed her. When he drew away, she tried to smile.

A glorious new sensation stormed through her system like rain in a desert, removing old scars of anger and mistrust. It gathered speed and force as wave after wave of dirt and cobwebs washed away in the tide of this new power. Strength settled in her bones, encircled her heart, and rejuvenated her limbs. For the first time in years, Adrienne tasted freedom.

They made their way from the chapel back to the rest of the family. Pops was sitting in a corner chair, elbows on the armrests and long legs stretched out in front of him. His fingers were laced together, one thumb making small circles around the other. It was interesting enough to hold Charles' attention who sat in the chair next to him.

When the doctor came into the waiting room, everyone stood. He was young—didn't look old enough to be a doctor—but Adrienne knew that was common in the ER. For a brief second, she wondered about his credentials, wondered if he was capable of treating a treasure like Sara.

He pulled the glasses from his face and rubbed them against his white coat. "Sara is suffering from acute dehydration." He slipped them back onto his nose. "She's stable and resting comfortably, but we're going to continue to pump fluids into her for the next couple of hours. After that, she should be fine to leave if she's feeling up to it."

The entire room breathed a collective sigh of relief. "Dehydrated? That's all?" Pops said.

The young doctor nodded. "Yes, it's not that uncommon in older people in stressful circumstances." His head tilted from one side to the other, no doubt a posture he'd practiced in the mirror a thousand times. "Sara told me she'd been burning the candle at both ends."

"Sweet Sara," Pops said. "Just try to slow her down."

The doctor chuckled. "Yeah, I can see why that wouldn't be easy. She's low on iron too. She said she's been dieting to get ready for the wedding, but I'm not allowing that anymore. I'm sending her with a week's worth of B-12 shots. They're simple to administer and will help boost her body's immune system and energy level." He pointed to Pops. "Plenty of lean, red meat for her over the next week or so will help her regain full strength."

Pops nodded. "We can postpone the wedding until she's feeling stronger."

"Actually," the doctor corrected, "you can't."

Pops questioned him with a look.

"Sara is adamant about the wedding going on as scheduled tomorrow." The doctor crossed his arms in front of him. "I think that would be in order. She should be feeling good by then . . . as long as she rests today."

Charles patted Pops shoulder.

The doctor's eyes narrowed on Pops. "I'm actually only worried about one thing."

Pops put his hands up in surrender. "We'll do anything so Sara can have her wedding day."

The doctor shook his head, but his mouth quirked in a smile. "I'm not worried about the wedding. I'm worried about the honeymoon."

A bright stain colored Pops's cheeks, as others in the group stifled snickers. Pops's mouth hung open.

"I'm just kidding, Tiger. She'll be fine." He shook Pops's hand, then Charles's and after throwing an appreciative look to Adrienne and ignoring Will, he left.

Pops scratched the back of his head. All eyes were on him. He opened his mouth to speak but changed his mind. Instead, he forced his hands deep into his pockets, grinned, and shrugged.

In a room next door to the bride's dressing chamber, a trio of men tugged at their collars and stared at their hands, wishing the time would move along more quickly.

"Are you scared?" Will stood to adjust Pops's tie.

Pops's gaze focused behind Will to an indistinct point. "No," Pops said, and the calm and serenity in his single word echoed that. His eyes locked on his grandson's. "I feel as though I'm on borrowed time. Life is best when you find someone to love, and you pour your heart and soul into it. Into *her*. Everything is sweeter. Everything is new, fresh. I got to do that not once, but twice. How could I be scared of what lies ahead when the whole world has been given to me and then given to me again?"

Will put his hands on Pops's shoulders. "You really are a poet, Pops." *Find someone to love and pour your heart and soul into it.* Will had fulfilled the first part. He loved Adrienne. Loved her more than life. She deserved someone who would pour his heart out for her. She deserved a man who could give her wings.

Some people were like pottery. They had been tested in a fire just hot enough to make them capable, but perhaps not durable. But Adrienne was fine porcelain. Delicate, yet purified in white-hot flame reserved for those who would stand every test thrown at them. He was fortunate to even know her. And more fortunate to love her.

She was the person he would pour his heart and soul into. But not just for him. For her. Because she deserved it. She deserved nothing less.

Pops lifted his hands so they rested on Will's arms. "But don't let the moment slip by," he said, tightening his grip.

Will frowned. "What moment, Pops?" He searched the older man's face.

Pops released a long breath and whispered, "You'll know. You'll know when it happens. You'll know when the time is right, and don't you dare back away from it. No matter what. You hear me, boy? No matter what or *when*."

Will nodded, and hugged his grandfather, the man who'd taught him how to love. Then he turned and hugged his father, the man who had taught him how to sacrifice. And now, Will was capable of letting Adrienne soar, but also catching her if she fell. For the first time in his life, Will really, truly knew what it was to be a man.

Cinderella's ballroom awaited the princess with an intimate gathering of thirty people. Will and Pops stood at the front of the room, wearing attractive dark suits, which caused each to stand a little taller. Adrienne walked down the aisle first, looking at Will, only occasionally leaving his approving gaze. His mouth had dropped open a little when she stepped in. She tried to hide a smile. Glancing around the room, she'd never felt more collective love than at this moment.

Taking her place opposite the two men, she pivoted and waited for Sara.

When Sara stepped in, there was a gasp that rippled through the crowd. A bouquet of white gardenias was clasped firmly between her hands. She drew in a shaky breath. Pops nodded admiringly, coaxing her forward. His face beamed with pride as he basked not only in her beauty but in the happiness emanating from her.

The ceremony began, Pops and Sara standing hand in hand, as the preacher spoke to them about love and commitment. Adrienne was lost in the fairy tale, wondering how weddings could be so similar and yet so different. Her eyes drifted to Will, the man she loved. Her mind strayed to the hospital. *Their* love was certainly unique. At the moment she thought Will would break her heart, he had instead cradled it, protected it. She remembered the poem she'd once shared with Sammie.

Where have all the poets gone?
Rhyme with passion left unsung,
Even now my heart it yearns,
Until my poet-prince returns.

Could Will Bryant be her poet-prince? Was it possible? Love was so much more than deep emotion; it was sacrifice, forgiveness. It was comfort. It was joy. She willed herself back to the ceremony as the preacher asked if there was anyone who saw any reason for these two not to be wed.

When she heard Will's voice, her blood stopped moving.

He stepped forward. "Pastor Vernon, I do."

Uncertainty darted around the room, bouncing off the candlelight.

Will swallowed, pulled a breath. "Until I say what I need to, I don't think this wedding can continue." He looked at Pops. But

Adrienne noticed Sara, who turned to Will with a delighted look on her face.

Adrienne's eyes burned from lack of blinking and being open too wide. A smile formed on Pops's lips and he nodded, urging Will on. Then, Pops turned and winked at Sara knowingly.

"Say what you need to, Will," she said.

Taking a deep breath, Will stepped past the couple and over to Adrienne, whose face was on fire. "I can't believe I'm doing this," he mumbled.

Pastor Vernon flashed a look that seemed to say, *"how did I lose control of my ceremony?"*

"Adrienne," Will took her hands in his. "Until recently, I didn't really understand what love was. But now I know. I'm not perfect. But I have two men who have helped me be—and will continue to help me be—the best man, the best husband anyone ever had."

She sucked in a breath. Here? *Now?* "Will, we should talk about this later," she whispered, eyes shooting to the group of waiting guests. Beside Pops, Sara beamed. Didn't she realize Will had just interrupted the wedding. *Her* wedding. Through clenched teeth Adrienne said, "Later, okay?"

"Everyone here is our family." With a wave of his hand he gestured to the crowd. "They love us and most of them would never forgive me for letting this moment pass."

Adrienne's pleading eyes went back to Sara but found no help as Sara anxiously awaited how this would play out. Then she turned to Pops—no help either. Surely, the preacher would be the voice of reason. But when her eyes met his, he had closed his Bible and rocked back on his heels, grinning and waiting.

"Adrienne, this is one of the things I learned from you."

Her brows went up, head jutting forward slightly.

"You're a risk taker. It's one of the things I love about you."

She heard Sara say, "She certainly is."

Adrienne felt faint.

Will rolled his eyes. "I mean, at first, it was one of the things that drove me crazy, but you're willing to put your heart on the line for someone else. How could anyone not love that?"

"*We* love it." Sara again.

Her mind spun. This wasn't happening. Couldn't be happening. Besides, her plans had already been set in motion. "Will, I'm leaving in three weeks."

The smile that had animated his face disappeared.

She shook her head. Yes, she loved him. But her life was moving in a different direction. "I was accepted at the school in Tallahassee."

"Fine." He nodded, taking only a moment to decide. "I'll go with you."

Again her breath left her. She swallowed hard. "You can't just pick up and move—your job, your house."

"There are banks in Tallahassee. Adrienne, you deserve to make your dreams come true. *Every* dream. And if the culinary school in Tallahassee is what you want, then I want to help make sure you get it." His thumb grazed her cheek. "But you also deserve a hero. You should have someone who understands your complexity and will let you act like a woman one day and act like a kid the next. I don't think I can trust anyone with that job but myself."

The lump in her throat wouldn't go down. "You . . . you would do that? Lose everything just to go with me?"

"I wouldn't be losing anything. I would be gaining everything." Will shot a quick look over to Pops. "Once, a really wise man told me that life is best when you find someone to love and you pour your heart and soul into them. Let me do that for you, Adrienne. Please."

She couldn't breathe. Couldn't move. He was *ruining* everything.

Will leaned into her, his words soft, only for her to hear. "Marry me. If Tallahassee is where you want home to be, then so do I."

Marry him.

The words rolled over and over in her head. *Marry him*, not so the world could revolve around him, but so his world could revolve around her. He was willing to do it. He was willing to sacrifice his whole world to make her dreams come true. The reality of this soaked into Adrienne. It was warm honey through her heart, slowly, completely and forever leaving its mark of sweetness. But sweetness had a way of turning bitter and . . . Quietly, she whispered, "That's not what I want."

All of the air left Will. His face became parchment, devoid of color. And she could see everything. Right there in his face and feel it in the breath he'd blown toward her. It was love and fear and pain.

Her head dropped, and she stifled a cry because she couldn't bear to see such hurt. "I don't want to go to Tallahassee. I don't want to leave here. Leave my family."

Will swayed toward her.

Adrienne gestured at the older couple. "I want to go on boat rides in the Gulf and eat vegetables out of Pops's garden. I want to sit on the porch swing and visit with Sara." Tears streamed down her face, landing on the silk dress she wore. "And I . . . I want to marry you."

He grabbed her, hugged her, held her. Sara squealed and clapped her hands.

"I'm already home," Adrienne whispered into his ear. She was only vaguely aware of the applause that rolled through the room.

Not wanting to let her go, Will reluctantly stepped back to his position as best man.

Pastor Vernon reopened his Bible. "Now, if no one *else* has any objections, I'd like to continue." He gestured to Sara. "I believe you have something to share?"

Sara nodded, then unfolded the letter in her hands with trembling fingers.

Dear William,

For many years I wondered what my life would be like if the man I loved were beside me. Many days I stared down an empty road, hoping you would somehow appear. Many nights I cried myself to sleep. For all the wondering and dreaming I've done, it doesn't compare to the joy in my heart. I promise to redeem the years. We may be old; our bodies may be tired and worn down. But I make you this promise: We will live, William. We'll devour every opportunity given to us. And if I'm whisked away on the wings of angels before you are, I'll leave you letters.

Tenderly, old hands found their way to her rosy cheeks, now wet with her own tears. Pops kissed her with all the passion of a man half his age.

After the vows, Pastor Vernon closed his Bible. "I now pronounce you man and wife." With a half-grin, he gestured to Pops. "You may kiss the bride."

"Now, turn and face the congregation while I present you," Pastor Vernon said, gesturing toward the audience. "Ladies and gentlemen, please congratulate Mr. and Mrs. William Bryant."

William and Sara made their way to the back, a shower of flower petals cascading over them as they passed each row.

Adrienne and Will came together in the front.

Pastor Vernon gestured toward Will. "I can run a fifty percent off special if you two would like to go ahead and tie the knot," he joked.

"I'm sorry for the interruption earlier." Will put an arm around Adrienne.

The preacher, who'd known the family since Will was old enough to get into fights on the church baseball field, smiled. "Never apologize for love. I think you gave your grandfather a terrific present by ruining his wedding."

His joke was lost on Will as he stared into the deep, brown, sultry eyes he loved. "No thanks on the offer. Adrienne's wedding is going to be for her alone. Whatever she wants, wherever she wants."

And he pulled her into his arms, burying his head in the soft throat that was truly, finally his.

Much later that evening, Will and Adrienne sat on the beach, still in their wedding attire. The warm embrace of love surrounded them, shielding them from the coolness of the air that danced off the Gulf water. Her toes were dotted with sand, as were his. Their shoes had been discarded nearby. The sun played on the sea, causing it to look like diamonds spread on silk.

"What about Hawaii?" She tipped her head so that she could look at him.

"What about it?" he teased.

"For a wedding?"

"I'd love to go!" He threw her a sidelong glance. "Whose wedding is it anyway?"

"Ours."

His heart jumped at those words. Ours. Adrienne would be his wife. "Oh, I'm terribly sorry, Miss Carter. But I'm afraid we can't possibly get married."

"And why is that?"

"Haven't you heard? We aren't even dating. It would be completely scandalous."

"Yes," she agreed, and left her chair to kneel in front of him. Her hands slid over his thighs, a sly grin on her face. "It would." She nuzzled her head into the deep hollow of his throat. "Didn't we agree that neither of us have enough scandal in our lives?" She forced out hot breath with each word—purposely—and the action had the desired effect.

His body shuddered. "Well," he growled, catching a handful of her hair in his hand. "For the sake of scandal."

Epilogue

Present day

Will pulled his daughter closer into the circle of his arms, drawing as much strength from her as she drew from him. A funeral wasn't the place for a three-year-old, but he'd insisted. "Will Great-Grandma Sara wake up?" Her eyes flitted to the casket once again.

They'd tried to explain, but death in terms of toddler life experience was impossible. When her toys died, Daddy put new batteries in them and they were good as new. Adrienne took Will's arm. "We should have left her with Sammie," she whispered.

He shook his head, gave his wife a sad smile. "No. She'll remember this—not all of it, but some. It's important for her to experience and to remember."

Adrienne slid her arm through his and squeezed. "How is Pops, really?"

Will glanced over her head to his grandfather, who stood between Will's mom and dad. As if knowing his grandson sought assurance from him, Pops looked over and winked. But the light had left Pops's eyes, and Will tried to resist the truth that he wouldn't have him much longer. "He's strong."

Three-year-old SaraAnn squirmed in her daddy's arms. "Can I go to Grandma Peggy?"

Peg heard and reached her arms out to take her grandchild.

Will's hands were now empty, and he wasn't sure what to do with them, so he pulled his wife closer and gently rubbed his fingers along her arm.

Pastor Vernon began to speak. "Seven years ago, I joined a man and woman in matrimony. They had the most endearing love story I've ever heard. Though they spent most of their time right here in Florida, during their seven years as man and wife, they visited three continents and countless countries. Sara Ambrosia Bryant was born July 11, 1928. Like Sarah of the Bible, she was gifted late in life with a family. Sara is survived by her husband, William Bryant; a son and daughter-in-law, Charles and Peg Bryant of Bonita Springs; grandson and wife, Will and Adrienne Bryant of Naples; and a great-grandchild, of the home. Sara loved fishing in the Gulf of Mexico. She and William would often take off on a fishing excursion early Saturday morning and not return until late that night. She caught a trophy sailfish last year, one her husband swears only bit on her line to torture him."

The pastor talked on, but Will turned his attention to Pops, who'd stood stoic throughout the service. When the memorial ended and they stepped outside, Will noticed Pops fumbling with something in his pocket.

"What have you got there?"

Pops stared down at the boat key. "Thought I'd go out for a bit this evening."

Concern drew Will's brows together. A cold wind whistled up his pant leg, setting his flesh on alert. Will stared up at the winter sky. "It's supposed to be cooler tonight, Pops. Why don't you wait and I'll go with you in the morning?"

Pops turned to face him fully, and something, some deep-seated reserve, caused the chill to pass through Will's entire body. "Nope. Going myself this time."

Will had fought the onset of tears and wasn't sure why now they insisted on burning his nose and stinging his eyes. "Really, Pops. I'd like to go. I'll go with you tonight. The grass will be slick when we get home."

But there was peace in his grandfather's voice as he spoke. "I'm eighty-eight, Will. I've lived through a war and buried the love of my life twice. I'm not afraid of a little wet grass." Quietly, he added. "I'm not afraid to live. And I'm not afraid to die."

Panic caused the sobs to tighten in Will's throat. He tried to speak, but fear so thoroughly froze him, no words came. Finally, he was able to say, "Pops. The dream." And this broke him. His tortured voice matched the terror inside his heart.

"How many times have I told you that's not the way I go?" He looked up at the sky, filled with encroaching clouds. "Me and the good Lord had a long talk about this some time back. One night I'll close my eyes and . . . "

He waited for Will to finish it for him. "And awaken in Glory."

Pops smiled.

But whether that day was today, a week from now, or a year from now, Will wasn't ready for it. There seemed so many things he should say. "I love you, Pops."

But his grandfather had already turned and started to walk away. "Love you too, boy." When he threw the look over his shoulder, Will saw it, the glint of a younger man looking out from Pops's eyes. "Take care of Adrienne."

Will's fist pressed hard against his mouth.

"And don't let SaraAnn forget about me, okay?"

Pops was a blur through the tears. Will couldn't answer. His head gave a shaky nod.

Later, much later that night, he heard the whine of the boat motor as he smoothed the hair from SaraAnn's face, tucking her into bed. "Tell me a story, Daddy?"

Somehow, Will found his words. "Once upon a time, there was a very brave soldier named William Bryant . . . "

He'd barely gotten into the story when Adrienne came running into the room. "Will, I hear the boat."

SaraAnn didn't notice her momma's panic.

Will watched as his wife rushed to the window and clung to the sill. He came over and placed his arms around her waist. "It's Pops. He's taking the boat out."

Her eyes widened in fear. "It's night, Will. The dream."

But he didn't answer, didn't explain, just stared out the window as running board lights disappeared, swallowed by the canal.

Frustration caused her to push away from him. "What are you doing?"

When the first tear trickled onto his cheek, she quickly moved back into his arms. "I'm learning to let go."

At 5:15, they got the call from the Coast Guard. The unmanned thirty-two-foot cuddy cabin was moored on Grace Island, one of Pops and Sara's favorite fishing spots. At 5:32, the coroner, a family friend, stopped by. "It's the strangest thing, Will. Your grandfather was lying on the beach like he was taking a nap, and I swear there was a smile on his face. I can't see any reason why he died." He rubbed a beard-stubbled chin. "The boat was tied, no signs of foul play. It's like he just stretched out to watch the stars, closed his eyes, and—"

"And awakened in Glory."

"We'll know more after the autopsy."

Will shook his hand. "He's with Sara. I know everything I need to know. Thanks, Dr. Baker."

Open windows filled the house with fresh air. Adrienne stood at the kitchen sink, rinsing the vegetables SaraAnn had picked from the garden. The five-year-old scurried outside to play when a fat squirrel entered her sphere of vision.

Adrienne laughed. "She still believes she'll catch that squirrel."

Will slid his hands around his wife, open palms grazing her growing belly and loving the fact their family was about to welcome a new member. He nuzzled her ear. "She's curious, like her mother."

She half-turned toward him, resting her head against his chest. "And stubborn, like her father."

With the pad of his thumb, he tilted her chin so he could gaze into her eyes. "You know, I've heard of men being attracted to pregnant women. I never fully understood until now."

She blinked innocently. "You weren't attracted to me when I was pregnant with SaraAnn?"

He scowled. "Ridiculously. But I think it's getting worse. I can't keep my hands off you."

A throaty giggle escaped her lips. "Well, who asked you to?"

He captured her mouth with his. Will angled so his body rested against hers. He lingered there, in that kiss, tasting the woman he loved until a swift knock hit him in the lowest part of his stomach.

Adrienne rubbed a hand over her belly. "Slugger's got quite a kick."

Will bent at the waist and addressed his unborn child. "Another few weeks, and she's all yours. But until you make your appearance, she's mine." He kissed her stomach, stood up, kissed her cheek, then dove for her mouth again, losing himself in her essence.

Later that night, Will sat at the antique bureau in their bedroom overlooking the canal. Beyond the open window, waves lapped the sides of the boat, and a strong breeze carried the scents of autumn. Throughout his life, he'd learned many things. But the one that most surprised him was the power of the written word. And that's why at night, when his family slept, he sat at the bureau and wrote letters.

Dear SaraAnn,

I'm watching you grow up before my eyes, and sometimes I wonder if I'm giving you all the advice you need. Life can be hard, but it's also beautiful. I expect you'll have your share of both, as we all do. But no matter what roads you travel, just one turn can lead you back home.

You and your momma are the loves of my lifetime. One day, I hope you'll find yours. Until then, make every day count. Live a life you'll be proud of. Be strong when life is a war. And be soft when a friend needs an understanding ear. Be yourself, SaraAnn, because there's nothing more beautiful than you. Of all the things I may be able to teach you, this one lesson is most important. Life is to be lived.

Your biggest fan,
Daddy

Acknowledgments

I wrote this book and placed it on a shelf. It was a book of my heart, and I was content to leave it there. But there were three people who read it and weren't satisfied with that. They insisted *One Lavender Ribbon* should be shared. For that, I thank you: Diane; my husband, John; and Julie Palella—who told me *One Lavender Ribbon* was her favorite book that she'd ever read. Those words forced me to lift it from the shelf, dust off the cobwebs, and dive back into the story of Adrienne, Will, Pops, and Sara. I'm so glad I did.

JoVon, thanks for your work, thoughts, ideas, and an unstoppable amount of enthusiasm.

Kelli, you took this book, nurtured it, cherished it, and helped mold it into something beyond what I dreamed. Your encouragement has made me a stronger writer, and your commitment to the project made it a much more powerful read. Thanks for being on this journey with me. If the pages sing, it's your song they're playing.

Sarah Sundin, thank you for sharing your knowledge of World War II and for being a beta reader for me. I'm so glad we connected.

A special thank-you to every man and woman who is now serving or who has ever served in the armed forces. You place your lives on the line so we can live without fear. You are my heroes.

About the Author

Melinda Hanks, 2012

*H*eather Burch writes full-time and lives near the beach in Southern Florida. Her debut novel was released to critical acclaim in 2012 and garnered praise from *USA Today*, *Booklist Magazine*, *Romantic Times*, and *Publishers Weekly*. Living in a house where she's the only female, Heather is intrigued by the relationships that form among men, especially soldiers. Her heartbeat is to tell unforgettable stories of love and war, commitment and loss . . . stories that make your heart sigh.